THE NEW WIZARD

"What are you doing?" Flayh shouted hoarsely.

Tahli-Damen grabbed for the magic pyramid. "I'm claiming what's mine!"

Suddenly a savage dog leaped out of nowhere for Tahli-Damen's throat. The young man threw up his arm, and the dog ripped his sleeve to tatters. Tahli-Damen clubbed the ferocious beast with his free hand and tried to scramble over the table, but the dog caught his leg in its jaws. Tahli-Damen's purple pants turned the color of his crimson tunic.

As quickly as it had appeared, the dog was gone. Flayh stood on the table in its place. But this was a different Flayh from the bald Elder the merchants had traded with through the years.

"By the dragon!" one merchant swore. "He has become a powershaper!" Then a ball of fire struck him in the chest.

THE
Wizard
IN
Waiting

Robert Don Hughes

A Del Rey Book

BALLANTINE BOOKS ● NEW YORK

for Johnny.
No matter now, to you,
    For you are gone.
And if you see, you see beyond
    All we do or say—
        But not with eyes.

Contents

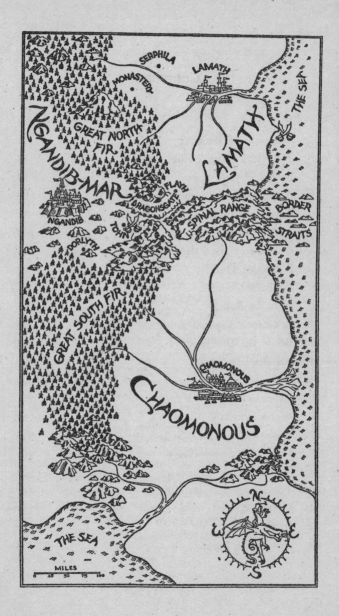

CHAPTER ONE

§   §

A Dream of Betrayal

—AWAKE AGAIN.

Those were the first words of the Imperial House of Chaomonous in over a thousand years. The second words followed logically from the first.

—Therefore, the dragon is dead.

The Imperial House did not speak as men do. How could it, lacking lungs and a mouth? Yet to one who knew castle speech, the groaning of aged doorsills or a whistling draft down a hallway would have expressed thoughts as clearly and purposefully as the words of human language. Condensation formed on all the interior walls of the palace as the House struggled for understanding, reaching for the memories stored within its drapes and dungeons—scenes that had been registered within it somehow, even when it had slept through the years.

The dragon was dead—that much was obvious. For untold centuries, the accursed Vicia-Heinox had been discussed and cursed within these halls. The dragon had straddled the Central Pass of the One Land, obstructing traffic and making a general nuisance of himself. Such a nuisance, in fact, that the One Land had been broken into three warring states, and the Central Pass had come to be called Dragonsgate.

1

The dragon had devoured humans voraciously in those days long ago. The House cared little about the consumption of persons, of course. With a few exceptions, one human was much like another, and it took real concentration to tell them apart. But the castle had been bothered considerably by the beast's utter lack of concern for structures. Some fine old manors had perished in the dragon's fires, in that first great period of burning. Indeed, some of the castle's own towers had been scorched by—

—Towers! the House exclaimed, and it quickly surveyed its own present condition.

—Amazing, murmured a window sash, as the castle noted a thousand years of home improvements. New spires jetted up from repaved courtyards. Reinforced parapets, gleaming in the sun from a recent whitewashing, gazed grimly down on the city that sprawled below. Gaily colored pennants fluttered in the breeze, at once festive and belligerent, throwing a bright challenge to anyone foolish enough to attempt to scale these heights. It was a stirring sight, to say the least, and the House wheezed with pleasure . . .

. . . A cold draft blew through the upper dungeon, chilling its inmates and puzzling the guards.

But of all the additions, by far the loveliest was a series of terraced gardens that climbed from deep within the castle's heart to the very roof itself. Fountains and walkways graced this artful wonder, and so glorious was the greenery it would have stolen the castle's breath away—had the castle any breath to steal.

—How odd, to grow so grand while sleeping!

The Imperial House took pride in its renewed appearance. Evidently it still stood tall among structures. Yet all was not as it should be. While its old walls and towers functioned just as they always had, as the castle's organs of touch and smell, sight and hearing, the new sections seemed devoid of life. There was no vision of the countryside from the new spires. The new pavements heard no conversation. Was it the House's imagination, or did these new constructions tingle, as if still asleep?

—Awake! the Imperial House ordered the new sections gruffly, and it sweated some more as it sought to force consciousness into these remodeled areas . . .

* * *

"Kherda!" Queen Ligne shrilled at her Prime Minister. "Do you see this?" She glided delicate, bejewelled fingers across a marble-tiled wall grown suddenly, inexplicably wet. "Just *what* is causing this?" She demanded as she rubbed her moist fingertips together in his face.

"I have no idea, my Queen," Kherda replied quietly, annoyed by her accusing tone. This wasn't unusual. Ligne's tone of voice regularly annoyed him and seemed to grow more annoying with every passing day. But just as regularly, Kherda swallowed his pique and smiled. Kherda was quite creative at inventing new ways to grovel. "Perhaps, my Lady, it's the weather?"

The House heard the conversation, and felt her caressing fingers, even as it registered a hundred other comments from a hundred other rooms. It focused its attention here, however, on this black-maned beauty and her parasitic Prime Minister. This was by force of ancient habit, really. Centuries of watching human behavior had taught the House that, in the minds of humans at least, the most critical conversations took place in the courts of Kings. That wasn't so, as the castle knew very well, having listened to years of sloppy drivel coming from this very throne room. It was often much more fun to hear what the messengers and consorts said outside the regent's hearing. Even so, it was a relief to find that the throne room had not been greatly altered.

—The foundations are the same, the House sighed, reassured. Still as firm, as impenetrable as the rock from which they had been carved. Indeed, while cosmetic changes had been made, the basic floorplan of the massive palace would still have been recognizable to Nobalog.

—Nobalog! The Imperial House winced, and a dolorous booming issued from the cistern beneath the kitchen, as the castle mourned the passing of its friend. More than a friend, really, for it had been the powershaper Nobalog— "the fat, bald one"—who had birthed consciousness in the castle so many years before.

—*How* many? the Imperial House wondered. How long had it been?

Not that it mattered, particularly, with Nobalog dead. While there had been many in that ancient age who sported with the castle, debating with it about current events or telling it meaningless human jokes, only Nobalog ever took the time to understand. More than that, of all the powershapers who had walked its corridors, only Nobalog had been sensitive to the damaging effects of magic upon the House. Nobalog had been a friend.

But Nobalog was long dead. That was the problem with humans. Eventually, they all died. Nobalog had been gone a thousand years by the time the dragon came, and put the castle to sleep.

The House listened again with some attention to the words of Queen Ligne, for her sharp voice had jogged its memory. It had heard her before!

—There have been dreams, the House said quietly, dreams that were not dreams at all, but rather stages of awakening. This is why some things are known.

Seeking to learn more, the House followed the woman's march down the hallway and onto the grand spiral. This was a gigantic curving staircase that formed the hub of all castle activities. Had she passed down the spiral, it would have taken her onto the dais of the vast great hall, where all of those within the walls took their meals. The House noted with some concern that the upper end of the spiral now opened onto the lowest garden terrace. Though beautiful, this new area was outside the castle's range of hearing. Ligne did not climb that high, however, turning off instead to stamp toward the royal apartments. She was bellowing orders even before she reached her attiring room, so that, by the time she slung open the door, a dozen attendants were already waiting to change her.

The House watched attentively as the army of maids stripped the queen bare. The castle's standards of beauty had all been drawn from the comments of men, and it was fully aware that many within the walls would have longed to watch this operation. To the House, however, the woman's shapely form was no more nor less entrancing than any of the other objects of art that lined its corridors or stood in its courtyards. While her imperious manner indicated that she truly believed herself the owner of this palace, the House knew better. Long after she passed from the scene, the House would continue to stand. Rather, the castle believed that it owned her, and was mildly pleased that the present regent was so comely in appearance.

And yet . . . was there not some question regarding her sovereignty?

The castle sweated to remember . . . There was a scene, perhaps months before, recorded in its semiconscious state . . .

"I look a mess!" Ligne muttered, but the vision in the mirror belied her words.

"You look positively regal, my Lady," Kherda gushed. The old feelings welled up in his heart again, those adolescent palpitations that had caused him to betray Talith, his rightful King, and lay the plot to elevate this woman to the throne. "It's little wonder King Talith chose you for his paramour!"

"Don't talk about Talith," Ligne mumbled. "I just ate dinner."

"But it's true, my Lady! Your beauty so ensnared him—"

"Turn it *off*, Kherda." The Queen scooped up her velvet skirts and paced toward the doorway. "You're sure Joss is coming?"

"It has all been arranged, my Queen," Kherda reassured her. "General Joss has accepted the terms of the agreement, and has promised to appear today, bringing the girl with him. Ah, there is one detail that I must—"

"But what guarantees do I have? The man has hated me from the first moment."

"He doesn't hate you—"

Ligne arched an eyebrow and shot Kherda a poisonous look.

"I mean, it may have looked as if he hated you," Kherda hurriedly clarified, "but you have to understand Joss. He's consumed with loyalty to the throne of Chaomonous, and he somehow sensed that you were a threat to his King. You must admit, he had cause to be suspicious—"

"So now he's going to turn his back on those old loyalties and surrender Talith's rightful heir to me?" Ligne accentuated her sarcasm by propping a hand on her jutting hip.

Kherda controlled his impatience, and—though he had explained this all a dozen times before—even managed a smile as he explained it once again: "Talith is dead, my Lady. There's nothing left for Joss to be loyal to. Why should he continue to support the House of Talith when the

King played such a critical role in his own downfall? After all, the King relieved Joss of his command the day before the battle—rather shabby treatment, in view of the General's loyalty. And you've certainly done nothing to injure Joss, apart from sentding a couple of raiding parties after him—"

"Which he destroyed," Ligne muttered.

"He is a shrewd tactician, to be sure." Kherda nodded. "There's little love between us, as you well know, and I judge it no blessing to have the man within the walls again. On the other hand, it's far better to have the General's talents with us than against us, and his great loyalty to the nation and the throne has convinced him that there would be no profit in a protracted civil war—"

"Yes, yes, so you've said. So where is he, then?"

"It isn't the appointed hour quite yet, and it's a long ride from—"

Kherda was interrupted by a series of trumpet blasts issuing from the gate of the Imperial House. He turned to Ligne with a self-satisfied smile. "You see? He's even early!"

"How very like Joss," Ligne mumbled . . .

The castle's memory of the dream faltered then, as if at that point in the conversation the House had lapsed back from semiconsciousness into a comatose state. Spurred on by an intense curiosity, the House pursued these fleeting wisps of thought. The thread of the dream picked up again . . .

They stood in the Hall of Peace: Ligne, Kherda, General Joss—and the Princess Bronwynn. Ligne made no secret of her elation. She trilled with laughter each time she spoke. "You can't imagine how delighted I am to see you again, Bronwynn," she sang. "I simply can't tell you how it pleases me!"

Bronwynn, daughter of Talith and true heir to the throne of Chaomonous, said nothing. Instead, she turned her startlingly blue eyes in a searing gaze on the General who had promised her a crown—and betrayed her.

General Joss avoided her eyes. It wasn't that he felt

guilty. He was doing the only sensible thing. The rights of one beautiful young woman could hardly take precedence over the right of an entire nation to peace—regardless of the royalty of her blood. Nor was he particularly bothered by her opinion of him. Joss had grown quite accustomed to hatred. But he had never been one to enjoy giving the *coup de grace* to a fallen enemy, as had some of his peers. He took no pleasure in this betrayal. And despite the girl's bedraggled hair and tear-stained cheeks, her accusing eyes were far too reminiscent of her father's to permit Joss to meet her stare. Instead, he turned his attention to Kherda. "You've informed the Queen of my condition?"

"What condition?" Ligne snapped, jerking around to look at her Prime Minister, who unconsciously stepped back under the impact.

"Ah, actually, the occasion never did arise to—"

"My Lady," Joss cut him off, "I made it clear to Kherda in our negotiations that the girl was not to be killed—"

"Not to be killed!" Ligne screeched, laughing no longer. "What kind of nonsense is this?"

"Kherda!" Joss roared savagely.

"It's true," the Prime Minister squealed, backing well out of the range of a possible swipe from Ligne's feline claws. He raced on: "It was a necessary concession to insure a successful result of the talks—"

"Not to be killed!" Ligne repeated, stalking Kherda's retreat and picking up speed to match his.

"I tell you it was necessary," the Prime Minister wailed, turning tail to scamper around behind the frowning General. Joss stepped in front of the enraged woman to block her pursuit.

"It *is* necessary," he said firmly, and Ligne turned her wrath on him instead.

"You . . . betray me!" she roared.

"You too?" Bronwynn piped up bitterly. "Perhaps we should start a club . . ."

"Ligne, listen to reason," Joss barked, and the authority in his harsh voice caught the Queen's attention. "You've nothing to gain by killing this girl, and much to lose. Her murder could only provoke more outrage from the populace and a possible insurrection. Place her under protective custody and let it be published that she's been deemed mentally unfit to rule. Do so . . . and I'll offer the full weight of my influence to back your claim."

"That girl is the only threat to my crown!" Ligne screamed.

"No!" Joss shouted back. "*You* are!"

The woman stared at him, shaken by his temerity. When she spoke again, she was calmer. "Just what do you mean?"

"It isn't seemly for a Queen to be so governed by her emotions," Joss answered evenly. "Perhaps if you would think this through, you'd see my point."

"Go on."

"Entrust the girl to me. You may find eventually she'll endorse your claim herself."

"That won't happen, Joss," Bronwynn said quickly. "I told you this morning—the throne is mine."

"Why such a change?" Ligne asked the General, ignoring the girl's comment. "You've always been so loyal. Tell me why you would make such a radical switch?"

Her tone was suddenly almost cordial, the General observed. That was a promising sign. "Evidently you *can* control your emotions—" he began.

"Of course I can," Ligne snapped. "Answer my question."

"I didn't have the strength to defeat you," the General admitted. "My army was hungry, the snow was cold, and victory was a hopeless fantasy."

"We could have won!" Bronwynn said heatedly. "If you'd contacted Pelmen as I told you to, we could have had the whole army of Lamath—"

"To ravage the countryside of Chaomonous?" Joss finished for her. "No, thank you," he snarled, and he turned back to Ligne. "I prefer Chaomonous to be ruled by Chaons, not fanatical Lamathians in long blue robes. You understand, don't you, my Lady?"

Ligne smiled smugly. "General, I understand perfectly. And your sensible explanation has brought a welcome focus to all of this. Kherda, you could take a lesson from the General."

The blood drained from the Prime Minister's face, then returned in a crimson flood. He would have spoken, but no words could express his humiliation and fury.

"General," the queen continued, "I extend to you once again the full command of the Golden Throng. Do with the girl what you choose." Ligne dismissed Bronwynn with a flick of her hand.

Joss recognized this as a bold gambit to assert her dominance in their relationship. Ordinarily he would have responded with equal coldness. But there was something about this woman, something compelling about the combination of her physical charms and her steel ambition, that caused him uncharacteristically to gulp. Ligne saw it and, before he could summon any reply, she spun on her heel and was gone.

. . . The House now remembered several other events of that same day, but they were matters of little importance. At the moment it was much more interested in discovering what had transpired in the weeks or months since that vision. Its curiosity had been thoroughly aroused.

It took only a moment to spot the Princess. While kings and emperors might redecorate their own apartments with regularity, few ever troubled to remodel their dungeons. The House found Bronwynn sitting at the bottom of the pit.

Though she sat in a darkness so total that she couldn't even see her own hands before her face, Bronwynn's knotted hair and the scrap of rag that passed for her dress could be clearly perceived by the House. The lack of light was unimportant, for the castle's sense of sight was no more like men's vision than its language was like men's speech. It was by a subtle—and totally unconscious—shaping of magical power. That same form of shaping allowed it to hear the rustling as Bronwynn pawed blindly through heaps of straw in search of a lost morsel of bread. "I know it's here someplace," the girl mumbled as she dug. She had dropped it hours ago—or maybe days—who could tell in this timeless hole?—and had been searching for it ever since. Her persistence was fueled by her hunger—and by the fact that she had nothing else to do.

The House felt no pity for her. Though it had witnessed pity before, it had experienced neither any need for it nor any inclination toward it in its centuries of consciousness. That humans imprisoned other humans within walls of stone had been among the first things the castle ever comprehended. The House saw little reason in the anger and frustration persons felt toward their imprisonment, however. It was, after all, a prisoner itself of sorts, and quite at peace with its immobility. One thing it did relate to, however, was the isolation that captives experienced. This Princess Bronwynn was doubtless lonely, and the castle decided to approach her.

—The object you seek is to your left and behind you, said the House.

Bronwynn jerked backward, landing prone in a pile of straw, staring up toward the grating that was the only entrance into the hole. The House chuckled, stirring the stale air with an incongrous draft.

—Now it is by your left foot.

"Is there someone there?" Bronwynn called. The raspiness of her own voice startled her momentarily; she had screamed herself hoarse during the first week of her captivity, and the constant chill of this dank place had added a persistent cold to her list of torments. But more startling by far was the sense that there was something present in the cell with her—something nonhuman.

—It is the House who speaks.

Bronwynn peered into the darkness, looking first one direction, then another. She succeeded only in making herself dizzy. "Who's there?" she whispered, fighting off the sense of vertigo.

—It is the House, the House said a bit peevishly.

Bronwynn could make no sense of the odd stirrings in the straw around her or the rapid changes of temperature in her cell. She only knew that some power or force had manifested itself toward her; she made the only assumption that seemed logical. "Are you the Power that Pelmen told me about?"

—The Power? the House asked. Such an idea was confusing.

"If you are—and I pray you are—I only ask that you let him know where I am and send him to rescue me."

Now the Imperial House had heard many pleas for rescue in its ages of existence—some even from those of royal blood. But all of these had been addressed to itself . . . not to some Power. Such a request made no sense.

—Must it be stated again? It is the House who addresses you. What do you mean by a Power?

"I began to wonder if you even existed. Haven't you heard me calling out for you all these weeks?" The Princess sounded cross, which made the conversation that much more perplexing. It was as if she didn't understand a word the castle said.

—Are you not listening? Or do the shapers no longer teach castle speech to the royal children?

"I, I know . . ." Bronwynn began, then she faltered, suddenly self-conscious about talking to nothing. She listened for a moment to the dark, then murmured: "Am I going insane, the way they want me to think? No!" she answered herself firmly, and she began again. "Of course, I know you haven't been active in Chaomonous in ages, but Pelmen always said he thought that was because of the dragon, and that the more people in this land learned of you, the more apparent your presence would become . . ."

—What are you talking about? Who is this Pelmen?

Bronwynn groped her way to her feet, stumbling against a wall in the process. It was wet with sweat. Odd, she thought, not realizing that her own inability to communicate had caused the wall's condition.

"If it is you, I'm begging you—take care of Pelmen. And take care of Rosha, too . . ."

The House hastily withdrew from the conversation, thoroughly bewildered by the strangeness of her notions. Bronwynn heard no more. She slumped against the moist wall and sighed. Her sensitivity, which had once caused Pelmen to suggest she might shape the powers some day, told her that the moment had passed.

"Or is my mind slipping . . ." she asked quietly. No one answered.

The House was experiencing some of those same feelings. It had slept too long. It needed someone to fill in the obviously sizable gaps in its understanding. Quickly, the House located the Queen. Evening had painted the sky purple, then black, and though the wind was chilly, Ligne now strolled atop the parapets.

—An explanation is required, the House demanded.

Ligne didn't even pause. She pulled her fur-lined cloak

tightly around her shoulders, and gazed downriver toward
the sea. The full moon had peeked above the eastern horizon, washing the countryside with pale light. The afternoon's vexations were long forgotten now. As the wind destroyed her careful coiffure, her eyes dropped slightly to
study the farthest reaches of her vast city, where distant
torches—tiny pinpoints of brilliance—seemed to reflect the
starry sky back at itself. Her thoughts were far away . . .

—Is there no courtesy anymore? Where are your manners? the castle snapped.

Ligne made no response. She was busy weighing the
qualities of her various lovers, clinically analyzing their
strengths and weaknesses. Her present prospects all bored
her. She wished for some new diversion to break up the
sameness of castle routine . . .

—Or has the world gone mad?

The House began to panic. Why would no one respond?

The castle had repressed the thought long enough. Now
it sprang to full, horrifying consciousness. The logical next
step was to turn to the present castle powershaper for counsel. The problem was, the powershaper quarters were missing. The apartments occupied by Nobalog and the other
shapers of old had been replaced by the terraced gardens.

With brutal impact, a new set of memories returned—
memories of the shocking years just prior to the coming of
the dragon. Wars abounded. The One Land, united for
ages, took only a moment to splinter apart. Shapers dueled
for no purpose save their own pride, urged on by Kings
and would-be Kings, and others who wished for no Kings
at all. Scholars who disavowed shaping asserted the pri-
macy of a world view based only on logic—and in this region, they had prevailed. For one brief moment, the House
relived those horrible days. It heard again the clamor of
arms in its hallways, felt again the inexpressible agony
wrought when shapers wrenched from its life force wonders sometimes splendid, sometimes terrifying, but always
excruciatingly painful. Then the memories passed . . .

Ligne still stood upon the battlements, gazing out at the
night. Bronwynn still rooted through the straw for a crust
of bread. And the castle was alone.

—Are there no more shapers? it asked the entire population that lived within its walls. Though a few hesitated in

their tasks with puzzled expressions, the vast majority of the citizens of this city within a city simply ignored the castle's question. No one deigned to answer. The castle's temper flared to rage.

—These questions *shall* be answered! it roared, and for the remainder of the night, the palace servants waged war with stopped-up plumbing, curious drafts, and pictures that seemed to leap from the walls.

—This House, said the Imperial House of Chaomonous, will *not* be ignored.

So completely did the House turn in upon itself that it missed what might have been a welcome visitation. For outside, at the very foot of one of its massive battlements, stood a lone figure draped in dark garments. And at various times, in various places, the man had proved something of a wizard.

The wind whipped his shoulder-length brown hair up on end as he peered up the facing of the clifflike wall. The sting of the cold watered his blue eyes, but he would not leave off his gazing. His lips moved. Was he speaking to himself? Or to some unseen listener? Then, as silently as he'd come, he disappeared into the winter night, heading south.

CHAPTER TWO

To Win a Way Within

"'. . . You MEAN that was your *daughter*, sir?' I said. 'But I thought it was your pet tree-monk!' Ah-ha-ha-ha!" Gerrig bent double, slapping his thighs as he pushed the sound of his mellow laughter out over the heads of his audience. As he straightened back up, a ripe tomato splattered across his face, spilling a juicy trail of seeds onto the red curls of his beard. Gerrig's laugh died, but a grim smile remained fixed on his lips.

"Why do you laugh at your own jokes?" taunted the peasant who had scored this latest hit.

"Because you are too dense to understand them, good fellow. I don't wish to show your neighbors how dull you are, so I laugh so that you may know when to join in." The peasant flushed, and his friends cackled at his discomfort. His only retort was another direct hit.

The laughing crowd took no notice of the dirty child who dashed out from behind the makeshift curtain to scoop up what was left of the two tomatoes. Nor did they hear her mutter, "Carrots," to Gerrig. The player nodded as the little girl scrambled down off the stage, and he looked out into the faces of his audience again.

"You, sir," he said, as he pointed at the peasant, "have

no imagination. Tomatoes! Why, any man can throw a tomato, or a turnip. They're round. But try throwing something oblong—a banana gourd, perhaps, or better yet a carrot. Now it takes a keen eye to—" Gerrig cut his words short and ducked. Two carrots whizzed over his head. A third bounced off his balding pate and rolled to the backdrop. The audience screamed with glee.

Gerrig stood slowly, rubbing his noggin and muttering, "If I hadn't ducked, you wouldn't have come close. You must try harder—" A barrage of vegetables filled the air, and Gerrig stooped, covering his head with his hands. The little girl scrambled onto the stage again, and began shoving the bouncing foodstuffs toward her mother, who waited in the wings. The audience had at last caught the fever, and now everyone was merrily participating—with one exception. Gerrig noticed the fellow as he knelt to roll a couple of turnips offstage. He straightened again and pointed at the man.

"You, sir! Don't you wish to join your neighbors in pelting the defenseless player? Wouldn't you like to show your own cultural appreciation? Join in. Lend a hand in this gracious reception your townsfolk have prepared for us."

The man raised both hands, palms up. An easily interpreted gesture—he had nothing to throw. But Gerrig looked again as the fellow pulled his ragged brown robe tightly around him, shielding his face. Gerrig thought he'd seen that gesture before.

"Potatoes," Sherina called quietly from the wings, and Gerrig launched into a new tirade of insults and abuse. Soon the villagers had exhausted their supply of rotting vegetables and rank fruit, and began drifting away, but he continued his monologue until the last peasant shuffled onto the road for home. Then he hopped off the stage of his wagon and started walking the twenty yards to where the brown-clad stranger still stood, watching.

"Show's over, friend," Gerrig called as he walked. "You can go home now." Gerrig was a big man, with thick, meaty shoulders and hands as big as shovel blades. His teeth were very white, and when the curtain of his bearded lips parted in a smile, it was impossible not to notice his gleaming canines. There was an implied threat both in Gerrig's gait and his appearance, and the stranger should

have been frightened—at the very least, a little startled.
Yet the brown-clad figure stood his ground and waited for
Gerrig to reach him, his posture alert but relaxed. Gerrig
slowed to a menacing saunter, and spoke more quietly: "I
said, you can go now." The threat was no longer implied.
Gerrig's tone of voice made it quite clear.

"You mean, that's all?" the stranger asked. "No performance?"

"You've seen the performance, and you've seen the reaction it got. Now be off with you!"

"But what of—of *Shadows of a Night at Sea* or *Tales of
the Six and One*?"

Gerrig raised an eyebrow. "You know those plays?
How?"

"Why, I've watched them, seen them performed."

"Oh?" Gerrig said. "Any particular—ah—rôles come to
mind?"

A low chuckle issued from the depths of the stranger's
plain garment. "The captain, of course, in *Shadows*. Who
could forget his final speech?"

"Yes, who could?" Gerrig nodded, pleased. The captain's
role had always been his own. But his icy manner swiftly
returned. "That was long ago. We don't play those tales
anymore." He jerked away, calling back to the line of wagons. "Sherina! Danyilyn! Is it cooking?"

"It's cooking," came some woman's yelled reply, and
Gerrig nodded. Then he turned back to the stranger.

"I cannot tell by your accent where you're from, but I
know you're no Southlander. Are you by chance a spy from
the court of the Queen?" Gerrig smiled as he asked this
question. There was, however, no humor there.

Again the stranger chuckled. "In a way, I do come from
the Queen. But not Queen Ligne, I assure you—nor do I
own any favor in her court."

Gerrig folded his arms, bringing one hand up to his face.
He tapped his teeth with his thumbnail for a moment,
thinking. Then he pointed at the stranger. "Nevertheless,
you have been there. Those were court plays you mentioned, rarely performed outside of Chaomonous proper.
You are from the capital."

"Perhaps."

"Not perhaps, you are!" Gerrig growled. "Now who are

you?" The actor reached out to jerk the stranger's brown cloak aside. Then he made a face. It reflected his consternation at not recognizing the brown stranger sooner.

"I must say, Gerrig, you do the soup scenario very well. Had I brought any vegetables with me, I surely would have thrown them at you."

"Yes, well," Gerrig grumbled, his voice rough and raspy, "I'll never surpass you at it. I make too big a target. Danyilyn! Sherina!"

"I told you, Gerrig, it's cooking," Danyilyn yelled back, annoyed.

"Set up another bowl then, wench. Pelmen's back again."

The troupe was smaller than he remembered. Even so, several of the faces were new. Half of the players Pelmen had acted beside for years were now gone. He glanced around him, taking roll, as Sherina set a bowl of steaming vegetable soup before him.

"There's even a little meat stock in it." The square-jawed Sherina smiled ruefully. "Coralai managed to snatch a bone away from a dog."

Pelmen smiled wanly, and looked over at Coralai, the little girl who'd been such an efficient collector of vegetable missles. "She's grown," he said quietly, experiencing that inescapable jolt of mortality he always felt when babies suddenly grew up. The other familiar faces gathered around him seemed unchanged by the year-long intermission. But children are the yardsticks of passing time, and Pelmen recognized it had been a while.

"Eat it, before it cools," Gerrig ordered as he shoveled a spoonful into his mouth. "It may be all you get for a while—if you plan on staying."

Pelmen took a mouthful as Sherina watched him expectantly. She'd never possessed the natural acting talent of some of the others in the troupe, but she could cook. One smile from Pelmen, and she was satisfied to go on happily about her business.

"The soup scenario is a summer ploy," Pelmen said to Gerrig as he cooled another spoon of the broth. "It's past the yule season—why aren't you wintering somewhere?"

"Did you, by chance, seek us on the coast?" Gerrig asked without looking up from his bowl.

"I did."

"We weren't there."

"So I discovered."

Gerrig still didn't look up. Pelmen understood. The man was embarrassed. "We've had a terrible year, Pelmen. The worst I can remember. We've been out of favor in the court ever since your *brilliant* final performance with us, when you called Ligne a traitor." Gerrig didn't hide his sarcasm. The troupe's last performance at court had been disastrous for all.

"She *was* a traitor," chirped Danyilyn, as she walked across the stage to the two men and droppped down to sit on its edge. "She still is. Hello." The last word she delivered into Pelmen's eyes in a husky whisper.

"Hello, Danyilyn. You're looking well, as always."

"Well enough to attract your attention, traveler?" She hummed.

"Danyilyn, you were always capable of that." Pelmen craned his neck to scan the line of wagons in both directions. "But where is everyone else? A year ago we were the best organized, largest troupe in Chaomonous. What happened?"

"One of us decided to meddle in politics, that's what happened," Gerrig growled, finally looking at Pelmen.

"We took a vote, Gerrig—remember?" Danyilyn said. "As I recall, we all agreed that we couldn't stand idly by while Ligne plotted to overthrow her lover. We agreed to make our opinions known."

"And a lot of good it did us," Gerrig snorted, draining the last of his soup and passing the bowl to Sherina for a refill. "Ligne is on the throne anyway, and we're reduced to begging peasants to pelt us with tomatoes so we can keep from starving."

"Then all of this is the result of our criticism of Ligne and King Talith?" Pelmen asked sadly.

"Not completely, no." Danyilyn sighed. "Though of course that did cost us our appointment to the court. But the confusion of Ligne's coup in the capital, the war on Lamath, the dragonburning—the year's events have thrown the whole countryside into confusion. The dragon burned most of this year's harvest, so there's no food, and it was bound to be a bad year anyway, since so many farmers were dragged off to the war. We're not the only troupe that's suffered."

"Though perhaps we're better complainers than most," broke in someone at Pelmen's back, and he turned around to greet Yona Parmi with a smile.

"Well, I'm happy to see you're still around," Pelmen said, and Yona snorted.

"Would I abandon my family? If I were to leave, who would Gerrig chew on?" Then he returned Pelmen's grin. Yona Parmi did not smile with his lips. They stayed fixed and frozen in a thin line. But when his cheekbones rose, and the skin of his fleshy face tightened across them, one could tell he was amused. Yona Parmi was a watcher of people, and what he saw in Chaomonous gave him little cause to smile. When he did, it was a joyous experience for his friends, compelling them to join in. In a moment the smile vanished, and Yona Parmi's cheekbones said he was serious again. "We all have tales of this past year's troubles to tell you, but I, for one, am far more interested in why you've returned." His tone was not scolding. Yona Parmi knew Pelmen as well as any man did and he knew Pelmen did nothing without purpose.

Pelmen glanced around him at this circle of old friends. There was some hostility there, and some bitterness, for it had been a difficult year, and Pelmen realized he bore much of the blame for their harsh conditions. "I'm here to apologize," he said quietly, "and to get you all back onto the main stage of Chaomonous."

A stunned silence greeted his announcemtnt. Gerrig recovered first. "And how are you going to do that?" he sneered. "I suppose you've brought us a gilt-edged invitation, won by your long-standing friendship with the Queen?"

"I've won nothing as yet, Gerrig," Pelmen responded evenly, "but I intend to. I've brought you all copies of a new play."

"Another explosive piece of political wizardry, I'll wager," Gerrig snorted bitterly.

Pelmen allowed himself a trace of a smile. "There may be a bit of wizardry in it." Only Yona Parmi understood the twinkle in Pelmen's eye.

"No!" Gerrig bellowed, slamming his hand on the wagon-bed. "You're not content with dooming us to exile, now you want to make sure we all roast over Ligne's fires!"

Pelmen ignored his huge friend's accusations. "Why not read it before you decide?"

"Sounds sensible to me," Danyilyn put in quickly.

"And to me," Yona Parmi echoed.

"Me, too," said a childish voice at Pelmen's feet, and he looked down into Coralai's unflinching brown eyes. He knelt down to look her squarely in the face.

"If I'd realized how big you'd be, I would have written a part for you." He grinned.

"So. Write me in." She shrugged, her expression solemn.

"I'll do it. That is, if Gerrig decides to give it a chance."

"Oh, Gerrig'll read it," Coralai advised. "You've just got to give him some time to blow off steam."

Pelmen glanced up at Gerrig's hairy face, not bothering to hide his smile. Obviously, Coralai knew Gerrig well.

Like all of Pelmen's plays, it was a work filled with bright color and strange images. The writer was in love with the sound of language, and some speeches thundered with a power that evoked deep emotional response. Most, however, brought the lighthearted tinkle of laughter, for the play was a comedy. It was a barbed comedy, however, poking merciless fun at an idiotic King too blind to see the machinations of his own advisors. With each line read, the target of the play grew clearer—the foolish King was obviously Talith. It was evident to every member of the troupe that the script would play quite well—yet the read-through grew steadily more uncomfortable with each new scene. By the final line only one actor was thoroughly enraptured with the piece—and that was Gerrig. Pelmen had quite deliberately made the King's mistress the heroine.

The reaction was not unexpected. Pelmen glanced up from his own manuscript and gazed around the circle of seated actors. "Well?" he asked. "What do you think?"

"I love it!" Gerrig exploded, a large grin spreading

across his beefy features. "It has pacing, it has style, power, substance—and humor, oh, I love the humor, such satire. And, of course, it will surely sell."

"It should." Pelmen nodded. He looked around the circle again. "Others?" he asked. No one rushed to respond. Pelmen glanced at Danyilyn. "What do you think?" he asked pointedly.

The actress bit her lip, forced a smile, then shrugged. "Reads great," she said.

"But?" Pelmen suppled for her, and she half smiled with embarrassment and continued:

"I mean it," she said. "The part you've written for me is excellent, and it'll be a fun role to play, but—but isn't it rather transparently Ligne?"

"Perhaps," Pelmen said.

"Not perhaps," Danyilyn blurted, warming to the discussion. "It's *her*. And she'll doubtless recognize herself—"

"Think she'll be pleased with it?" he interrupted.

"How could she help it?" Danyilyn snorted, making her own feelings for Ligne quite apparent. "She comes off smelling like a rose instead of the manure beneath one." Suddenly her eyes narrowed. "What's happened to you in the last year, Pelmen?" she demanded. "This isn't like you."

"Perhaps it wasn't," he said quietly.

"How can you support that woman, when she's—"

"Could I say something here?" Gerrig broke in, and Danyilyn snapped:

"There's no one here big enough to stop you."

"I think it's just the piece we've needed," he argued. "Oh, perhaps it doesn't reflect our own political opinions, but we're entertainers, not politicians, and—"

Danyilyn uttered a rude comment about Gerrig's ancestry. Had it been said by a stranger in a pub someplace, Gerrig would undoubtedly have sent the fellow home over the shoulders of his mates—if not directly to the local cemetery. When Danyilyn said it, however, Gerrig simply shut up. The image presented by the exchange was that of a poodle pursuing a Saint Bernard, for though Danyilyn's figure was ample, she was really quite small. She had a giant-sized temper, however, and now that it was roused, she turned it back on Pelmen.

"After leading us to expose this trollop, you want us now to become her pet players?"

"I want you to consider performing this play," Pelmen answered quietly. "As you've said, she's sure to like it, which should win the troupe a new appointment to the court. Once there, you may find more freedom to do the plays you really do well."

"Freedom!" Danyilyn spat. "Freedom bought at the expense of the true Queen."

"I've heard that she's dead." Sherina said it so quietly, it was almost a whisper.

"She's not dead," Gerrig interrupted authoritatively. "She's just missing. The merchants took her north and sold her as a slave to the new ruler of Lamath."

Pelmen wondered briefly where Gerrig got his misinformation, but quickly dismissed the thought. Gerrig was sure he knew everything about everything. What details he lacked could easily be supplied from his rich imagination. Pelmen focused his attention on Danyilyn. "Is freedom to influence public opinion something to be sneered at? What help can you offer the true Queen from this far south?"

Danyilyn stared at Pelmen, her forehead furrowed by an ugly frown. "I just can't believe this is coming from you."

Yona Parmi witnessed this whole encounter silently. While others spoke, he watched Pelmen's eyes, searching the wanderer's face for a clue to his real purpose. He saw none, for Pelmen had frozen his features into a grim gaze that gave away nothing. However, that was sufficient to assure Yona Parmi that Pelmen's concern extended far beyond the mere showcasing of a new play. And he trusted Pelmen's judgment. He now spoke up in favor of the project, though he loathed the thought of Ligne as Queen more, perhaps, than did Danyilyn. "I think we should do it."

The volatile actress spun around to face him. "You, too?"

Yona Parmi's eyes were close-set and very weak, yet they contained a quiet wisdom that made Danyilyn pause. He pushed a shock of black hair out of his round face and squinted at her. "Accepting, as we all surely must, the clear parallels in this piece to recent events—has Pelmen misstated the case? He's presented Talith as a fool—which he was—and Ligne as a clever manipulator of fools—which she is. The tale is entertaining. The moral is simple—don't be a fool. Has he said any more than that? Has he endorsed Ligne's method of claiming a crown? I think not. But Ligne may, and she will perhaps be pleased enough to invite us into her home. Is there anything wrong with that?" Yona Parmi's small black eyes hooked Danyilyn's in a challenging stare. Though soft-spoken, he had taken what was for him an adamant stand, and Danyilyn could not dismiss it lightly.

"You . . . really think we should do it?" she asked, her wrath fading.

"I do. But . . . I have a question."

"Ask it," Pelmen said quickly.

"Queen Ligne knows your face, and the two of you did not part as friends. How do you intend to survive long enough to play this piece before her?"

"Ah." Pelmen smiled. "The Talith role is obviously that of a fool. Correct?"

"Certainly."

"That's how I'll play him, then. In the whiteface of a fool."

"You'll wear it at all times within the walls?"

"Exactly."

Yona Parmi nodded. "Might work."

"Fine." Gerrig smiled, clapping his giant palms and wringing his hands in anticipation. "We'll take our time and do it right. By late spring we'll be ready to—"

"I want to premiere it at the Pleclypsa Winter Festival," Pelmen interrupted.

"The Pleclypsa Winter Festival!" Gerrig roared, aghast. "That opens next week. Every troupe in the region will be competing—"

"And so will we."

"There isn't enough time," the beefy performer bellowed.

"There is if we start in the morning," Pelmen shot back. He glanced around at the once proud troupe, now clothed in threadbare garments. "That is, unless you prefer the soup scenario to the kitchens of the Imperial House."

Gerrig swallowed hard, then looked down at his copy of the script, handwritten in Pelmen's familiar looping scrawl.

Then he looked back up. "If anyone wants me, I'll be in my wagon. I've a lot of lines to learn. The rest of you had better do the same." The man turned and lumbered off in the direction of his wagon. Heeding his good advice, the remainder of the troupe dispersed to their own rolling homes. Danyilyn, however, lingered long enough to regard Pelmen with friendly suspicion.

"I know you. You didn't write this to please Ligne."

"I didn't?" he responded blankly.

"You're up to something," she went on. "And I'm going to find out what." That said, she tucked her script under her arm and strolled away.

"She'll not do it easily, if she does," muttered Yona Parmi, as he joined Pelmen. "Nor, I imagine, will I."

"What are you talking about, Yona?" Pelmen asked innocently.

"I thought not," Yona grumbled good-naturedly. "Your couch still awaits you," he said, referring to the fact that he and Pelmen usually shared a wagon whenever the wanderer chose to put in an appearance. As they walked toward it, he was planning his first questions. It would take time, but he would find out.

After a week so busy it seemed to sprint past without being noticed, Yona Parmi had learned much about Pelmen's role in the events of the last year. He was no closer, however, to discovering Pelmen's purpose in rejoining the troupe. The playwright could be exceedingly stubborn when he chose to be. Still, Yona hadn't given up trying.

They were encamped in the meadow of a small village only a few miles south of Pleclypsa. While no one in the troupe felt truly prepared, Pelmen's plan called for them to premiere the play that night, before this rural audience. It would be their last chance to correct any trouble spots before the opening of the competition in the regional capital.

The wagons were formed into a circle, with only a single opening. Yards of cloth had been wrapped around the outside of this ring to insure that those who wished to watch had to pay for the privilege. The troupe had learned long ago to give the largest boys in the village some trifle and free admittance to keep nonpaying customers from crawling under the wagons. This small investment in security always paid off, for the challenge between the older guards and the younger lads not so chosen made the mobile theatre the center of a village's attention for days. People flocked in from the fields to participate in the excitement imported by these painted actors from far away.

It was midmorning, and already the guards beyond the wagon walls were shouting authoritatively and feeling important. Younger boys lay in the bushes and plotted in whispers how they might gain entrance into the circle. Within the ring, however, activity was at a minimum. The players had rehearsed far into the night and were now exercising their age-old prerogative of sleeping late.

Pelmen wasn't asleep, but he was resting comfortably on his low couch. The two friends had been locked in conversation until late the night before. Yona Parmi had resumed this morning as if sleep had never intervened.

"So you attempted to thrust this Rosha lad into the role of dragon slayer, but were forced to do the task yourself when his garbled speech enraged the beast?"

"It wasn't by choice, Yona," Pelmen replied, as he scooped his manuscript up off the floor and began studying it. He found it terribly difficult to memorize lines he'd written himself. He tended to want to rewrite in the middle of a performance. "It simply had to be done. Even so, it was a group effort. Without the cooperation of my companions, I would surely be in the belly of the beast today."

"Still avoiding the hero's role, aren't you?" Yona Parmi frowned. "It rather annoys me, Pelmen, each time you return, how you diligently praise your various comrades in arms, while disavowing any real role in changing history yourself. It's especially aggravating that you seem never to include us in your plans—"

"Please, Parmi." Pelmen winced. "Haven't we had this conversation before?"

"A number of times, I'll grant. But we never seem to finish it. You always disappear, off to perform some new feat of magic that sets the forces of nature in balance again. And then you return, humbly denying having had anything to do with it."

"What about Coralai in the second act? Is she stealing too much of the focus for the point to get across?"

"Or else you attempt to change the subject."

"I think the pacing of that act is a little ponderous . . ."

"What I can't understand is why you should even bother with us."

Pelmen glanced up at him. "I told you, Parmi, I feel responsible for getting you back into more comfortable surroundings."

"A well-intended gesture it is, and I'm duly appreciative. But I can't shake the feeling there's some grander scheme behind it all."

"Think Danyilyn is too obvious in her impersonation of Ligne?"

"I didn't think she could be too obvious, as far as you were concerned."

"Just so long as she's not offensive to the Queen."

"That puzzles me as well. Why this sudden devotion to a shallow woman ruled only by her unrepressed lecheries for power and for young men?" Yona raised a sparse eyebrow in mock horror. "You haven't fallen in love with her yourself, have you?"

Pelmen laughed aloud. "I think you know me better than that."

"Yes, yes, and there's this Serphimera woman you told me about. But who could be sure?" Yona Parmi shrugged. "For all we know, you could be one of Ligne's chief advisors by this time."

Pelmen rolled off his divan and strolled past Yona Parmi to the door. He pushed it open and glanced outside. "Another cold gray day," he said. The clouds looked ominous. "I hope it doesn't rain."

Yona struggled to his feet and came to peer out over Pelmen's shoulder. "That would make for a rather soggy performance. Why not raise a wind and blow these clouds away?" He said it teasingly, but carefully studied his friend's reaction.

There was little to study. Pelmen only chuckled mildly and climbed back into the wagon. He sauntered to the dressing table and scooped water from the bowl there to wash his face.

Yona persisted. "I know you need to get into the Imperial House of Chaomonous," he announced, and Pelmen stopped washing and looked at him.

"How do you know that?"

"It's the only thing that makes any sense. That's why you've rejoined us—to get within the walls. But I don't understand why you don't just transform yourself into a falcon and fly in. You can still do that, can't you?"

Pelmen toweled off his face. "That would be shaping, Parmi, and you know I've never been able to shape the powers in Chaomonous."

"I know you've always said you couldn't. Does that mean there are no powers here to shape?"

Pelmen shrugged—a bit too elaborately, Yona Parmi thought—and said, "All I know is that I've never shaped any powers in Chaomonous."

Yona Parmi turned testy, for he knew from Pelmen's veiled eyes that the traveler knew far more than he was saying. "You'd never been a Prophet in Lamath before last year, either!"

"That was different. I had nothing to do with that. The Power did that through me."

"The Power being that One who met you on a mountain-top long ago?"

"The same."

"Do you think the Power you speak of is not powerful enough to cross Dragonsgate?"

Pelmen met Yona Parmi's eyes. For the first time since he had returned, he let Yona see the worry he'd hidden inside. "You aren't going to give up, are you?" he sighed.

"You've given me no reason to believe I should." Yona Parmi waited a moment, then prodded, "What's troubling you, my friend?"

"I'd prefer not to involve you, if I can help it. The less you know, the less you can be held accountable for by others."

"Meaning, by Ligne."

"By Ligne, by her advisors, by whomever, Yona. My concern extends well beyond the borders of this supposed Empire of Chaomonous. There are others in other lands who oppose me."

"Pelmen, I'm already involved. I'm part of the troupe that's going to get you within the walls. But answer my question, man! Pelmen Dragonsbane has slain the dragon and opened the pass for traffic to move freely between the three lands. Cannot the Power pass Dragonsgate as well?"

Pelmen thought for a long time before answering. "The Power *has* passed."

"Ah . . ." Yona Parmi sighed, his dark eyes lighting up.

"As have other powers."

Yona looked puzzled. "What other powers?"

"Those that have been shaped by Mari powershapers for these many centuries," Pelmen intoned quietly. He turned his gaze on Yona Parmi again, and showed his friend an expression of quiet desperation. "And I never seem to know which is which."

"You mean—powers from Ngandib-Mar are free among us?" Yona Parmi asked with a shudder. Suddenly he felt an urge to glance around him and beneath the bed.

"Or so it seems." Pelmen nodded. "A week ago I stood outside the walls of the Imperial House. There's something *there,* Yona. I felt it."

Yona Parmi swallowed hard. "But the Power is around too, isn't it?" he asked. His tone demanded some reassurance.

"At times." Pelmen nodded. He half smiled at the expression of panic that threatened to take over his friend's features. "Now are you sure you want to know the rest?"

"Not knowing is worse than knowing," Yona Parmi mumbled. "I think," he added.

"The result of it all is that I'm bound up inside. I don't want to shape, for fear of shaping the wrong thing. Nor can I feel any confidence that I won't be seized any minute by one greater than I and experience again that curious elation of *being* shaped myself."

Yona Parmi just stared at him, a bit glassy-eyed.

"And all of it seems to stem from the death of the dragon—for which, as you say, I bear the ultimate responsibility."

"But how did that . . ." Yona's sentence trailed away. He really didn't know the right questions to ask.

"Why did that make a difference? I don't know. I have a theory, though, that the opening of Dragonsgate has played a part. For a thousand years only the merchant families have moved between the three lands—merchants, thieves, and vagabonds like myself. And merchants, of

course, have showed little interest in powers of any kind—
except their own power over the people. They've isolated
themselves from everyone else and isolated, too, the librar-
ies of the past. They share no knowledge between the
lands, save that which serves their purpose. But there's
traffic now, Yona, of common people—a trickle, true, but
movement all the same. I know of a dozen freetraders who
made the crossing before a gang of rogues plugged up the
pass. And more will make the journey after the spring
thaw, in spite of the thieves' high tariffs. And with them
come questions, and with the questions . . . powers." Pelmen shook his head and sighed. "The world is changing,
Yona Parmi. And I can't say what the result of it all might
be." He looked back at his friend. Yona Parmi was gazing
off into nowhere. "Yona? Parmi, are you all right?"

Yona Parmi looked at him, licked his lips, then muttered, "You said something about going over the second act
again?"

Pelmen understood the reaction. How well he understood
it!

"What power! What magic! What grace!" Gerrig was
talking about his own performance, naturally. The gray sky
had thundered throughout the play, but never made good
its threat. The local peasants had gathered, enjoyed, ap-
plauded, and departed to their homes and pubs, leaving the
players to clean off their makeup in the diminishing light
of early evening.

"I thought it went rather well," Pelmen agreed.

"Well? It went marvelously! Didn't you hear the shrieks
of laughter, the thunderous applause?"

"Thunderous?" Danyilyn snorted. "From a few hundred
peasants, outside, on a damp afternoon? I'm pleased, certainly, but let's save the idea of thunderous for tomorrow
night."

"Yes," Pelmen quietly agreed. "Two thousand pleased
urbanites in a packed house—that's thunderous applause."

"Say what you will, I thought I was superb," Gerrig
gloated with characteristic modesty. "The play's good too."

"The play is excellent," Yona Parmi growled. "If a bit
distasteful, still," he added.

"I only wish I knew what we'll be competing against," Danyilyn muttered, as she examined her charming face in a small mirror.

"Regort will be there with his troupe," Gerrig advised, "And of course Shavor-Brot's band, who performed so miserably last year—"

"I thought they were good," Yona Parmi mumbled, but not loudly enough for Gerrig to hear. It was an old argument, one there was no sense in repeating. Sherina heard him, though, and she smiled her agreement.

"—then the local group will be performing—Eldroph and Berliath, are those their names?"

"He's excellent." Danyilyn nodded. "Her I can do without."

"—plus a half-dozen other troupes. I've heard there's even one coming from up on the Straits Coast. Should be a worthy competition."

"It's likely they'll all be rehearsing tonight, somewhere in the city," Yona Parmi said. His eye was on Pelmen. "It would certainly be nice to know what they're doing in advance." Pelmen heard him, but didn't respond.

Gerrig chuckled. "I wouldn't mind stealing a good line or two myself. Wishful thinking, though—we couldn't make Pleclypsa until well after midnight. What say we find the local tavern instead?" His feet were already on the path toward the village, and Danyilyn and the others were following.

Yona Parmi hung back to ask Pelmen: "Are you coming?"

"Not tonight," he said loudly. "I think I'll turn in early." The wandering wizard faked a yawn.

"Ah," Yona Parmi muttered quietly, "but just what will you turn in *to*?" A few minutes later, as the group of laughing players reached the edge of the village, Yona Parmi heard a screech and looked up in time to see a falcon passing high overhead. When many hours had passed, and he arrived back at their wagon, Yoni Parmi found Pelmen lying on his couch, comfortably wrapped in a fur.

"Well," he asked. "How's the competition?"

"Yona," replied Pelmen as he turned his face to the wall, "we have nothing to worry about." Already he was planning his first move once they got within the castle.

* * *

For days, the Imperial House had sweated to grow as an entity, seeking to extend consciousness into those useless parapets and towers built since the sleep first came. Buried within its subconscious were memories of those spells muttered ages before by Nobalog, when he enchanted the House into life. The castle drew upon this knowledge, dredging wondrous power from the air. After long absence, the magic had returned to Chaomonous, and the House reveled in a renewal of activity. There were conversations to listen to, Drax games to comment on, unknowing clowns to chuckle at, trysting lovers to spy upon. But before all of that came the work—the slow, intense process of moving awareness into new areas of its own structure. The task consumed its energies—consuming also any opportunity for that dreaded thought to arise once more: that no one could hear. It could not tolerate being alone forever. And so it kept on working.

Weird drafts frequently puffed down the hallways now, as the castle laughed in celebration of each new sign of progress. Such phenomena unnerved the occupants of the massive edifice. Being descended from those who had disregarded all supernatural experiences, most Chaons had little use for superstition. Yet a sense of the strangeness of the past week had stolen over scholar, soldier, servant, and stranger alike. None could tell the origin of his feelings, nor did anyone attempt to give expression to these sensations, fearing the mockery of his fellows. But the sensations persisted, and it pleased the House no end to witness the discomfort of those who lived within it. They would know its presence.

The Imperial House had at last gained control of the perimeters of the gardens. It had possessed the terrace walkways to the point that it could overhear every garden *tête-à-tête*. It could even enjoy the fragrance of the blossoms. Although it was beginning to notice a peculiar irritation on its rooftop, its mood was jovial as it relaxed and watched the butterflies flutter from flower to flower, much as the Queen moved from man to man in her court.

Suddenly its attention riveted on its lower dungeon. In a flash, its pleasant mood disappeared, replaced by a fearsome wrath. An invader had appeared from nowhere! The

House was understandably shaken, for throughout its waking years its walls had resisted every challenge, and its inward sanctuaries had remained inviolate. It had never thought to examine its own foundations for cracks. Yet cracks there were—cracks that had been there for centuries.

There was one man who knew them all, much as a rat knows its secret pathways into the larder. Like his brother rats, this man now scurried along hidden corridors in the darkness, oblivious to the curses the Imperial House heaped upon him.

The castle's record as a fortress was impeccable. And yet, in its twice a thousand years of existence, it had housed a score of short-lived dynasties. The old records that lined the dusty shelves of its library detailed a murky history of plots and counterplots. As a result, secret passageways carved of rock, dark memorials to those sinister doings, met and diverged in the black silence beneath the castle's dancing floor. Many had been dug since the coming of the dragon, and thus the House was blind to them. But all were known to the man who now added his inaudible tread to the weight of the heavy quiet.

He had an affinity with darkness. The black of the hellhole of Chaomonous could not compete with the inky darkness of his heart. His face was the stuff of nightmares. His name was Admon Faye.

He searched for something. Gliding from door to door in the dungeon, he hovered and listened to the movements within each cell only long enough to be sure its occupant wasn't his quarry. It was a testimony to his expertise in the art of silence that the denizens of this dank place, their ears sharpened by the absence of light, never heard him pass.

He left one corridor, slipping cautiously into the torchlit stairway to descend even further into the pit. He tiptoed into a fetid chamber, half lighted by a torch in the stairwell behind him. On the far side of the room, the dark side, he found a grate in the floor and knelt to listen.

"Here," he thought to himself. From the cell below the grate he could hear the shallow breathing of a child—or a woman. He struggled to lift the heavy grillwork. It wasn't fastened down.

"Food? Food at last?" Bronwynn called up weakly. "Where's the torch?" When he didn't answer, she whispered, "Who's there?"

"Hush!" he ordered in a sharp whisper; then he uncoiled a length of rope from around his waist and tied a loop in one end of it. "Wrap this around you," he whispered again, and he dropped the rope into the emptiness. It slapped the straw below, and he heard the woman shuffling toward it. She did not speak again until she stood beside him in the chamber.

"Who are you?"

Admon Faye kept his face turned from her and the dim torchlight to his back as he bent to murmur, "Grab my belt and follow me out."

They quickly left the dungeon and soon were into the subterranean maze. As they made their way through it, there was only one exchange between them. "Pelmen?" the young woman whispered, and Admon Faye stifled a snicker.

There was a convenient crevice in the rock just a few feet above the level of the river. Admon Faye did not hesitate when they reached it, but vaulted out of the crevice to land in a rowboat secreted below it. The young woman popped her head out, wincing in the first sunlight she'd seen in months, but determined to discover who had rescued her. Once she saw the legendary face of Admon Faye, she was tempted to climb back inside.

"You!" She spat.

"Into the boat, Lady Bronwynn," Admon Faye ordered quietly. "I'm in no mood to get an arrow through my back, and, I trust, neither are you."

Without another word Bronwynn wedged her body through the crack and tumbled into the boat. Though she had little stomach for what lay before her, it was surely better than what she'd left behind. She lay back in the small craft and enjoyed the sun on her face, while Admon Faye merged them effortlessly into the anonymous traffic of the great river of Chaomonous.

The Imperial House watched it all in fury.

CHAPTER THREE

※　※

In the Slaver's Sewer

IT'S ONE OF THE IRONIES of large cities that frequently the pockets of greatest lawlessness are found in the very shadow of the seat of law. The heart of the criminal sub-culture of Chaomonous lived within a five-hundred-yard radius of the palace. Bronwynn's escape by boat had lasted all of four minutes—long enough for Admon Faye to steer them from the foot of the castle's granite foundation to the mouth of a nearby sewer. Chaomonous was proud of its sewer system, but no one in the city felt prouder than the thugs and thieves who made it their private highway. Within minutes of her rescue from Ligne's dungeon, Bron-wynn found herself locked away in yet another cell. As far as she could tell, her circumstances hadn't altered a bit. She'd only changed locations—and jailers.

Now she stood behind the door with a small rough stool in her hand, awaiting Admon Faye's return. She heard the scrape of an oar against the sewer wall, then another scrape of wood on rock as a boat was moored in place. There were some mumbled words, but no reply. She hoped that meant he'd come alone.

Not that it made any difference. She'd tangled with Ad-mon Faye before, far to the north in the land of Lamath—

and her cheek had borne the imprint of his teeth for weeks afterward. Rosha mod Dorlyth had nearly killed the hideous slaver on that occasion, knocking Admon Faye headlong into a pit as dank and dark as this one. But the cutthroat was a powerful man—he'd survived. In her much-weakened state, Bronwynn knew she had little chance of escaping him. But she could surely let her feelings be known.

The key turned in the lock, and Admon Faye thrust his stomach-churning visage inside. Then he jerked back, yelping in pain, as Bronwynn sent the stool crashing savagely off his forehead. He slammed the door open and kicked the bouncing stool aside, then grabbed Bronwynn by the collar of her filthy dress. He hoisted her up until her face was scant inches from his glaring eyes, and spat out, "You may be a Princess, dearie, but a strap will peel your hide as easily as it will a slave girl's!" She trembled with fury and fear. Then inexplicably, he dropped her, and all anger drained from his face. He righted the stool, shoved it over to a rude table, and motioned her toward it. "Sit down. I've brought you some breakfast."

"Why are you keeping me here?" she screamed. "Are you planning to sell me back to Ligne, is that it? So you can finally make a profit on my death?"

Admon Faye rotated his little finger in his ear and shook his head. "Really echoes when you yell in this place. Sit down and eat."

"I'm not eating anything until I find out why I'm here!" she screamed again with exaggerated shrillness.

"Just what do you think I've come down here to do?" Admon Faye yelled back. It was Bronwynn's turn to stop her ears. The slaver laughed. Then he ducked out the door to the boat and quickly returned with two tankards of drink, a loaf of bread, a pot of honey, and several chunks of cheese. Bronwynn's mouth watered involuntarily. It seemed like years since she'd tasted anything but stale bread-crusts in gravy. She plopped onto the stool, tore the bread in half, and soon had her mouth crammed full of the heavenly stuff. Admon Faye went out a second time, returning with another stool. He closed the door behind him, sat on the stool, and leaned his back against the wall. "Surely you understand, girl, that I don't act as barmaid to

all my captives. Don't think I'd trouble myself to steer that
boat down here through the slime just to watch you feed
your belly."

"Then why have you come?" Bronwynn asked, her
mouth full of cheese and her fingers dripping with honey.

"We need each other, Bronwynn. You and I."

Bronwynn was startled. For the first time, Admon Faye
had revealed to her his crooked excuse for a smile. The
sight threatened to rob her of her appetite, but the smell of
the cheese won her back, and she quickly stuffed more of
both it and the bread into her mouth. "I need you?" came
her garbled reply. "What for?"

"To rescue you from Ligne, for one thing."

"Some rescue! I've just been switched from one dungeon
to another."

"I wouldn't complain," Admon Faye said defensively.
"Here you have furniture, at least, and a torch for light—"

"And the delightful smell of a sewer drifting by my
door," Bronwynn snarled. "Truly one of the garden spots
of Chaomonous."

"You won't be staying here long. It's the safest place in
the city for you right now. Joss will be combing the streets
above us within the hour—and Joss uses a sharp comb."

"Joss!" Bronwynn whispered savagely, then she spat.
"Joss, the turncoat!"

"The very man," Admon Faye sneered. "So you see, you
do need me."

"I don't," Bronwynn chirped. Admon Faye had frequently seen the mirror image of her haughty expression
on the face of her father. "Pelmen would have rescued me
in time—and if not, then my Rosha."

"Pelmen!" Admon Faye snorted, then he chuckled. The
sound of it gave Bronwynn a chill. "Your mighty powershaper is meandering over the countryside, trying to pick
up the pieces of his acting career. He has no intention of
saving you."

"That's not true," Bronwynn protested. "It's only that
his supernatural powers are limited here. You know magic
won't work in Chaomonous. At least, it never did."

"All I know is that Pelmen is hundreds of miles away,
hunting a troupe of actors to join. If that's a powershaper,
then I'm irresistibly attractive." Once again Admon Faye's

spine-shivering cackle filled the cell, and Bronwynn turned away from his twisted smile. "As for your tongue-tied sword lad, don't expect him before the winter thaw. Dragonsgate is clogged with snow. Besides, the merchants in Ngandib-Mar tell me that while you've been starving in the dungeon, he's grown fat with winter feasting. The lad has his pick of every blushing maiden in the Mar. You think he'd sacrifice all that to come crusading after a skinny wench like you?"

Bronwynn's voice was cold. "If you belittle Rosha again, I swear, beating or no, I'll brain you with this stool."

Admon Faye's smile died, but quickly revived. He shrugged his shoulders and waved a hand at one tankard as he grabbed the handle of the other. "Wash that bread down so I can understand you. We've much to discuss, and I'll not mention your Rosha if you'll keep Pelmen out of the conversation. It's time for you to face some realities."

"What realities?"

"To start with, Ligne wants you dead."

"Then why hasn't she killed me? She's had me in that pit for months."

"Kherda and Joss prevented her. Both feel some fondness for you still, since they watched you grow up."

"Some way to show it," Bronwynn whined, remembering the shackles Joss himself had clamped around her wrists.

"More than that, though. They feared a popular uprising if you were killed, and Ligne believed them."

"Now that makes more sense."

"Good." Admon Faye smiled. "You do have some grasp of political realities."

"Of course I do!" Bronwynn snapped. "I grew up in court, didn't I?"

"Then you'll not be surprised when the Queen changes her mind and orders Joss to murder you on sight."

"So when are you going to sell me to him?"

"Realities, child, remember?" Admon Faye growled. "I have no need of gold. There's as much gold stowed in these sewers as there is in the vaults of the palace. What I covet is freedom to operate my businesses in peace, and that's something Ligne won't give me. She wouldn't be a bad ruler, but for one great flaw. She bears grudges. No Queen can last long who bears a grudge—especially not a grudge

against me! Simply because I failed to carry out her orders
to the letter, allowing you and Pelmen to survive, she has
determined that I must be put to death. She may fancy
herself an invincible regent, but that's one sentence she'll
never live to witness."

Bronwynn returned to the bread and honey. "You seem
to come and go in the castle easily enough. Why not just
slit her throat in bed?"

Admon Faye smiled again. "A plan not far from my
own, little Bronwynn. And I would have done so already,
but I lacked two things."

"What things?" Bronwynn mumbled.

"A sufficient force to secure the castle from within—
and a legitimate ruler to set on the throne in her place."

Bronwynn stopped chewing, then began again, more
slowly. "You mean to give me back my kingdom," she said
matter-of-factly.

"You are quicker than your father was." Admon Faye
chuckled.

"So was my mother," Bronwynn observed. "That's why
Ligne disposed of·her." She raised her eyebrow meaningfully, then took a deep draught from the tankard and
wiped her mouth. "What makes you think I would give you
any more freedom than Ligne has?"

"A certain . . . awareness on your part."

"Awareness of what?"

"That I could kill you just as easily as I'm going to kill
her." Admon Faye smiled. The cruelty in his sunken eyes
made her stomach float.

Bronwynn kept silent for a long time, finishing the loaf
of·bread and licking the honey from her fingers. Admon
Faye waited until she had finished and looked back up at
him before saying, "I assume you've been considering the
idea. Are you agreeable?"

The young woman tossed her golden-brown hair back
over her shoulders and shrugged. "Certainly," she said.
"Until."

"Until what?"

"Until the situation changes," she said evenly, her blue
eyes meeting his. "Realities, remember?"

Admon Faye searched her face, waiting for her strong
gaze to weaken. It never did. "As I said, girl, you're

quicker than your father." He stood to leave, and turned toward the door. Then suddenly his fist shot out of nowhere, cracking Bronwynn across the side of the face and bouncing her off the wall and onto the floor. She screamed in shock, then gasped at the pain. He waited until the echoes of her shriek had died before he spoke. "But I trust you won't try to take advantage of our old family friendship." The last thing she heard as he left was his chilling chuckle.

Pleclypsa was a walled city which no longer needed its walls. At one time it had been the fortified capital of a nation hostile to Chaomonous, but now, far from being hostile, the native Pleclypsans did all they could to curry favor with their imperial overlords. If anything, the citizens of Pleclypsa were more snobbish about being Chaons than were the citizens of Chaomonous itself. It was this peculiar conceit and the real municipal inferiority that undergirded it which prompted the leaders of Pleclypsa to pay out exorbitant sums each year to import the finest players in the kingdom for a dramatic competition.

The actors loved it. They viewed the Winter Festival as a kind of theatre convention, the one time in the year when they all could come together and compare notes. Stuffy matrons, normally repulsed by the acting profession, vied with one another in providing sumptuous banquets for the players to feast upon while awaiting their night to perform. The whole region turned out to watch the new plays premiere. The local merchants had shrewdly scheduled a carnival to coincide with the Festival, so that cultured and uncultured Southlanders alike crowded into the city's inns—raising, naturally, the prices of lodging and board. The streets swarmed with people; gold changed hands, and much of that gold found its way into the pockets of the troupe that won the accolades of the judges. The color, the crowds, and the drama of the moment appealed to these actor types. As a result, the Festival lasted longer each year, as more and more troupes clamored for their night upon the boards.

The first night of the Festival was almost as tense as the last, for on that night every competing band performed a short segment of its dramatic offering for the year. The

judges rated these scenes against one another, and produced a schedule for the remaining days that was calcu-
lated to build the Festival to a thrilling climax; the troupes
performed in reverse order, beginning with the least impressive. It did not always happen that the cast who performed last received the Festival prize—some troupes actually preferred to be scheduled in the middle of the run,
hoping to put pressure on the casts to follow while relieving
some of their own anxieties early enough to enjoy the carnival atmosphere. But there was a psychological advantage
at being offered the final night that could not be ignored.
That made the first night all the more hotly contested.

Pelmen stood backstage in the shadow of the green-
velvet curtain, watching Gerrig. His giant friend joked and
sparred with Regort, who had been a cordial enemy for
years. Pelmen wasn't fooled by Gerrig's relaxed demeanor.
The pressure building inside him caused the man to laugh
too loudly, to wink too broadly. The light banter between
the two adversaries crackled with repressed hostility and
promised a night of electrifying performances.

Danyilyn didn't bother to hide her nervousness. She
paced the stage, belting out lines to test the acoustics of the
hall and the mettle of her voice. These were old lines,
speeches she'd spoken so many times that her phrasings
bore the ruts of much use. She wouldn't dream of letting
slip any new lines, nor would any of the other actors and
actresses who paced in circles around and beside her, making their own adjustments to this theatre. No one wanted to
tip his troupe's hand to the others—good lines got stolen
that way.

But Pelmen was quietly confident. He had dared to take
his alter-shape the night before; on falcon wings he had
come to investigate the final rehearsals of the competition.
In a way, he felt a bit troubled at his unfair advantage, for
he was a man of integrity, and the act smacked of cheating. But Parmi had reassured him this morning that it was
only good sense. "Your purpose—whatever it is—surely
warrants your using every power available to you," Yona
had said. "Besides," he'd added, "it's not as if you're going
to steal any of their garbage." Indeed, the other offerings
seemed a cut below average this year—perhaps as a result
of the unstable national conditions. It was difficult to re-

hearse consistently when starving. As he'd described what he'd seen to his friend, Yona had agreed that they need feel little anxiety this year. "Our material is better," Yona Parmi had grunted, and Pelmen was inclined to agree.

That's why it puzzled him to see Yona Parmi acting so strangely. The short player prowled the dark backstage area, peering behind dusty flats and regarding the clutter of props suspiciously. Pelmen strolled up behind him.

"Are you looking for something?" he began. Yona Parmi jerked at the sound of his voice.

"No," Parmi snorted gruffly. "I'm looking for nothing. That is, I'm hoping to find nothing."

"You're sure to find that back here." Pelmen smiled. He felt sure that he knew, now, the reason for Yona's strange behavior. He didn't mock him.

Yona ducked to peer behind a cutout of a tree. "Seems like a legitimate enough place for powers to be lurking," he mumbled.

"In my experience, powers don't lurk. They act. I think they'd prefer to be out on the stage than back here in the dust."

"And why is that?"

"That's where most of the people are." Pelmen shrugged. "And they're fascinated by people."

"Oh." Yona Parmi glanced about him, then smiled in tight-lipped amusement. "Then I prefer to be right here."

"You're afraid of them."

"Aren't you?"

"No. Not the powers themselves. More of the people who use them."

"Yet you use them. You did last night."

"I know," Pelmen replied quietly.

Yona Parmi understood. "You're afraid of yourself."

Pelmen nodded, then arched a friendly eyebrow. "And as long as I remain so, I feel rather confident that I'm nothing, really, to be afraid of. It isn't the powers you need to fear, Parmi, for if they're here and you don't know it, you'll never notice them. And if they're here and you do know, they're yours to mold. But those others who know, and who mold—they're the people I fear. They'll shape to suit their whims—and I've seen too much of mankind's doings to feel encouraged by that."

Yona Parmi froze his ironic smile into place. "Your words are encouraging me to dig a deep, cool hole and bury myself in it."

"I've considered it," Pelmen joked, but there was more than a hint of seriousness in his words.

"And yet you say you fear *being* shaped. Explain that."

Pelmen blinked, then his eyes looked beyond Yona, as if gazing at a reality beyond human sensation. When he spoke, it was in hushed tones heavy with mystery. "Sometimes I fear that. Perhaps it comes so unexpectedly. I sense a power, I begin to shape, then somehow, inexplicably, it begins shaping me. And then when it happens, I'm elated. Once it comes, I fear nothing at all. I never know exactly what I'll do then . . ." Pelmen's eyes finally found their way back to Yona's. "And that's a rather frightening prospect in itself, don't you think?"

"Not necessarily. That is, I'm not convinced you really believe it so, since you persist in chasing the experience. But tell me, these religious followers of yours—"

"They're not mine."

"—of the Prophet's then—"

"They're not his either."

"All right, have it your way. Of the Power . . ."

"That's got it."

"Do they experience this—ah—being shaped as well?"

"Some do," Pelmen said with the quiet confidence of one who knows he won't be believed. "Not all. Not all of them have discovered yet that this is what it's all about. Some grab at the trappings of faith without experiencing faith itself."

Yona Parmi nodded thoughtfully. "So you entrusted the new Prophet with the task of helping them?"

Pelmen met his eyes. "*I* didn't."

Yona Parmi looked away in discomfort. "Pardon me," he muttered, "but it's rather difficult to shift one's entire view of the world in a moment."

Pelmen nodded. "It isn't easy to attribute actions to something other than people, when you've been used to seeing them as the only movers. As I say—it's people who do most of the shaping, consciously or unconsciously. And much of that turns out badly," he added with sadness. His mind wandered then, briefly, to Lamath, and the gentle plowed fields of that earnest, hard-working region. Then he continued. "I guess you could say that Erri the Prophet is responsible for being himself—and for letting others see in him the difference between shaping and being shaped."

Yona Parmi cocked an eyebrow. Even in the dark, Pelmen could see clearly his quizzical expression. "Doesn't Erri shape?" he asked.

"Not often." Pelmen smiled. "That's why he's the Prophet, and not I. I'm much too impatient. I prefer to shape my own destiny."

"Which, in turn, makes you dangerous." Yona Parmi nodded wisely.

Pelmen looked at him, a bit startled at this insight. Then he also nodded. "Exactly."

"Yet if you didn't battle these others, these various powershapers who inhabit Ngandib-Mar, who would?"

"Perhaps the Power would," Pelmen replied thoughtfully. It was evident from the way he said it that this was something not fully clear in his own mind.

"Then why battle at all?"

"Because there are people I care about who are in trouble," Pelmen answered. Quiet determination lent backbone to his words, as he finished. "And it might be through me that the Power chooses to aid them." It seemed to Yona Parmi that Pelmen's eyes blazed out of the shadows. He felt enormous relief when Danyilyn scurried over and grabbed each of them by the arm.

"We've drawn the third slot for tonight!" she announced, sure that her news bore the same critical importance for them that it did for her. For her sake they both pretended it did and joined her in the harsh green limelight to begin warming up their voices. A few moments later, Pelmen slipped quietly away to paint his face the color of the moon.

Pezi belched. Now it wasn't unusual for the obese merchant to belch—in fact, some of those who knew him argued that he never uttered a sentence without punctuating it with a burp. What was unusual was that Pezi had a miserable bellyache. Pezi's stomach rarely ever bothered him—it had swelled to enormous proportions long ago to accommodate the triple platefuls of food the merchant gorged down at every meal, and it no longer troubled to register any protest at such routine ill-treatment. But Pezi's latest binge had been monumental. It had amazed every occupant of Tohn's castle. Nor was it over; a half-empty platter of roast beef lay on the bed beside him. On the floor next to his bed sat a pitcher of ale. On the cabinet just beyond the pitcher, a towering sandwich leaned, threatening to topple at any moment. In his hand was a raw white onion, which he munched between belches as if it were an apple. Pezi had a problem. And when he had a problem, he ate.

Like most of Pezi's problems, this one concerned his uncle Flayh. He and his uncle fled Lamath on the day the dragon died, fearing reprisals from Pelmen the Prophet. Since they were merchants of the House of Ognadzu, they had found refuge here, in the family castle administered by Pezi's uncle Tohn. The ensuing months had been tense, as Flayh and Tohn had wrestled for control of the family's fortunes, but it had really been no contest. Though this was Tohn's castle, and its occupants were from his line of the family, Tohn suffered from a weak heart. The combination of a harsh winter and unceasing tension proved too much for the old warrior. They'd buried him in the snow.

Once firmly in control again, Flayh had returned with a passion to what had once been his favorite hobby—he'd involved them in the politics of Chaomonous. Not that Pezi minded that at all—he rather enjoyed dabbling in politics himself, and staunchly believed that the House of Ognadzu needed to reassert its dominance over the Chaon markets. While he and his uncle had been manipulating events in Lamath—or trying to—the rival House of Uda had established a virtual monopoly in Chaomonous, and it truly irked Pezi to have to buy his favorite candies from the competition. This very moment, a plot launched by Flayh was supposed to be bearing fruit—they'd contracted with Admon Faye to steal Bronwynn from the dungeon of Queen Ligne. But that was Pezi's problem. Where *was* Admon Faye? And why hadn't he contacted them?

Pezi got up to pace the floor. Two paces convinced him he'd better lie back down again.

Three days ago, Flayh had told him, "Keep me aware of

every development." Then he had disappeared into Tohn's old library and hadn't come out again. That concerned Pezi. Before they left Lamath, the old man had been showing definite signs of mental instability—and also signs of budding shaper power. It really didn't matter to Pezi whether the old goat was a powershaper or was crazy— both possibilities gave him the hives.

"Is he in there practicing his magic?" Pezi belched at his onion. "Or has his mind come unpeeled?" Or, he thought without saying it, has he gone to join Tohn wherever the dead gather? He stifled that thought—which was really more of a hope—and tried to fill his mind with something else. Flayh had also learned a bit about reading minds.

So what was Pezi to do? Interrupt his uncle to inform him merely that there was no news? Keep waiting until Admon Faye chose to notify them of his success or failure? Eat another sandwich? Truly a dilemma. Pezi definitely did not wish to interrupt Flayh. He thoroughly enjoyed his uncle's periods of absence. Yet if he didn't interrupt him, and Flayh was expecting him to . . .

Pezi sighed. Then he rolled off the bed and waddled toward the door, shoving piles of wadded garments aside with every step. He stopped with his hand on the door-latch—did he really want to do this? "Might as well," he grunted. He knew if he lay back down he'd only have to eat some more. He took one more bite of his onion and stuffed the rest into his pocket. Then he shuffled out into the hall and made his way to the door of Flayh's study. He hesitated there, steeling himself against the expected flood of colorful curses that always greeted him when he disturbed his uncle, and knocked on Flayh's door. No reply. He knocked again, a bit louder. Still no reply came from within the room. He crouched down to plant his ear on the keyhole, but could hear nothing. Straightening himself back upright—no mean task in itself—he put his weight behind the blows and pounded a chubby fist against the oaken barrier. Then he stepped back out of the way, so he wouldn't be clobbered when Flayh came boiling out.

Nothing happened. Pezi began to be concerned. He tried the doorlatch with little enthusiasm, sure that Flayh had locked it from within. As expected, it was locked.

"Now what am I going to do?" Pezi mumbled. Then he

recalled seeing a ring full of keys dangling from the belt of the castle's seneschal. He hurried away to find the man. He was trying not to get his hopes up . . .

He puffed around the corner into the seneschal's office, his cheeks turning the color of ripening plums, and skidded to a stop before the man's desk.

"Yes?" the seneschal asked rudely. Flayh's treatment of Tohn mod Neelis had created an abundance of ill will toward Pezi and his uncle. The castle staff feared Flayh far too much to reveal it to him. The bumbling Pezi felt the brunt of their displeasure.

"I need your keys," he demanded, thrusting his palm in the seneschal's face.

"My keys!" the man snapped. "Whatever for?"

"My uncle's been locked within the library for three days. He could be dead for all we know."

"I'll turn blue before I give you my key ring!" the seneschal spat savagely.

Pezi shoved his nose into the man's face and bellowed, "I said, give me the keys!" Pezi didn't expect the reaction he received, for the seneschal very nearly did turn blue. He choked, coughed twice, then thrust his keys into Pezi's palm and bolted from the room. Pezi straightened up, a bit puzzled but thoroughly pleased. "I guess I told him," he muttered as he turned to saunter back down the hall, his confidence boosted by this quick response to his firm authority. He never gave a thought to the onion in his pocket that had made it all possible.

After several attempts, he found a key that turned the lock, jerked open the door with a mighty heave and stepped inside. He knew immediately it was a mistake.

Candles and smoke were the first things he saw—an abundance of candles that filled the room with flickering light. Then he glimpsed Flayh, who had for the first time noticed him. The old man's bald pate glowed in the eerie illumination, and so did his beady eyes. Flayh's expression in that first brief instant was one of desperate surprise— Pezi had caught him with his magical pants down. A split second later a horrified Pezi stared down the throat of a savage dog, who hurtled through space toward his neck. Pezi shrieked and fell backward. To his great good fortune, the lean gray animal slammed nose first into his tummy and bounced head over heels into the courtyard. Pezi saw the dog bounce out, but it was Flayh who rushed back inside, slamming the door behind him. He regarded his nephew with wide-eyed surprise.

"I did it!" he gasped.

"You *almost* did it," Pezi gasped back, as both hands sought out his threatened throat. He had to plow through a series of chins to get to it.

"Do you think anyone saw?" Flayh pleaded.

"I did," Pezi spluttered.

"I mean anyone important." Flayh ducked back outside to check the hallway in both directions, then danced back inside, a frightening grin spreading across his wrinkled face. "I *did* it! I found my alter-shape! Oh *thank* you, Pezi, you can't imagine how delighted I am."

Pezi squirmed in terror. His crazed uncle had actually embraced him.

Flayh scampered across the room, clapping his hands like a schoolgirl. "A dog! I'm a long, lean hound! Something powerful! Not a mere insect, like Mar-Yilot, or a lizard, like that fellow Joooms—a hound! A powerful hound!"

Pezi stared, open-mouthed. At last his uncle ceased his raving and turned to stare back at him. "What are you gawking at?" Flayh snapped, and Pezi, relieved, closed his mouth. That had sounded like the uncle he knew. "What are you doing here? Why did you burst in unbidden? What's the meaning—"

"I came to give you some news." Pezi blurted out as loudly as he could. If his uncle was going to turn into a dog whenever he got angry, Pezi was determined to keep him pacified.

"News? Of Admon Faye? What is it?" Flayh demanded in crisp brittle tones.

Now Pezi was in a quandary. "Ah . . . there's *no* news . . ."

"No news? You interrupt me to bring me no news?"

"That's the news," Pezi whined. "That there's no news . . ."

Flayh charged toward him, grabbing this nephew whose great girth dwarfed him by the collar of Pezi's tunic. "You loathsome—"

"Please, uncle," Pezi cried, and Flayh backed quickly to the other side of the room.

"What have you been eating?" Flayh asked in horror.

Pezi stared at him, then shrugged and began listing, "A half of a ham with cherry sauce, a broasted fowl's breast marinated in a mint jelly with—"

"Enough!" Flayh shouted. "What possessed me to ask such a question of you . . ."

"Please, uncle," Pezi rushed on to say, "I only wanted to keep you aware of the situation as you told me to—"

"Get out! And stay out until there's some development worth telling about. And give me those keys." Flayh held his nose and stalked over to jerk the key ring from Pezi's hand.

"But the seneschal—"

"Out!" Flayh roared as he shoved his nephew backward and slammed the door in his face. The key scraped into the lock, and the tumblers shifted noisily.

Pezi just stood there for a moment. He noticed again that his belly ached. He felt of it, and sighed. "Must be hungry," he muttered. He finished his onion on the way to the kitchen.

Bronwynn sat against the wall of her prison and daydreamed. She'd gotten good at that during these months of darkness. Months? It could as easily have been weeks or years, for all she knew. No, not years—her hair hadn't grown long enough for that. But it had been plenty of time for her to imagine a hundred different means of rescue. And every dream starred Rosha mod Dorlyth.

Rosha, her intended—warrior of Ngandib-Mar. At first she'd been embarrassed to fantasize about him so extravagantly. Now she just leaned back and enjoyed it—imagining him breaking the door down, crushing her in his arms . . .

The door slammed open, jolting her out of her pleasant vision and back into the ludicrous reality of her current predicament. In all her dreams of rescue, none had seemed so improbable as this.

"Resting easy, are you?" Admon Faye asked with a mock cheeriness that made her groan. "No? Pity. I've come to bring a little sunshine into your life. Get up."

"Why should I?"

Adom Faye didn't reply. He just reached down to grab Bronwynn by the shoulders and hoisted her up. He spun her around to face the wall and, before she could react, was slipping a leather strap around her waist.

"I'm not going to be tied!" she shouted and she rammed her elbow back into his gut. He grunted, then boxed both of her ears in response. She stomped on his foot, spun around to rake his face with her fingernails, and got a punch in the eye for her trouble. That dazed her—it also calmed her down. Admon Faye went on about his business, moving the strap up and wrapping it around her bust first, then dropping it down to her hips. "What are you doing?" she asked, though it was already perfectly obvious to her.

"I'm measuring you for some new clothes. Or would you prefer to keep this rag?"

"Why didn't you just say that, then?"

"Oh, Princess Bronwynn, may I take your measurements, *please?*" he mocked in a squeaky falsetto. Then he snorted. "Suppose we get it straight between us who does the asking and who does the telling?" He read the last measure, then slung Bronwynn into a corner of the cell and pocketed the tape. He pointed his finger at her. He said nothing, just pointed that finger and looked at her. Then he left as quickly as he'd come.

Bronwynn didn't bother to get up. She lay back where she was and tried hard to think about Rosha. But the thoughts now only filled her with despair. For while Ligne's dungeon was far blacker than this place, at least there she had felt that Rosha, or Pelmen, or someone on her side might be able to find her. No one knew she was here, save Admon Faye. And at the moment, it seemed even Ligne's hole might be preferable to serving the whims of the slaver. She didn't cry—Bronwynn wasn't much for weeping. But it might have helped her feelings. Bottled inside her chest was a lump of disappointed hopes—and nothing could make that lump go away.

Still fuming, the House watched in silence as Joss climbed a small, private stairway into its upper levels. It felt enormous frustration; though it had warned its occupants in every consceivable way of the invasion and escape of the intruder, not a soul within its walls had paid any heed. It had been hours before the theft of the captive had even been discovered. The warders who made that discovery then took another few hours to decide how to inform the Queen. Finally they'd drawn straws, and the luckless loser carried the message to her quarters. Now, after wasting a day, the Queen had summoned her Lord of Security to inform him of his failure. The castle hoped she'd have the man hanged. His guards! Ineptitude had besmirched the honor of the Imperial House of Chaomonous!

The terraced gardens spiraled up out of the bowels of the castle to the very rooftop itself. Overall, capping the pleasure park's floral splendor, arched a gigantic aviary wrought of iron and delicately colored glass. It stretched up to a height almost equaling the loftiest of the castle's towers, which were themselves the tallest in this land. This rooftop cage was the warmest spot in the palace, kept so for the sake of the brightly plumed birds that fluttered from one man-made branch to another. Just as exotically plumed as the birds were the colorful courtiers who walked and talked beneath. This was one of Ligne's favorite spots, for she felt the gorgeous gardens, illuminated by the multicolored light from above, served as a perfect setting for the jewel of her own beauty.

She greeted Joss with a forced smile, and quickly got down to business. "I hope you haven't regretted entering my service, Joss," she said as she tossed a handful of seeds before a peacock. "For a man of your integrity, such a transfer of loyalties must have been most difficult."

"I would be lying if I denied it, my Lady Ligne." Joss nodded stiffly. He always felt out of place in this garden. He was much more at home in the armory, many floors below.

Ligne smiled, her blue eyes sparkling. "And General Joss never lies."

"Only for the sake of Chaomonous," he affirmed. She waited for him to elaborate, and unwillingly he obliged. "It was not so difficult to turn my back on Talith, once the King proved himself a fool. I determined that when he would not listen to reason, he was beyond any help that I might offer."

"When he refused to believe I was about to overthrow him, you mean?" she supplied, still smiling.

"That is correct, my Lady." Joss nodded, his discomfort growing. Ligne was a capricious woman with a taste for cruelty. He had no intention of crossing her.

"I've been pleased with your performance, Joss, ever since you saw the futility of resisting me. You may relax. Your marvelous military talent—which Talith so wastefully misused—has proved much to my liking. I feared you as an enemy, Joss. I feel far more secure with you as a servant." She turned away from him, scattering seed with a wide sweep of her arm. "But I cannot seem to shake this tiny whisper of doubt that nags at me whenever I consider your service." She spun around to face him, her blue eyes suddenly hard. "I mean your continued affection for Talith's daughter Bronwynn."

Most men would have flinched under Ligne's gaze. Joss merely acknowledged it with one of his own. Then in deference to his Queen, he dropped his eyes and inclined his head. When he looked up at her again, his expression was humble, but frank. "As I've stated, it would be a lie for me to say I feel no lingering sense of shame regarding my break with the late royal family. But I must simply remind my Queen that it was I who duped the Lady Bronwynn into believing I would lead her army of rebellion, and who then brought her to you, bound in a criminal's chains. My Queen should examine only my actions to determine my faithfulness. My feelings are a private matter, which I never allow to interfere with the business of state."

"Never?" Ligne demanded, shouting in his face.

Joss blinked, but did not draw back. "Never," he murmured tonelessly.

Ligne continued glaring for a moment, then her eyes softened, and she turned away. "I believe you," she said at length. "If you suddenly protested that you hated Bronwynn, I would certainly doubt your sincerity. After all, I always considered her a likeable child, didn't you?"

"I did," Joss answered, very aware of those eyes fixed on his.

"Regrettable that I've been forced to confine her to the dungeon, don't you think?" Ligne didn't blink.

"If my Queen feels it is so, yes."

"And what do *you* feel?" she snapped.

He hesitated briefly, then breathed heavily, "I never allow my feelings to enter into the affairs of state."

"Good," Ligne snarled, suddenly angry, "for I'm going to need your absolute loyalty to return her there!"

"Return her?" Joss barked, his body cocking rigidly to attention. He realized now that he had just passed a very serious test. He realized, too, he was now facing a stiffer one.

"She's gone," Ligne spat. "Stolen from my hole. My foremost rival, the only threat to my security in this position, and she's vanished!"

"I heard no alarm."

"No guard was fool enough to give any. Nor did I call for one when the warder finally made it known to me in my chambers, some hours ago." She gazed at Joss, and motioned toward a sparrow that glided overhead. "When the bird has flown, is there any point in screaming in anger?"

"None, my Lady," Joss acknowledged curtly.

"Of course, the guards say they didn't see a thing." Ligne sneered. "So I'm having their useless eyes extracted. But though their cries might soothe my temper, they won't change the situation. Oh!" she seethed, balling her fist and shaking it above her head. "I ought to wring Kherda's neck for keeping me from killing her while I had her!" Then she glared at Joss accusingly.

Joss cleared his throat. "My Queen, I have no love for Prime Minister Kherda, as you well know, but I did agree with that policy. To assassinate the Lady Bronwynn publicly would certainly build no confidence among your subjects—"

"Don't lecture me!" Ligne shouted, pointing her finger at Joss. Then her voice softened. "How can you expect me to consider public confidence when a free Bronwynn presents a clear and present threat to my reign? I am no longer concerned with appearances. I want Bronwynn dead, and I want you to kill her." She moved to him again, shoving her face into his. "I'm satisfied that your feelings will not be allowed to interfere." Her eyes left no room for objection. Joss offered none. "I have given this assignment before, I think you're aware."

"Yes, my Queen. To Admon Faye."

"There are few men in this land capable of stealing a captive from my prison. Admon Faye is the only one who comes to mind."

"Yes, my Queen."

"When you find the man, put an end to him as well. We did not part on good terms."

"Yes, my Queen."

Ligne looked up at him. "Well? Go!"

Joss turned to leave the aviary, pushing a peacock aside with his boot.

"Oh, one more thing," Ligne called, and Joss turned to listen. "I've had the warder gutted. Display his body in the armory for several days. I want the palace defenses to have something to think on. Consider it yourself, Joss—won't you?" She clapped her hands together to rid them of the last of the bird seed, then turned to walk swiftly down the garden path. Joss walked just as swiftly down the interior stairway to the lower levels of the castle. The further he got from the woman, the cleaner he felt. But duty was duty, and she was right. Chaomonous could not afford two Queens.

Bronwynn gingerly fingered her eye and the swollen flesh surrounding it. She longed for a mirror. Not that anyone was going to see her down here—thank goodness. The way she looked now, a rescuing Rosha would probably gag and just leave her behind! But a mirror would have been nice. There was something comforting in knowing exactly how ugly she looked. In her imagination, the whole right side of her face was twice its normal size, and as black as a ripe avocado. Admon Faye had punched her hard. But it was the memory of his pointed finger, and the threat implied in it, that made her shiver. Understandably, she didn't leap for joy when she heard his boat mooring outside her door. She fixed a sneer on her bruised features, but he ignored her as he stepped inside and tossed her a linen bag. "Put them on," he muttered, then he left the cell, slamming the door and locking it behind him. She heard him get into his boat. She waited, listening.

"Put them on!" he ordered through the door, and she decided she'd best comply. She opened the drawstring of the linen bag and dully examined its contents. Her interest grew suddenly sharp.

It held a new pair of suede boots, well-made by the look of them; a pair of soft leather trousers, styled like a man's but tailored to fit her; a shirt woven of wool and dyed a dark green, and a tan waistcoat to go over it; and a floor length cape, fur-lined within and coated without with pitch, to keep her both warm and dry in harsh weather.

"Where are you taking me?" she shouted.

"Are you dressed yet?" he yelled back.

"Not yet—"

"If I have to come in and strip you myself, I guarantee you won't like what follows."

Bronwynn got dressed. She was more than happy to abandon the rag she'd been wearing for months, and the quality of these new clothes convinced her that Admon Faye's sewers were indeed lined with gold. The cape felt especially good. She hadn't been warm in weeks. "I'm ready," she called, and Admon Faye flung open the door and grabbed her by the wrist. He moved too quickly for her to resist him effectively, binding her arms behind her with an expertise born of years of slaving.

"I thought you were going to make me a Queen!" Bronwynn cried.

"And I will. If I don't skin you first. Get into the boat."

Bronwynn obeyed without argument, and Admon Faye poled them away from the wall. He turned the bow of the craft into the stream and began pushing it against the gentle current. Bronwynn gagged at the sight of the waste and rubbish that bobbed along the water surrounding them. She decided even Admon Faye's face was preferable, and looked back at him. "Is it always this deep?"

"Often deeper," the slaver answered. "Be glad you chose to be a good little girl. I could have left you behind—and in the spring thaw you'd have drowned in the stuff." He chuckled lewdly.

Bronwynn turned away from his ugly smile. Maybe the garbage was better. "Where are we going?"

"You'll know it when we get there."

"It must be somewhere in the Spinal Range, or you wouldn't have provided this cape—"

"I told you once, girl. You'll know it when we're there."

It was clear Admon Faye would say no more. Bronwynn snuggled back into the cloak and rested, watching reflected light dance on the granite vault above her. The rhythm of the pole ramming into the sewer bed and the gentle rock of the boat made her drowsy . . .

Then she was wide awake, as many pairs of hands lifted her out of the rowboat. She was carried like a rolled-up carpet up a flight of steps, under the rough arms of several most ungentle porters. They sniggered, pinching and tweaking her flesh all the way across an underground stable toward a waiting horse. There they tossed her skyward, and she instinctively spread her legs to slam down into the horse's saddle. Her hands were untied, then quickly bound again in front of her, and someone slapped the animal on the rump. It moved sluggishly out of the stable, into the sunlight.

Bronwynn squinted. This was only the second time she'd seen the sun in months. She ducked her head, protecting her eyes against the glare, but they soon adjusted, and she saw that she was just one of many riders, mounted and ready to move. She heard many shouts and cries around her, but easily singled out Admon Faye's voice above the rest.

"What about Joss?"

"He rides to Dragonsgate. The barman at the Bull's End told him your plans."

Admon Faye swore savagely, then muttered, "Have you dealt with that barman?"

"His body floats in the sewer."

"But Joss knows," Admon Faye snarled, and he cursed again. "Very well. We'll have to go by way of the Great South Fir. That's well out of our way—but no matter. We'll break from the woods due south of Tohn's castle. Joss will find nothing in the pass but a lot of snow." Admon Faye chuckled. "Wonder how he'll justify that to our gracious Queen?" Admon Faye spurred his horse to move abreast of Bronwynn's. "Well, little girl, are you ready to ride?" Before she could answer, he grabbed the reins of her horse and dug his heels into the flanks of his own. Bronwynn clamped her knees tightly onto her saddle and leaned forward, as Admon Faye's band of rascals charged westward toward the Great South Fir.

CHAPTER FOUR

A Swordsman's Surprise

"PERHAPS YOU didn't hear me the first time, Rosha. You—are—*crazy!*" Dorlyth mod Karis' face was redder than his beard.

"I d-did hear you the first time, father. And every t-time since."

"Then why do you persist in making a fool of yourself. There's a blizzard outside!"

Rosha mod Dorlyth, pretended champion of Heinox, friend of Pelmen Dragonsbane and a bear's-bane in his own right, did not reply. Instead he cinched the saddle of his war-horse a notch tighter, then turned to fetch his saddlebags.

Dorlyth ran his hand through the unruly curls that ringed his mouth, and sighed. "Son, I know it's very difficult to come home once you've become a hero, but—"

"It's not difficult to come home, father. It appears the d-difficulty is in leaving again. Would you hand me that?" He pointed to a scabbarded greatsword that hung on the wall. Dorlyth nodded and pulled it down, fingering it lovingly before passing it to Rosha across the horse's back. He had given the sword to the lad only six summers before, and already it was the premier weapon in the land. King

Pahd mod Pahd-el, ruler of Ngandib-Mar, had honored it with a name, making it the first named sword in Dorlyth's memory. "Thalraphis" he had dubbed it—"the eyeneedle" —for though the weapon was five feet long, it had been no more than a needle in the eye of the great dragon, Vicia-Heinox. With this very weapon, Pelmen had slain the mortal enemy of all mankind.

Rosha took the sword and strapped it to his saddle. Then he glanced around the stable, trying to think if he were forgetting anything.

"Rosha—son—think it over! If she really did call you her treasure, the woman's not going to run off and marry someone else before spring!"

"It's not just B-bronwynn, father. It's s-s-simply time to go!" That was true. From the moment he had arrived home he'd been wined and dined by every wealthy family in the land of Ngandib-Mar. King Pahd had given him the biggest banquet anyone could remember. His stomach still felt bloated.

The celebrations of his heroism had barely passed before the yule season arrived, and once again the lords and barons of all Ngandib had clamored for his presence. He was so tired of eating and of honors that he hoped never to see another breast of pheasant or golden goblet again. Being a hero had grown boring to him, at last, so he'd ridden home to the comfort of his father's fire.

Dorlyth and Rosha had watched the yule log dwindle together, wrapped in bear furs, and had finally talked themselves out. Rosha learned a sad truth. Being a hero was much less satisfying than doing heroic things. It grew dull and stale in a hurry.

And then there was Bronwynn. Princess of the Golden Kingdom of Chaomonous, far to the south, her last words to him had been a declaration of her love. Then she'd ridden away, to reclaim her throne from the false Queen Ligne, and he hadn't heard another word from her. Day after day he had watched the southern horizon for a blue-flyer bearing a message, but those carrier birds that did arrive at the castle brought only more invitations to dinner.

Worst of all, he was stuttering again. He had to go!

He stepped to the doorway of the stable and gazed out the open gate. Large flakes of snow tumbled gracefully from the sky, adding to the three-inch blanket of the stuff that already covered the cobblestoned courtyard.

"Only a fool would ride east in this weather," Dorlyth growled, "and I didn't raise a fool." Rosha slung himself up onto the back of his war-horse. "On the other hand," Dorlyth muttered, "maybe I did." Rosha wheeled his mount and would have ridden out, but Dorlyth shouted, "Wait!" and grabbed the reins.

"No, father!" Rosha yelled, then he clasped his arms tightly around his horse's neck, as the animal reared to protect its master. The horse had been a gift from King Pahd, and was nervous and spirited.

An old warrior like Dorlyth hadn't lived to become old by being stupid. He beat a hasty retreat to the far side of the stable, and Rosha's warning shout disintegrated into a chuckle. The young swordsman slipped down to the ground and caught the beast's head in his hands, saying. "It isn't good to trample your master's father, my friend. Relax." Then he turned to look at Dorlyth, still twenty feet away.

His father made a wry face. "Can I come tell you goodbye without getting stepped on?"

Rosha grinned, and spread his arms wide. Dorlyth mod Karis hugged his son powerfully, then stepped back to look at him. "Can't blame an old man for being lonely," he said gruffly. Rosha understood what Dorlyth was truly saying to him . . . "Go with blessings." The young man nodded. Then he laid a hand on his father's shoulder and squeezed it.

"Take c-care of yourself, will you?"

"Me, take care of myself? Lad, *I'm* not the one going out into a snowstorm!" Dorlyth frowned. Then he winked, and growled, "I thought you said Pelmen was coming to visit?"

"He said he was. B-but you know P-pelmen."

"Indeed I do." Dorlyth nodded sourly. "If he says he's on his way, that means don't expect him." Rosha climbed back onto the horse's back, and the animal allowed Dorlyth to come up close without moving. "One thing more," Dorlyth muttered, and Rosha looked at him expectantly. "If you get married, at least let me know. Fathers are interested in that sort of thing."

Rosha laughed, and with a twist of his hand was gone, out the stable door and into the crisp air of early morning.

In a moment both horse and rider had disappeared into the swirling snow.

"Merciful, that," muttered Dorlyth to himself. He hated long good-byes.

Admon Faye did not permit his troop of brigands any rest until they swept past the last cultivated field and entered the edge of the Great South Fir.

The three lands were divided from one another by two great natural barriers. The Spinal Range, a wall of rock that separated Chaomonous from Lamath, started in the sea itself as the formation of islands called the Border Straits. From the coast it ran one hundred and thirty miles inland to the west. Its granite cliffs were unbroken, save for that one legendary pass known as Dragonsgate. At Dragonsgate, the mountain range divided, and separate arms extended into both sections of the other geographical barrier—the Great Fir. This band of rugged forest was fifty miles wide at its narrowest point, but that was around the base of the mountains, where it was also so dense as to be impenetrable to all but wood creatures. The mountains formed the dividing line, separating the Great Fir into northern and southern sections.

Eighty miles southwest of the Spinal Range, the Great South Fir could be passed. But few people attempted the feat. Most of those who did were slavers. Any other small party travelling alone in the Great Fir was likely to finish the journey with slavers—in chains.

The Great Fir was the closest thing Admon Faye had to a home—or it had been, until his recent conquest of Dragonsgate. Scattered through the forest were his cleared campsites. Some of these were of enormous size but so skillfully hidden in the thickets as to be unrecognizable to all but the trained woodsman. It was not until they reached one of these hidden shelters that Admon Faye let his weary band stop.

His little army of forty swords had more than tripled in this latest visit to Chaomonous, and now a hundred and fifty men scrambled for the best of the tent sites, and fought one another for firewood.

Bronwynn, however, stayed astride her horse. Though exhausted by the journey, she refused to budge until someone cut her bonds and lifted her down. If she were to be the Queen of this ragged rabble, they could begin now to show her a little respect.

"Are you planning on going somewhere, girl?"

Bronwynn stiffened her shoulders at the sound of Admon Faye's voice. He was behind her, but she refused to turn her head. "I'm going nowhere until someone does me the courtesy of cutting my bonds and getting me down."

"Take that attitude about it," he growled, "and you may be sure no one will. Get off." She didn't budge. "I guess you must like it up there," he said after a moment.

"Like it?" Bronwynn snapped. "My bottom is black and blue."

"If it isn't, it will be," he threatened, "unless you hop down off that horse and start collecting some firewood. Your hands are tied in front of you. You can get off easily enough."

Bronwynn sighed, then kicked her right leg over the horse's head and pivoted on the saddle, dropping easily to the ground. She groaned. The insides of her thighs were raw, and her legs were cramped from clamping tightly onto the saddle. Admon Faye chuckled behind her. She turned to glare at him, loathing everything about him.

He chopped a point on one end of a branch with a heavy knife. Then he reversed the stake and lopped off two forking branches at the other end, leaving the fork in it to hold a spit of meat. Then he looked up at Bronwynn. "You want your ropes cut? Here's the knife." The weapon came flipping at her end over end, and Bronwynn jerked away, but it buried itself harmlessly in the mulch several inches short of where her foot had been. "Wouldn't have hit you, your Highness." Admon Faye snickered, as did the other outlaws who happened to be standing nearby. Then the slaver turned his back on her and buried the point of his stake at the edge of an old firepit. Bronwynn picked up the knife and, after an awkward moment of pushing and reaching, managed at last to cut through her bonds. Then she looked around. No one was watching her. Admon Faye's back was turned, as he leaned on the stake, driving it into the ground.

Bronwynn was angry, and that anger clouded her good sense. Dismissing the possible consequences of success, she grabbed the knife in both hands and vaulted toward Admon Faye's broad back. But before she would reach it, that back had moved—the stake wasn't in place anymore either. Admon Faye sidestepped her charge and brought the stick arching around behind her. At the very instant she realized he had moved, the stick cracked painfully across her backside, and she fell most ingloriously into the ashes of the firepit. It wasn't the blow that hurt her most. It was the shout of laughter that greeted her humiliation.

"Remarkable, isn't it," Admon Faye remarked to a comrade, "how they all try exactly the same thing?"

"Get up, girl," someone laughed, "and take comfort in the fact that you aren't the first who's pitched headlong into a firebed."

"My Lady," Admon Faye mocked her, "I hope you are appreciative. I did at least wait about starting the fire until after you took your tumble."

Bronwynn felt certain that no fire could burn as hot as her cheeks did right now. She could hear the laughter rippling through the far side of the camp as the news was quickly relayed.

Admon Faye stepped down into the pit—it was shallow, only a foot or so deep—and dragged her stumbling and choking to her feet. She cowered away, expecting another blow to blacken her other eye. Admon Faye felt her jerk—and grinned. He was, by both instinct and training, a bully. And he knew from long experience that to withhold an expected blow sometimes struck the soul with more savagery than a punch. He withheld this one. He shoved her away with a derisive snort, and left her standing in humiliation in the ashes.

Bronwynn felt the intended shame—she wasn't even worth hitting! She dragged herself out of the pit and sat down on the edge of it. For the first time in a long time, she filled her hands with hot tears.

Rosha thoroughly enjoyed his first day of travel. The snowstorm, moving rapidly westward toward the High City of Ngandib, passed over him by midmorning, and when the sky cleared, the rays of the sun turned the snow-blanketed landscape a dazzling white. Though many miles away still, he fancied he could see the summit of Dragonsgate far to the northeast, and his heart quickened at the memory of the recent triumph there—a triumph in which he'd played a leading part. He booted his mount, and they plunged onward at a trot. Snow sprayed up around the hooves of his war-horse as they journeyed down through shallow valleys and over small hills, past small stands of trees denuded by the winter cold.

They passed few castles, and Rosha gave these a wide berth. It wasn't that he feared danger from them. He just couldn't shake the memory of a dozen ugly daughters, girls who'd been pushed at him by the most influential rulers of the land in fits of fatherly matchmaking. Rosha swore under his breath that he would not attend another banquet. However, should he be spotted by the lords of these local manors, he feared he would have no excuse not to. He pushed on, stopping little. His goal was to be at Dragonsgate inside three days.

Launched at last on a new adventure, his spirits rose, and his thoughts turned from the past to the future. The sound of hoofbeats was muffled by snow, and nothing moved in the white stillness to interrupt his deep deliberations.

He wondered about the world. With Vicia-Heinox dead, the barrier that had separated the three lands for centuries was gone as well. There had been only war between the lands for so many centuries—could peace really be possible now? His father thought not. But Dorlyth was old, and his foreign adventures had left him bitter toward all ideas that weren't Mari in origin. Could his father and the other leaders of Ngandib-Mar ever look with favor on the words of a Lamathian?

Of course, Dorlyth listened to Pelmen, and Pelmen was —no, Rosha thought. Pelmen wasn't really a Lamathian. But he wasn't a Mari either. Still and all, Pelmen was a powershaper, and didn't that make him Mari, at least in part?

More critical for Rosha, of course, would be Mari reactions to Chaons. His Bronwynn was the Chaon Queen—or would be soon. For a moment Rosha speculated on the reactions of those wealthy lords who had hosted him, once they heard of his marriage to the ruler of their hated southern rival.

"Let them talk," he announced to his horse's mane. "I *will* marry Bronwynn!" Rosha smiled, pleased with himself. He hadn't stumbled on a single word.

His second and third days out were as miserable as his first day had been fun. A new storm struck about noon of the second day, forcing him to pitch his tent early to wait out the worst of it. Within the confines of its fish-satin walls, he and his horse got better acquainted—a bit too well acquainted for Rosha's tastes. He broke camp early the next morning and pressed on, but the storm had been followed by a dreadful drop in temperature, and Rosha recounted ruefully his father's pleas for him to wait until spring. The sun came up at last to light his way, but its heat never penetrated the bitter cold. Rosha's breath froze on his face, and even the layers of bearskins he wrapped around himself couldn't slow the chatter of his teeth.

He began to long for a companion, anyone to talk to, to keep his mind off the chill. He talked to his horse for a time. Then he told his plans to his sword. Finally, for want of anything better to do, Rosha began to sing. The afternoon of the third day found him riding up the short incline of the western mouth of Dragonsgate, singing at the top of his lungs while his teeth chattered merrily between choruses.

Had Tibb been sitting any closer to the fire he would have been in it. "Why'd I ever let you talk me into this?" he chattered.

"Greed," his companion snorted, as he clapped himself on the shoulders in an effort to keep them from freezing. "A pure lust for stolen gold. That's the only thing that could ever budge you from Lamath."

"Yeah, well, when am I gonna see some of it?" Tibb responded sourly. "You promised me there'd be piles of it in this cave. There's piles all right . . ." Tibb turned his baleful gaze upon the enormous mound of dragon-droppings that lined the back of their freezing abode. "Does that smell like gold to you?"

"We could have had the gold, if we'd gotten here quick enough," Pinter snapped. "But no. You had to wait around to loot the Temple of the Dragon."

"How was I to know the funny little Prophet was gonna board it up?"

"Piles of gold and diamonds, hoarded in this cave for centuries, and you pass it up to steal altar cups!"

"Those cups were pure gold! A goblet in the hand is worth two piles of dragon dung any day!"

"Yeah?" Pinter snapped back, now flapping his long arms like a bird. "Well, you'd better be glad we've got it here to burn, or you'd be a solid block of ice."

"And that's my fault, I suppose?"

"Yes, it's your fault. If you hadn't wasted time we'd be with Admon Faye now, wherever he is. I'll wager he's not freezing."

"So let's go find him, then."

Pinter regarded Tibb with sheer revulsion. "Two Lamathians in Chaomonous? We'd be in irons by tonight."

"Then let's go back to Lamath," Tibb pleaded.

"Through the snow?" Pinter stomped to the entrance of the lair and pointed down at the Dragonsgate Pass, fifty feet below them. "Look at it!"

Tibb didn't need to. The pass had been snow-clogged for weeks. "We can't just sit here," he mumbled.

"Oh, yes we can," Pinter challenged. "We can just relax and wait for Admon Faye's return, as we agreed. Spring can't be very far away . . ." he added mournfully.

Tibb hunkered down closer to the small fire. It was giving off more smoke and stench that heat, but it beat no blaze at all. "What if he doesn't want us?" the stocky thief inquired sensibly. "What if he decides to sell us instead? It's been done," he protested.

"Tibb." Pinter sighed in exasperation. "You're talking about Admon Faye. This is not just some small-fish cutthroat. This man is a true outlaw. He's got class, style, taste—"

"We talking about the same Admon Faye? Mean fellow with a mug that would scare the wrinkles out of tugolith's hide?"

"Tibb, this is a man who is truly free. He bows his knee to no King."

"Still ugly, just the same."

"And when he returns, we'll offer him our swords—"

"And hope he doesn't use 'em on us."

"—and offer him the tribute we've collected in his absence," Pinter finished loudly, glaring at his comrade.

"Which is exactly nothing," Tibb snorted.

"There'll be some," Pinter affirmed confidently. "There will!" he repeated in the face of Tibb's snide expression.

"Oh, certainly." Tibb nodded. "Piles of it."

Pinter suddenly straightened up. "Do you hear that?"

"Hear what?"

"I hear singing . . ."

Tibb smiled uneasily. He'd been fearing it . . . the combination of the snow and these cramped conditions had caused his friend to come unravelled—

"Listen!" Pinter shouted. "Don't you hear it?"

"Sure, Pinter, sure," Tibb responded with exaggerated calm. "Why don't you come sit—" He cut off. Now he was hearing it too.

"A merchant!" Pinter shouted, and he jumped with excitement—an unfortunate move, since he was tall, and happened to be standing under the low lip of the cave's entrance. He yelped as his head grazed the rock and he landed hard on his rear. But the blow couldn't faze him. He was too thrilled. "Come on, we've got to stop him."

"It's, ah, it's probably not a merchant," Tibb argued nervously. "Why would a merchant be coming through now?"

"Get the weapons! Throw me my helmet! We have to get down and stop him before he gets through." That would be no easy task. Vicia-Heinox had favored this particular cavern for its inaccessibility. Its entrance, fifty feet up the sheer face of Dragonsgate's northern cliff, had proved a formidable obstacle to the pair when they'd first arrived. Sheer desperation for some protection against the cold had finally driven Tibb to scale the wall—that, and his expectation of diamonds and gold. Once inside, they'd discovered the remnants of Admon's Faye's encampment and a neatly rolled rope ladder of hemp. Now Pinter danced from one side of the cave mouth to the other, shouting orders while he tried to toss the ladder out and down. In his haste he succeeded only in turning the neat roll into a tangled, knotted pile.

Tibb was loathe to leave his fire—especially for a fight.

"I'll bet he's a cutthroat. Nothing but a cutthroat. Has to be a crazy cutthroat to try to pass Dragonsgate under these ridiculous conditions."

Pinter jerked feverishly at the pile. "Quit blithering and get that equipment over here. He'll be past us before we can even get off this cliff."

"What purpose will it serve?" Tibb demanded, stalking stiffly across the cave floor toward a pile of arms. "We'll get nothing but trouble out of this one. He's a cutthroat, I guarantee you. No one but a cutthroat would be in this pass in the wintertime."

"We're here, aren't we?" Pinter snarled, freeing one knot with a mighty jerk, and putting in two more in the process.

"That's what I said," Tibb yelled.

"We're not cutthroats," Pinter barked. "We're outlaws. Outlaws!"

"So you keep saying," Tibb muttered as he shuffled across the cave toward Pinter, his arms loaded. He slammed the load of weapons and gear onto the stone and turned around to look for the rope ladder to lower them. "Where's the rope?"

"Where do you think it is?" Pinter yelled in exasperation. "Where does it look like it is?"

"It looks like it's in knots," Tibb observed. Pinter roared in frustration as yet another tangle came into the ladder; in anger he buried the toe of his boot in the pile of gear. It plummeted over the edge, turning end over end to the canyon floor and landing in a snow drift.

"Now why'd you do that?" Tibb scolded. "I bet your precious Admon Faye doesn't kick his weapons off cliffs."

"Say one more word to me, Tibb, and I'll send you down the same way!"

"You bent my sword!" Tibb griped, peeking over the edge. His sword was sticking point down in the snow. "Look at it. You ruined it."

"Would you help me untangle these knots?" Pinter screamed. "He's getting past."

Rosha stopped singing. He had seen the large bundle tumble from the cliff face, and it aroused his curiosity. He focused his gaze on the cave entrance above him and shouted for joy when he saw a rope ladder drop freely from it, followed by two scurrying figures, who fought to keep from falling as they hurried to the ground. "Ho there!" he cried. "At last here's some company!"

Dragonsgate was wide at this point, nearly a quarter of a mile from cliff to cliff, so Rosha could easily have avoided the ragged-looking characters who now wrestled with the bundle in the snow. But he was so eager for the company of others that the thought of danger never entered his mind. He guided his horse toward them through the drifts, climbing leisurely to meet the two thieves who hustled to block his way. "Greetings, my friends," he called as he reached them.

"Halt there!" cried Tibb, waving a sword in his face.

"Stay your mount, or I'll cut his forelegs," Pinter added, seizing his weapon in both hands and swinging it back to strike.

"And touch not your blade," Tibb went on sourly. "Or I'll drop you here." This mounted warrior had dragged him away from his warm fire, and the stocky thief was determined to make him pay for it.

Rosha hadn't thought to reach for Thalraphis. He was trying to control a cackle. The sword Pinter waggled at him was bent at a ridiculous angle. "Your weapon, sir," he managed to get out, "is somewhat . . . misshapen."

"Yes, well," Tibb grumbled, talking his eyes off Rosha and glancing up the blade of his sadly bowed sword. He shouldn't have. Rosha's left foot had slipped its stirrup, and now slashed out to crack across Tibb's knuckles. The sword in question sailed into the air, turning slowly and flashing once in the sunlight before clattering against the near cliff and dropping into the bank. Both thieves followed its flight in surprise. There was plenty of time for Rosha to jerk out Thalraphis if he'd wished to, but he left it where it was. He was enjoying this encounter.

Tibb put his hands on his hips and frowned at Rosha. "I don't imagine you've helped its shape any by that."

"Who knows?" Rosha grinned. "The blow just might have straightened it."

Tibb stomped angrily after his sword, tossing up a shower of snow with every stride, and Rosha turned back to face Pinter, who watched him uncertainly.

"Here now," Pinter said nervously. "Don't try any tricks. Get off that horse, or I'll maim you both."

"Oh, I shouldn't bother this animal if I were you, my friend." Rosha smiled. "He's a very special horse, you see, and he doesn't take kindly to anyone who threatens me." Rosha was pleased with the performance of his tongue. Perhaps it was because he was on his own again, but for some reason he felt very confident in his speech today. "What are you two doing out here, anyhow? You ought to be sitting by a fire someplace."

"I was," Tibb called, "until you showed up." He picked up his sword and gazed at it in disgust.

"We are defending our pass against intruders like yourself," Pinter shouted. "You'll not leave Dragonsgate without paying the toll you owe us."

"Toll? You make it sound like you owned the place."

"And so we do."

"Own Dragonsgate?" Rosha said, incredulous. "No one owns Dragonsgate. Not since Vicia-Heinox died. If anyone could claim title to it, it would be my friends and I. After all—we evicted its last owner."

"What? Who are you?" Pinter queried aggressively.

"Rosha mod Dorlyth, bear's-bane," Rosha said flatly.

Pinter was visibly shaken. He swallowed hard, then shouted, "Tibb!" He took several awkward steps backward in the snow.

"I'm coming, I'm coming," Tibb mumbled as he slogged his way back toward them, turning his battered blade over in his hands and shaking his head in disbelief.

"This is one of them!" Pinter shouted, suddenly dancing and weaving from side to side as if he expected Rosha to fall on him any moment. "This is a companion of the dragon killer!"

Tibb looked up at Rosha with a new admiration. While in Lamath he had followed Pelmen's prophetic ministry with some curiosity—and here was one who had travelled with the Prophet. "Really?" he asked.

Rosha had heard that tone before, and it made him wince. He half-expected Tibb to ask him the same insane question he'd left Ngandib-Mar to avoid: "What was Vicia-Heinox really like?"

"You—ah—you put your hands in the air, bear's-bane!" Pinter shouted nervously. He was growing breathless. In spite of his long legs, it was difficult to dance and shuffle in this snow.

"Why?" Rosha asked sensibly.

"We need some tribute from you—(puff!)—to present to our master—(puff!)—when he returns."

"Oh?" Rosha smiled. "And who is this master of yours?"

"Admon Faye, of cour—" Pinter's voice abandoned him in midsentence. The point of Thalraphis was suddenly hovering two inches from the tip of his nose.

"How did you do that?" Tibb asked Rosha, admiringly.

Rosha ignored him. "Where is he?" he demanded. All humor had left his voice.

Pinter minced no words, quickly spitting out, "He's in Chaomonous."

"Where in Chaomonous?" Rosha demanded.

"I don't know." The sword tip moved an inch closer to Pinter's nose. "I don't. Who can know where—"

Rosha touched his heel lightly to the flank of his warhorse, and they were gone in a burst of powdery whiteness. Both Pinter and Tibb were left lying on their backs in the drifts.

"How did he do that?" Tibb asked again.

"You were certainly right about one thing," Pinter choked, staring at the sky. "He was nothing but a cutthroat!"

Joss studied the road carefully. "I begin to disbelieve the barkeep. Either he lied, or Admon Faye has changed his plans." He turned to look thoughtfully at his squire. "Would you care to wager that he's riding hard toward the forest?"

"Couldn't we cut him off?" the boy wondered.

"Not a chance. He knows the Great South Fir better than a tree gnome. I should have jailed that barman."

"Because he lied to us?"

"Yes—or because he lived to suffer for telling us the truth. Probably dead already. We'll camp here."

The young man wrinkled his nose in confusion. "I don't follow."

"We've come this far, and the slaver isn't ahead of us. We'll camp and wait. He may surprise me and ride into a trap. Summon my staff. I want an ambush set up within the hour."

Three hours passed, and Joss dismissed the idea of trapping Admon Faye. But as the sun was setting, his squire raced to him with great excitement. A single rider had been spotted approaching from the north. Joss mounted his charger and rode out to meet him.

Joss did not come to his lofty rank by battle alone. He had risen through the Golden Army on the strength of his disciplined mind and a memory that held a tight grip on detail. Had he never met Rosha before, he still would have recognized the young warrior, for Bronwynn had described him at great length. But Joss had met Rosha—in Dragonsgate, only a few hours after the conquest of the dragon. And there was no doubt. This was the man.

Rosha rode through Chaomonous with an arrogance born of innocence. He was, after all, a hero, and heroes never travelled any other way. When he saw General Joss waiting for him in the road, he drew Thalraphis and saluted with it. "Greetings, my friend," he called, and he reined in his charger thirty yards from the General.

"Greetings, Rosha mod Dorlyth," the General replied, his face fixed in a smile.

"You know me?" Rosha said, flattered. He urged his war-horse forward a few yards.

"Of course I know you," Joss called gravely. "But I see that you do not remember me!"

"Do I know you?" Rosha asked suspiciously.

"But of course you do. I am from the court of the Queen!" Joss watched the lad closely as he said these words. He was pleased with the boy's reaction.

"Bronwynn?" Rosha touched his horse gently and the animal trotted to within a yard of Joss. Rosha eyed the General, then nodded in recognition. "Yes. You were the man who took her from the pass."

"I am." Joss smiled.

"Where is she?" Rosha demanded.

"Why, in Chaomonous, I believe," Joss said smoothly.

"I'm—I'm surprised. I didn't expect you to put her on the throne so quickly. I expected to be—ah—needed, somehow, in the struggle."

"The Queen," Joss responded with a sly grin, "came to

the throne quite unexpectedly. I humbly confess that the Queen has been most appreciative of my assistance."

"The Queen," Rosha muttered, trying to accustom himself to seeing Bronwynn in that light. "That sounds—quite good."

"But, of course," Joss said, "her problems are not at an end. It seems that Admon Faye has rescued the false Queen from the dungeon and plots to place her on the throne of the land." The General found he was enjoying this deception.

Rosha seized the pommel of Thalraphis with a fierce frown. "I am aware that Admon Faye is still abroad in the land. I met two thugs in Dragonsgate who told me so."

"Oh, then he is there." Joss nodded.

"No, only those two. They told me he's somewhere here, in Chaomonous." Rosha drew Thalraphis again and held it out before him. "I ride to pledge my sword to the Queen," he said, "to help to rid this land of the plague of Admon Faye."

Joss smiled broadly. "I can think of nothing that would please our Queen more." For the first time in many days Joss felt the urge to laugh aloud. He resisted it, as he led the proud young warrior into his camp.

Rosha was pleased. Throughout the ride to the capital city his tongue had not stumbled once. In fact, it had wagged as freely this day as any day in his memory. He heard himself telling General Joss of personal things he'd never revealed to anyone before. Of course, there was no harm in that. After all—this was the man who had placed his Bronwynn on the throne.

Joss was a patient, attentive listener. His interest in Rosha's background never seemed to flag. When Rosha exhausted one area of discussion, Joss would ask a pointed question that would open up a whole new area, then would nod encouragement to the young warrior and listen for another hour. Rarely did Rosha have an opportunity to ask Joss a direct question, so skillfully did the General steer the conversation away from himself. He also tended to avoid conversation regarding Bronwynn. Joss' standard reply to any question regarding Rosha's beloved was, "That will be known when you meet with the Queen."

Rosha talked at length about his attitude toward Bronwynn's crown. "Perhaps it would appear unseemly to you for someone of my rank to aspire to marry your Queen. But the crown of Ngandib-Mar doesn't pass from generation to generation as your crown does. Bronwynn told me that the throne of Chaomonous always passes to the oldest male heir. Isn't that correct?" Joss would only nod. "But Ngandib-Mar isn't so well organized," Rosha went on. "It's ruled by a confederation of chieftains, who must agree who will rule in the High City of Ngandib."

Joss smiled grimly, his eyes on the road ahead. "And how well does that system work? Does it prevent war?"

"Prevent war?" Rosha asked, surprised. "Not a chance. But it's a rare Mari who wants to prevent war."

"I had heard that." Joss nodded.

"My father does—but since the dragon's death, I've dined with above fifty of the Mari chieftains, and most of them encourage battle."

"To what end?"

"Why— to have the opportunity to test one another and to gain glory in victory."

"And what if they lose?" Joss asked, cocking his eyebrow.

"Then they wait impatiently for the next battle, for a chance to redeem themselves." Rosha grinned over at Joss. "The discussion over who should be King provides plenty of opportunity for battle."

"Then I would imagine you Maris have a new King every year."

"Oh no. Pahd mod Pahd-el, the present Lord of the High City, is the third Pahd mod Pahd to rule as King. And he's been King since he was my age."

"It sounds as if the Pahds have gone far toward establishing their own dynasty. The family of Pahd must be very strong."

"Not really," Rosha shrugged. "My father says Pahd is a very powerful swordsman on his own, but he's not an especially strong ruler. He's King now because, whenever the confederation of chieftains tire of fighting one another, Pahd seems a harmless enough compromise choice. Besides, he's already moved into the palace, and it would take a considerable army to crack *that* citadel.

"What I'm trying to say is that any Mari can aspire to wear the crown. He may not be powerful enough to take it—and it may be worth little to him if he does—but it means there is no royalty in Ngandib-Mar—and a person can marry whomever he chooses."

"Are there no slaves in Ngandib-Mar?"

"Of course there are! All of my father's vassals are freed slaves."

"Then there is a royalty in Ngandib-Mar," Joss said quietly. "It consists of any who are free."

Rosha thought. "What you say is true," he replied grudgingly. "But not royalty as you speak of it."

"Perhaps not."

"You don't think it will cause any problems for me to marry Bronwynn, do you?" Rosha asked.

Joss did not meet the young warrior's eyes. Calmly, he replied, "That will be known when you meet with the Queen."

Rosha made a face. "And when will that be? It appears Chaomonous is much further away than I thought."

"Perhaps you underestimated the size of our nation," Joss suggested. "With all respect to your native land, our Chaomonous is by far the largest, most powerful state in the world."

"Oh? Then how do you explain the Battle of Westmouth? My father and a few thousand Maris destroyed your whole Golden Army!"

General Joss' expression didn't change. He replied quietly, "The Golden Throng had no leader on that day. Had I been allowed to guide them as I'd planned, the outcome might have been very different."

Rosha watched the General's face, his hand moving to the pommel of Thalraphis. "Do you deny the achievement of my people?"

Joss chuckled. "You may take your hand off your weapon, Rosha mod Dorlyth. I intend no insult to your father or your King. I only suggest you may be surprised by what you find in Chaomonous."

Rosha sat back into his saddle with a haughty laugh. "I've seen Ngandib and I've seen the city of Lamath. Nothing can surprise me anymore."

Joss smiled and turned to look at the powerful young

warrior. "I imagine you believe that. But, of course, an expected surprise wouldn't be a surprise at all, would it?"

They did not reach Chaomonous by nightfall, camping instead some thirty miles from the city. When he awoke the next morning, Rosha was informed that Joss had preceded him, to prepare the way for his arrival. When Rosha rode into Chaomonous later in the day he was grateful that Joss wasn't beside him. He had forgotten how impersonal and intimidating large cities could be. Rosha was so frightened his hands shook—and he was stammering so fiercely that no one could understand a sentence he uttered.

Late in the afternoon, Rosha was waiting in a marble-floored hallway in the third level of the royal palace. He devoutly wished that Bronwynn would hurry up and grant him an audience, for the strangeness of the place was making him tremble. This was not at all what he had imagined during those cold nights in his father's castle. It was nothing at all like what he'd planned.

No one said Bronwynn's name, and no one but Joss' squire addressed him directly. They all spoke only of the Queen, and with such reverence that he was hard pressed to hold in mind that picture of his little golden-haired comrade of many travels. He longed for a glimpse of her friendly face, and considered breaking into her apartments. After all, hadn't she called him "Rosha mod Bronwynn"— Rosha, Bronwynn's treasure? Did Bronwynn's treasure need to wait for a summons?

As he considered this possibility, the double door down the hall clacked open, and Joss, smiling, walked toward him. "I know you have been kept waiting for some time, bear's-bane. I have had some difficulty convincing the Queen that it is truly you. She's suggested that if she could see the sword which slew the dragon, she would believe me."

"S-see my s-s-sword!" Rosha answered sharply. "All she has to d-d-do is look out the d-d-door!"

Joss gave him a patient smile. "Nevertheless, she is the Queen, and we must do as she suggests. Please?" He held out his hands.

Rosha angrily ripped Thalraphis from its scabbard and laid it across the General's palms. Joss nodded slightly and turned on his heels. The door closed behind him, and Rosha was alone in the hall once more.

He had felt only awkward before. Without his weapon, he felt naked. But Joss returned with merciful swiftness, wearing a wide smile. "The Queen will see you now," he said and he motioned the young warrior forward.

"Bronwynn?" Rosha bubbled as he ran to the door. "Bronwynn!" he cried as he bolted into the throne room.

The woman who slouched on the ornate chair of office had beautiful blue eyes like Bronwynn's. But there the resemblance ended. Rosha stopped in the center of the room, then turned all the way around, his eyes scanning the line of armed warriors who ringed the walls. Then he looked back at the woman, his handsome face twisted with disappointment.

Ligne smiled maliciously, fingering the flat edge of the sword she held on her lap. "Unfortunately, Bronwynn is no longer with us," she said. Then she passed the sword to an aide, stood up, and smoothed her tight dress over her hips. "Will I do, instead?"

"A very handsome creature, isn't he?" Ligne said later, as a bound and gagged Rosha knelt before her, shivering with rage. Four men had suffered broken bones before the company of guards had managed to subdue him. One guard still lay unconscious in the infirmary on the floor below them. Joss had appealed to the Queen to allow him to chain the boy in the dungeon right then, but Ligne was a connoisseur of the male body, and would not part with this one so readily.

"I assure you, my Queen, he is a savage, handsome or no. It would be best for your safety if you would allow me to cage him immediately."

"Come now, Joss, he's only a boy—"

"Who is an extremely competent swordsman. Please remember that he has battled Admon Faye and has survived—"

"Pity you didn't kill him," Ligne whispered to Rosha, walking behind the trussed youth and gliding her hand along his bare neck. They had tied him and forced him to his knees. Now she knelt beside him, admiring his legs as Rosha strained against the ropes. "He's like a mountain cat—or a bear—sleek and shining and powerful." Ligne's eyes glistened with excitement.

"He's a bear's-*bane*, my Lady, and most dangerous," Joss continued, eyes following every thrust of the young man's arms as Rosha wrestled to get free. "I must ask you to allow me to—"

"And I order you to keep silent!" Ligne snapped. Then, more softly, she added, "I want to play with him awhile."

Joss struggled to hold his temper in check, then said tersely, "Is it that you favor the lad so much? Or do you just treasure what is Bronwynn's?"

Ligne stood up and looked at her chief warrior, her blue eyes icy, her jaw jutting out sharply. "Do you dare repeat that?"

"There's no need, my Lady. You heard me."

Ligne studied the man for a moment, then turned her head away. "You are too valuable to be wasted, Joss. I choose to take no offense in your words. But in the future, you will refrain from involving yourself in affairs that do not concern you."

"Any threat to the security of my Queen must involve me, my Lady, and the young barbarian constitutes such a threat. Should he manage to free himself from those ropes, he will seize the nearest weapon and turn on you."

"I know." Ligne smiled, shifting her hips salaciously and running her fingers through Rosha's curly dark hair. "It's a most incredible feeling. Quite enjoyable." She glanced back at Joss' leathery face and shrugged. "Perhaps the fact that he came seeking my rival does play a part in the excitement—I'm amazed the skinny little witch could interest such a magnificent creature." She looked back down at Rosha, who had jerked his head free and now focused his fierce gaze on her hand, longing to bite it. "But I think he would interest me in any case."

"He's dangerous—"

"Exactly," Ligne finished, cutting her General off. "If it would make you feel any better, give the order to remove all weapons from this room—if you feel that would minimize the threat."

Joss gave an angry wave, and the armed warriors began clearing the room. "As you say, my Queen. But I feel certain that the man could easily break your neck with his hands alone."

Ligne's teeth sparkled as she flashed a smile. "The very idea gives me chills." Joss followed her gaze to the struggling form of the young warrior. Rosha had flipped onto his back and now was kicking at his captors with his bound legs. "He's so aggressive!" Ligne husked, watching a pair of unarmed soldiers wrestle Rosha back into a kneeling position. "Tie him like that," she ordered, "so that he's forced to remain on his knees. Then leave the room."

"My Lady Ligne!" Joss protested.

"Joss, be quiet!" she ordered, as her mail-clad guards produced more rope and bound Rosha more securely. Then they went out, leaving only the captive, the Queen, and the General behind in the throne room.

"Queen Ligne, please reconsider—"

"Leave us, Joss."

"He is enraged and frightened, the most dangerous—"

"I said get out!"

Joss nodded curtly, and Ligne's hard look softened a fraction. "Believe me, General. If there is anything I am equipped to handle, it is a man." She winked at him and dismissed him with a wave, then went back to sit on her throne. As Joss reluctantly closed the door behind him, he could hear her saying, "Now, Rosha. You and I are going to become very well acquainted . . ."

CHAPTER FIVE

Birds of a Feather

THE REAR OF PLECLYPSA'S GRAND PLAYHOUSE was honey-combed with small attiring rooms. About midmorning, the troupe crowded into one of these to stare at one another in shock. The Winter Festival had been rocked by scandal—and they were the victims of it. It made little difference that they had the sympathy of the vast majority of the Pleclypsans. They'd been had—and they knew it.

Their splendid scene on opening night had won them the last night on the program. So thoroughly had they carried the evening that several Pleclypsan officials had suggested they be acclaimed immediately as winners. Unaccountably, this notion won the support of Eldroph-Pitzel and his wife Berliath, the leaders of the local Pleclypsan troupe. They suggested that the competition be held, but for second place only, and that Ligne's Lord of Entertainments be invited to attend, to witness a wonderful play inspired by the Queen's rise to power. Grudgingly, the other troupes gave in—they, too, had been impressed with the competition.

Lulled by such praise, the troupe had made the most of the Festival. They had starred at a half-a-dozen parties, hobnobbing with the regional governor himself. They had attended each evening's performance as spectators rather than competitors, watching with the smug self-confidence of judges. On the night before their own final, triumphal performance was scheduled, they were briefly reintroduced to Maythorm, Ligne's Lord of Entertainments, before going in to witness Eldroph-Pitzel and Berliath perform. They were laughing and joking as they took their seats. Their laughs turned to gasps, however, as they watched the troupe from Pleclypsa perform Pelmen's play about Ligne. It had been stolen.

Oh, it was a pale copy, true. They couldn't duplicate the cleverness of Pelmen's lines. Obviously they hadn't managed to steal the script. Yet the basic structure of the show was the same—and so was the reaction of the crowd. Berlaith, who had made a point of picking Danyilyn out of the audience, smiled directly at her throughout.

That had been last night. And this morning the news had swirled through the city that Maythorm had already departed for Chaomonous with his enthusiastic report for the Queen. No one had bothered to tell him that tonight was the final night.

Apparently, the Pleclypsan troupe had not been able to get to all the organizers—already the troupe had received a public apology from an apoplectic Minlaf-Khen, director of the Winter Festival. But as far as an invitation to court was concerned, the damage had already been done. The actors were bitter.

"It must have been that skinny peasant who stood just to the left of the stage," Gerrig spat.

"No," Danyilyn snorted, "it was Berliath herself. She stood back in the shadows by Sherina's wagon through the entire performance. She probably even took notes."

"What difference does it make who stole the play?" Yona Parmi asked. "Someone did, obviously."

"But who'd have thought they'd be interested in us?" whined Gerrig.

"Of course they'd be interested in us!" Yona Parmi's aggravation was evident. "We've taken the prize three years out of the last five. This year they'd counted us out, then suddenly got word we had entered late. Of course they'd be interested in us. I'm just disgusted with myself for taking so much for granted. The Pleclypsans didn't do this to us— we did it to ourselves."

Danyilyn rose from her stool and stalked around the room. Players shuffled their feet to let her pass, as she paced the full length of their cramped space. Suddenly she stopped and spun around to look at Yona Parmi. "Where's Pelmen?"

Yona glanced around the room, then shrugged. "Not here, evidently."

Danyilyn's jaw clenched. "I'm getting tired of all this secretiveness, Parmi! Is Pelmen with us or isn't he?"

"Danyilyn, it's his play that was stolen."

"Then where is he? Why isn't he here, helping us plan what to do next?"

"Plan? What's to plan?" Yona Parmi's tight-lipped expression was hard. "We have a play to perform tonight. He'll be here for it. Until then, I suggest we let Pelmen do whatever he thinks best." Yona struggled down off his high stool and dodged through the legs to the doorway. There he paused, and looked back over his shoulder. "If past experience is any guide, he'll probably surprise us."

Riding an up-draft two-hundred feet above the Chaomonous Road, Pelmen struggled to maintain his alter-shape without becoming exhausted. He had already spotted his quarry—Maythorm and his bodyguard. Now he was choosing a spot to make his play. He'd been up and down this road a hundred times in his lifetime, but this was the first time he'd ever flown it. As always, he felt a powerful temptation to turn aside from his human responsibilities and explore the scene below for the sheer joy of it. Fighting that temptation added to his growing weariness—yet he had far too much to do today to succumb to exhaustion.

A powershaper did not choose his alter-shape. When it came, it came in a moment of insight—of inspiration. There was no midpoint of being half-human and half-shaped. Normally, a wizard took the shape the first time almost by accident, when some conscious or unconscious need for that identity arose. Thus Mar-Yilot had become a butterfly when she learned the boy she loved collected them, and Joooms became a lizard when trapped in a windowless cell. One day Pelmen had needed to stop a blue-flyer before it could deliver a dangerous message. He'd flown up and caught it before realizing what he'd done. Since that time, he'd been able to take his falcon-form anytime he chose—as long as there were powers present to shape.

The very presence of those powers in Chaomonous prompted him to haste. Never had he sensed the forces now loosed upon this land—and he felt hesitant to use them. It was as if he expected someone or something to say any minute, "You can't do that here," and spill him from the sky. Then, too, since his religious vocation had claimed him the year before, he'd felt a kind of moral dilemma each time he'd shaped. He had to wonder now, with every act of magic, if his molding harmed or angered whatever power he made use of. For some strange reason, the closer he got to the Chaon capital, the greater his hesitancy grew. Clearly, he needed to deal with Maythorm in a hurry.

His falcon eyes were far superior to his human vision. The road had passed a large manor and into a small forest. Forty yards off the road he spotted a thatched roof among the trees, and swooped down to investigate. It was a charming peasant dwelling, cheery and clean, with whitewashed walls and a carefully swept porch. Pelmen circled the house, dropped down behind it—and stood on the earth, a man. There was no glass in the single window; and, though it was a brisk morning, the green shutters were open. "Hello?" he called. There was no answer. He circled the house on foot, knocked on the door, and at last went in. The householders were gone—though, by the warmth of the soup pot sitting on the hearth, they'd not been gone long. "Probably plowing," Pelmen murmured. If so, they would be at it all day. "I hope you'll not mind if I borrow your home," he announced, "and a bit of this cooling soup. I promise to make it worth your while." In a small pocket on his sleeve was a golden coin—he'd brought it for just this purpose.

His garments belied the wealth tucked into that sleeve. He was clothed in rags, specially selected from the costume cart late the previous night. Through the early hours of the morning he had carefully sculpted lines of age into his face by candlelight, until he looked every bit the aged peasant he would soon portray. His artistry with makeup had nothing to do with wizardry. It was stage magic, a skill that had often proved useful to him—and which would need to again, if he were to survive within Ligne's castle.

It didn't take long for him to feel that he knew the small cottage as well as its owner. That done, he shot through the

open window on flashing brown wings. He had a rendez-
vous planned with Maythorm, and he wasn't about to miss
it.

Maythorm did nothing in half-measures. He either *loved*
something or he loathed it, and he had *loved* the play he'd
witnessed the night before.

"Wasn't it marvelous?" he gushed to Craglump, the taci-
turn, stolid soldier who'd drawn the unenviable task of
guarding Maythorm's body on this trip. Craglump didn't
usually talk much, which made him the perfect companion
for Maythorm, since the handsome Lord of Entertainments
rarely stopped. "The class of the Festival, obviously. Such
elegance on stage! Berliath, as Ligne, caught our hearts as
if they were doves and held us, fluttering, until the final
curtain!"

"Yeah." Craglump nodded.

"And Eldroph-Pitzel! Such thunderous power as the
shrewd tactician who engineered her rise! His voice, like a
fist of iron, hammered upon our senses with the ringing
zest of a joyful blacksmith!"

"Right."

"Who's that?"

Craglump sat up rigidly in his saddle. Maythorm's
change of tone startled him—he realized he'd been half
asleep. "Who? What?"

"There." Maythorm pointed. They had topped a tiny
rise, and he'd spotted a ragged, barefoot peasant racing
away from them.

"Oh. Just a peasant," Craglump muttered, almost disappointed.

"But why is he running?" Maythorm asked, and he
spurred his mount to pursue the retreating figure. "You
there," he shouted when he came abreast of him. "Why are
you running?"

"To get out of the storm!" the peasant shouted, and he
scurried on ahead as Maythorm reined in and tossed a
puzzled look at the sky.

"Storm?" he asked. He chased the peasant down again,
this time blocking the old man's path. The winded runner
leaned on his knees, gasping for breath. "What storm?"

Maythorm sneered, winking his amusement at Craglump, who had now caught up.

The peasant looked up to meet the courtling's gaze and puffed, "The one that's on its way!"

"Why, there isn't a cloud in the—"

Lightning tore open the heavens, and Maythorm's eyes jerked upward in disbelief and terror.

"Took my wife just that way not four years ago. I'm to my cottage!" the old man yelled and he raced toward a clump of woods just ahead of them. Maythorm and Craglump took one horrified look at each other and pursued him. Actually, they arrived at the single-roomed dwelling well before he did, and were comfortably inside when he huffed up to the doorstep. He saw them crowded together at the open window, peering skyward. Had they been watching the ragged peasant instead of the bright, clear heavens, they might have caught the quick flash of a smile he allowed himself as he closed the door behind him.

Maythorm and Craglump had an eventful morning, to say the least. Balls of colored fire danced before their eyes with hypnotizing power. At times their peasant host disappeared, and a screeching bird of prey swooped over their heads and glided between their legs. Each time they dashed for the door to escape, bolts of lightning collapsed upon the cottage, threatening to rend its rafters from their moorings, and the two cowered in one another's arms. The dizzying whirlwind of incredible occurrences spun round them faster and faster, until both were giddy with confusion, and they dropped, unconscious, to the stonework floor.

They remembered little of the morning's activities when they came to themselves later that afternoon. They were seated in their saddles, their horses casually plodding the dusty road toward Chaomonous. Each felt a bit embarrassed at dozing off, and hoped the other hadn't noticed. Maythorm compensated by bursting into a new review of the previous night's performance, using even more superlatives than before. "I've *never* seen Gerrig so powerful! What a wondrous instrument he's made of his voice! And Danyilyn! The exquisite delicacy of her performance could curl the hairs of a cavern bear! I certainly must look that luscious beauty up when they arrive in the palace," the lady-killer drooled.

Craglump wasn't listening. He was watching with a curious discomfort the lazy flight of a falcon, as it skimmed the treetops to their left, heading southward toward Pleclypsa.

That night, a weary peasant woman found no soup left in her pot—but the gold piece she found in the bottom of the kettle more than made up for the loss.

Through tedious days of silent enchantment, amid much earnest effort and sweating of walls, the castle had managed finally to regain full consciousness of its rooftop areas. It wished almost immediately that it hadn't. A good part of its motivation for moving into these rebuilt upper structures first was to get at that strange annoyance it felt marginally aware of, but couldn't quite comprehend. Now it understood thoroughly. Too thoroughly. And at that moment, the indignity was happening again.

Plop.

The Imperial House of Chaomonous reacted much the same as would anyone else who awoke from a long nap to find someone had built a birdcage on his head. It cursed. Eloquently.

—Filthy, loathsome, tasteless, stupid . . .

Such phrases could not begin to translate adequately the castle's lucid descriptions of the fowls who befouled its roof tiles. Its vocabulary of expletives was extensive, involving unfavorable personal comparisons that might have both shocked and delighted Chaon historians. Unfortunately, they were lost on both the stupid, feathered objects of its wrath and the stupid human officials who might have been able to do something about the problem. Which simply infuriated the castle further.

Plip-splip.

—Despicable pigeon! May a sadistic eight-year-old pluck your feathers! May your beak rot off! May your eggs crack even as you lay them!

In spite of such venomous outbursts, the birds that populated Ligne's aviary continued to consume their birdseed, and persisted in all of their other normal biological functions

Plip.

—That pigeon has sealed its fate! the House cried aloud

to no one but itself. In fact, it wasn't a pigeon at all, but rather a long-tailed, two-colored warbler. It was an exotic specimen, as were all the birds in Ligne's aviary, and was a real prize, having been brought from somewhere far away upon a merchant's spice-ship. The castle couldn't have been less concerned with such distinctions. A bird was a bird, and while the House could tolerate a certain degree of relationship with such necessary winged creatures as hunting falcons and blue-flyers, nothing in its long experience had prepared it for such regular, repeated humiliation.

It had already concentrated much attention on the gigantic grillwork itself. In its vivid imagination the House fantasized the cage toppling from the roof to the cobblestoned streets of the city far below. What foul-feathered flutterers managed to survive in the twisted wreckage would be free, then, to fly off and besmirch some other, less august manor!

Yet the cage itself had thus far resisted the castle's every effort at control. Thus far, the House could only look at it, and suffer under it—and curse.

There was one bright spot in all of this. Though its colorful curses were quite untranslatable into human speech, they were nevertheless perfectly audible to human ears. Whenever it cursed, every servant's bell in the entire palace threatened to ring itself right off the wall.

"Those *bells* again!" Ligne snapped, as fourteen guards, nine serving girls, four butlers, a maid, and the bearer of royal chamber pot came scuttling breathlessly into the throne room. "When is Kherda going to fix those bells?" she screamed. The collection of servants all disappeared as hastily as they had assembled—except for the pot bearer. Experience had taught him to move deliberately.

"Have *you* any idea why they ring so?" she asked her sinewy young captive. As usual, Rosha made no reply.

He felt little motivation to—there was nothing to be gained by replying. Nor, in fact, would he gain anything by not replying. He'd been cut off from his love, cut off from his sword, cut off from his land—all those things that had made his life worthwhile. And now he was cut off even from looking at the world, for Ligne had ordered her chief falconer to fit the young man's head with a hood of brown leather. It covered his face down to the bridge of his nose, cutting off all light. His arms were manacled behind him above the elbows. He'd been kept so for three days, and was gradually losing interest in anything but his own thought. His difficulty with speech had always made talking a chore. He felt little inclination to engage in meaningless conversation now.

Prime Minister Kherda came dashing down the hall, holding his long skirts out of the way of his feet as his sandals clipped along the tile floor. When he reached the doorway of the throne room he paused, leaning against the richly carved walnut doorjamb to suck in gulps of air between stammered phrases: "I don't . . . understand why . . . these bells . . . keep ringing so!" He panted momentarily, then continued bravely in the face of Ligne's ice-cold stare. "I've done . . . my best . . . to find . . . someone who's qualified . . . to find the problem. No one knows!"

"Then why not send to Ngandib-Mar for a sorcerer?" Ligne asked sweetly. "Surely a powershaper could find the problem." The Queen was mocking him, Kherda realized. Ligne didn't believe in magic any more than he did.

"There are no powershapers," he muttered wearily.

"But there must be powershapers," she continued, sneering. "Who but a powershaper could have witched this castle to behave so?" Suddenly Ligne dropped her mocking pretense and snarled: "I don't want to see your face until you find me a craftsman who can fix those bells. Unless, of course, you wish to be strangled with a bell cord?"

Kherda had grown accustomed to such threats from his tigerish monarch. Even so, he retreated from her chamber hastily. Ligne turned back to her captive in time to catch the shadow of a grin chase across his lips and disappear. "And what are *you* laughing at? Are you laughing at me?" she demanded.

Rosha said nothing. But Ligne imagined that she saw in his tight-lipped frown an expression of self-satisfied derision. It both irritated and inflamed her. Her voice softened. "You're the only one who dares. Why do I allow it?" She ran her hand down the length of one of his bound forearms, and he balled his fist in response—a silent signal, but one she clearly understood. "I know. You don't like for me to touch you." To tease him, she began massaging the corded muscles in his back and shoulders, cautiously staying out of the short range of that fist. Rosha would swing at her, given the chance. That was the reason for his chains. "Why is that, Rosha mod Dorlyth? Do you hate my entrails so passionately that you've never noticed my more visible physical attributes?" Ligne felt she had good cause to boast in her appearance. She was still a young woman, and her oval face was free of any trace of those lines of care so frequently in evidence on the faces of more responsible monarchs. Her blue eyes could be dazzling if she chose to charm, dangerous if she chose to threaten—but never could they be dull. It was on the basis of her great beauty that she had vaulted to her exalted position—by way of Talith's bed, of course. Nor did she feel any shame in that. It fact, it fed her ego to recall how she'd seduced the late King not only into bed, but into his grave as well—assuming anyone bothered to bury the proud oaf. Ligne carefully cultivated her saucy, brazen appearance, clothing herself in scintillating materials of shocking colors, tailored to expose to best advantage those portions of her figure she thought most entrancing, while hiding those flaws visible only to herself. With flowing hair the color of a raven's inky cloak, Ligne was far more than just striking. She was more than just lovely. Hers was the perfect standard of beauty, against which all the men who knew her measured their wives and lovers. She praised her own appearance by that unconscious arrogance of one who has never been anything but beautiful.

Yet it was all lost on Rosha. And for a perfectly obvious reason.

"How am I to s-s-see your f-f-fabled beauty while you c-constantly keep this hood on my h-head?" His frustration nearly gagged him.

"You know I'd gladly remove that mask, my pretty friend. Such a shame, to hide such handsome dark curls. But how can I, when you've promised that the moment I do, you're going to kick me in the face? Can you tell me if that good night's rest on the cold floor of my dungeon brought about some change of heart?"

Rosha had subsided again into silent attention. His lips wore the patient expression of a carnivore on the prowl—mute, passive, but ready to strike any time.

"I thought not," Ligne answered herself, smiling with feigned indifference. "I suppose I should give my guards permission to burn or club you into submission to me . . ." She tried to make it sound like a threat, but it wasn't, and Rosha knew it. Ligne sighed. "But, of course, I couldn't do that, any more than I could beat the spirit out of one of my falcons. Would you like to visit the falcons again, Rosha? Would you like to have fellowship with your brothers under the hood?"

Rosha shrugged. It meant nothing to him. He heard Ligne summon a guard and soon felt a tug on the chain that encircled his chest. That meant he was to move forward. Rosha obeyed without a struggle—waiting patiently.

The mews where the royal falcons were kept contrasted sharply with the giant aviary that stood on the roof nearby. Where the floor of the aviary was lined with white dung, the floor of the mews was spotless. While the aviary rocked with the constant chaotic screeching and fluttering of brilliantly plumed birds from exotic jungle climes, the mews was as silent as a cliff. Its gray and brown occupants stood on their perches at quiet, sightless attention, like feathered soldiers awaiting orders to charge. Maliff, the falconer, shuffled from bird to bird, giving vigilant attention to each scrape of a talon or fluffing of wings.

"Hushhh . . ." Maliff whispered softly. "Hush now. Be carm." His voice soothed his feathery charges. "You'rr see. You'rr get some fine red chunks of dinner soon, when my boy crimbs back up from the kitchen." The birds seemed satisfied by his words. They were not bothered by Maliff's inability to pronouce the middle consonant of his own name.

The falconer heard the wicket gate open behind him and scowled. "Took you rong enough!"

"Just what do you mean by that?" Ligne snapped, and Maliff whipped around to apologize to his Queen.

"My Rady! I had no idea! I thought it was my boy fetching me some broody meat for my farcons!"

Ligne had already dismissed the falconer from her mind,

and was strolling down the line of birds as if reviewing a perfectly disciplined regiment. "Here, Rosha," she said to the young captive who'd been dragged in behind her by a guard. "How orderly, how obedient your winged brothers are. They wait only for my command." She reached forward to stroke a tercel.

"Stop," Maliff said without thinking, and won himself a cold hard look.

"What?" Ligne asked icily.

"Prease, my Rady, they don't rike to be stroked," he said bravely.

"They are *my* birds, Maliff, and I'll touch them if I choose!"

"Yes, my Rady." The falconer nodded. "Onry I must warn—" he said involuntarily as she reached out to the peregrin again.

"I don't recall giving you or anyone else permission to instruct me, Maliff!"

"Of course not, my Rady, and I'm not, but you did keep me on as caretaker of these rovery birds, and I'm aiming to do the best job possibre. Ret one ride on your fist, but don't stroke him. You'rr put him off if you do rike that."

Ligne leaned on the perch of a young eyas and propped her head on her hand. The eyas scraped down to the other end of the bar. "You're just full of instructions, aren't you? Well, tell me then, oh mighty trainer of the hunting bird, how do I get *this* one to obey me?" She jerked her head to the hooded Rosha. Maliff averted his eyes from the hood. He'd made it himself, but he hadn't enjoyed the chore.

"That's a man, not a farcon," he muttered softly.

"I know that!" Ligne exploded, and the room's occupants responded with fluttering and flapping.

"Hush! Hush now!" Maliff soothed and the commotion subsided. Ligne was gazing at him angrily, and he looked away as he explained, "I was hushing my charges, my Rady. Not you."

"Well?"

"If he were a bird, I'd free his wings and train him to my fist. But I fear if you were to roose this one, he'd kirr you sure as gord. You'd be safer if you ret him fry free. That's Mariff's advice."

Ligne gazed intently at him for a moment, translating

his words. Then she shook her head and dismissed him once again from her mind. "I refuse to listen to a man who can't even pronounce his own name. Tosha, this bird-minded fool has a clumsier tongue even than you!" The young warrior's muscles corded across his back as he strained relfexively at his bonds.

Ligne noticed, and chuckled. "Got you again, didn't I. A sure means of angering you at will—mention your stammering speech." Rosha jerked toward her but was stopped short by the length of his chains. Ligne had turned her back on him, and reached for a leather glove that hung on a peg above her head. "I'll take this one," she told Maliff as she slipped the glove over her right hand, motioning toward the untrained eyas whose perch she had disturbed.

"He's not furry trained yet, can't I get you—"

"Enough!" Ligne shouted, and Maliff stepped back submissively and let her have her way. She unwrapped the thong that tethered the eyas to its perch, then touched its underbelly with her gloved hand. Blindly it climbed aboard, and the Queen spun around and stalked out of the mews into the bright sunlight of the castle's roof.

"Prease," Maliff called after her, "don't ret go of that reather rash rine!" But the woman was gone, and he was speaking only to the backs of Rosha and of the guard who hurried the youth through the wicket gate after the Queen. "He'rr fry away . . ." Maliff worried aloud. He shook his head sadly, and turned back to his silent falcons.

The Imperial House watched as Ligne crossed the few steps to the outer door of the aviary and shouldered her way inside it. Its hot rage at this dull, ignorant Queen with her total disregard for its feelings had faded to a cold distaste for her. The House didn't mind her cruelty—it could be quite cruel itself. Nor was it particularly offended by her arrogance. It expected such foolishness from human monarchs. It was just that she was so shockingly rude! The Imperial House had not yet admitted that no one could understand it. Rather, it felt sure it was being snubbed.

At the moment, however, it was more concerned with thinning the population of the cursed aviary than anything else. Its halls felt a great draft of mirth at the welcome sight of a falcon being carried into that gigantic cage.

It watched, too, as Rosha was pushed inside the outer door behind Ligne. The guard followed them in, closed the outer door behind them, then all three stepped through the inner door into the aviary proper. The House listened as Ligne trilled to the anxious bird on her fist in the syrupy singsong of baby talk: "Ho ho, you know where are you, birdie? In the midst of a hundred other little birdies who are scared to death of you. Yes, they are. You could crush each one of these little darlings in your bad old claws, you know that? Ah, but you *can't*, can you, birdie? Because you're like Rosha here, birdie—you can't see a thing, and I've got a tight hold on your leash. Would you like me to free you, birdie?" The falcon slapped its wings tentatively as if in answer, and Ligne laughed harshly. "You would, would you? Not a chance!" She aimed this last at Rosha, who stood passively where his guard had positioned him.

"There you are, my Lady, I've been looking all over for you." Kherda came walking toward them from the interior entrance, herding a pair of arrogant peacocks before him.

"What is it now?" Ligne complained, wrapping another loop of the leash around her left hand.

"Maythorm has returned from Pleclypsa with a report on that play that—"

"Who's Maythorm?" Ligne demanded testily.

"Maythorm is a member of your court, my Lady—surely you remember him? Lord of Entertainments? Smells of lilac?"

"Go on," she sighed. She began to stroke the falcon absently. It stepped away from the offending hand, but she paid no notice. When the hand continued stroking, the hooded bird fluffed its feathers and carefully stepped back to its original position on the leather glove, settling there to endure this torture stoically.

"Maythorm has returned from Pleclypsa with a report on that play that—"

"What play?" Ligne snapped, turning her eyes back to the bird.

Kherda forced an indulgent smile onto his aging features. He'd made it a practice lately to avoid mirrors. The tensions and irritations thrust upon him by this unappreciative tart of a Queen had ravaged his face with premature wrinkles. Nevertheless, he kept on smiling . . . "There were reports of a play—rather complimentary toward yourself—being performed in the southern reaches . . ."

"Play? Is Pelmen in on this?" she demanded, arching an eyebrow.

"According to Maythorm's confused accounts, the play is performed by Pelmen the Player's old company, but that—"

"I want him arrested! I want him brought here, immediately, to stand trial for high crimes against the state!" Ligne's pretty face was red, her lips were curled into a savage snarl.

The Imperial House watched this conversation with interest. It watched the uneasy movement of the alarmed falcon from one end of the Queen's glove to the other. It noted the way the woman's hand alternately clenched and released the loop of leather bound to the falcon's fesses, which held the predator in check. It also watched with a consuming hatred the swoops and dives and twirls of that cursed two-toned warbler; that bird had just spattered the pavements again, and its song seemed to the House to be a trill of mocking laughter.

Kherda held his tongue in check by clamping it between his teeth. He had become a master of that art. He smiled again with exaggerated graciousness, and replied, "I think the Queen will remember that this Pelmen is firmly installed in a position of power as the Prophet of Lamath. It would seem most ridiculous for a man in his—" Kherda broke off, for Ligne had turned her back on him, and was looking with suspicion at Rosha. The young warrior was smirking—to himself, he thought, unaware that he held Ligne's irritated attention.

"You know something we should know?" she demanded, and Rosha closed his mouth and banished his mirth. "I've seen that stony expression too often lately!" Ligne shrilled and she lashed a foot viciously into his bare shin. Rosha winced briefly at the unexpected pain but didn't budge from his place by the cage wall. That mask of rock settled immediately back onto his features.

"Talk to me! I demand that you speak! I'll rip that expression off you . . ." Ligne tore off the leather hood that covered the head of her falcon, and would have thrust the frightened bird into Rosha's face had not Kherda and Rosha's guard caught her by the shoulders and pulled her off.

"My Lady! Ligne, please! Control yourself," Kherda shouted as the woman cursed him and struggled to get free. The falcon fluttered around their heads, beating its wings to keep from falling, while surveying for the first time the rainbow-feathered feast that filled the aviary. Maliff had only lately trained him to the lure, and here was live meat wherever he turned his head—none of it further than twenty strong beats of his wings.

The Imperial House watched all this with fascination.

The Queen at last succeeded in controlling her own temper and turned her attention to controlling the falcon. She'd kept a tight rein on its leash primarily because she'd clenched both fists in her rage. Now she looped it again around her left wrist and spoke soothingly into its ears. When she turned her face back up to the others, her lips wore a flippant grin. "I don't know why I let myself get so angry when you won't speak to me," she told Rosha. "Why should I want to listen to you maul the language, stumble over every word, stutter and stammer through the simplest of speches?"

The guard groaned inwardly as he struggled to restrain Rosha's automatic reaction. This was the hardest part of his job—holding the powerful warrior in check when Ligne was in the mood to bait him.

Kherda took a deep breath. "My Lady, if you could leave the lad for just a moment, perhaps we could deal with this play business and I could then leave you to your game." Kherda ignored Ligne's sharp look, continuing blithely, "Of course, Maythorm always tends to exaggerate, and he seems rather more addled after this last trip than any previously—still, he swears loudly that this play is a masterpiece. The fact that this troupe was at one time connected with Pelmen may be dismissed as entirely coincidental. In my analysis, this event holds no danger whatever. Rather, it would indicate that these players are attempting to win their way back into court favor—which implies public acceptance of your legitimacy as ruler. Perhaps you would like for me to issue tham an invitation to court?"

Ligne was still gazing at him when he finished. Her sapphire eyes made no secret of her annoyance. "Must you bother me with such petty details? Can't you invite this troupe by yourself?" She turned her back on the Prime Minister, effectively dismissing him. Kherda stiffened, and turned his own back on her.

"Kherda," she said sharply, and he froze. "What are we going to do with this pretty young warrior who can't seem to talk?" Ligne chuckled at Rosha's strugglings to get free. It was easy to see that he longed to get his bound hands loose and to wrap them around her throat.

"You know very well what I think you should do with him!" Kherda snarled.

"That's right. You want to lock him away, don't you, so that I can't look at him? You'd prefer me to get my mind back on affairs of state, wouldn't you? Well remember, Kherda, I *am* the state now—" She paused and touched Rosha's shoulder affectionately. "—and this is one affair I can handle all by myself."

"So you say," Kherda snorted, "but I've yet to see him in your bed—" Kherda swallowed the rest of his statement, shocked that he would allow himself to be so dangerously familiar.

Ligne's eyes were on his once more, and Kherda braced himself for the lash of her tongue. Remarkably, it didn't come. Ligne was smiling instead—a girlish, almost modest smile. "Nor will you, when he finally is," she said, and she raised her eyebrows flirtatiously. Kherda would have preferred the tongue-lashing. She'd just revealed how much she cared for this savage young captive—and such affection was dangerous.

"My Lady, the boy's a killer! He is a consort to your rival, and a known follower of your enemy Pelmen. Lock him away at once, before he wriggles free and strikes you down."

"Lock him away, Kherda?" Ligne snarled. "Lock him away in my dungeon, so that he can be stolen away in the night, as was my rival? I never have gotten a clear explanation of how that happened, Kherda. Do you have any idea?" Ligne advanced on him menacingly, keeping her voice low to keep Rosha from guessing what had happened to his love. Kherda stepped backward, nearly tripping over the back of a curious peacock that craned its head around his knees for a look at the angry Queen. "As to Pelmen, you say he's far away, in Lamath, no longer any threat. Is that true, Kherda? Do you know that, for certain? Or are you trying to lull me into a false sense of security, plotting against me, just as you once plotted with me?"

"My Lady, you know the measure of my loyalty. I've supported you in every way—"

"See that you continue, Kherda! And keep your pointed little nose out of matters that don't concern you!"

"Yes, my Lady." He nodded vigorously.

"Now get out of my aviary!" she screamed, and he whipped around to obey. He didn't leave very quickly, however. He knew Ligne well, and had learned always to expect further orders after being abruptly dismissed from her presence. She acted now true to form. "Kherda," she yelled, and he turned back to face her. "Anybody in that troupe any good?"

"Ah . . . I believe . . . the heavy player—Gerrid, Gerrig, something like that . . ."

"Gerrig, really?" Ligne said, pleased. "I remember him from *Shadows of a Night at Sea*—yes, he will do nicely. Summon his troupe to court."

"Then you are interested?" Kherda growled.

"Of course I'm interested. Who wouldn't be intrigued by a masterpiece based on oneself? After all, Kherda—I'm only human. Besides, it will certainly be an improvement to listen to someone who can talk without gagging on his own stumbling tongue."

Ligne jumped at the bellow of rage behind her, and spun to see Rosha hurtling blindly in her direction. Her jibe had caught the guard by surprise. Rosha had jerked the chain leash free from the soldier's hand and now aimed his hooded head like a battering ram toward the sound of Ligne's voice. She threw herself out of his path, banging her elbow on the cage bars and crying out in pain. Rosha's head plowed into the gut of the wide-eyed Prime Minister, knocking him backward, and both of them landed in a heap on the back of the squawking peacock, who suddenly had occasion to rue its own curiosity.

There was a brief whisper of pulsing wings as a brown form shot skyward, then a shriek and a fluttering of colorful feathers. Ligne gasped and looked at her hand in disbelief—the falcon was no longer bound to her. "Kherda!" she screamed. "Do something!"

But Kherda was locked in a desperate struggle with an aroused peacock, who was intent on clawing his tired face to ribbons. He did not see the brilliant wave of birds flock first to one side of the cage and then to the other to avoid the darting and swooping of the falcon. He did not see the lightning-quick flash of that hunter as it caught and crushed a second exotic show bird, then a third, and a fourth. The falcon was only doing what it had been trained to do—and doing it very well.

Three floors below, Maythorm happened to be walking down a hallway when a cold, whistling wind hit him in the face. The Lord of Entertainments immediately broke into a cold sweat, and dashed back to his sumptuous apartment. It had been a very curious week, altogether. Maythorm resolved not to come out of his room again until it was over.

After a brief taste of spring, a sudden sleet storm hit Pleclypsa, coating everything with a thin layer of sheet ice. The troupe huddled together for warmth in Gerrig's wagon, which still stood parked behind the theatre. Gerrig's temper seemed to rise with every drop in temperature. "When are you going to wipe that silly greasepaint off your face?" he growled at Pelmen.

Pelmen turned his head slightly to study his reflection in Gerrig's large mirror. "When it's time," he said quietly.

"I think it's time now!" Gerrig snapped. "You look like a fool!"

Pelmen smiled. "That's the idea, isn't it?"

"You put that stuff on to hide your identity from Ligne, didn't you? Well it's certain we won't make it to the court this year, so do us all a favor and clean it off." He seemed enormously aggravated.

"I'm not as certain of that as you seem to be," Pelmen calmly replied. "We did win the Festival, after all—in addition to a public apology from the Festival organizers."

"So what?" Danyilyn snorted. "Maythorm didn't see us win it! As far as he's concerned, our play belongs to Eldroph-Pitzel and Berliath!"

"They've not received any court invitation as yet . . ."

"How do you know?" Gerrig muttered. "We've been shut up in here all day."

"The sleet probably delayed the blue-flyer," said Danyilyn morosely and she leaned back on her couch and gazed at the ceiling. The paint was peeling. It seemed a fitting comment on their recent fortunes.

"That's possible." Pelmen nodded. He glanced down to the far end of the wagon where the troupe's smallest member played earnestly on the floor. "Coralai," he called, "how's your mother?"

"She's sick," the child answered. She didn't miss a beat in the game she played, and her solemn expression never changed.

"Is she not feeling any better?"

"Nope."

"Perhaps I'll visit her," Pelmen announced as he stood up.

"Don't slip," Danyilyn warned. "That ice is wicked."

Pelmen was nodding at her as he opened the wagon door. He didn't see the shivering messenger beyond it until the door caught the man in the chest, skating him backward across the ice and down. Pelmen hustled out of the wagon and moved gingerly over to offer him a hand. The messenger grabbed it too vigorously, and Pelmen skidded down beside him. The white-faced player laughed aloud and suggested, "Maybe we'd better not help each other up." After a few moments of slipping and sliding, they both struggled through the door of the wagon to safety. The group crowded around expectantly, for the man wore the livery of Minlaf-Khen, the premier organizer of the Winter Festival.

"Well?" Gerrig demanded after a moment. The messenger shivered so hard that he couldn't get a word past his teeth. "You have a message?" the big actor prodded. "What is it?"

"Give him a chance, Gerrig," Yona Parmi scolded. "Can't you see he's freezing?"

"Just nod yes or no. You've a message from Minlaf-Khen?" The messenger nodded. "It must be important . . ." The man nodded again. "Does it have to do with the court?" The messenger nodded once again, and Gerrig could no longer contain himself. He seized the fellow by the collar and hoisted him into the air. "What *is* it, man?"

"Put him down," Pelmen ordered, and Gerrig set the man back on his feet.

"Minlaf-Khen received a flyer from the Queen," the man chattered, determined to deliver his news before Gerrig assaulted him again. "You've been asked to appear at the Imperial Court."

The messenger was quite unprepared for the ensuing commotion. Shrieks of surprised joy greeted his words, and he found himself the target of another of Gerrig's assaults; the bearded player engulfed him in a massive bear hug, then dropped him on the floor and raced on to embrace Danyilyn, Yona Parmi and the others in turn. Now ignored, the messenger crawled to a corner of the carriage and huddled there, awaiting a safe route to the door. He would spend no longer with this crazed assembly than he had to.

Yona Parmi grinned widely, gasping for the breath Gerrig had squeezed from his lungs, as he glanced around at the celebration. His smile faded when he caught a glimpse of Pelmen's face. Despite its clownish paint, the expression there could not have been more solemn. Yona Parmi followed Pelmen's gaze to the dancing form of Coralai, who rejoiced with the rest. He slipped over to his friend's side. "You should be pleased," he muttered quietly. "You've done it."

"No, Parmi," Pelmen responded. "I've only begun it." Then he turned to look Yona in the eye. "We'll need to leave Coralai and Sherina here. Sherina's too sick to travel . . ." He looked back at Coralai. ". . . And the court's no place for a child."

"I'd sooner fight a bear than be the bearer of that news." Yona Parmi smiled sardonically. Coralai could be a terror when aroused. "But come—don't you feel at least some joy in this accomplishment? After all, you've launched your plan."

"I've launched it, Yona. But what have I launched us toward?"

"Evidently, to the court of the Queen." Yona Parmi shrugged.

"The Imperial House." Pelmen nodded, his eyes and his thoughts focused somewhere far away. "Within the walls."

"And what do we do once we're there?"

Pelmen looked over at him, allowing him a hint of a smile. "You never give up, do you?"

"I haven't yet." Yona Parmi smiled back.

The springtime sun returned the next day, bringing with it a glorious thaw that set every heart in the troupe singing—all, save the littlest one. By late afternoon the train of wooden wagons had departed for the north, leaving a disappointed little girl and her relieved mother behind. Sherina knew nothing of Pelmen's purpose and still less of his unusual powers, but she'd known him long enough to be sensitive to his moods. This trip to court was far more than it appeared to be on the surface. She felt perfectly happy to be left out of it.

CHAPTER SIX

A Pair of Rogues

IT WAS EASY to pretend she was flying. Bronwynn's long golden-brown hair, newly washed in a chill stream fed by the melting snow, had dried in the flying wind. Now it fanned out behind her like the plumes of a peacock, as her mount careened through thickets and past naked trees, keeping pace with a pack of racing rogues. Admon Faye's cutthroats were extravagant riders, daring disaster just to make riding fun. They formed no orderly columns, picked no single best path, felt no compunction at breaking rank. For there was no rank. Admon Faye's band attacked the forest before it in an unending cavalry charge, each man abreast of every other. Ducking tree limbs, jumping hedges, they threatened a hundred collisions every day, yet miraculously their horses never seemed to falter or brush flanks.

Bronwynn, no longer in bonds and perfectly free to fall behind and be lost if she so chose, had to ride her hardest to keep up. She found the experience exhilarating and would have thrown back her royal head and screamed in excitement were it not for the treacherous, onrushing trees that demanded her constant attention.

They had hit the snow line days ago, and the wet, white blanket had deepened now to a layer a half a foot thick. It deadened the sound of five hundred pounding hooves, giving emphasis to the weird crackling of scores of cold-deadened twigs, as horses and riders shattered branches aside.

Browynn had given up tracing their pattern of flight, for patterns were anathema to Admon Faye, and he followed none. They rode northeast one day and due west the next, stopping one day at noon, the next at dusk, and the next not until long after midnight. Wherever they stopped, however, she could be sure of three things: a campsite would appear out of nowhere; she would be ordered to build a fire; then for the rest of the night she would be the butt of a torrent of abusive jokes. Admon Faye roared with the rest of them at their nightly critiques of her slender anatomy, adding his own lewd comments to those of his band. But he let no one touch her. Only one man had tried, and he now wore his arm in a sling. The chief slaver did not rule this band by guile or smiles or charisma. He ruled it by force, powered by simple, raw cruelty.

Bronwynn had come to realize that it was that cruelty which insured his protection of her. It wasn't that he didn't want her to be abused. It was rather that she was his private preserve—no one could torment her but him.

And torment her he did. A slap here—a boot in the backside there—an insidious pinch just as she was dropping off to sleep—these were daily occurrences. And try as she might, she couldn't force herself to grow accustomed to such humiliation. Sometimes she screamed, sometimes she cursed, but always with the same result. Admon Faye laughed.

"Get used to it, girl. You surely can't believe things will be any different when you're the Queen, and I'm your Prime Minister." Then his eyes would freeze, and his face would twist still further as he'd mutter, "I pulled you out of that hole, little girl. Your life belongs to me. Forget that, and you can forget your next breath as well, for I'll garrote you myself." His threats never failed to terrorize her. His frigid eyes and loathsome face plagued her dreams each night.

But the wind and the flying snow and the cracking brush had washed out of her mind all thoughts not directly tied to the moment. She couldn't tell how far they'd come since dawn, nor what direction they travelled. She only knew that she was riding expertly with a troop of experts, and was thrilled by that recognition. The smells of horse and of new leather filled her with a strange sense of power. A masculine feeling? she'd wondered briefly, then quickly discarded the idea. She was no less a woman because she rode with brigands through the snow and cold. Perhaps, indeed, she was more of one. And certainly Ligne herself had proved that a hunger for power was not a masculine preserve. Bronwynn admitted to herself a growing compulsion within. She was starting to want to be Queen.

A cry went up from the left flank of the charging brigade, at once loud and indistinct. Then, with a powerful leap, her horse cleared a large bush, and she understood for herself. For the second time in her life, Bronwynn rode through the enchanting fields of Ngandib-Mar.

Not that she recognized anything. Pelmen had brought her past this place only the spring before, but that had been another wild ride, and mostly under the cover of night. Besides, the numbing uniformity of the snowy counterpane at their feet erased all memory of spring landmarks.

Freed now from all obstructing trees, the troop of riders took on the semblance at least of an organized band. The flanks dropped off and the center pushed forward to form a vanguard. Bronwynn whipped her horse gratuitously as it bounded along a few yards to the rear and left of Admon Faye. Before her were the many hills and valleys of the heart of Ngandib-Mat, but she saw the men were wheeling away from that heartland, turning eastward toward the line of high, stony cliffs that she knew formed this face of the Spinal Range. They were riding, then, to Westmouth—the field where her father had died.

On Westmouth before Dragonsgate, her father had led the grand Golden Army to an equally grand defeat. Somewhere under the melting snow lay Talith's unburied bones. That thought chased through the young woman's attention, but she gave it no warm, sad welcome. She dismissed it. Her relationship with her father had never been good, and his death had resulted directly from his own foolish arrogance and his greed. Bronwynn was much more concerned with where they were travelling now, and why.

They stopped only once to rest their horses on the banks

of a small stream that curled through the colorless country-side. Then they were off again, a wedge of racing riders several hundreds of yards wide, plowing up plumes of snow in their wake. The sun was setting back of her left shoulder, turning the hilly horizon a glorious magenta, before they dipped down at last into the wide flat plain that was West-mouth, and she saw where they were going. Some miles beyond stood a single castle, its gray walls painted a dull orange by the setting sun.

She urged her exhausted mount forward, drawing abreast of Admon Faye once again, and shouted: "Whose is it?"

"It's a merchant manor," the slaver called back. "It be-longs to the family of Ognadzu. It once was the home of Tohn mod Neelis, but now it's ruled by his cousin."

"Who's his cousin?" Bronwynn yelled, her eyes watering in the whipping wind.

"Flayh," Admon Faye answered, and it seemed to Bron-wynn that for the first time today she finally felt the cold. She had heard much about Flayh, and in her mind his name had long been linked with that of Admon Faye as a foremost agent of wickedness and villainy. As they gal-loped across that last stretch of flat space that separated them from the castle, Bronwynn felt very much the small girl, a long, long way from home.

The castle was not an impressive edifice. Its tallest tower rose barely forty feet above the ground. It was from this spire that Pezi spied the large group of approaching riders. He had been taking his evening constitutional after a heavy dinner—his one concession to the need for diminishing his blubbery bulk. His stringent exercise program called for his climbing the steps to this rooftop one time, resting several minutes to get his breath back, then returning slowly to the castle floor. On this particular occasion, however, he pushed himself into a trot on his way down, crying "At-tackers from the south!" His cry stirred tremendous activ-ity in a brief space of time, and Pezi felt rather proud of himself as he waddled hurriedly toward the gate. The ex-citement ceased as quickly as it began, however, when the sharp-eyed warrior who was officially on watch recognized that it was Admon Faye's band of outlaws, and shouted the information down.

Pezi was a bit embarrassed and he didn't look at the faces of those castle dwellers who walked past him on their way back to their places. He heard several snickers behind him, and his visage clouded. He broadened his stance before the gate—no easy task, given the stubbiness of his pudgy legs—and shouted, "Open up!" to the two men who operated the winches that raised the portcullis.

From their vantage point atop the wall, they could see the fast-approaching cloud of Admon Faye's crazed riders, who had targeted on the gate and now rode for it five abreast. They could also see the petulant figure of the unpopular Pezi, standing directly in the path of the incoming riders. They smiled at one another gleefully, and opened the gate . . .

"What happened?" the fat little merchant asked plaintively when he awoke several minutes later. His comment drew raucous laughter from those gathered around. He opened his eyes and rolled his head to the side, to find he was lying on a table in the great hall. Scattered around the room were outlaws and slavers guzzling ale and leering at the serving girls. Suddenly a giant form blocked his view, and he followed it up to look into the repugnant face of Admon Faye. Pezi winced at the sight.

"Well now. Awake, are you, Pezi? Very brave of you, lad, to attempt to hold off our charge that way. Bit foolhardy, however, to stand alone against a hundred and more riders. I trust you'll forgive my clubbing you aside, but I thought you might prefer a split noggin to the hooves of half a hundred horses on your belly."

Those standing near enough to hear the slaver guffawed at that, and Admon Faye joined in lustily. Pezi lay back and closed his eyes, wishing he were somewhere else. He raised a tentative hand to his forehead and found it was—well—lumpy.

"No, lad, you can't laze around on the tables like that!" Admon Faye grabbed the cloth of Pezi's blue and lime shirt and hoisted him into the air. "Stand up, Pezi, steady on you feet! You want to start a rumor that the merchants of Ognadzu are a pack of drunks?" The slaver set the chubby merchant on the floor, but Pezi found standing anything but steady. "Bit addled, still?" the slaver asked solicitiously. "A little ale might help," he offered and he scooped a tankard off the table. Pezi reached for it woozily, but Admon Faye wasn't handing it to him. Instead, he upended the tankard over Pezi's head, and the merchant's eyes shot open in cold shock. Boisterous cheers welcomed the sight, and Admon Faye collapsed snickering onto a bench.

Pezi wiped some of the liquid out of his eyes, and glanced around to find the swiftest route of escape. He started down the aisle, but Admon Faye shot a booted foot out to block him between the benches. "Can't let you run off, Pezi. These good people tell me you're the man in charge."

"Flayh rules in this castle, not me," Pezi grumbled and he turned to try to escape in the other direction. Admon Faye glanced at one of his cohorts, and the man nodded and straddled the aisle at the other end of the row. Pezi understood. He sat across from Admon Faye, leaned back on the table behind him, and propped his aching head in his hand.

"That's the problem, my friend," the slaver continued. "Where is Flayh? I've ridden a long way to meet with him. Is this how he greets his guests?"

"Uncle Flayh comes and goes as he chooses, and he expects his guests to do the same. Would it be too much to ask to let me do that, as well?"

"In a moment, Pezi. In a moment. Surely Flayh is here in the castle somewhere?"

"Surely he is," Pezi agreed, "but I couldn't tell you where. Uncle Flayh is . . . different, lately."

"Ah yes, I'd heard something about that. A powershaper now, is he?"

Pezi raised his eyes knowingly and finally met Admon Faye's amused gaze head on. "Scoff if you choose, but he *is*." Pezi looked around to see who might be listening, then leaned across and spoke earnestly: "And he's a dangerous one."

Admon Faye leaned forward too, thrusting his face down into Pezi's. "I'm pleased to hear it. I trust dangerous people. They don't fold up while defending your flanks."

Pezi scooted back on his seat, discomfited. Admon Faye let a lazy smile spread across his features and he, too, sat back. But his eyes never left Pezi's, and the merchant felt that gaze would sizzle right through him. "What about you, Pezi? Are you a dangerous man?"

Pezi shifted on his balloonlike bottom. "I—I carry my weight—" He hadn't intended that to be funny, but those who ringed him found it hilarious. "I can handle myself!" he shouted, and the tone of his voice silenced his mockers. Pezi wasn't lying. Perhaps he was a bit chunky and certainly he didn't move with the grace of a wild buck, but he fought like an angry boar when cornered—and he was feeling very much cornered at the moment. Pezi felt for the pommel of his dagger and snarled, "I can be as cruel as the next man, should the need arise."

"Can you now?" Admon Faye asked quietly. "Yes, I see a bit of fire in your pudding face at that. Then are you saying I can trust you, Pezi? Because I don't think much of that hand upon your dagger."

Pezi thought a moment, then dropped his hand to his side.

"Good," said Admon Faye. "I like that. A moment of hesitation to show spirit—then a demonstration of reasoned caution. Very good, Pezi. Perhaps we can work together." Admon Faye waved a hand at the man who guarded the aisle, and the fellow went back to join his mates. Pezi stood up, hitched his pants, and started to leave. "Bring me the girl," Admon Faye shouted behind him. Pezi didn't look back, but stalked straight for the door. It opened before he reached it, and two beefy rogues pushed a woman into the hall. It wasn't until they collided that they recognized each other.

"Pezi!" Bronwynn snarled.

"Princess?" Pezi replied, and he quickly stepped back, for Bronwynn's face registered a long-harbored rage.

"You—scum!" she shrilled, and she buried her balled right fist three inches into his stomach. Bronwynn had been saving this up for a long time and so, without hesitation, she buried her left fist in the same spot. Pezi doubled over, the wind knocked out of him. He could hear that, once again, his antics had the whole hall hooting. "You're the one who got me into all this mess!" the girl screamed in his face, and she boxed first his right ear, then his left.

"Come on, Pezi," Admon Faye cheered. "Show us your renowned fighting spirit."

"You . . . mudgecurdle!" Bronwynn spat into his ring-ing ears. "You're nothing but a mudgecurdle!"

The description was accurate enough. A mudgecurdle was a small animal who appeared to be the mirror image of a cute, cuddly bunny—until a person tried to pick one up. Then it sprayed a double-barrelled dose of potent liquid odor so offensive it could render a person senseless in a matter of minutes. The term had entered common usage long ago as an epithet for a traitor. Certainly Pezi had proved himself such when, with Ligne's help, he'd kid-napped Bronwynn from her father's castle so many months before. Ever since that day, Bronwynn's life had been a series of escapes from one danger into another. Except for a few wonderful weeks she'd spent in Lamath as the initi-ate of Pelmen the Prophet and the companion of Rosha mod Dorlyth, Pezi's action had caused her nothing but grief. During those eventful months she'd learned some-thing about self-defense, and Admon Faye's abuse had helped sharpen those skills and given her a powerful thirst for revenge. Now she put every trick she'd learned into action, kneeing Pezi in the ribs and cracking his balding pate with her knuckles.

These harsh slave-traders loved nothing better than a fight after dinner, and a circle rapidly formed around the two combatants. Benches were overturned and tankards kicked aside, as spectators scrambled for a good view. The everpresent dogs who made the straw-covered floor of this hall their home all barked merrily, thoroughly enjoying the excitement though not understanding its cause. No one no-ticed, then, when a lean, graying hound bounded through the open door, past the crowd, and up onto one of the ta-bles.

"Is this the way you treat the manor of your host?" The voice seemed to come from everywhere at once, and the fighting stopped immediately. All eyes turned to the center of the room. There, atop a table, stood Flayh, formerly a merchant of Lamath, now a powershaper, resplendent in a white robe of fish-satin, and a red cloak of the same pre-cious material. He seemed to glow with an eerie iridesc-ence—a bluish aura outlined his body against the darkness of the room.

So devastating was his entrance that no one dared to

speak for several seconds. Then there was the casual clapping of a single pair of hands, followed by a low chuckle.
Admon Faye was amused. "Very good, Flayh. Most impressive."

"You were asking for me previously, slaver—better said,
you demanded my presence. Am I one of your slaves, Admon Faye, to come running at your command?" Flayh
scowled, and threw his red cloak wide. "I am Flayh the
powershaper!" The words rang around the walls of the
room, and echoed off the high ceiling.

Admon Faye glanced around with studied calm. "Pity,"
he said after a moment. "I'd expected a thunderclap after
such a declaration."

Flayh's arms dropped slowly to his sides, and he smiled.
"I'm working on that. And with the progress I'm making, I
expect to have it soon."

"Good, good," the slaver encouraged. "Since we've gotten that out of the way, can we get down to business? I do
believe that it was you who summoned me here, and not
the other way around. Or would you prefer to posture some
more beforehand?"

Those standing next to Admon Faye saw him jerk
slightly, then watched as his jaw clenched and his fingers
formed into fists. Flayh was smiling grimly, his eyes locked
into those of the slaver. There was silence in the hall until
Flayh's body went slack, and Admon Faye gave a great
sigh. Flayh had been attempting to draw fear out of the
ugly slaver. He'd failed—but just barely.

"So," the powershaper said quietly.

Admon Faye wiped his sweating forehead. "So," he
agreed. In that contest a mutual respect had formed between the two men. Ironically, no one else in the room
really understood what had happened.

"You have buried your fears deep, Admon Faye. I
couldn't pull them to the surface. Quite."

"And you, Lord Flayh, are much more than an aging
merchant." Flayh noted with approval the slaver's respect-
ful mode of address. Admon Faye had a host of negative
qualities, Flayh thought to himself, but stupidity wasn't one
of them.

The thought brought Pezi to Flayh's mind. "Nephew,
since you seem to be momentarily out of trouble, why don't

you seize the opportunity and go change your suit?" Though asked as a question, Pezi recognized Flayh's statement was a command. Guarding his stomach from Bronwynn, he stepped around the girl and out of the room. Flayh shrugged at Admon Faye. "Pezi's making a single-handed attempt to give all merchants a reputation for slobbishness. I hope he's at least amused you."

"Oh, that he has," the slaver chuckled, and he stalked across the room to sit on a bench at Flayh's table. The powershaper climbed down to join him. Admon Faye noticed with surprise Flayh's small stature, but immediately put the thought from his mind. He had learned long ago that height is not the measure of a man—particularly if he's a sorcerer. "I notice you aren't wearing the colors of your house . . ."

"Indeed, I've abandoned the blue and lime of Ognadzu except for state occasions. This feels more fitting to my individual tastes." Flayh raised his hand and a servant far across the room scrambled toward the kitchen.

"And yet you continue to call yourself a merchant . . ."

"Of course. You're a rogue and a brigand and a cutthroat, yet you remain a businessman throughout. There's nothing inconsistent there, nor is there any in my being both wizard and merchant. These vocations, these skills— they're nothing more than the tools with which we impress ourselves on the world. So let's bargain together, you and I. I assume you've brought the girl?"

Admon Faye beckoned toward Bronwynn, and the two nearest slavers seized her under her arms and hoisted her over the benches to stand at Flayh's side. The powershaper turned to look her over thoroughly.

"So this is the famous Bronwynn, daughter of Talith of Chaomonous. I had hoped to meet you long ago, child, but my fool of a nephew bungled the job. You've cost me dearly and, were I less forgiving, you'd suffer for it. But I've decided to make you Queen instead." Flayh jerked his head. "Throw her in the pit—"

"Ahhh—" Admon Faye grunted, raising his hand, and the two slavers who held Bronwynn froze. Flayh frowned, and Admon Faye smiled. "I've found that I enjoy the little girl's company. She stays with me—or none of us stay."

"You're giving orders? In my house?"

"The girl is my captive . . ."

"Whom I ordered seized."

"Freed by my skill and knowledge," Admon Faye roared. Then his voice softened. "What's the matter, Flayh. Don't you trust me?" he asked sarcastically.

Flayh stared at him. Then he, too, smiled. "Of course I do. It's the girl I don't trust." He waved an arm. "Take her away," he muttered, and Bronwynn was escorted out of the hall. Flayh's eyes jerked back to meet Admon Faye's. "And what if she runs?"

Admon Faye chuckled. "She won't run away. Where would she go?"

"To the castle of Dorlyth mod Karis, of course. The father of her boy lover."

"Ah yes, you mean Rosha mod Dorlyth." Admon Faye was familiar with the family. "Actually, I'd rather welcome another encounter with young Rosha," he said. "His sword left several new scars on my face."

"Why should you care?" Flayh sneered. "Who could possibly tell?"

Admon Faye's eyes flashed. "My respect does not entitle you to comment on my appearance, Flayh. Mock me, and I'll kill you." The statement was so frank that Flayh was shocked.

"No one threatens me like—"

"No one comments on my features!" Admon Faye snarled, rising to crouch over the table.

Flayh looked him in the face, then shrugged. "Nor would I. The girl is your responsibility. But I warn you—if she slips away I hold you accountable, and should anyone seek to rescue her from us, I depend upon your blade!"

"So be it." The slaver nodded, eager to get on to other matters. "The plan is simple. I assassinate Ligne, and place Bronwynn on the throne. I'm doing that for myself—Ligne has become as much a bother to me as she is to you. I understand you will profit from the move as well?"

"I will profit greatly from it. Jagd and the merchant house of Uda have monopolized all business in Chaomonous—that mudgecurdle. How could I have trusted him?"

"You didn't," Admon Faye chuckled. "You thought you could control him."

"So I did. I assume he's still living at the palace?"

"Under the warm protection of Queen Ligne, yes, or he'd be in his grave already. He's been cutting into my markets as well as yours. I assume we'll plan to assassinate Jagd, too?"

"Perhaps that won't be necessary," Flayh muttered. "I've summoned a meeting of the Council of Elders of the merchant houses. Unless he's willing to be stripped of his position, he's obliged to attend."

"You think he'll come? Knowing your feelings?"

"What has he to gain by staying sealed up inside the Imperial House? He'll have to move against me sometime, Admon Faye. The question is when. I think he'll come."

"Which brings us to something that greatly interests me." Admon Faye smiled, lacing his fingers together and placing his hands on the table between them. "What do I get from you?"

"Of course, you've guessed it already, or you wouldn't be here." Flayh also smiled. "As all of us know, the dragon is dead. That means the slave market has dropped off considerably, threatening your business." Admon Faye nodded. "It also means that anyone can pass Dragonsgate, which is certainly threatening ours. We merchant families have held a monopoly on all trade for so long, I'm afraid we've become rather used to it. I, for one, don't relish the idea of losing that to a new influx of independent traders. Of course, we could field an army to hold the pass against all others, but that would surely rouse the common people against us, and eventually one of the three lands would send in a larger army to drive us out. Bad reputation and bad business. However—" Flayh cleared his throat. "I understand that you and your little band control the pass at this time."

"I do."

"There's great advantage to us in that—or will be, if we can agree. Of course you could never resist an army, any more than we could, but your strike and run tactics are such that any army that drove you from Dragonsgate would have to remain there to keep you out. The state that attempted such would draw immediate response from the other two, resulting in international incidents, and war. No one would want that."

"True," Admon Faye said quietly.

"While you, being an outlaw known to all three lands, would actually be a kind of buffer for all three."

"I take the dragon's place. Get to the point."

"So what is it that you want, you who can take whatever you choose? Respect. Respect, and real power. A seat on the Council of Elders. Your own merchant house."

Admon Faye smiled broadly. "You understand perfectly."

"The Council has been summoned, and you will naturally be elected to it. You have what you want, we have what we want . . . and between the two of us, we eliminate Jagd from the competition. What more could you ask for?"

"Only one thing," Admon Faye said.

"And that is?"

"Your seat, Flayh. As head of the Council." The slaver grinned as he said it. Flayh raised an eyebrow, then returned the grin.

"That, my friend, is why it pays to be a powershaper."

CHAPTER SEVEN

❦ ❦

Opening at the Palace

AN HOUR BEFORE DUSK, the chain of wagons rumbled over a cobblestoned bridge into the heart of Chaomonous and turned east down the main thoroughfare. The broad street climbed steadily to the base of a huge chunk of granite. On top of that rock stood the Imperial House itself.

As the road wound up out of the city, one could see that the center of town was constructed on a little sliver of land, a peninsula bracketed by two giant rivers. On the far side of the castle the rivers joined, rolling as one to the sea many miles beyond. But the arriving players paid no heed to the rivers. All eyes were fixed on the massive fortress that rose before them.

It was impossible to tell where the rock stopped and the structure began, so closely had the castle's walls been married to their granite foundation. Though the setting sun did curious things to the color of the palace, it was clearly not of a single shade of gray. Rather, it seemed the battlements were of patchwork construction, a testimony to the long years the castle had been in the building. The tops of its spires disappeared into a cloak of fog that clung stubbornly to its ancient stonework. The Imperial House of Chaomonous towered over the capital, drawing all eyes to itself.

From a distance it appeared to float above the world, unrelated to the city clustered at its feet. But from the perspective of the approaching wagons, the castle looked anything but ethereal. It squatted on its granite slab in heavy silence, brooding over the confluence of the two rivers like an ill-tempered titian.

Pelmen rode atop the second carriage with Yona Parmi. Flocks of excited children raced beside them, and he smiled and waved to them, maintaining the clownish persona he had assumed in Pleclypsa. But there was no smile behind his white face. The closer they got to the malevolent presence of the castle that dominated the landscape, the more sure he grew that some nameless power lurked within its walls. But what power? And how did it come to be here?

Gerrig's wagon led the parade, moving at a pompous snail's pace. Gerrig stood on the top of his carriage, waving both hands in the air and shouting at the startled shoppers who thronged the city's markets. Gerrig loved nothing so much as acting and at the present he was giving a lively performance in the role of the conquering hero.

"He'd better sit down before we start up the incline," Parmi mumbled, "or he'll scatter pieces of his head all over the cobblestones."

"Are you reading my mind again?" Pelmen asked solemnly through a fixed, forced smile.

"It isn't hard, you know. Your thin mask doesn't hide worry well."

"Is it that obvious?"

"To one who's watched you for so many years, it's certainly obvious." Parmi cocked an eyebrow and gazed up at the castle's heights. "Are there powers here you fear?"

"Perhaps."

"Still not going to tell me why we've come?"

"Why should I cause you to worry, too?"

Yona chuckled nervously. "It's comments like that which make me worry." He was silent for a moment, then he went on: "Just promise me this. If you need some help, will you call on me?"

"That I can promise."

"Fine." Yona nodded and leaned out to wave at a meat merchant who peered at them from under a red and purple awning. "I must say," he muttered, noting the colors, "it looks as if the house of Uda has taken over this city entirely."

"Does it matter?" Pelmen wondered.

Parmi regarded him with a curious smile. "By that you mean?"

"Only that despite their colors, one merchant is very like another."

"You've not gone to war with the Council of Elders!" Yona blurted in astonishment.

"Not exactly. But they may have gone to war with me."

Yona Parmi swiveled back to stare glumly at the rear of Gerrig's ascending wagon. "Battling dragons seems ridiculous enough. But battling business?" He heaved a heavy sigh.

"It's all right, my friend," Pelmen said. "Don't worry about it."

"Come now, Pelmen, how can you expect me not to?"

"I can't! That's why I haven't told you any more than I have. One thing I do hope, however . . ."

"And that is?"

"That you won't call me Pelmen within the walls."

"Ah—" Yona grunted, and he slapped his forehead. "Sorry. Henceforth you're Fallomar in my every thought."

The road tilted up sharply, as it began its zigzag climb of the castle mount. Gerrig finally took his seat—grudgingly, since many new spectators had just rushed into the streets to watch them. They were obviously headed for the Imperial House, and these city dwellers were fascinated by the sight of anyone privileged to pass beyond those forbidding walls. The climb to the outer gate took ten minutes, and the two players passed it in silence. Then they were inside. Their wagons were wheeled away to the massive royal carriage house. Their animals were led the other direction to a gigantic stable. Then they were permitted to climb the thirty-foot stairway to enter the main gate.

They walked through hallways lined with masterpieces of paintings and sculpture, across carpets of inch-thick pile. The ceiling, twenty feet above their heads, was inlaid with a continuous mosaic pattern interweaving blue, green and pink stones—and plates of beaten gold. The halls glowed with a golden shimmer, as those polished plates reflected the light of long white candles, held in place by brackets of still more gold. The halls twisted and turned at sharp angles; at the head of each turn was a pair of slotted windows. These were arrow slits, and through these apertures the troupe could see the watchful eyes of the palace guards following their progress intently. This mixing of luxurious grandeur with raw force was designed to intimidate each entrant of the castle, and the design suceeded admirably. "This house could never be taken by force," Pelmen murmured to himself.

He felt a strange sensation then—as if the walls had heard his words and approved. He put the thought out of his mind when he noticed a curious condensation on the wall. The fitted stones glistened with reflected candlelight . . .

The other veterans of court performance stalked along grandly, joking with one another over the awestruck expressions of their newer companions. "Don't get too excited," Danyilyn complained casually to one. "This is the front half of the palace—for important people. We're nothing but players, so they'll stick us in the servants' quarters in the back."

For that, Pelmen was very grateful. The further out of Ligne's path, the less chance of her seeing through his thin disguise. As they turned another corner, he smiled clownishly and waggled his fingers at the guards beyond the wall. He thought he saw one pair of eyes smile back.

Moments later they were standing on the tile floor outside of the Chamber of Peace. Here they waited for half an hour. A harried-looking court attendant finally stepped out to greet them, his hands fluttering as he apologized. "I'm so sorry the Queen isn't here yet, but she's been delayed by some very important business that can't be interrupt—"

"I'm warning you, Kherda, the next time you hold me up like that when I'm closing for the kill, I'm going to have someone cut off your hand!" Pelmen recognized the voice immediately as belonging to Ligne. It was coming from the spiral staircase at the far end of the hall, and growing louder as she descended. He edged his way back among other members of the troupe, positioning himself behind Gerrig's broad back.

"I don't know why you're complaining," Kherda protested defensively. "You won, anyway."

"Much to my dismay," added a little man coming down the stairs behind Kherda and Ligne. His scarlet and purple cloak marked him immediately as a merchant of Uda. As the little group walked toward them, Pelmen noted the cloak's material and its costly cut and guessed him to be not only a merchant, but an Elder as well. "In fact," the man continued, "I think Kherda was really trying to help you, Ligne, not harm you. When he replaced his losses with his star instead of his disc, it was me he was arming to battle with, not you."

Pelmen smiled to himself. The important business that had kept the Queen from meeting with them sooner had obviously been a game of full Drax. It was the language of this three-sided table game that they were speaking.

"Say what you like, Jagd, he was deliberately undermining my strength. I had a chance for total conquest." Ligne spat at Kherda in disgust. "But you knocked it down to a marginal victory."

"Which is, as they say, just as much a win." Jagd smiled beneficently. "Besides, Ligne, you appeared to me to be totally unaware of my cube, and I fear—"

"My Lady," the court attendant tremulously interrupted, "the travelling players have arrived, and—"

"I have eyes, don't I?" Ligne bellowed at the man, and he swiftly bowed his way out of their presence, backing into the Chamber of Peace. Ligne looked at the group before her with a hint of distaste playing around her lips, then abruptly smiled a warm smile. "Welcome! Gerrig, hello! Yes, I remember your face," she said to Yona Parmi, waving away his bow. She looked into Danyilyn's eyes for a moment, craning her neck as if to see into the darker corners of the actress' mind, and asked, "Weren't you here before, too?"

Danyilyn scraped the floor with the hem of her skirt as she curtsied gracefully. She smiled a pleased, awed smile, perfectly conveyed her joy that the Queen should deign to remember her. Of course, she was a professional, but Pelmen still had to admire the skill with which Danyilyn communicated that feigned pleasure.

Now Ligne brushed past Gerrig and stared into Pelmen's face, squinting to try to see through the greasepaint. "And you?" she began, almost with a tone of suspicion.

Gerrig broke in hastily. "This is Follomar the fool, a new addition to our troupe, and this is Magrol, Jamnard . . ." He continued, moving through the group. Ligne didn't follow him. She reached out to try to touch Pelmen's face, and he ducked out of the way.

"Why are you wearing makeup?" she demanded.

"Why do you?" he quickly responded.

"To improve my appearance, of course."

"There's my reason as well."

"But you've covered your whole face."

"An improvement, believe me. But if my Lady doubts my word, let me propose a contest. Let her remove her makeup and I'll remove mine, and we shall see who needs it the most."

Ligne's sharp blue gaze threatened him only momentarily; then the woman blinked and her nose wrinkled into a grin. "A genuine fool! How amusing, Kherda." She turned and pointed a finger at her Prime Minister. "Listen, you sour old parchment pusher! Lose me another game like that, and I'll put this one in your office!"

"You didn't lose," Kherda groused. He sighed with exasperation.

"Everyone else in the group is new," Gerrig broke in nervously. "It's been a hard year for us, and some of our best drifted off to join other organizations. But we are ever so grateful to you, Queen Ligne, for allowing us to—"

"Spare me," the Queen said, and she turned around to stalk into the Chamber of Peace. Gerrig looked inquiringly at Kherda, who jerked his head toward the door and frowned. Gerrig followed Ligne into the opulently furnished chamber. "I hear you now perform a masterful play with me as the subject." Here Ligne turned, and her cold blue eyes ran Gerrig through. "Your last appearance inside these walls was not so masterful."

"But, they, I . . ." Gerrig stammered, flustered by her manner.

"Don't stammer at me! I'm tired of hearing mumblings that make no sense."

Gerrig shut his mouth, and resolved to keep it closed unless she asked a direct question. His tongue had long been his fortune, and he was anxious to keep it safely in place.

"I recognize that at that time this wasn't my court, and that you were under the influence of that tedious Pelmen. I trust that during your present stay you'll refrain from commentary on my morals and my politics?" She looked at Gerrig expectantly, and he nodded with all the sincerity he could manage to muster. "Fine. I've a number of things on my mind these days—I'm in no hurry to see you perform. Perhaps you won't mind sampling the pleasures of the court for a few weeks?"

"Wh—why, my Lady, we would be *honored* to spend—"

"To spend my gold on your extravagant appetites? Of course you would. Realize, however, that when I do wish entertainment, I require it at a moment's notice. You may find it wise to be prepared when I call on you. Craftsmen who disappoint me often find my displeasure—painful." Ligne then glided grandly out of the Chamber of Peace, passed the troupe without a glance, and headed back for the staircase, calling over her shoulder, "Come on Jagd. Let's play another."

Kherda followed her, his sandals flapping as ever. "My Lady, there is a drought in the southeastern provinces and—"

"You told me that at breakfast."

"If you could give your approval for the relief goods to be accompanied by a contingent of the Golden Throng, I could dispatch—"

"Have you ever tried the sweep-flip opening, Jagd?" Ligne asked the merchant as they reached the stairs and started up. "Someone told me that in Lamath it's called the Hanni opening, because that house originated it."

"Doubtless a Hanni merchant who told you so. It originated with Uda. I don't think very much of it myself, however, since it wastes too many valuable pieces early in the . . ."

Pelmen strained to hear the rest of Jagd's explanation. He was a Drax player himself, though it had been months since he'd played. Even then, it had been only a game of Green Dummy Drax he'd played against Dorlyth. But the hall was ninety feet long, and Jagd's quiet voice didn't carry very far. The merchant and the Queen disappeared into the upper levels of the palace.

Kherda stood at the foot of the stairs, shaking his head.

Almost as an afterthought, he turned to call back to the actors: "Go see the Lord of Entertainments. I'm sure one of you will remember where his office is. He'll give you lodgings, and I'll give you a more thorough orientation in the morning." Kherda sighed; then, scooping up his skirts, he assumed a dignified expression, and flapped up the stairs.

Gerrig spun around to look at Pelmen, his face the color of a freshly laundered sheet. "Do you think she recognized you?"

"Recognized whom?" Fallomar answered him. The eyes of the clown peered back at Gerrig curiously, as if the huge actor's words were totally devoid of meaning.

Gerrig understood. He nodded, then took Danyilyn by the hand. "Come, lady. Let's go find some rooms." They started for the stairway, for Maythorm's office was on the floor above. Pelmen was gone, swallowed whole by Follomar the fool. Gerrig was surprised at how much he already missed him.

Maythorm had been advised of their arrival by the serving girl who'd been bringing his dinner to his room. She felt sorry for the poor man—the slightest noise made him jump, and he seemed uncommonly suspicious of everyone and everything. Besides, he was so good-looking . . . perhaps someday he would notice her! She made a special effort to roust him out of his quarters to meet the players when they arrived at his office. As they surged into his room, he stood to meet them, his handsome, almost pretty face radiating a dazzling smile. "Welcome, welcome, Gerrig and Danyilyn, so *pleased* that you could accept our—" There he stopped, dumfounded. The puzzled troupe waited for him to regather his wits and finish his sentence. "Why, you're not Garrig and Danyilyn!" he gasped, his forehead knitting in indignation. "You're . . ." he stopped again, and this time his face went blank. Then his eyes widened and he blurted out, "You're Gerrig and Danyilyn!"

Gerrig arched an eyebrow. "I've always thought so . . ."

"But I was expecting Danyilyn and Gerrig!" he gasped. "I mean, I was expecting . . . who was I expecting . . ."

"Apparently, sir, you were expecting us," Gerrig grunted, and he produced from a pocket within his tunic a tiny cylinder of parchment, which he unrolled and read aloud. "Summoned to the court—by invitation of the Queen—Gerrig, Danyilyn, and the acting troupe thereof."

"But there must be some mistake!" Maythorm pleaded. "The troupe I invited were to win the Winter Festival in Pleclypsa!"

"We *did* win," Danyilyn snapped.

"No, but they performed a play based on the Queen's rise to power!"

"That's our piece," Gerrig smiled, his teeth bright against his bushy red curls. "Masterful work it is, too." He winked at Pelmen. Fallomar the fool regarded him curiously, and once again Gerrig was reminded of the need to conceal Pelmen's identity.

"But . . . but . . ."

"The man's obviously distraught," Follomar explained to the others.

"Do I know you?" Maythorm asked the painted clown suspiciously.

Fallomar peered into Maythorm's face. "Why, I think so. Weren't you at the recent convention of All Fools?"

"Are you calling me a fool?"

"Not actually, no. Would you like to take this opportunity to prove yourself one?"

"I know that voice!" Maythorm snarled. His pretty features quickly turned red.

"Better, I hope, than you know Gerrig and Danyilyn—"

"Are you related to a peasant in the south?"

"Are you related to a buzzard in the north?"

"What? Who said anything about buzzards?"

"Well, you brought up pheasants—"

"I said peasants!"

"Absolutely unrelated."

"What?"

"Peasants to pheasants."

"You are an *idiot!*" Maythorm roared.

"I'm a fool, actually."

"You certainly are!"

"I thank you for that good review!" Pelmen smiled.

"Get out of my office!"

"But you invited us."

"I . . ." Here Maythorm hesitated. The blood drained

from his face as swiftly as it had flooded in. "I invited . . . you?"

Gerrig stepped forward and passed him the parchment slip. "Posted by blue-flyer to Minlaf-Khen. You see—right there—the seal of the crown."

"I . . . authorized this?" Maythorm murmured as he circled his desk-table and slumped onto a stool.

"We came to get our room assignments," Danyilyn announced impatiently. "Can we get on with it?"

Maythorm raised his eyes slowly, a slack-jawed expression robbing his features of energy. Then, abruptly, he smirked. He pointed at Gerrig and laughed aloud, then said, "I get it. You're after my job, right? A cream-puff post, you think, frosted with power and weighted with wealth, am I right?" His finger swept the whole troupe. "You're all in on it, aren't you? Plotting in private to pry me out of my office."

The actors exchanged bewildered stares. "Maythorm," Gerrig began, "as Danyilyn said—"

"She's not Danyilyn!" Maythorm yelled. "I know who she is—she's Danyilyn! I know all of you!"

"What a relief," Fallomar sighed heavily.

"And I know you, too!" Maythorm shouted, pointing now at the fool. "You're the peasant who ambushed me on the road, who summoned the thunder and changed to a falcon and threw balls of colored fire at me all morning!"

The entire troupe stared open-mouthed at Maythorm—all, that is, save Yona. He was regarding the painted fool with some alarm.

Gerrig cleared his throat. "Ah, Maythorm . . . perhaps the Queen's been working you too hard—"

"Ah-ha! You see?" Maythorm crowed. "Insinuating that I, Maythorm, am a bumbling incompetent! And naturally, you could do better?"

The bellowing of the Lord of Entertainments had attracted quite a crowd in the hallway outside. Now the serving girl bustled into the room, plowing her way through the troupe to Maythorm's side. As she led him out, she apologized, "He hasn't been himself since he got back from Pleclypsa."

"Oh that's all right." The fool shrugged. "According to him, we haven't been ourselves either."

"I'll get you, fool!" Maythorm shouted, pointing back at Fallomar. "I'll be watching you like a hawk!" Then Maythorm and the serving girl disappeared into the hallway, leaving the cluster of actors staring at Pelmen.

"I love the palace," he sighed. "It never fails to restore my faith in government."

A steward finally assigned them their lodgings. They all were given rooms in the craftsmen's quarters, on the third level of the Imperial House. While Yona Parmi, Danyilyn and Gerrig were given large rooms very near the grand stairway at the castle's center, Pelmen received a small cramped cell well to the backside of the palace—indicative of the fact that Maythorm, though perhaps a bit addled, was not without influence. This was really much to Pelmen's liking, for he was right around the corner from a servants' stairway, which descended directly into the slave's quarters and the kitchen. He intended to get well acquainted with the castle's slaves; as in every palace, it was they who knew best the business of the royal occupants. He felt sure that if Bronwynn was anywhere within the Imperial House, she was in the dungeon, but he wanted to be sure before attempting the dangerous entry. He hoped the slaves could either confirm or deny that Ligne had imprisoned her there.

It was the only possibility that made any sense. One day, she and Joss had ridden together from the forest in a guerrilla attack on one of Ligne's weaker outposts. The next, she had disappeared . . . and Joss was suddenly once again the Lord of Security. Pelmen was positive she was here.

Something else was here as well. Pelmen lay back on a dirty cot and gazed toward the ceiling, listening for something, anything, that might give him a clue as to its nature. As he tuned his spirit to listen, he felt a telltale uneasiness in his chest—his breathing grew shallow. It wasn't fear . . . more a sense of anticipation. "Who are you?" he finally whispered. "You're surely not the Power . . ."

—What do you mean by that? replied the Imperial House brusquely. It had been watching this gaily painted character ever since he'd entered its walls, but it had taken a special interest in the fool after witnessing the exchange with Maythorm.

Pelmen listened intently. He heard nothing. "I wonder," he mumbled.

—Speak up! How can you expect this House to respond if it cannot hear your comments?

Pelmen just gazed at the ceiling, and argued with himself. "Just your imagination," he muttered.

—What about imagination? asked the House. Come, come, speak up! This Maythorm fellow seems to think you a powershaper. Is that so?

The player was silent. It had been a long day of travelling. He'd fallen asleep.

Pelmen woke with a jerk. He was sweating. The air in his tiny room was stale and close, but he found himself gulping great mouthfuls of the stuff. He felt strangely terrified, as if someone—or something—had laid a hand on his shoulder as he slept. He peered into the black corners. There was nothing here. That terrified him even more.

He jumped up from his mattress and shuffled cautiously for the door. Though these craftsmen's rooms had never housed captives, they were built sturdily enough to double as jail cells if the need ever arose. He put his weight to the unvarnished wood, and swung his heavy door outward.

It was dark night. No sunlight filtered down the hall from the slits in the outer walls. Some very dim light flickered off the masonry beyond the corner, the evidence that one of the torches still burned. But no one moved in the hallway. The castle was as quiet as a forgotten tomb.

Then it began. The irregular flicker of that torch around the corner suddenly grew patterned. The light began to flash—evenly, regularly, as if beating time to some unheard orchestration, written for ears other than man's. Pelmen dismissed it as the result of a draft. But there was no draft in this ancient hall, and he knew it.

His first impulse was to run. But Pelmen rarely followed his first impulse in anything. More often than not, he followed the dictates of his intuition, but he refused to be a slave to those illogical feelings that mediated his sensitivity. He waited. He leaned against the rock wall and listened.

A chill tiptoed down his back as the stone under his

hand turned a slimy cold. He jerked away—then the hand returned, feeling of the suddenly moist rock. He shook his head in bewilderment. The torch suddenly went out.

Light disappeared. Everywhere was shadow. And still Pelmen listened, while the awareness grew in him that his whole body was trembling with tension. He took a deep breath of the cooler air of the hallway and shook himself to bring on relaxation. When he was quiet again, he listened to the emptiness. Nothing stirred. Pelmen heard only his heart.

This was not the Power, of that he was sure. There was a cruel humor to this, and he had never experienced such in his communication with that Being who had made him a Prophet. But he was equally sure there was something here alive, something or someone who wished, it seemed, to talk with him. Not the Power, no. But certainly a power.

Pelmen abruptly slipped back into his room and closed the door with a heavy thud. The sound was reassuring. He leaned his back on the wood, as if barricading himself against the force in the hallway. But the act was unconscious. He knew full well that the presence was in here as well.

Pelmen stretched his hand out before him, palm up. Though only inches from his face, it couldn't be seen for the utter lack of light. Using his shaper power, he needed only to speak a phrase or think a thought, and above his invisible palm would grow a glowing ball, any color he chose, to light his way in the darkness. Pelmen would have thought nothing of doing so in the land of the Maris. Felt there, these strange sensations would simply prompt him to begin shaping. Yet here, he hesitated . . .

This was but a power—like all the others, probably—and if he chose . . .

There was a long dark moment of decision.

. . . But he did not choose. Pelmen lowered his hand to his side. Instead of shaping, he spoke. "I know you're here. Whether you are a Mari power, travelling far from home, or some other kind of power I know nothing about, still I feel you, and I know you're here. Perhaps you enjoy teasing me, but if you—"

He cut himself off. An idea broke into his chain of thought, and he stopped himself in the midthreat. Perhaps he could shape this power—but did he need to? And should he shape it, would this power be harmed? He remembered the terror he always experienced just prior to being seized by the Power—and though the joy that always followed inevitably flooded away any scars, he knew that joy proceeded from the Power's nature—it wasn't due to the nature of shaping.

"I'll let you be," Pelmen said softly. "But I have an important day tomorrow. I have a friend who must be freed from a woman's enforced will, and a land to be freed from her tyranny. Plus a dozen other problems I'm sure you're no more interested in hearing than I am in listing. What I'd like to do is get some sleep, and forget them for a while. Now—" Pelmen tried to say it nicely, but a hint of unintended annoyance crept into his tone, "would you let me get some rest?"

He threw himself on his mattress, and crossed his arms on his chest in aggravation.

Sleep came again quickly. This time, it was undisturbed—except for one thing; his dreams were all oddly colored, as if a ball of blue flame burned all night, just beyond his eyelids . . .

CHAPTER EIGHT

A Sudden Duel

STILL HOODED, Rosha was led down the long, glass-enclosed corridor that separated his quarters from the upper apartments of the Queen. Ligne had placed him in the room she herself had occupied as Talith's mistress, near the aviary on the castle's roof. There was apparently only one entrance, and that way led down a series of steps through Ligne's gigantic suite on the lower levels. There had at one time been many entrances, which Ligne herself had installed to accommodate the hosts of men who visited her in Talith's absence. These she'd ordered walled up before depositing Rosha there. The Queen wanted this lad all to herself.

Rosha heard the guard grumbling as they descended the by-now familiar stairway into Ligne's suite. They passed on through the apartment, evidently greeting no one. Then doors opened before them, and Rosha heard the sounds of people moving about in the halls. He was led around corners and down corridors until he felt his hand being placed on the railing and knew he was descending the grand spiral in the very heart of the castle. This staircase was twenty feet in diameter. It had been designed to permit impressive royal entrances to the great hall, for it opened out onto the

Queen's dais. Rosha and his guardian stepped down into the aroma of frying bacon, stewed beef and a clamor of other delicious smells. But Rosha wasn't hungry. For some reason he felt particularly hostile today.

"Good morning, Rosha," he heard the Queen call, her voice dripping with honey.

"Is it?" he snapped. "I wouldn't know." A chair was pushed up against the back of his legs, and he sat in it. Then he stared sightlessly out over the noisy throng that crowded the hall and radiated his hatred at any who cared to look.

"Good morning, Fallomar," Yona Parmi said cheerfully, looking up from a plate piled with sausages and bread. "How did you sleep?"

"Not as well as I might have liked," Pelmen grumbled quietly, as he crawled over a long bench to sit across from his friend. "And you?"

"I fared quite well, thank you," Parmi answered.

"No dreams of powers?"

Yona stopped eating and looked up from his plate again. "No . . . why?"

"As I said, it proved a somewhat sleepless experience for me."

"I should guess so, on that sack of straw they gave you for a bed, in that rat warren of a room. That should teach you not to mock the Lord of Entertainments when he's making room assignments. I slept on a feather mattress myself."

"I couldn't be more pleased with my location—though it does concern me that Maythorm seems to have recognized me somehow. I intend to stay well out of his way, henceforth—his and Queen Ligne's."

"You should have little difficulty losing yourself in this gigantic barn. And of course, if you're caught you can always fly away—though I wager that would leave the rest of us with some difficult explaining . . ." Parmi noted an uncertain expression flick across his friend's features, and his brow creased in concern. "What is it?" he asked.

"Nothing . . ." Fallomar murmured.

"You'll not convince me that way!" Parmi grunted, and

the fool had to gesture to him to hold down his voice. "This mention of powers . . . is the Power here?"

"Yes—and others."

"Other powers?"

"At least one."

"Ah. And you're uneasy about your shaping."

"Would you keep your voice down, Yona!" Pelmen whispered with intensity. "You'll soon have the Queen herself listening in on our conversation!"

"I don't notice anyone paying us any mind." Yona shrugged as he consumed a sausage. "And as for the Queen, she's far too interested in that hooded captive seated next to her to pay any heed to us."

At the mention of a captive, Pelmen's eyes shot up to the dais. A quick glance at the unfortunate creature next to Ligne assured him that this was no petite female and, with passing pity for the poor wretch, he turned back to the plate of food before him. As he turned, Pelmen caught a glimpse of the young prisoner's arm twitching—and suddenly the miserable captive had grabbed his total attention. He stared at the dais, his jaws clenched in shock and his eyes wide in horror.

"Fool!" Parmi snarled, pulling Pelmen's gaze back across the table to him. "You want to attract her attention? You certainly will if you stare at her that way! You have no idea how thoroughly that whiteface underscores the brilliance of your eyes!"

Pelmen stared at him for a moment, then began sneaking peeks at the royal table, to make sure he wasn't mistaken. He wasn't.

"What's the matter with you." Yona Parmi demanded ferociously.

The painted fool sighed, and took a bite of a sausage. "You remember the young man I told you of?" he said, chewing without tasting. "The stuttering warrior who helped me slay the dragon?"

"I do. Rosha something."

"That's him under the hood."

Yona Parmi stared this time. "You're sure?"

"He moves like Rosha. Has Rosha's build. No, I don't know for sure, but his jaw is the mirror image of Rosha's father, Dorlyth. I'm afraid it's him."

"But . . . what's he doing here?"

Pelmen glanced up at the stage, then looked away in revulsion as he muttered, "At the moment, he's being spoon-fed."

Indeed, Ligne was feeding Rosha herself. Joss would not permit him to handle eating utensils, since they could possibly used as weapons against the Queen, so Ligne had taken to feeding him. She'd come to enjoy this little symbol of her domination; she viewed this humiliation as just one more bit of leverage that would eventually, inevitably, force Rosha to yield to her demands and become domesticated.

"Did you know about this?" Parmi whispered, and Pelmen shook his head from side to side. Yona waited for a moment, then asked, "What are you going to do now?"

His appetite gone, Pelmen stared at his breakfast. "Parmi," he sighed, "I wish you hadn't asked me that.

A disheveled Kherda, late from his bed, joined Ligne on the platform and seated himself in the vacant chair between the Queen and Jagd. As always, he brought a sheaf of documents with him, which he hoped to dispose of during breakfast. It was the same stack he'd carried with him to every meal this week. As yet, he'd not been able to hold the Queen's attention long enough to take care of any of this business, and the frustration was beginning to gnaw on him. "Good morning, my Lady. I have here a number of matters that we could dispense with in just a moment if you . . ." He trailed off. The Queen had paid him absolutely no mind. "Well," he muttered bitterly, "I see she's still taken with her toy."

Jagd, who might have assumed this was addressed to him, didn't respond. The merchant mulled over his own problems. Jagd was tired of this castle. Not that the food wasn't excellent or the company never boring. He just wanted to get back to work. But through his network of spies Jagd had learned of Flayh's planned assassination attempt, and above all else, Jagd wished to keep on living. Early that morning, in the utter stillness of predawn hours, he and Flayh and Flayh's obese nephew had carried on a tense conference by means of a trio of ingenious, pyramid-shaped crystals. Flayh had issued him a summons to attend a conclave of the Council of Elders, to be held in Ngandib-Mar. Although he was fully aware that this invitation was a trap designed to lure him from the castle to his death, still the temptation to attend was strong. He was tired of walking the floors of his guest apartment, wondering if or when Ligne watched him from secret chambers beyond the wall panels. He was weary of interminable bouts of Drax—not to mention being short of gold, since Ligne always demanded that he wager, and it wasn't in his best interests to defeat the woman. As Jagd nervously gulped down a frosted spice cake, he squirmed in his seat, watching the doors for a messenger from the roof. He was expecting a missive from his protegé in the Mar, Tahli-Damen. On the basis of that word, he would decide whether to go or to stay.

"Have you ever heard the like?" Kherda seethed, bumping Jagd with his elbow to get the merchant's attention. "Why, she babbles over him like a merchant's daughter—" Kherda stopped, and looked at Jagd. "Pardon. I . . . wasn't thinking. Just an expression, you understand."

"Doesn't offend me." Jagd shrugged. "I have no daughter." The merchant went back to his breakfast. Kherda leaned toward the Queen to try to overhear her conversation with the boy.

"You seem exceptionally stubborn this morning," Ligne was chiding. "Come on now. Eat."

"D-don't you ever t-tire of this game?" Rosha snarled.

"Why, whatever do you mean?" she mocked, her voice lilting.

"This n-nonsense of trying to feed me!" he exploded. "Untie my hands and let me eat!"

"Can't do that, my sweet. Joss is afraid you'll fork me to death. Come on now," she teased. "Aren't you hungry, darling?"

"Yes! Hungry to move, hungry to see!" he spat savagely. "My m-muscles are turning to sponge!"

"Kherda!" Ligne screamed. Kherda rose a couple of inches off his seat as he clapped his hands over his ears. "Oh, you're here already," she noted. She continued without apology: "See that Rosha gets some exercise today. He says his muscles are getting spongy, and we certainly can't have that."

"Yes, my Lady, I will. Now as to the abundance of ver-minous insects in the northern edge of this region, I have a document here for the Queen to sign that abhors the pres-ence of such insects and authorizes the use of national funds to eradicate the pests. Just sign here—" Kherda had been looking at the document, not the Queen, and he now realized that he was talking to her back. Ligne was heatedly whispering something in Rosha's ear as the lad frowned grimly. Once again, all Kherda could see was her back— that beautiful dark hair spilling down across her shoulders from a garnet-encrusted circlet. They were beautiful shoul-ders—fetchingly white against her russet and tan dress— gorgeous shoulders, as he'd known for many months. But Kherda felt a sense of despair, for this seemed to be all he saw of Ligne lately. Apparently today would be no dif-ferent. And there was so much that was crying out to be done, real issues that needed to be dealt with! He couldn't even get her to sign a toothless royal decree!

Kherda hurled the document onto the table in disgust— clearly a mistake. The rolled sheet bounced crazily, striking the underside of a crystal goblet and freakishly capsizing it. Kherda stared in horror as red wine splashed onto the table and streaked for the Queen! He grabbed for something to stop its tide, and came up with the document. Its parchment-like texture absorbed nothing, however, and he reached be-low the table for the tablecloth and began sopping up the liquid. He was just sighing with relief when he remem-bered there was *never* a tablecloth at breakfast, and he stared at his hands in horror. The wine soaked material was russet and tan—he'd sopped up the spillage with Ligne's skirt!

A gasp rose in chorus from all over the great hall. Kherda held the material, dumfounded, and raised his head to meet several hundred pairs of eyes that reflected back his shock, along with a good deal of amused curiosity at what he would do next. He turned his white face toward Ligne, and saw—once again—her back. For once he was glad. She continued chattering merrily at Rosha. She hadn't even noticed.

A titter now began in the front of the hall and worked its way all the way to the back. Kherda stuffed the soiled dress back under the table, and rubbed his stomach. "I

. . . feel a bit . . . ill . . . my Lady . . ." He rose un-steadily to his feet, and jerked toward the grand spiral, muttering, "I hope . . . you . . . will pardon me . . . "

Ligne didn't notice him go.

Neither did Jagd. Unnoticed by most of the dining crowd, a lad clothed in red and purple had bolted into the hall and raced quickly to the dais. He passed Jagd a balled-up message and got a curt dismissal for his trouble.

Jagd stood and moved away from the table, then un-crumpled the note and read it quickly:

> SUSPICIONS CONFIRMED. ARMED SLAVERS TO ATTACK YOU IN DRAGONSGATE. ADVISE CAUTION. AWAITING IN-STRUCTIONS. TAHLI-DAMEN.

Jagd didn't hesitate for a moment. He shot for the stairs as swiftly as his old legs would carry him and scrambled upward past several floors to the lowest level of the gar-dens. Ignoring the stairs, he raced around the ascending ramp that rose from this lowest level to the upper gardens and the aviary on the rooftop. Puffing with exertion, he passed through the aviary's double doors, circled the mews, and ducked into the hutch of the Lord of Signals. This enclosure was constructed on the same floor plan as the falconer's mews, except for a wide hold in its ceiling that opened onto a cloudy sky, and the fact that its perches were thick with hundreds of brilliant blue-flyers. Jagd stuffed the wadded message into a pouch of his cloak, and grabbed a fresh sheet and a stylus off the spattered table. Quickly he scribbled:

> EXPECTED THIS. WILL REMAIN HERE. DEMAND THE PYR-AMIDS BE REVEALED TO THE FULL COUNCIL AS PLANNED. JAGD.

Jagd scooped a bird off the perch and ignored its flutter-ing protest as he bound the message in a tight cylinder to its left leg. Then he cupped the blue-flyer in both hands, held them to his head, and imagined: he was rising out of th castle—turning north—crossing the great South Fir to-ward Ngandib-Mar—passing over the castle of Tohn, where Flayh now ruled—three miles beyond, to the palace

of Uda in Ngandib-Mar. Jagd pictured in his mind the turrets of that castle, and most especially the face of Tahli-
Damen. Then he pulled his hands away from his face,
opened them, and looked at the small blue bird.

Its black eyes peered back intelligently. Good. He had
gotten its attention, and it understood its route. Jagd gave
the bird a toss, and it was sky-borne, beating its way
through the hole in the roof and up into the clouds.

Pelmen did not witness Kherda's hasty exit either. He
was busy making one of his own. Maythorm had spotted
him across the great hall and had jumped up to pursue
him. Pelmen spent the morning slipping quietly from one
endless corridor to another, reminding himself of the floor
plan of the castle while eluding his pursuer.

It was easy to lose oneself in this monstrous construction. There were thousands of places to hide that anyone
could find, and Pelmen felt certain that there were still
other hidden passageways secreted in the walls. Certainly
he could have avoided the wrathful talent agent easily
enough on his own. But a few brief conversations with
passing slaves had provided him with a new resource he
felt sure could prove valuable in accomplishing his true
purpose. Maythorm's handsome features had all the female
servants swooning, and the man had cut a wide romantic
swath through the wives and girl friends of the entire male
population of the castle. As a result, Pelmen needed only
to mention that Maythorm was chasing him to a male
slave and he'd receive immediate assistance. Maythorm's
pursuit did not greatly concern him, but it was proving a
helpful tool, introducing him to potential allies and revealing some of the choicest hiding places. The elaborate game
of hide and seek could have been fun—were it not for his
dismay over Rosha's captivity. As he leaned against the door
of a broom closet, his mind raced ahead, seeking some plan
to get the young man free. Getting Bronwynn out of the
dungeon had appeared difficult enough. This new compli-
cation threatened to make the task impossible. Yet he
couldn't leave the treasure of Dorlyth enthralled to this
amoral queen.

"You can come out now," whispered a caustic voice

from beyond the door. "The pretty boy's past, trailing a pack of slobbering wenches behind him."

"Do you mind if I rest here a moment?"

"Matters nothing to me. You'll not bother my brooms. But if you'd really like to duck this greasy wife-thief, why not just wash your face? I could bring you a bowl of water . . ."

"Thank you, my friend—but what's a fool without his face? I'd be the greater fool to reveal what's beneath it." Pelmen weighted his words with meaning, and the helpful slave proved to be quick as well:

"Your secret is safe."

Pelmen listened carefully as the whisper of the broom receded down the hall, leaving him alone in the closet.

"I suppose you're here," he muttered. He wasn't addressing the power which inhabited this palace. Rather, he spoke to the Power who had met him upon a mountain, anointed him a Prophet, and aided him in battle with the two-headed monster. There was resignation in his tone of voice—as if he'd known all along this taxing task could never be accomplished in his own strength alone. There was also a hint of what would be viewed in human circles as simple, genuine warmth. Pelmen spoke as he would to a Parmi or a Dorlyth—he spoke to One he knew as a friend. "I needn't explain it to you. You know. The trouble is, I don't. Is Bronwynn in the dungeon? How do I get Rosha free? And what about this other presence? Do I dare shape it in the process?"

The Imperial House of Chaomonous heard every word of the player's muttered monologue—but this morning, it didn't respond. It couldn't. It was in desperate pain.

The delicately crafted pyramid through which Jagd the merchant talked to his rival was not simply a clever gadget, as Jagd thought it to be. It had been shaped many years before by gifted artisans—and energized with power by the foremost shaper of that age. The pyramids shaped power . . . and as a result, Jagd's pyramid pulled its dynamism from the stuff that gave the Imperial House its being. Like excess acid in a human gut, any shaping within the walls burned the castle with savage intensity. The Imperial

House gasped, so to speak, in misery—yet the pain went unrelieved. Like a bubble of gas, an incandescent blue glow continued to suffuse the room of the merchant of Uda, searing the insides of the palace. It would have cursed —every bell would have rung out its agony—had the pain not so thoroughly robbed it of the strength to cry out. Instead it waited helplessly for succor—and none came. The humiliation of a shower of bird droppings had been completely forgotten. The Imperial House faced its first major crisis since awakening.

It listened intently to the clown's odd mutterings. Hadn't the painted fool admitted, just last night, that he was a shaper? And if a shaper, then surely he understood castle speech . . . though he seemed to be feigning ignorance. If the castle could but communicate the measure of its pain . . .

—Strange conversation indeed, the Imperial House gasped when Pelmen finished. Was it the other power the jester referred to? The castle winced at the notion of this fool shaping it.

—Isn't there pain enough already? Obviously, the man is not addressing the Imperial House! But if not, then who? Despite its agony, the House mustered all of its senses and listened closely for any reply the fool might make.

There was none. And yet, when he finished speaking, the one named Fallomar bolted out of the closet, seemingly refreshed and emboldened. Though the Imperial House had plainly heard him tell his friend at breakfast that he wished to avoid the arrogant Queen at all costs, the castle now watched him stride purposefully toward her very throne room.

—Strange business, this, the Imperial House muttered to itself. Then it winced. It longed for a mouth of some kind—if only it could burp . . .

The inside of Kherda's mouth had the consistency of cotton, and beneath his voluminous cassock his bony knees knocked together. Ligne's rage was terrible to behold— especially when directed at him.

"Look at this!" she shrilled, holding her stained skirt out for inspection. "Ruined!" Her cheeks were as scarlet as the blotch left behind by the spilled wine. Ligne's eyes narrowed to cruel slits. "Do you know something about this, Kherda?"

A commotion at the door drowned his strained response, and snagged the Queen's attention. "What's going on?" she snapped. Then her pretty eyes widened as the colorfully clothed fool stumbled into the throne room. He stood up and straightened his garments, then glanced casually around as if he owned the place.

"Do you know," he began without preamble, "one of those guards actually tried to make me believe I couldn't come into this room? Why, he almost dared me to prove him wrong. So I did." The fool bowed deeply, then raised his head and winked.

The Queen was aghast. "Nobody comes in here unannounced!"

"That must be me, for I came in without announcement, and I'm certainly a nobody."

"You'll be a sorry nobody before you dare such impudence again!" Ligne thundered.

"Oh, but I quite agree! Why, I'm already the sorriest individual imaginable. Is someone eating this?" he asked, as he scooped a grape off a nearby plate and popped it into his mouth. "For who could be sorrier than a fool? Especially, a fool without an audience to amuse—"

"I'll give you an audience! An audience of warders, who'll cackle at your cries and smirk at your every scream!"

The painted jester winked at her once again. "Ah, but, my Lady. Why let them have all the fun?" The confident twinkle in his eye proved infectious. Ligne's smile started with a tiny curling at the corners of her lips, then broadened until her teeth gleamed brightly and her eyes sparkled. She fought to control it.

"You are a presumptuous lout."

"Obviously." The fool nodded. "And I presume by the softening of your tone that you'll not dispose of me immediately?"

"Not immediately. But why take such a chance? Why not let yourself be introduced in the proper manner?"

"My manners have never been proper, my Lady. And as to being introduced—it seems this Maythorm fellow has taken a dislike to me." He leaned forward, cupping his hand to his mouth and whispering loudly, "Confidentially, I think he's jealous of my face." That drew a laugh from those close enough to hear, for everyone in court knew the handsome Lord of Entertainments, and certainly this pasty-faced character offered him no challenge. "Besides, that takes such a long time—and I couldn't stand to wait another moment for another glimpse of your radiant beauty."

Ligne cocked a carefully sculpted eyebrow. "I see for all your foolery, you're not afraid of flattery."

"Indeed, my Lady, a fool who cannot flatter flatters himself to think he'll long remain a fool. To be honest, my mistress—ah, my Lady—when I beheld you at breakfast, I felt I had found one I could flatter in good faith."

The lilting of his tongue had hypnotizing power—but his mention of breakfast jarred Ligne's memory, and she looked down again at her soiled dress. "Ah, yes. Kherda and I were just speaking of breakfast. Weren't we, Kherda?" Her sharp manner had returned.

The Prime Minister choked. For a moment he had been permitted to hope that this insolent player's interruption might distract the Queen indefinitely. It wasn't to be. "Ah . . . my Lady . . ." he began.

"What would you do, fool, to a careless, clumsy dolt who cannot even keep his glass upright!" Though she'd addressed the jester, her scorching stare did not leave Kherda's face.

"Why, I'd give him a medal and a promotion," the fool answered.

Ligne whipped around to face him. "What? Why?"

"For choosing such a delicately colored wine to spill! My Lady, the color of that stain truly enhances the tint of your cheeks. You really ought to thank him."

The Queen put her hands on her hips and stared at Fallomar for a moment, a small frown on her lips. "How long has it been since the court had a jester?" she snapped suddenly. Her question could only have been directed at Kherda, but it caught the Prime Minister off guard. "Well?" she demanded.

Kherda seized the opportunity to deflect attention from himself. "Of course, there's not been a court fool since you took the throne, my Lady, but I believe there were three during the reign of your predecessor—"

"And where are they now?" Ligne's eyes didn't leave Fallomar's, nor did her frown fade.

"Ah . . . ah . . . I believe . . . why, I hadn't thought of any of them for years, but . . . ah . . . unless they've died . . . all three are still in the dungeon."

Ligne's nostrils flared and her eyes narrowed. "Now, fool. Are you certain you wish to continue this game?"

"I'll play, my Lady, so long as I remain ahead and not beheaded."

"Then beware your clever tongue, my friend. Let it grow too sharp, and it'll cut your saucy head off."

"Ah, but if it grow too dull, what then? Will you make me wear a hood like that stumbletongue in the corner?"

Rosha had been leaning against the wall, taking advantage of this interlude from Ligne's prodding to daydream of freedom. This comment brought him to life with a roar. He lunged toward the center of the room, jerking his unsuspecting guard off his feet and dragging the poor man across the rug. The fool danced nimbly aside and casually watched the warrior charge past. He turned back to watch Ligne's smirk grow wider. It revealed the Queen's thorough enjoyment of this diversion.

"My stumbletongue, as you call him, is more prone to take offense than I," she gloated.

"Perhaps because he's more offensive?" the clown asked, and Rosha again charged the sound of his voice. Rosha's guard, prepared this time and reinforced by soldiers from the doorway, pulled the raging captive up short. Rosha jerked at his chains, but they held. He vented his wrath in a shout: "You may d-d-duel with your t-tongue, fool, but give us both d-d-daggers, and we'll soon s-see who st-st-stands!" His muscles knotted, straining at his bonds. The fool gazed at him lackadaisically.

"How did you know the lad's tongue betrays him?" Ligne asked.

"I heard him tripping over his sausages at breakfast."

"Queen!" came Rosha's strangled cry of frustration. "Give me leave to k-k-kill him!" The days of inactivity and frustration welled up inside him, begging for some release. It seemed possible the Queen might let him take out his rage on a meaningless upstart of a jester.

"An amusing idea." Ligne nodded. "What do you think of it, fool?"

Fallomar chuckled nervously. "You'd let a hotheaded youth rob you of months of amusements?"

"You're assuming you'll lose!" the Queen crowed. "Does your dagger wit not match your dagger work?"

"In truth, my Lady, I'd rather not see blood—especially not mine!"

"Ah, but you've made me curious. Is a fool's blood white, like his face? Bring two swords!"

"My Lady, you can't be serious!" Kherda protested.

"Oh I can't?" Ligne snarled, shooting him a dangerous scowl. "Perhaps you'd rather Rosha spill *your* blood for exercise?"

"Ah . . . no, my Lady—"

"Then get out of my way!" the woman bellowed, and Kherda did just that, backing into the corner Rosha had vacated. "Loose his hands!" Ligne ordered Carlad, Rosha's guard, plunging the man into a dilemma. Carlad took his orders from General Joss, and the Lord of Security had instructed him never to free Rosha from his bonds in the presence of the Queen. But Joss was far to the north, investigating some matter of national security.

"My Lady," Carlad pleaded, "if . . . if I loose him and unhood him, he may kill you—"

"I said nothing about unhooding him! Just tie his hands in front of him, so he can hold a weapon."

Carlad obeyed her, managing with some help to get Rosha's hand bound before him just as another guard sprinted back through the double doors with a pair of swords—one a short Chaon stabbing sword, the other the named great sword Rosha had brought with him. Thalraphis. Pelmen had a good idea which weapon he'd be handed. This he hadn't planned on.

Rosha stretched his arms above his head, then made a quick grab for the buckles that held his hood in place. Carlad and his fellows jerked the warrior's hands down and filled them with the haft of Thalraphis. Then they ducked away, as Rosha whirled the five-foot long weapon above his head with an audible whisper.

"Now, fool," Rosha said icily, "let's see who stumbles first." The confidence that came from the sword in his hands seemed to run straight up his arms to his tongue. Rosha never stuttered in battle.

Fallomar had watched all of this with growing consternation—while a gleeful Queen watched him watching. "Well, fool?" she cackled. "Take your sword." A worried guard handed the clown the shorter weapon, keeping well out of range of Rosha's wheeling scythe. Fallomar took the weapon soundlessly and backed out of the way. He happened to move toward Kherda—trapping the old man in his corner.

"I must protest this, Ligne!" the Prime Minister squealed. "You're going to get us all killed!"

"No real loss in your case," the Queen snorted. Her face flushed with a sensual excitement. At the sound of her voice, Rosha leaned in her direction.

Pelmen saw the move and acted quickly to keep the raging warrior from hewing the woman down here in her own throne room. "I'm over here!" Rosha squared around to face his voice and started toward him slowly, still whooshing that long, flashing blade. Pelmen slipped quietly to his right, leaving the Prime Minister directly in the path of the on-coming savage.

"He's moved!" Kherda shouted. "He's moved to your left!" Rosha stopped advancing and turned his head tentatively to his left.

"Come, clown. Where are you?" he muttered.

"I'm here," Fallomar called warily. "But where now is your tangled tongue!"

"This is my tongue!" Rosha shouted, brandishing the great sword before him.

"I'd rather duel the one in your mouth!" the clown said.

"So would I!" the Queen agreed.

Once again Rosha turned in the direction of Ligne. Pelmen skipped quickly behind him. "Back here!" the clown shouted and he slashed his sword toward Rosha's broad back. Before it could arrive, Rosha had reversed, and he caught the blow on his own sword with a chilling clash—as Pelmen had known he would. The fool skittered backward then, dodging the three swift swipes he knew would follow. That was a family technique that Dorlyth had ingrained in his son through constant practice. Pelmen had learned it directly from the source.

Rosha stopped then, puzzled. He's expected to cleave the clown into quarters . . .

"Come, come, my friend," Fallomar teased. "If you're the expert—"

Rosha charged again, and once more Pelmen ducked and scampered to his left.

"You speak like a butterfly!" the fool shouted. "Can't sit down on a word and make it stick!" He said it mockingly, but he hoped Rosha would mark his words and not their tone. It was the echo of something Dorlyth had said to the lad the last time the three of them had been together.

The hooded swordsman never paused. He whipped around and attacked in earnest, and the painted clown was hard pressed to keep from being diced.

Pelmen was not a poor swordsman. In years past, he'd battled Dorlyth and survived—no mean feat in itself—and with a single, well-placed stroke had slain the legendary Vicia-Heinox. He could have killed or maimed Rosha a dozen times, given the handicap of the young man's blindness. But Fallomar the fool was not a swordsman—and could not be allowed to appear one. Pelmen ignored one opportunity after another—and suddenly found himself pinned into a corner. Rosha kept pressing, and their swords rang together three more times before a crashing blow knocked Pelmen's sword flying from his hands. The hooded warrior smiled as he heard it clatter away, then he shoved his pommel into the fool's gut, cracked it down on Pelmen's head, dropping him to the floor, and planted both his knees on the player's chest. He found the fool's neck by feel, then quickly swung the tip of his weapon into place.

Pelmen stared up the length of a blade poised to slit his throat.

CHAPTER NINE

At Blade Point

"WELL?" said Ligne. "Do it!"

Rosha leaned back. "Kill him? I think not."

"Why! He insulted you! Cut his throat!" Rosha stood up, allowing the fool to breathe. "Go ahead and kill him!" Ligne screamed.

"No."

The Queen stared at him. "Why not?" she demanded.

"It j-j-just came to m-me. If this ma-ma-man be so honey-tongued, p-p-perhaps he could train me to sp-sp-speak." Rosha had greatly exaggerated his stutter—and Pelmen sighed with relief. Sometime during the fight, Rosha had recognized his voice. Pelmen thanked the Power for the young man's quickness and good sense. "B-besides," Rosha continued, "he s-s-seemed to b-b-be amusing you."

Ligne gazed at the grinning fool, a bit puzzled by this turn of events. But she was nothing if not capricious. She decided to be pleased. "Yes. Yes, he rather does amuse me." The Queen caught Carlad's eye and pointed to the sword Rosha still held loosely before him. The guard nodded and crept up behind to snatch it away. Surprisingly, Rosha offered no resistance. Once again, Ligne was puzzled. "You seem . . . so docile, suddenly," she said. "Are you injured? Ill?" She seemed genuinely concerned.

"I'm n-neither."

"Perhaps the lad is . . . winded," offered the fool from the floor.

"Winded? B-b-by the likes of you?" Rosha snorted. "B-better thank your g-good fortune I d-d-didn't cut *your* wind altogether, funnyman. D-don't forget that I st-still could."

"I won't! I won't!" Fallomar answered earnestly.

Rosha turned sightlessly toward Ligne's voice. "My Lady, s-since you have this fool to entertain you, c-c-can I be allowed to lie down?"

"Certainly, poor dear!" Ligne gushed, nodding permission to Carlad to take him away. "I'm afraid you might be sick!"

"Only sick of you," he muttered.

"What was that?" she asked. She really hadn't heard him.

"N-nothing. P-perhaps you're right. Fool!" he bellowed.

"Right here," said Fallomar, who had gotten to his knees.

"I'll be expecting those lessons—if the Queen permits?"

"Of course I permit," Ligne assured him. "I think it's an excellent idea. But I want you to rest yourself today. I'm afraid this fighting has tired you . . ." Her hands fluttered in the manner of a mother who feels helpless to help. As Rosha and Carlad disappeared through the door, she turned and made her way back to sit on her throne. Pelmen watched as she leaned on an armrest and propped her chin on her hand. The young man's sudden change of mood perplexed her.

"My lady, I appreciate the reprieve—"

"Don't thank me," she muttered. "Thank him."

"I shall. And . . . I will give him lessons in speech—"

"Leave him alone for now," Ligne growled. "Something's the matter with him."

"Nothing, I trust, that couldn't be cured by a little light . . ."

"What are you talking about?"

"The—ah—leather helmet."

"Oh," Ligne said glumly, leaning back to gaze at the

muraled ceiling. "I leave that on him because he wants to kill me."

"Perhaps, if he could see you, he'd be less inclined to slay you." As he spoke, the fool frowned at Kherda and motioned him out of the throne room. The Prime Minister stared at him, affronted, until he realized the fool was trying to help him escape before Ligne remembered her fit of pique. Kherda scooped up his skirts and scooted out the door, nodding gratefully to the fool as he passed. Pelmen winked, then went on: "After all—he could have killed you just now—and he didn't."

Ligne studied the mural high above her head with great attention. "You really think so?"

"My Lady," the fool said, "I had an excellent vantage point."

The woman's eyes drifted down from the ceiling to settle on the fool. "So you did." She thought for a moment then, chewing absently on a fingernail. "Say something funny," she suddenly ordered.

"Something funny."

"That's right."

"I just did."

"What?"

"I said, 'Something funny.' And to some, it would have been."

"What?"

"Funny. But evidently not to you."

"I said, say something to amuse me, not to confuse me," Ligne snarled.

"Ah, yes. But, I ask myself what amuses the Queen. The pain of others, it would seem, just by observation. Perhaps I should fall on my face?"

"Now that would be funny." Ligne smiled.

"I thought as much." Fallomar smiled back. "People laugh at different things. So I will need to stay on my toes at all times—remembering always that what would most amuse my Queen is watching those toes be pulled off."

Ligne chuckled, then suddenly grew serious. "You know, I knew you were coming," she said with a dreamy, faraway look in her eyes.

If her words stunned Pelmen—and they did—he didn't

show it. "How? You have a fortune teller stashed under your throne there?"

"Close." She smirked mysteriously.

For the second time that day, Pelmen felt a little dizzy from the shock.

Though the winds were high, the blue-flyer that Jagd had dispatched wasted no time. Like every other bird of its species, it would not rest until it had accomplished the task that a human had assigned. Jagd's special attention to his protegé's face meant that the bird would surrender its message to no one but Tahli-Damen—a security precaution that Jagd intended to remind the young merchant of the next time they spoke.

The journey took the bird all that day and into the morning of the next, but it did not rest until it saw below the five-turret arrangement that matched the picture Jagd had placed in its mind.

The bird alighted on a broad cross painted in blue on the roof of one of the turrets. A handler stooped immediately to pick it up, but it eluded several attempts, and the handler soon realized this bird was intended for someone special. As Tahli-Damen was the highest ranking member of the family present, the bird handler started down the interior stairs to find him, and the bird hopped along behind from stair to stair. It was quite oblivious to the comic image it presented as the handler escorted it into Tahli-Damen's presence with a grin. The blue-flyer nonchalantly hopped onto Tahli-Damen's desk and extended its foot. As the promising young merchant untied the message bound to its leg, the blue-flyer dismissed the trip from its mind. It had accomplished its task. It had earned a good meal and a rest.

"From Jagd?" asked a young woman standing by a window on the far side of the room.

"That's right," Tahli-Damen replied, studying the page intently. Then he looked up. "He's not coming."

"As we expected." She nodded and smiled furtively. "I can't say I'm disappointed. This will make you the ranking member of Uda's delegation!"

"I appreciate your confidence in me, Wayleeth." He smiled grimly. "But I'm afraid I don't share it. I am too young to exercise any influence with the other houses, and I fear I won't have much more say with our own. He hides it well, but your father is still angry that I was promoted over him."

"You deserved to be!" said Wayleeth. "I love my father dearly, as everyone knows. But everyone also knows that he's been a do-nothing supervisor, who's been outmaneuvered by Tohn mod Neelis ever since we were moved to Ngandib-Mar!"

"Don't be unfair," Tahli-Damen scolded. "He was a good leader in Lamath. He couldn't help it if Jagd matched him against a man more Mari than merchant!" Tahli-Damen had cared little for Tohn mod Neelis. The man had very nearly cost him his life by not allowing him sanctuary in the midst of a battle. "Naturally Tohn did a better job of meeting Mari needs—he knew the Mari mind as well as the Mari market. But he's gone now, and Flayh's as Lamathian as your father. We'll reestablish Uda's dominance here, and we may do it this month. In fact, I'm sure of it."

Wayleeth's eyes glowed. "I'm sure of it too—with *you* in charge."

Tahli-Damen blushed and deflected the compliment with a brusque, "We need to be on our way. The conclave doesn't begin until tomorrow, but there will be informal preliminary negotiations in the halls and corridors tonight, and I don't intend for Uda to be ignored." He grabbed his scarlet cloak, slung it around his shoulders, and would have swept past her and out the door had she not caught him by the waist and pulled him around to face her.

"Go well," she husked, "but return swiftly! You know there's nothing to do in this castle when you're gone!" She kissed him, and Tahli-Damen then charged out of the room, calling for his seconds and for his horse.

About the time Jagd's messenger bird delivered its tiny epistle, Pelmen slipped away to the roof of the Imperial House to send one of his own. He'd spent the rest of the previous night amusing the Queen—with perhaps too much success. She'd insisted on him spending this entire morning with her as well. Pelmen was learning that the best way to entertain Ligne was not to dazzle her with his own wit, but to appear dazzled by hers. It was his lot to laugh apprecia-

tively as she drilled barb after barb into the members of
her court. Thus far, she'd seemed thoroughly pleased with
his presence. If she had any idea of who he really was, she
hadn't revealed it. Perhaps she hadn't seen the troupe perform enough in the past to be able to know him by sight—
Pelmen hoped that was the case. But there were many
other courtiers who would recognize him—so his face
would keep its white coating.

Pelmen waited in vain for Ligne to explain why she'd
expected him. He didn't press the issue, and she seemed to
forget about it. But her chance remark had created a
powerful curiosity within him. He longed to be about his
business, to get on to the dungeon and investigate it—but
she wouldn't let him loose. Only by pleading for time to
take care of private matters had he won this small respite.

He did not enter the hut where the platoons of blue-
flyers gathered. He stopped a few feet behind it instead—
and gave a silent, mental summons.

—Here now! What are you doing? asked the Imperial
House, for this soundless call, if not an actual act of shaping, was certainly prelude to one.

In answer, several blue-feathered birds fluttered out the
open roof of their crowded coop and landed on his shoulders and outstretched arms. Pelmen looked at each one of
them in turn, then with a thought dismissed all but one.
The chosen flyer hopped onto his palm, and its black eyes
studied the clown intelligently.

—What cheek! Talking to birds, but ignoring the Imperial House.

Pelmen could have sent a rolled note, as Jagd had done,
but he had much to say, and security was essential. Instead, he planted his message in the little bird's mind:

"To Erri, the Prophet of Lamath. Hello, my friend. I am
within the castle, as we'd planned—but events have conspired to obstruct me. I've not been able yet to check the
dungeon—there's a curious power here, quite unknown to
me, that's inhibited my abilities somewhat. Bronwynn may
yet be beneath me but, if so, her presence is a closely
guarded secret. Worse news—Rosha *is* here, and is a captive of the Queen."

Here Pelmen paused, and briefly held a picture of the
hooded Rosha in his mind. The blue-flyer looked at him

curiously. Then Pelmen began forming mental sentences again:

"As we guessed, this land is suffering from a lack of leadership. The Queen spends her time seeking diversion from her responsibilites, while the common people starve. In the wake of last year's crippling of the Golden Throng, there's a sense of defenselessness among the peasants. There is a void here that needs to be filled. And I need help. Send someone to me—someone you trust. Don't dispatch a flyer—I'd rather not arouse the suspicions of the Lord of Security any more than necessary. Send the one of your choice to 'a fool' in the Imperial House. One thing more—where is Serphimera? Pelmen."

Pelmen held the bird away from him and looked at it inquiringly. The flyer patiently awaited its directions. Once again, Pelmen held the bird close to his head and imagined a route of flight that would take the magical little creature due north across the peaks of the Spinal Range, over the desert in southern Lamath, past the lower river to the capital city itself. Then he imagined the layout of the city, the location of the old dungeon of the King, and a certain window of that dungeon. Erri had taken the place over and made it his new monastery. Pelmen imagined the tiny cell beyond that window—Erri's office. Finally, he held in his mind an image of Erri's face—and tossed the bird into the sky. In seconds, it had disappeared toward the north.

He glanced around to see if he'd been noticed. No one was in sight, and he sighed with relief.

—Down here! Look down here! growled the Imperial House from its roof tiles.

Pelmen happend to look at his feet. He was startled to see that the roof had suddenly become slick. "Has it rained?" he mumbled, glancing skyward.

—No, it has *not* rained! Would you pay attention?

But Pelmen's thoughts had already travelled back downstairs, as he prepared himself for his next performance in the throne room.

—You will gain nothing by ignoring this House! the castle theatened, but it gave up when Pelmen turned to walk briskly into the aviary. One thing was clear—this painted fool could shape, for dispatching a thought message by flyer demanded a confidence in one's mental abilities common only to powershapers. But the castle grew more suspicious of this character with each day. Why such secretiveness? Why not openly display his abilities, and help the House? Was he in league with the hideous thief who had robbed the castle's dungeons?

—Why will you not reply!?

Pelmen was trotting down the garden ramp when he chanced upon a sight he had to stop and look at. On a stone bench beside a beautiful fountain sat Gerrig, in ardent pursuit of a giggling lady of the court. He wore a costume so flagrantly colored and so incredibly tight that he most resembled a fat flamingo. Carnelian sequins glistened in the light, calling most unflattering attention to the actor's chubby backside. Pelmen chuckled.

Gerrig wheeled angrily around to see who laughed. His face flushed when he saw Pelmen and, with words as immodestly passionate as the color of his pants, he begged his lady friend to excuse him momentarily.

A peacock joined Pelmen on the walkway as Gerrig started toward him, and the fool leaned over and asked the bird, "Do you think those are sewn on, or painted on?"

"Where have you been?" Gerrig demanded in a fierce whisper. "We had a rehearsal last night, and another this morning—or do you think you're too good for rehearsals?"

"Calm down, my friend. I've been entertaining the Queen."

"Doesn't it matter to you that Ligne said—you've been what?"

"Entertaining the Queen."

"Are you crazy?" Gerrig spat quietly. "What if she recognizes you?"

"I've always wanted to be buried by a stream—"

"Be serious!"

Pelmen grinned. "You're wearing *that,* and expect me to be serious?"

"I thought you were avoiding the Queen!"

"I'd intended to. But she seems to have taken a liking to me, so my services are in demand."

"Doesn't she know you?"

"Evidently not. Though I wouldn't be surprised to have Ligne play with me, as a cat plays with a mouse . . ."

"I hope not—for *my* sake! Listen, this Maythorm fellow

is combing the castle for you. You've offended him, some-how—"

"Take care you don't steal his ladies." Pelmen winked, nodding toward the pouting woman on the bench. "Or he'll be after *you* instead."

Gerrig glowered. "I try to help you, and all you do is joke!"

"I'm a fool, remember?"

"Yes, well, don't fool yourself into thinking you can per-form without rehearsing—even if you did write the play."

"I'm surprised you've had time to rehearse. How long did it take to stitch those onto you? Did a tailor do it, or a magician?"

"Get out of here!" Gerrig bellowed, and his lady friend twisted around to stare at him. "Not you, my dear," he soothed, as he minced his way back toward the fountain.

Pelmen looked down at the peacock, who watched the actor's retreat. "Nothing to be alarmed about," the fool said. "He's broad in the tail, true, but nothing to compete with yours." As if in answer, the peacock fanned his feath-ers and stalked proudly away.

Bronwynn paced along the battlements, gazing westward toward the sunset. Somewhere out there was Rosha. But where? Why hadn't he shown himself? Had he already for-gotten her in all his feasting and honors, as Admon Faye sneered at least once every day?

A cool breeze swept along the parapet, and she tugged her wrap tightly around her shoulders and hung her head. She could hear a dull roar issuing from the open door of the castle's central hall. Merchants had been arriving all day long from every direction, and the carnival atmosphere had driven her out into the twilight. The din the slavers normally set up at mealtimes had now multiplied into a head-splitting cacaphony. She'd run from the room in des-perate need of some peace and quiet.

It wasn't just the noise. The tension had been growing all afternoon as well. As every new contingent arrived at the gate, the rope of relationships tautened another notch. Smiles there were in abundance, and the jokes flowed around the tables as freely as the ale. But there was a chill-ing lack of humor to all this, and true good will seemed totally nonexistent. These men, whom Bronwynn had always supposed to be the best of friends because of the closeness of merchant cliques, were far from friendly. This assembly could be the most powerful force in the world, having far more impact on history than the grandest of her forefather's armies. It depressed her to discover that not one of these merchants seemed to have a friend—only momentary allies.

A lean dog had joined her on the walls, and it stood panting by her side, obviously begging her attention. She scratched its head absently and thought of the houses she had already seen represented here.

The conclave certainly didn't lack for color. Besides the ever-present blue and lime of Flayh's own house of Ognadzu, a sizable group wore purple and red, the symbolic garb of Uda. Hann was here, in their solid burnt-orange tunics, and so was Blez, the house of pink circles on a field of gray. The Elders of Wina had arrived the night before, and Bronwynn had quickly grown used to seeing their dark brown diamonds superimposed on a rainbow assortment of backgrounds. Wina was a young house, only a couple of centuries old. It had forged a reputation as being a house that cared for the common peasant, and its patriarch had been leery of establishing too sharp a distinction in dress between Wina's merchants and the people they served.

And yet, for all the cheery colors and all the cheerful talk, there was not a single breath of honest cheer anywhere in the castle. Bronwynn could feel the oppressive weight of the tension even out here. A dark mood clung to her—she couldn't shake it. As she stared up at the purpling sky a tear glistened on her cheek. "Poor old thing," she said to the dog. "I guess all those people in your hall drove you out, too."

"Actually I came looking for you," said Flayh.

Bronwynn jerked away, grabbing her chest to still her pounding heart. The bald powershaper, gowned in red and white, stood where the dog had been.

Bronwynn glared at him, then turned her back and clutched both arms across her chest. "I take it you weren't expecting me?" Flayh gloated. Bronwynn said nothing, and Flayh frowned. "You don't seem very impressed."

"Perhaps because I've seen the trick before," Bronwynn snarled, "done much better, and not as a childish prank. Excuse me," she said, and she started past him for the stairs.

Flayh was a small man, but his fingers had steel in them. He grabbed her arm, and she yelped and stood still. "I said I came looking for you."

"Ow!" Bronwynn cried aloud. "Say your peace then, I'm listening, but let go!"

Flayh released her arm, but gripped her eyes in his own. He challenged her will, drawing up the fear inside her as he'd attempted to summon Admon Faye's. Bronwynn gasped, robbed of breath. She was seized by a sudden terror that the sorcerer found quite appropriate. "Good. You will continue to fear me, Bronwynn. I like for people to fear me."

His eyes were swallowing her! Bronwynn choked, and her legs trembled helplessly.

"I've come to tell you why you're here, Bronwynn. Perhaps Admon Faye has already made it clear, but hear it again—from my lips. I intend to make you a Queen—my *own* Queen, to be precise. Do you understand?"

Bronwynn nodded fearfully as she backed away from this creature who so terrified her.

"Stand where you are!" Flayh ordered, and Bronwynn's sandals became one with the stone. "You've been chosen for this task only because it is expedient—not because I feel you in any way suitable. I want nothing from you but obedience—the obedience that proceeds from fear."

"Yes . . . my Lord," Bronwynn muttered, amazed that she would say such words, yet too frightened to resist.

"I assume you referred to Pelmen, when you belittled my power. I don't know what spells he possesses, or what beast is his alter-shape, but I can assure you: when we meet in open battle, it is I who shall walk away, and not he. Mention of Pelmen provokes me! Do you understand!"

"Yes! Yes, I do!" the young woman choked out in a barely audible whisper.

"Very well then. You will accompany me to the hall. I want you present at each session, so that you'll know my policies when I place you on the throne." Flayh stepped closer and thrust his nose into Bronwynn's face. "I desire to control all the three lands, and this time neither Pelmen nor any other meddler will obstruct me. Come." Flayh spun around and descended the stairs, and Bronwynn found herself following him quite docilely. It shocked her to realize how easily she'd broken under his eyes—but he was, after all, a powershaper. As they entered the brightly illuminated hall, she thought of something she'd heard Pelmen say months before: "Why is it that one who owns so much should want to control even more? It seems to me it would get boring . . ."

"All I asked for was a single day off—a single day! Just to celebrate my daughter's birthday with her and perhaps go visit my brother down the river. What does he say? What he always says. 'No chance, Carlad. Get back to your post.' Now what do you think of that!"

Rosha didn't respond. He just rolled his hooded head away and leaned against the wall behind him.

"That's what I thought, too!" Carlad snarled. "Wouldn't even take it up with the General! Never gave it a chance. So, here I am, chained up inside this tower—"

"Wait a minute," Rosha interrupted. "For your information, I'm the prisoner here, Carlad, not you."

"Oh yeah? Well, has it ever occurred to you that I'm just as much chained to you as you are to me? Hunh? Has it?"

"How could I help it, Carlad, since you remind me of that every single day? Usually when you're complaining about your sergeant."

"You'd complain, too, if he was your sergeant!"

"I think I've got plenty to complain about," Rosha grumbled.

"Yeah, yeah, just because you're a prisoner here, you think you've got it rough. You get the best off the table, don't have to work, you got that gorgeous Queen pawing you all day . . . real hard duty!"

"I don't see you wearing a leather hood, Carlad," Rosha said quietly.

"You don't see me wearing . . ." That suddenly struck the guard as funny, and he cackled. "No, I guess you don't *see* me wearing one, do you!" He laughed again, and Rosha joined in.

"Nor do I see this gorgeous Queen you keep raving about." The warrior smiled ruefully.

Carlad looked at his prisoner a moment, mulling over something. "Why is it you only stutter when you're around her?"

Rosha's smile turned grim. "Why is it you never seem to hear your sergeant unless he's in the room with you?"

Carlad chuckled and leaned back against the wall beside Rosha. "That's what I thought."

"Carlad?" Rosha asked. "Take it off?"

The guard licked his lips and looked over at the repulsive headgear. His fingers twitched. "No," he grunted suddenly. "Orders not to."

"Carlad," Rosha pleaded. "Come on."

"What if my sergeant comes in?"

"You can tell him I overpowered you." Rosha grinned.

There was a knock at the door. "You see?" Carlad argued. "I bet that's him now!"

"No, it's probably the Queen, wanting me to come strut through the throne room."

It was neither. The white-faced fool popped his head inside. "Can I come in?"

"Certainly," Rosha called. "C-c-come on in, c-clown."

Carlad looked at his smiling charge, and hid his own snicker.

"I've come to give you a lesson."

"W-w-wonderful. I'm ready t-t-to d-d-do m-m-m-my b-best."

Carlad groaned, and the fool looked over at him. "What's wrong?" Fallomar asked. The guard shook his head, and waved off the question.

"C-c-can you r-r-really m-make m-me t-t-talk like a m-member of the c-c-c-c—"

Carlad groaned again, more loudly, and once again Fallomar looked over at him. "Are you ill?"

"Yes, C-a-carlad, are you s-s-s-s—"

"Am I really going to have to sit and listen to this?" the guard demanded of Rosha.

"Why, whatever d-d-do you m-m-m—"

"Come on!" Carlad pleaded, and he leaned against the wall and shrugged at the fool. "He's trying to drive me crazy!"

"Who c-c-could t-t-tell?"

"You see?" the guard asked Fallomar.

"You know, you c-c-could always ch-chain me to this c-c-c-c—"

"Chain you to the clown, yeah, yeah," Carlad sighed. "Then in walks my sergeant, and what does he say?"

"P-probably couldn't tell the difference!" Rosha cackled.

"All right. All right. I've had enough of this," Carlad announced, fighting a laugh of his own.

"Why don't you chain me to him?" asked the fool. "You could lock the door from the outside and take a break—"

"I can't believe you!" Carlad shouted, staring at Fallomar in surprise. "Yesterday this man was trying to kill you, and you want to be chained to him?"

The fool gazed at him a moment, then raised his eyebrows. "Good point. But—ah—he could have, and didn't."

"That doesn't mean he won't! Listen, I've been around this fellow long enough to know, and believe me—"

"C-come on, C-carlad! Leave m-m-me with him!" Rosha smiled a tight, treacherous smile, clearly visible to the guard under the edge of his hood. "Just for a few moments . . ."

Carlad looked at Rosha, then at the fool, then turned his face away to smirk at the wall. That was it! Rosha had changed his mind, and wanted a couple of minutes with this white-faced idiot in private. "That's why the speech lessons," he murmured in Rosha's ear.

"That's right . . ." Rosha whispered back.

"What? What's that you're talking about?" asked Fallomar, feigning ignorance.

"Well, I don't imagine it would hurt to leave for just a *little* while." Carlad smiled. "Wouldn't hurt *me,* anyway . . ."

"Fine Carlad, then get—I m-m-mean, g-g-g-go ahead . . ."

The guard stifled his chuckle as he unlocked his own waist shackle and fastened it around the fool's hips. "Have fun," he said as he skipped out the door and locked it behind him.

They were silent for a moment, leaning together against the wall. Pelmen broke it.

"Great performance. Want to join an acting troupe?"

"Any chance we could get out right now?"

"Not much. Not since we're chained together and locked inside as well."

"Keep your voice low," Rosha advised. "Carlad says there are secret passageways all through this place."

"He's right, but at the moment Joss is still somewhere north of the city, and I left Ligne at the Drax table."

"Ligne!" Rosha spat.

"A devious woman." Pelmen nodded.

"Would you get this thing off my head?" Rosha pleaded, and in minutes the leather hood was unbuckled and tossed onto the floor. Rosha squinted at the glare, even though the room was lighted only by a single torch.

"Feel better?" Pelmen asked after a moment.

"Much. So when do we get out of here?"

"That depends."

"On what?"

"On where Bronwynn is, for one thing."

"Bronwynn! Where is she?"

"If I knew that, I might be able to plan better! I don't."

"She's not dead . . ." Rosha asked uncertainly.

"We'll hope not. No, I fear she's in the dungeon below us."

Rosha stared at him. "Ligne's said nothing to—"

"But she wouldn't be likely to, either. Would she?"

"I'd expect her to kill Bronwynn, not imprison her."

"That's a possibility." Pelmen sighed. "But, we don't know. I'd like to search the dungeon."

—She's not there, announced the Imperial House. Nobody listened. Nobody ever listened. It went back to cursing a green-jay.

"How do you intend to do that, since you've become such a close friend of the Queen?"

"I'm going to depend on you to distract her."

"Me?" Rosha asked. "How am I going to distract the old witch?"

"By pretending you like her."

There was a brief pause before the explosion. "What!" the young warrior screamed. Carlad, outside the door, chuckled to himself, imagining it to be the fool's death cry.

"Somehow, I expected that would be your reaction . . ." Pelmen sighed.

"Ask something else, anything, but don't ask me to do that!"

"Not even to provide rescue for your Lady?"

"We don't even know she's in the dungeon!"

"And if she is?"

Rosha's pained expression reflected the battle going on inside him. "Come, Pelmen, don't—"

"Fallomar," the fool broke in quickly. "I am always *Fallomar*. Remember it."

"Got it." Rosha sighed, then he leaned back against the wall and shook his head. "I don't know if I can," he mumbled.

"Stiffen up, mod Dorlyth," Pelmen said quietly. "Being a hero demands many kinds of courage."

"Oh, but you don't know that woman!" Rosha groaned.

"I'm coming to know her better and better," Pelmen whispered harshly. "And learning to loathe her more. Time, Rosha. I need time to go below."

Rosha sighed. "I'll . . . try."

"And keep up that stutter in her presence—perhaps it will discourage her."

"That's simple enough. When she gets too close, it comes back on its own."

Carlad pounded on the door. "Rosha! You finished with him yet?"

"Ah—hold on!" Rosha called. "What about the hood?" he asked Pelmen.

"You want it back on?"

"Are you joking?"

"Then I'll take it with me. Wear it into Ligne's presence and tell her I stole it from you to get her attention. With you warming up to her, she'll not put it back on you."

"I don't know how I can . . ."

"Duck your head, and call the guard back."

"Carlad!" Rosha called, and the guard came back into the room, grinning. He stopped when he saw the fool's face still intact.

"Come on, man, set me free!" Fallomar ordered as he jumped to his feet and stretched the chain to its full length.

"I expected—"

"I know what you expected, but I talked him out of it! Now, get me loose before he changes his mind!"

"Just as well," Carlad mumbled as he rushed to unlock the shackle. He didn't want his sergeant walking in while the exchange was taking place. "Would have been difficult to explain."

Fallomar stayed to help Carlad chain himself back in. Then he skipped toward the door, pausing only to scoop the hood up off the floor before dashing out.

"Hunh?" Carlad shouted. He twisted around to look Rosha full in the face for the first time.

"So that's what you look like," the young warrior smiled at the astonished guard.

"He's got your hood!" Carlad shouted, and he bolted toward the door.

This time it was Rosha's turn to pull the chain up short.

CHAPTER TEN

❧ ❧

Into the Bowels

THE NEXT DAY began strangely. Ligne did not appear at breakfast. When Rosha didn't either, Pelmen became alarmed. Brushing aside Yona Parmi's questions, he left the table and began questioning various friendly servants he found seated near him. A few quick conversations relieved him. General Joss had returned late the night before, Pelmen was told, and Joss and the Queen were said to be locked in critical conversations behind closed doors. Since she hadn't summoned Rosha, the warrior had chosen to take breakfast in his room. Pelmen felt sure he knew why—Rosha would delay as long as possible revealing his hoodless condition.

A few minutes after breakfast, the fool appeared outside the throne room door. "The Queen won't see you!" a guard announced, blocking the entrance with his pikestaff. Pelmen recognized the man as one who'd been on duty two days before, when he'd made his unannounced entry into the Queen's presence. Obviously, the fellow was determined not to allow it to happen again.

"Something wrong?"

"That's no concern of mine or yours. Move along!"

Pelmen wasted no time in obeying those instructions. He

made his way swiftly to the kitchen. For the last two mornings he'd arisen early to cultivate a friendship with the cook. He hoped to make that friendship pay off—the path to the dungeon led right through the kitchen.

"Ho, fool!" the cook cried cheerily when he saw the painted clown come down the steps. "You're back quick today!"

"The Queen's grown tired of my company. I hope you've not?"

"No, indeed!" The man smiled, showing his toothless gums—the result, he'd explained to Fallomar, of sampling too many pies in his youth. "This is a time I can enjoy you. Breakfast's over, and it'll be a while before we begin dinner in earnest—though I do have a few treats in the oven." The cook slapped the stonework lip of the cistern that held the castle's water supply. "Sit down. Talk to me."

"I've little to say this morning. I fear this fool has had his fill of fooling for a time."

The cook nodded. "I get tired of my own cooking sometimes. You've no need to entertain me."

"Ah—but I hope you'll not stop feeding me?"

The cook snickered, and slapped Fallomar on the back. "Don't you worry. In fact, I may have something for you to nibble on now. Let me check my ovens." The man walked to the far side of the giant kitchen where stood the rows of rounded ovens.

"There you are!" Pelmen heard someone shout behind him, and he whipped around to see Maythorm plunging toward him.

"Oh, no." He sighed.

"Playing up to the Queen, aren't you?" Maythorm shouted, shaking his finger. "Trying to make me appear incompetent!"

"Maythorm, you really don't need my help for that—"

"What are you doing here?" the cook roared, and Pelmen turned in time to see him set a steaming dessert on the cutting block and seize a meat cleaver imbedded in the wood beside it. The cook started forward.

Maythorm stopped his own charge and regarded the oncoming cook with some alarm. The man was twice his size and frowning nastily. "I . . . I have no quarrel with you."

"But I have one with you! There's the little matter of my

niece!" The cook was picking up speed. With his head lowered and his ample belly flopping, the cook strongly resembled a charging tugolith, Pelmen thought.

Maythorm proved himself quite nimble. He vaulted a table, putting it between himself and his attacker, and cried in a high-pitched shriek, "Who *is* your niece?"

It was the wrong thing to say. The cook stopped and stared, his eyes bulging with rage. "You mean you don't even know?" the cook bellowed. He started over the top of the table. Maythorm raced for an exit—any exit. "You come into my kitchen again, and I'll drop you down the cistern!"

Maythorm was gone.

The cook grinned toothlessly at his painted friend. "Moves quick, doesn't he?"

Pelmen's eyes twinkled. "I'd heard he was fast with the ladies. Seems he's rather swift of foot as well. Ligne ought to send him to the Merchants' Games next year."

"If the Queen would send me and my cleaver as well, we'd be sure to win," the cook cackled.

Fallomar smiled, then looked down into the dank darkness behind him. A cold draft blew up from the cistern's depths. "Would you really drop him in?" he asked.

"Not likely," the cook muttered, brandishing his famous cleaver and slashing it through a chunk of red meat. "Not unless I wanted to follow him down it. The Queen would probably drop me in after him, and you'd hear nothing of either of us again."

"It's just a well, isn't it?"

"Not exactly. It's a reservoir, carved out of the rock. It's fed by the river, when the water's high. Spills through an iron grating on the south wall." The cook slammed his cleaver into the cutting board, and it quivered there as he went on: "It's poor water, believe me. All the filth of upper Chaomonous spills through that grillwork. We have to boil every bucket we raise!"

"It's safe though," Pelmen muttered to himself; then, when the cook gave him a puzzled look, he explained, "I mean secure for the Imperial House. I assume no one could get through the grate?"

"Who'd want to?" the cook snorted. "No. Not big enough. So there'd be water enough to last out any siege.

Though whoever would be fool enough to lay siege to this fortress would be a fool indeed. Oh, no offense intended," the heavy man added, in deference to Fallomar's profession.

"And none—" Fallomar cut himself short when he saw Ligne bolt rather furtively from the door the steward had just exited. She hurried through the kitchen and down another corridor. She held her cloak around her as if that might hide her identity from the very people whose jobs demanded they watch her every move. "There's the Queen," he announced to the cook. "I think I'll go amuse her." He got up.

"I wouldn't," the cook warned, raising his heavy brow.

"That's why you're the cook and I'm the fool!"

"What if she's not amused?"

"Then come visit me occasionally. And bring a pie."

"Be careful!" the cook called as Fallomar danced down the hall.

Ligne had already turned in through the dungeon door. That was good. He hoped to bluff his way past the guards, but it would only succeed if she were out of earshot, on her way into the lower depths. He paused briefly outside the door, then plunged in.

As with every dungeon he'd ever visited, the initial impact was more olfactory than anything else. A rank stench hit him with suffocating force, stopping him in the doorway. He forced himself forward.

"Ho, fool, what goes?" a warder called out of the fetid shadows. "I've been expecting you, to be sure, for hardly a fool comes into this court who doesn't finally join us here. But I expected you to come in chains and under guard—not by yourself!"

Fallomar chuckled. "I came early to inspect the rooms. I wanted to reserve a good one before they're all taken! Did the Queen pass through here?" He started to circle the guard, but there was the *ching* of metal striking stone, and he found his way blocked by a pikestaff.

"Stop!" the guard snapped. His voice softened immediately as he continued with concern, "Where do you think you're going?"

"Why, to prison, of course," Fallomar offered.

"And that quickly, unless you give me a reason for this!"

The guard leaned toward him. "Hear me. Quit your fooling and take yourself somewhere else. This is no place for you, especially not now."

"Why should now be different?" the jester inquired, shrugging elaborately. "It always seemed to me that dungeons were ever awful. Are some hours more bitter than others?"

"The Queen is within," the guard whispered, and Fallomar reacted with shock.

"You mean, she's sent herself to jail?"

The guard laughed at that, and Pelmen took advantage of his laughter to try again to get past him. He stopped when the business end of the pike was leveled at his nose. "You halt!" the guard roared, and Fallomar did just that.

"I . . . just thought . . ." he began lamely, and the guard slipped the pike under his left arm and slung him toward the door. He crashed against the masonry and down to the floor. The guard became solicitous.

"Did I hurt you?" he asked with sincerity.

"Only my backside," Pelmen answered honestly, "and it quickly heals . . ."

"Then take it out of here!" the guard ordered.

"But I only wanted to amuse the Queen! I know many humorous tales about dungeons and I thought this the perfect venue—"

"Shut up!" the guard ordered. Pelmen responded to the authority in the man's voice. He shut up. "How many times must I tell you, clown, that this is not the time?" He said this quietly, but with great force.

"Then another time—"

"Hush! No. No other time. No one enters this dungeon without authorization either from Queen Ligne or the Lord Joss. Anyone who succeeds in entering it otherwise will never get out—do you understand me?"

"But I only . . ."

"Quiet! By my orders you should be in a cell already, for attempting unlawful entry. Get out of here before she returns and makes me keep you!"

"If you could tell me why—"

The guard sighed in exasperation and lowered his voice into nothing more than a whisper. "Security is incredibly tight. Ever since the Princess—" The guard slammed his mouth shut, then cursed. The deadly look in his eyes, though only dimly perceived in this foul gloom, convinced Pelmen it was time to retreat. He bolted up off his knees and out the door into the corridor. He didn't stop running until he'd reached the safety of the kitchen.

Once again into its safe, well-lighted expanse, Pelmen leaned against the wall to catch his breath and ponder his options. The guard had let slip "the Princess—" . . . so Bronwynn *was* an occupant of the dungeon. In the choking silence of the catacombs, somewhere below his feet, Rosha's lady lay in chains. What other explanation fit the facts he'd uncovered? Pelmen imagined the treatment she surely must be receiving from the jealous Queen's hand—perhaps this moment—and his jaw clenched. Was there no way to get to her?

"I thought you'd be back in short order," the cook said. "The Queen is very particular about who visits her dungeons and who don't."

Pelmen turned around to watch as the cook dropped sliced olives and cashew nuts atop a curious looking culinary concoction. "Who feeds them?"

"What?"

"The prisoners. How are they fed?"

The cook shook his head. "I've got no idea. All I know is, we never have any leftovers. The Lord Joss has all leftovers collected off the trenchers before they even come out of the great hall of washing. That's all the more I know about it." The cook sauntered toward the bank of ovens on the far wall and shoved his creation into one of them. "If you'll pardon me, Fallomar, your interest in the doings below us seems quite unhealthy to me. Are you planning an act that might land you there? It's not that infrequent for fools, you know . . ."

"So the guard informed me."

"But it used to be, with Talith on the throne, that the old man's temper would subside after a time, and folks would be let out. Since this Queen's come to power, I've seen a lot of souls go below—but not a one's come up again."

Pelmen spun the possibilities in his mind, hoping that the random swirl of ideas might produce some new, unconsidered option. "You say the dungeon stretches below us here?"

The cook frowned at Pelmen and held that frown on his features as he took a steaming pie from another of the ovens. The kitchen filled instantly with its delicious aroma. "Do like me, Fallomar. I forget it's there." The culinary expert turned away then and walked slowly toward the pantry in the back end of the kitchen. It was nearly time for his servants to begin arriving, to start preparing the midday meal. The cook felt sure that Ligne had at least one spy, maybe two, scattered through his host of helpers. He hoped to discourage the clown from any further inquiries into the matter.

Pelmen's eyes cast around the kitchen in desperation. They fell on the low stonework wall that formed the lip of the cistern. It wasn't twenty feet from where he was standing. If the dungeon stretched directly below them . . .

When the cook came out of the pantry, Fallomar was gone. "Good," the cook muttered to himself. "He's decided to keep himself out of trouble."

Jagd usually had a dozen cloaks in his closet, all of them either solid purple or solid red. At the moment, however, his closet was empty. His guest rooom in the royal quarter of the castle resembled wash day at the laundry, for he had hung all his cloaks on the walls, on a dozen strategically placed pegs. He hoisted the last one into place and stepped back to look. It appeared that all textured surfaces were covered. Since spy holes normally were hidden in the textured panels to prevent discovery, and the only wall space now visible to him was smoothly plastered, he felt relatively safe. He did not know if secret passages circled his room, but he always assumed their presence in a castle of this age. Ligne could attempt to spy if she liked—all she would see would be darkness.

He doused the oil lamp that sat on the ornate table beside his bed, then set it on the floor. Then he pulled a heavy chest out from under the bed. He found its buckles by feel rather than sight. The latches sprang open in his hands like living things, and he opened up the chest.

The precious object inside glowed dimly. He pulled it out and set in on the table before him. As he peered into its glassy face, the strange blue light within it fanned into a new, brighter life. This was one of three very precious crystal pyramids possessed by members of the Council of Elders. Used together, they permitted instant communication between three members of the Council, wherever in the world they might be. While Jagd valued it as a complex machine of very fine craftsmanship, he had yet to recognize it for the awesome magic tool it really was.

"I see you've finally deigned to join us." That voice, mediated by the pyramid, made Jagd wince in irritation. It belonged to Flayh, who possessed the second of the three objects.

"I must be careful," Jagd replied sarcastically, peering into the crystal's depths. "Remember I'm no longer free to live in my own house, since certain persons seem disposed to try to assassinate me."

"So you've said," Flayh answered. As the parties each concentrated on the objects before them, the link between the three grew more stable. Jagd could now see Flayh's sneering face on the inner left-hand facet of his pyramid. On the right-hand facet he saw the sluggish, dull features of Flayh's obese nephew, Pezi. "I called a meeting of the Council, Jagd, in part to deal with your problem. I fear your absence will mean that problem gets very little attention."

"I do appreciate your consideration," Jagd replied snidely, "but perhaps that's the best I could hope for. Had I attended, I'm sure the problem would already have been resolved—much to your satisfaction."

"Whatever do you mean by that, Jagd?" Flayh asked with pretended civility.

"It would have been finished in Dragonsgate, with me on the sharp end of a slaver's sword. Thank you, Flayh, but I'll find my own solution."

"You hurt me deeply," Flayh mocked. "Such accusations . . ."

"Can we drop the pretense and get on to business? I notice your fat puppet is there beside you still—"

"What do you mean—puppet!" Pezi barked. "I'm no—"

"Shut up, Pezi," Flayh growled, and Pezi obeyed without question. "Of course Pezi is here. He is the owner of the third pyramid."

"The pyramids belong to the leaders of the Council, as you well know!" Jagd exploded. "When we first put them to use it was resolved that each should be held in trust by the most influential merchant in a land! You've broken the framework of their usage twice now, first by stealing the Lamathian pyramid and carrying it into Ngandib-Mar, and now by entrusting the pyramid of Tohn mod Neelis into the pudgy hands of this pasty-faced glutton! Do you dare contend that this overweight marionette is the most influential merchant among the Maris?"

"I'm no marion—!"

"I said shut up, Pezi!" Flayh said again, and Pezi bit his lip and sulked into the pyramid. "Are you quite finished?" Flayh asked Jagd. "For if you are, let me inform you that the pyramid has merely been entrusted to Pezi for safekeeping until the conclave begins tomorrow morning. The issue was to be high on the agenda."

"Was to be?" Jagd snorted.

"Of course, with your absence, you certainly wouldn't care to have it brought up in Council. Certainly your forces would find themselves outvoted—"

Jagd's sharp, derisive laughter cut Flayh off. "You larcenous liar!" he shouted. "You would never bring these devices up on the floor, for fear of losing your own! But I can guarantee, Flayh, the pyramid issue will be brought up!"

Flayh's gaze grew cold. "Then I can only assume you have broken the terms of your possession as well, by revealing it to someone outside the circle!"

"Yes, I have," Jagd cackled, "and we shall see how the Council as a whole reacts to your usurping of extraordinary powers!"

"I'll show you extraordinary powers!" Flayh shrilled, and his eyes bored into Jagd's. The merchant of Uda felt as if hot stakes were being driven into his skull. He tossed up his hands to block that penetrating gaze and suddenly realized he was screaming. He was marginally aware of Pezi shouting, "Uncle! Uncle, stop!" as well as of that mysterious clanging of bells that periodically disturbed the quiet of the Imperial House.

Jagd screeched: "I'll force the issue to the floor despite you!" Then he rolled backwards on his bed and away from the pyramid, effectively breaking the link and freeing his mind from the blood-chilling cruelty of Flayh's eyes.

The object dimmed to its original soft shimmer. No longer were the faces of the other two merchants visible in its facets. Jagd knew from experience that he, too, would be glowing with that quiet blue radiance for a while, and that to rush out into the hall was to court unwanted stares and difficult questions. Someone pounded on his door and called, "Are you all right in there? Did you ring for service?"

"Go away!" he managed to shout, and the pounding stopped. He could hear the ringing continue throughout the castle and shook his head at the imponderable mystery of it. But the noise was only one of a host of mysteries that plagued Jagd and was of minimal importance compared to the shock and terror he felt now. His worst fears had been confirmed.

"Tahli-Damen," he muttered, "your budding talent is about to meet its stiffest test. I hope you're equal to it, lad. For somehow, old Flayh has made himself a powershaper."

—What pain! What utter, agonizing pain! groaned the Imperial House, and it swore mightily through its bells. It gasped, and its foundation stones ground together. Candles guttered, torches flared, and wind whistled in the corridors.

A bit ostentatious, perhaps, for an attack of gastritus. But pain is pain, and this castle had never subscribed to a stoic philosophy. It reacted violently to the events taking place in the room of the little red-clad merchant.

—Pest! the Imperial House shouted at Jagd. Vermin! it shouted again. But, like all its other stupid occupants, this one didn't understand. He just lay on his bed and sparkled like a luminous fish! And every shimmer radiated more of that searing energy, the substance from which magic was drawn—the substance that burned the castle's insides!

—And there's no mouth to belch! screamed the House. It was no stranger to magic. Indeed, the House held more remembered spells locked in the patterns of its stonework than any being existent, it felt sure. But so much magic concentrated in one room, with no path of escape! Excruciating!

—At least open the door! the House pleaded. Just to dissipate it a bit will help! But like a gasping sturgeon, the merchant lay on his back and glistened.

—Not even eyes to weep! moaned the anguished castle, and it turned its attention away from this insensitive knave to the one it had been watching for days. Though arrayed as a fool, this man showed a wisdom and sensitivity the House hadn't seen in a millennium. Perhaps this one could dissipate the magic, and bring some relief!

—*If* he survives his fall, that is.

Pelmen's survival was very much in question. It hadn't occurred to him to wonder if there might be something in the subterranean cistern until he was plunging through the darkness into it. He had only time for the thought. Then his heel struck the water, and he was under. Immediately he churned for the surface, totally blind in the pitch black cavern. He gasped for breath as his head popped out, his heart pounding loudly. He thanked the Power he was still alive.

It struck him a moment later that his thanksgiving was a bit premature. He felt something grip his leg, and he was under water once again.

He kicked at the thing with his free foot, but with little result. The water dragged on his leg as he swung it, robbing his kick of any force. He squeezed his lips and eyes tight, holding onto his air as he sought once again to kick the terrifying thing that had gripped him. Success! He fought to the surface, a maelstrom of flailing legs and arms. He jerked the air into his lungs—but again the force grabbed him and dove for the bottom! What was it? And what was it doing in the cistern?

Actually, it was nothing more than a dumb fish. But it was a big dumb fish. The grating was far too small to permit the access of a monster like this. But when it had entered the cavern beneath the castle, it hadn't been a monster—just a man-wise denizen of the river, who found the cavern's cool, quiet pool preferable to the currents of the busy waterway. Other fish had found the grate as well, and these it had eaten, along with the ever-present garbage that floated on the surface. And after a time, it had grown too big to pass out the grate and into the main stream. Much too big. It was now much, much bigger.

Pelmen kicked again—a fruitless move, since he'd tried it twice already, and the fish now expected it. The scaly beast gulped as Pelmen kicked at it, and Pelmen's other foot wound up inside its mouth.

Panic seized him. He clenched his fists, bent at the waist, and tried pounding on the dull beast's spiky skull. The fish gulped again, and Pelmen realized he would soon be swallowed. In a rage born of terror, Pelmen extended his arm and bubbled some words toward the surface. For the briefest of instants, a ball of fire burned underwater! But it doused immediately. What was a powershaper to do?

"I *am* a powershaper," Pelmen encouraged himself, but little encouragement came. "And about to be a drowned one!" As his lungs clenched in a mute scream for air, Pelmen invoked the Power. And the Power aided him.

—He *is*! said the Imperial House with a jolt. Everyone in the castle felt its shock as a slight tremor. A number of wild-eyed servants wandered far from their tasks—the afternoon had taken on an apocalyptic character.

—A powershaper again! the castle crowed gleefully. A door slammed in the Hall of War, and Lord Joss put the soldiery on alert.

—It's boiled carp for dinner than, chuckled the Imperial House, and—though it burned—it put its knowledge to work.

Pelmen had fought the temptation far too long. He prepared to yield to the pressure of the deep. Suddenly, however, they were hurtling for the surface, and in much faster time than Pelmen had managed earlier! Fish and fool broke the surface together and continued into the air—a giant leap into a cavern filled with steam. Pelmen's legs came free in midair, and he plunged toward the water, rejoicing. His joy turned to screams, however, when he struck with a scalding splash. The water around him frothed and bubbled. Apparently, he was not only going to be eaten—he was to be cooked first!

Pelmen's reaction came purely by intuition. His hands shot into the air, and a rush of wind blew in through the grating and tore him bodily from the water. He rode a raging whirlwind through the blackness of the grotto, until good sense convinced him that a light was needed, and a ball of fire burst into existence above his outstretched palm.

His eyes scanned the walls in panic, looking desperately for a cleft or prominence, something he could cling to when the wind died, as he knew it must in a moment. Already it was dropping him toward the boiling water again, and he could only sustain it—

There! A hole in the wall. He sailed through it and skidded along the uneven floor, scraping his already raw body. He gasped, exhausted. He had expended tremendous resources in those brief, bleak moments of terror. Now he slept.

Behind him, in the pool, the giant fish continued to leap and struggle in the boiling froth, until at last it was forced to yield up its long life and die.

Someone in the kitchen, passing by the cistern, sniffed twice, then called across the large room to the cook: "I thought we were roasting a pig today! Why is it I keep smelling fish?"

CHAPTER ELEVEN

A Chaotic Council

BRONWYNN FOLLOWED ADMON FAYE into the central hall of Tohn's castle and took a seat beside him. They sat on the dais, as befitted honored guests of the meeting, but not at the head table itself. It was reserved for members of the ruling Council alone—the foremost merchant of each house, plus the leader of the dominant house in each land. For many years that had meant that the house of Ognadzu had seated two representatives at the head table. Flayh had represented the blue and lime both as chief Elder and as the most influential merchant in Lamath. Tohn mod Neelis had also been seated, for his expertise in Mari culture had thrust his house far above all competing houses in Ngandib-Mar. But Tohn was dead now, and though his noninvolvement in the recent Mari-Chaon war had won many new friends for Ognadzu in the Mar, its supremacy was far from unchallenged. There was much consternation, then, when Flayh took his central seat at the ruling table and Pezi, smiling sheepishly, took the seat on Flayh's right hand that had been Tohn's. The muttering that swept through the lower level of the hall forecast a stormy meeting, but no one had ever expected it to be peaceful. A major power shift was shaping up, and the fever of politics had infected the host of younger merchants who now attended a conclave for the first time.

Another storm of whispers issued when an obviously youthful merchant in purple and red strode purposefully to the dais and took the seat on Flayh's left as if he owned it. Flayh had been waiting for a hush to settle on the crowd before starting the session. That hush fell quickly when he turned to address Tahli-Damen sharply:

"What do you think you're doing? Go to your place!" He pointed a long, bony finger at the rows of tables on the floor, where the lesser members of the families sat by houses, ranked according to their influence.

"This is my place," Tahli-Damen replied evenly, and those nearest to the dais—the older members—gasped at his brazenness. "I am representing the house of Uda in Chaomonous—I think it's no secret which house is dominant in the Golden Land."

"Nor is it any secret who is the leader of that house!" Flayh snarled. "That he refused to come is his own business! He's forfeited his voice thereby, and he knows it!"

"He refused to come because you ordered his assassination!" Tahli-Damen shot back, and all the merchants present roared in shock—not because it wasn't true—they all knew that—but because the young man had the gall to say it aloud!

"Order!" Flayh shouted. "I command order!" He banged on the oaken table with an empty tankard, and order was quickly restored, as merchants of every age and color leaned forward to hear his response. He disappointed all of them, for he turned his back on Tahli-Damen, choosing to pretend he wasn't there, rather than confront the lad before the assembly. He could do that much more effectively in private. "Brother merchants!" he began, his voice carrying with surprising strength for so small a man. "I have summoned you to this meeting to consider grave matters that threaten our livelihood! The dragon is dead!"

The response pleased Flayh. The gathering seemed to forget the upstart's embarrassing intrusion, and turned its attention to the real problem.

"This has already cost us," Flayh warned. Pezi was surprised at how dignified his uncle sounded. "We are faced with a problem unlike any our fathers faced before us. For a millennium our families have been the feeders of the dragon, and in return we've built a style of life unmatched by the noblest of nobles, unmatched even in the courts of the three regents. My friends, our position has been gravely jeopardized by Vicia-Heinox' death! Lest any of you miss its significance let me hasten to explain. With no dragon in Dragonsgate, trade between the three lands will become utterly, disastrously free. Any ignorant lout who thinks himself a salesman can now take it into his head to transport goods between the three lands. Of course, he could never hope to compete with our volume and experience. But he will soak off some of our profits, and if enough free traders begin to move, our monopoly will unquestionably be broken."

A hiss swept the hall, and Flayh stretched out his palms to hush the whisperers. "There is more at stake than just our businesses, however. Our very lives are threatened as well." Shock greeted this statement. What Flayh had said so far was generally acknowledged as the truth. This was a new thought. All eyes riveted on the bald speaker. "We have never attempted to ingratiate ourselves with the populace of any land. We are, therefore, unpopular. But peasants in all three lands have been forced to tolerate us, for we were the only source of the goods and services they needed. The crowns have called us arrogant, but never to our faces. They've been aware of our power, and of the fact that our united front could topple them from theirs. But the dragon is dead! What happens now?"

The question raised immediate response. Brab mod Crober of the house of Blez leaped to his feet in great agitation. "They'll kill us and take our lands! They've always wanted to—what's to prevent them?"

"Not so!" shouted Klaph, a Hanni merchant in charge of his family's operation in Lamath. "As all of you know, our land has just endured tremendous social and religious upheaval—yet we remain free to trade, and the Prophet of Lamath has offered no interference—"

"Yet!" Flayh thundered, his eyebrows knitting fiercely. "You remember, Klaph, that I am originally of Lamath. Yet I and my house were hounded from that land by these religiously motivated rebels. You know yourself that La-mathians are fanatics, feeding themselves to the dragon to obtain religious satisfaction—"

"That was before! The dragon is—"

"Dead, yes!" Flayh continued aggressively, leaning down the table toward Klaph and emphasizing his points with a shaking finger. "But what happens if this worship-crazed Prophet should choose tomorrow to throw you out? Do you think you would survive the night? I doubt it!" Flayh turned to the assembly and thundered in a voice strangled by rage, "Be reminded, you merchants from Lamath, that this new Prophet is but a pawn of the dangerous Pelmen, who brought this entire problem on all of us!"

The hall rang with agreement, and Klaph sank back into his seat under the weight of the crowd's abuse.

"I repeat!" Flayh trumpeted. "What are we going to do? Before anyone else speaks," he went on quickly, "I'd like to offer a suggestion that I feel will meet with your unanimous approval."

"That's yet to be seen," Tahli-Damen put in quickly, and Flayh made a great show of ignoring him.

"What is needed," Flayh said, "is, quite simply, a replacement for Vicia-Heinox." Stunned silence greeted him.

After a moment, a lesser merchant of Ognadzu meekly began: "You mean we need to seek out another dragon—"

Flayh cut the man off with a sharp look. Then he surveyed his audience and explained: "I have taken the liberty of inviting an old friend to attend this gathering. Though you may not know his name, you all will surely recognize him as—"

"By my face, Flayh?" Admon Faye asked sharply from his seat to Flayh's far right. Bronwynn suddenly felt trapped in the wash of eyes, as everyone turned to look at the slaver seated next to her.

"I meant nothing by that, my friend. I refer only to the fact that you are as widely travelled as a merchant—as any *other* merchant," Flayh amended carefully. He turned back to the delegates. "My brother merchants, I give you the dragon's successor in Dragonsgate: Admon Faye." Flayh pointed at the slaver, and once again Bronwynn shifted in her seat, wanting to hide from the eyes that turned toward her. She could see them associating her with the hideously visaged slaver—his girl friend perhaps, some of them were thinking. Bronwynn didn't feel at all flattered.

Admon Faye rose in his place and bowed courteously. Then he sneered, and the assembled merchants, for the most part, quickly found something else to look at.

"What . . . exactly . . ." Brab mod Crober began, and Flayh nodded to him politely and went on:

"Admon Faye is an expert slaver. Of all those who ply his unpopular but essential trade, he is the best. Or *was*. The death of Vicia-Heinox has caused the demand for slaves to drop drastically. He is in need of a new line of work.

"We are all familiar with the continuous sword-rattling that passes for diplomacy between our several nations. With Dragonsgate clear, no nation can feel safe. I predict that we will soon see a build up of troops in every mouth of the Gate—a build-up that will continue unabated, sapping the economic strength of each land, until the inevitable war results. We cannot have that—not least because those border lands closest to the pass have always belonged to us! We don't want soldiers building barricades across our farm lands!"

"No!" roared the assembly in one mighty voice.

"However. If someone occupies the pass—someone non-threatening to national security, but powerful enough to resist all but the severest of raids—my guess is that rulers of security in all three lands will be able to relax, and life will soon return to normal. I propose that Admon Faye and his horde of henchmen be installed in Dragonsgate to form such a buffer—and to discourage passage to anyone save merchant houses recognized by this Council!"

A round of cheers broke out then, lasting for several minutes. Flayh actually smiled—an honest smile of pleasure, something Pezi couldn't remember ever seeing on Flayh before. The cheering was interrupted by Klaph of Hann, who jumped to his feet waving his burnt-orange sleeves.

"A moment! A moment please!" he cried, and the merchants quieted to hear him. "Just what does Admon Faye want in return?" he asked. He didn't hide his suspicion.

"Very simple," Flayh replied. "A tribute from each caravan—something each of us should feel quite comfortable with, since that was our arrangement with the dragon as well—and a secret seat on this Council." Flayh gauged the reactions of his audience and decided that he was home free. Protests were few. He continued: "It must be a secret seat, for if it became known that Admon Faye formally belonged to the Council, public sentiment might force one regent or another to move upon him and chase him from the pass. As long as the general populace remains convinced that he's acting only in his own interests, each regent can publicly deplore his presence, while privately offering him every incentive to continue." Flayh turned toward Admon Faye and smiled. "You surely don't mind being deplored, do you?" he called.

"Mind it!" Admon Faye hooted. "I've made a career of it!" The comment brought a hearty laugh, and Flayh confidently moved for an immediate vote. The response was unanimous approval. Even Tahli-Damen endorsed it heartily, admitting to himself that Flayh's genius had produced the perfect solution. Besides, his argument was not with this.

Tahli-Damen braced himself for the next item on the agenda to be announced. Flayh cleared his throat. "Now to the matter of other seats on the platform." Flayh spun around to face Tahli-Damen and drilled his eyes into those of the young merchant. "I demand that you vacate that position!"

Tahli-Damen came out of his chair ready for a scrap. The adrenaline pumped through him with such force that he felt no fear at all. In fact, he felt strangely elated.

"And I refuse!" He turned to the crowd and announced, "I have been deputized to this chair by Jagd of Uda, who refused to attend on threat of assassination!"

"Your patron's paranoia is none of our concern!" Flayh screeched, but the young merchant kept on talking.

"My Lord Jagd has refused to attend in person, but has authorized me to challenge Flayh to produce the two pyramids he holds in his possession!"

"What are you talking about?" Flayh shrilled, and he grabbed Tahli-Damen's shoulder and tried to wrench him around.

The Udan merchant winced, but continued talking to a sea of rapt faces. "Flayh knows very well what pyramids I refer to, though he's conspired to keep them secret from all but a chosen few of the merchant Elders—"

"I must protest!" shouted Brab mod Crober, pounding his hand on the head table. "This knowledge is privileged, reserved only for those seated on this dais!"

"No!" shouted some younger merchants in the back of the hall, and Tahli-Damen was forced to scream to make himself heard over the heckling.

"No longer will these magic objects be hidden! If you would hear Jagd himself endorse an open and free discussion of these precious crystals, then help me to force this man to produce the two pyramids he holds in his possession! Then Jagd of Uda will himself speak to you, from his sanctuary in the Imperial House of Chaomonous!" Tahli-Damen pointed at Flayh, but did not look at him. He did well in that, for the merchant powershaper was livid in his wrath and glared at his young accuser with every intention of crushing the young upstart under the weight of his own terror. But he needed to grip the lad's eyes!

Flayh was oblivious to the bedlam the young man's words had unleashed. Fist fights had broken out in three sections of the room, scufflers clothed in blue and lime against those in scarlet and purple. Admon Faye shook his head in disbelief, a grin traced on his hideous lips, while Bronwynn tucked herself behind his body, fearing the benches would soon start flying. Gradually everyone became aware of a heavy pounding on the table, and order was restored. Surprisingly, the pounder was none other than Pezi, who had been so seized by the excitement of the moment that he'd acted with an uncharacteristic authority. He even earned his uncle's attention. But when he noticed Flayh's peering eyes, his courage faltered, and he shoved Flayh's ale-cup back into his uncle's shrivelled hand and sank into his seat.

Flayh was nonplussed. Skeptical expressions had replaced the cheers of a moment ago, and his normal sourness returned with a rush. He frowned at the gathering, then opened his mouth:

"I cannot comprehend the —"

"Don't lie to us!" someone shouted.

"We won't be silenced!"

"We want the truth!"

"Show us the pyramids!"

"Produce them!"

"We demand to see the objects!"

The cries rang out from every corner of the hall, each one clearly audible.

"I . . ." he began again, and someone else shouted:

"Don't deny it! Brab mod Crober has already admitted they exist."

That was true, and Brab blushed and hung his head. His face turned the burnt-orange color of a Hanni tunic.

"Very well!" Flayh snapped. "I will fetch the objects before our next session! But first I—"

"No!" Tahli-Damen roared, jumping to his feet once again. "You've hidden them from us long enough! Produce them now, or forfeit your credibility entirely!"

"Do you threaten me?" Flayh shouted, spittle flying from his contorting lips. Now it was Tahli-Damen's turn to ignore Flayh, and the young man did so with a flair. The chorus of support he received immediately from the tables on the floor made it apparent that Flayh would have to yield.

Flayh realized his cause was hopeless. "Go fetch them," he spat, and Pezi waddled for the door at top speed—which was, of course, necessarily slow.

Flayh sank back into his seat to wait, steaming with frustration. As half a hundred excited conversations began, he cursed quietly. "I'll have you peeled," he growled through his teeth at the young adversary seated beside him.

Tahli-Damen faced stolidly forward. "No doubt you would—if you were able."

"Oh, I'm able, boy. And you'll suffer as I prove it to you."

"Threaten all you like, Lord Flayh. I only seek an equitable solution to the problem of our warring houses. I was taught in our own merchant's conservatory that interhouse wars were the deadliest of sins, because nothing is so harmful to business."

"You lecture me, as well as threaten? My child, your education is only beginning! You obviously view yourself as a political comer, but I assure you, you've come to nothing but a dead end here!"

"We shall need to let the Council decide that."

"Oh no. It's already been decided. By me."

"Perhaps you think too highly of yourself, Lord Flayh." Tahli-Damen angled his eyes even further away from Flayh's as he said it.

"And perhaps, my boy—just perhaps—you don't regard me highly enough."

Their verbal sparring ceased then, but the taut silence between them was as charged with meaning as any conversation. At last Pezi rushed back into the chamber, carrying two oddly shaped velvet bags with drawstrings of gilded rope. As he passed Admon Faye, the slaver had to fight the urge to trip him and barely resisted the temptation. Admon Faye was determined to appear respectable—though after what he'd already witnessed, he wondered why he bothered.

Flayh glowered at his nephew as Pezi deposited the first of the pyramids before his uncle. The chubby trader unsacked his own device and plopped himself onto his chair. Then he leaned forward and would have begun the process of clearing his mind to form the link, had Flayh not grabbed him by the ear and viciously twisted his head away from the surface of the object.

"Not yet, idiot! Wait until I instruct you to begin!" Flayh released his nephew and straightened to look into the upturned faces below him, suddenly grown silent once again.

"I do this under protest—No!" he broke off, pointing at a younger merchant who had started to jeer. His angry scowl dismayed the lad, and the young man quailed and turned pale. Flayh paused for a moment and scanned the room for other sneers. They all disappeared, and he continued. "These objects have been a secret trust, and I am horrified that a member of the ruling Council would so frivolously reveal their existence—"

"Not frivolously," Tahli-Damen murmured, and Flayh turned to stare at the man. Tahli-Damen maintained his composure, fixing his eyes on the table top.

"May I be granted the courtesy of finishing my statement?" Flayh demanded. Tahli-Damen didn't reply, and Flayh turned back to the crowd and shouted: "These objects are precious implements which permit—as has been pointed out—conversation at great distances. They are reserved for the three foremost merchants, the head of the dominant house in each land—"

"Then why has Pezi got one?" someone shouted, and Flayh was forced to wait again for the confusion to subside before he could go on.

"Pezi uses the pyramid entrusted to Tohn mod Neelis, the late lord of this castle!" His savage mood was very threatening, yet interruption came in spite of it.

"Is this a permanent arrangement?" someone questioned, and Klaph spoke up through a clamor of boos:

"Then we might expect some reassignment will take place?"

"Certainly," Flayh snapped, "should any reassignment prove necessary!"

"I think it very likely that it should!" Klaph bristled. "Since you've left Lamath, my family has done a thorough job of reorganizing the regional markets! I feel that I am entitled to hold the Lamathian pyramid!"

"You haven't even seen the device work yet!" Flayh snarled. "Are you entitled also to the dangers of its operation?"

The suggestion that the pyramids might be dangerous as well as useful caused Klaph difficulty in swallowing. Klaph was a conservative man, like most merchants. Caution drove him back into his seat.

Flayh surveyed his audience and found them a little less restive. "Yes." He smiled, "I thought that might bring a bit of hesitancy to some of you. Are you entirely certain you want this demonstration?"

"Don't be put off by him!" Tahli-Damen challenged. "This is another ruse to keep us from exercising our rightful powers!"

"I'm getting tired of you," Flayh breathed, for Tahli-Damen's statement had once more swung the Council against him.

"And I've been tired of you since before I arrived," the young merchant shot back. His obvious success with the Council had emboldened him to the point of cockiness. Flayh noted this, and marked it well.

At last Flayh nodded to Pezi and leaned toward his own pyramid, complaining, "I'm not sure if this will even work . . ."

"It'll work," Tahli-Damen said confidently.

As Flayh peered into the cloudy blue crystal before him, and the gathered host gasped at the sudden blue flame that sprang to life within both it and its twin, Flayh cursed himself for having allowed Jagd and this young merchant so totally to outmaneuver him. By the time the pyramids cleared, he'd already plotted his vengeance.

Once again, the bells rang throughout the castle. "I'm going to have that Kherda fried!" Ligne barked—then she smiled at Rosha, and patted him on the hand. "I'm sorry, darling, I know I shouldn't go on like that. But this incessant ringing is driving me insane!"

Rosha thought of the obvious insult, but resisted saying it. Ligne had returned from her visit to the dungeon only a few moments before and found him without his hood. Instead of being angry, she seemed positively thrilled. He would say nothing to earn it back on.

He glanced up at the wall of the game room, where the servants' bell hung, and watched as it noisily rocked up and down. Its pull rope swayed from side to side, untouched by any human hand. He had heard this clamorous ringing many times in the past, but this was his first view of the phenomenon. It chilled him. There were powers at work here—strange and angry powers.

"Try to ignore it, dear," Ligne ordered, an irritated smile gracing her elegant features. "It's your move."

Rosha tried to turn his attention again to the game—a difficult task, since he felt as if some invisible presence stared over his shoulder. They played a game of Green Dummy Drax, the weak, two-handed version of the three-sided table game so favored by the Queen. Rosha, while not an expert, felt himself a competent player, for he and his father had often shared the winter nights playing Green Dummy next to the fire. But he pretended now to learn the game anew, and Ligne had eagerly assumed the role of instructor.

"No, no, not like that!" she scolded lightly, as he purposely made an impossible move. "Your column can't take my disc while it's still on the base triangles! Look, I'm on the inversions here! Remember, base triangles are white, inversions are yellow. It's simple!"

"Oh," Rosha replied. "I g-get it n-now." He replaced his column, made a proper move, and pegged the expended move on the reference plank.

"Very good!" Ligne cried, clapping her hands in delight. Her eyes sparkled as she made her answering move.

His suggestion that she teach him to play was proving a shrewd ploy. Thus far, the game had kept her mind off his body. She seemed to be receiving this sudden thaw in his feelings for her as the natural result of her invincible charm. She could think what she liked—he didn't care. He was determined to make this sacrifice for Bronwynn's sake. Moments before, he'd made a convincing fuss over the Queen in the presence of Jagd. Perhaps too convincing, for the merchant had popped into the throne room only for a moment and had popped out again a moment later with the speed of a nervous rodent. Before he could get away, Ligne had wrung from the merchant a promise that he would soon return. Rosha hoped he would hurry, for while he'd sworn his determination to convince the Queen of his affection for her, he didn't know how he could endure it if she started pawing him again. He had always solved his problems violently, and though his hands were still bound before him, it would take little effort to break the woman's pretty neck. Pelmen's words convinced him there was little to be gained from such a rash act, and much to lose. He had to resist the temptation.

"It's your move," Ligne chirped, and without thinking Rosha skillfully attacked her cube and removed it from the board. Ligne gasped. "That was . . . very good." She frowned. While she wanted him to learn this game, Ligne did not like losing. Suddenly he threatened to defeat her.

"It was?" Rosha covered. "J-j-just lucky, I g-guess."

"Yes," she replied evenly. "Very lucky." With a sweep of her hand she cleared the board of all pieces, then she turned to look at the door. "This game really isn't worth finishing. It's only Dummy Drax, after all. Where is Jagd? I expected him to come join us in a full-sided game!"

Rosha shrugged. He hoped the man returned quickly. He couldn't hide his disgust from her forever.

The Imperial House bellowed. It was happening again! The miserable runt in the violet knickers had resumed his torture! Oh, the House had been prepared for it, of course, for the verminous merchant had never taken his laundry off the walls. Only once had he left his room, and that only for a moment, to give the Queen some lame excuse for his absence. Then he'd raced back to that sparkling shape on the table that commanded his constant attention.

All morning long, the House had watched Jagd watching the pyramid. The feeling of dread grew during the afternoon, until the House decided that the pain would be preferable to the suspense. But when the object finally flickered to life, the Imperial House immediately changed its mind. A new round of cursing had set off less confusion in the castle than before, for the servants had grown accustomed to these outbursts. This unfeeling, blasé attitude on the part of the help incensed the castle still further. Who did they think they were working for, after all? The Queen?

—That's exactly what they think, the Imperial House said bitterly. In the ancient past, the House had frequently despised its occupants, but this supposed monarch seemed exceptionally stupid. The House sighed for a return to the good old days . . .

Then it jerked, causing doors on every floor to slam mysteriously. The conversation between Jagd and the blackguards who held the other pyramids grew heated, and the magical energy released was building up an excruciating bubble of gas in the castle's bowels.

—A lot of good that did! the castle moaned, for the servants were used to its wincing now, too, and they casually reopened the slammed doors without another thought.

—You! Powershaper! Can't you tell you're desperately needed? Wake up!

The castle was not entirely pleased with its clownish powershaper's performance. All the lazy lout had done so far was snore. It had cost the House enormous effort to save the fool, and what had he done in return? He'd made use of magic, that's what, searing yet another painful hole in the House's inner lining—and then had promptly gone to sleep!

—Oh! The House cried out. Wake up! it yelled at Fallomar the fool. It really wasn't sure why it had moved to save the rascal in the first place. The possibility was there, of course, that this Fallomar fellow might wake from his deafness and offer the House some fellowship. But even if the fool did learn to speak, there was no assurance of his help. The House had dealt with many powershapers through the ages, and the majority had been only selfish thieves, greedy for new ways to swell their powers. Some had even tormented the House for spite, so great was their cruelty. The House chuckled through its pain—the last sorcerer to try such got a chandelier implanted in his forehead!

—Any chandeliers? the House wondered, running a quick check of Jagd's room.

—No such luck, it groused. The lighting fixtures had all been replaced in the last twenty years—besides, Jagd was twelve feet away from the nearest one.

A lot of bells rang in the castle.

—Wake up! the House shouted, but the powershaper slept on. This one might be different, the House said, hoping desperately for some relief. If only he could be roused! The castle remembered how the man had responded to its teasing with a polite but confident warning. That he was truly a powershaper he'd proved in his wrestling match with the old fish.

—True, your magic proved painful, the House pleaded with the sleeping magician, but at least it dissipated out the grating. Not like this agony!

For Jagd's heated conversation continued still, and his room was shut up tight!

—Arise! The Imperial House screamed, agonized. The Imperial House wants you!

Tohn's hall hummed with power, as the two pyramids on the front table crackled with brilliant blue intensity. Many merchant mouths hung open in disbelief, as the recognizable voice of Jagd, Elder of Uda, echoed off the giant beams overhead. Jagd and Flayh had abused each other for a quarter of an hour already, and neither seemed ready to stop. Poor Pezi rubbed his broad forehead feverishly—the stress had given him a splitting headache.

"Naturally you hold me responsible!" Jagd screamed. "You always hold me responsible for all your misfortunes!"

"This is not a misfortune!" Flayh screamed back. "It's

an impossible situation deliberately created by your complicity with this strumpet of a Queen!"

"The entire ruling Council agreed to our plan to place Ligne on the throne! Can I help it if you and some of the other houses so overplayed your power that she's come to favor Uda alone?"

"Yes, you can help it! You were the representative of the whole Council in the court, not just your own organization! You've demonstrated your disloyalty to your brethren here by siding against us. Your very absence from this meeting indicates your true loyalties!"

"That's a lie, Flayh, and you know it! You think I take pleasure in sitting around this castle doing nothing? It's your assassins who have imprisoned me here, dooming me to interminable games of Drax with a vain Queen and her stuttering young warrior! You think I—"

"What!" roared a female voice from one side of the dais. The assembled merchants tore their eyes from the mesmerizing crystals to see Admon Faye holding a kicking, screaming Bronwynn in the air. He'd been holding onto her since early in the conversation, for in the exchange between Jagd and Flayh she'd learned more about her own kidnapping than in all the months since it happened. She'd known, of course, that she'd been ripped from the Imperial House with Ligne's aid. But the cold-bloodedness of it had enraged her anew.

Now that rage exploded into new dimensions. "What did he say?" she shrilled. "I want to know what he said!"

"What's going on there?" Jagd asked, holding his head.

"Don't distract us!" Flayh ordered. "You'll make us break the link!"

"Oh, my head . . ."

"Shut up, Pezi!"

Bronwynn broke loose and rushed over to crowd between Pezi and his uncle. "I want to know what he said!"

"Said about what?" Jagd asked, as a disembodied woman's voice lanced painfully through his head.

Admon Faye suddenly understood, and a grin spread from one ugly ear to the other. He stalked up behind Bronwynn and spoke to Flayh, "Ask what he means by a stuttering warrior."

The object's lock on Flayh's mind made these other

voices intolerable. It seemed a thousand people clamored
for his attention at once. Pezi, feeling the pressure too,
moaned aloud. Flayh relayed Admon Faye's question to
Jagd, hoping to end this bitter interruption.

"Some young bruiser from the north is all I know!" Jagd
shot back. "Name is Rosha, and he stutters. He's the
Queen's latest paramour! Can we get back to business? My
head wants to explode!"

"Yours isn't the only one," Pezi added mournfully.

Admon Faye, still grinning, led Bronwynn back to her
chair. There she sat, stunned and shaken, throughout the
chaotic events that followed. Perhaps it had been only an
interruption to the others in the room, but this news
crashed in on Bronwynn with the suddenness of a death
message. It took much the same toll on her heart.

—They talk about pain! the Imperial House roared. *This*
is pain! A strong wind whistled through the subterranean
passageways, the only audible evidence of the castle's
screaming in these caverns.

—Powershaper! Wake up! the Imperial House pleaded.

Pelmen jerked to awareness. The dream was gone, but
not the blue light. He identified it instantly, for he'd heard
these threeway conversations before. "Of course," he whispered aloud. "Jagd has his pyramid with him here!" He
wondered momentarily why he'd not heard Jagd using it
before—then he recalled for the first time the bright blue
dreams that had plagued his sleep and understood. Pelmen
thrust all thoughts from his mind except those he heard
issuing from the bright azure ball behind his eyelids.

"Wait!" Jagd yelped. "Someone is listening!"

"Of course someone is listening!" Flayh bellowed.
"There's a room full of people here!"

"This is someone else!" Jagd said anxiously. He felt a
pair of eyes fixed on his back, and longed to turn around
to see if one of his cloaks had fallen from its peg.

"I feel it too!" Pezi wailed. "Someone powerful is listening! Ohhh . . ." he moaned, his head spinning. "I can't
take any more of this . . ." Pezi reeled, rocked forward,
banged his forehead noisily on the table, and passed out
beneath it.

The link broke immediately, with a flare of light and a loud snap.

Flayh cried out in anguish, then ordered Pezi: "Get up from there, you dolt!" The fat merchant didn't budge. "You swine! Can't you manage to do anything right?"

"Of course he can't," Tahli-Damen said as he leaped from his chair and swiftly circled behind Flayh to seat himself over Pezi. "He isn't qualified! Jagd! Jagd!" Tahli-Damen peered into the pyramid as he'd seen the others do.

"What are you doing?" Flayh shouted hoarsely. With a vicious shove, he pushed Tahli-Damen off the seat and onto the floor. Or rather, onto Pezi, who didn't seem to notice.

"I'm claiming what's rightfully mine!" Tahli-Damen yelled back, jumping nimbly to his feet. "You've been so busy manipulating people that you haven't been keeping up your business! Uda has just this month edged Ognadzu in total Mari sales, so this pyramid is mine!"

Klaph started to suggest that since his house was now dominant in Lamath, he should get one, too. He never got the sentence out.

Suddenly a savage dog leaped out of nowhere for Tahli-Damen's throat. The young man threw up his arm in shock. With a snarl, the dog ripped his sleeve to tatters, taking with it a strip of flesh. The dais emptied immediately, save for Pezi, who smilingly slept on, and Bronwynn, who continued to stare dully into space. Tahli-Damen clubbed the ferocious beast with his free hand and tried to scramble over the table, but the dog caught his leg in its jaws. Tahli-Damen's purple pants turned the color of his crimson tunic; but despite his wounds, he kicked the beast off and rolled on across the head table, dropping onto the dais floor. He kept on rolling until he dropped off the dais, into the waiting arms of family members who'd rushed past the scattering merchants to his aid.

As quickly as it had appeared, the dog was gone. Flayh stood on the table in its place—but this was a different Flayh from the bald Elder these merchants had traded with through the years. The figure who stood astride the two pyramids was awesome. Gone were his blue and lime garments. Gowned in gleaming white, with a red cape flowing from his shoulders, Flayh the powershaper tossed multicolored balls of energy at his enemies as they all plunged wildly for the doors.

"By the dragon!" Klaph swore, using an outdated Lamathian oath. "He's become a powershaper!" Then a ball struck Klaph in the chest, and he raced down the line of emptying tables and grabbed a pitcher of ale to douse the sudden flames.

Tahli-Damen's cousins bore him rapidly from the hall, ducking the burning missles and shoving other merchants aside. As they passed through the door, Tahli-Damen turned his head to gaze back at Flayh. He watched the powershaper's lips move, and saw how a pointed finger could snuff out fires created by a thought mere seconds before. Tahli-Damen was bleeding, but it wasn't his wounds that concerned him. His heart wanted to pound its way out from between his ribs. Tahli-Damen was terrified.

CHAPTER TWELVE

Below the Dungeon

PELMEN GROANED and grabbed his head. "I wish they wouldn't do that . . ." he muttered to himself.

—You think *you* do! the Imperial House replied.

Pelmen didn't hear it. He only felt a chilly breeze. From where he stood, he could see a bit of sunlight sneaking in through the grating on the far side of the pool. That meant he was on the dungeon side of the cistern, and he sighed with relief. He felt as if he'd been sleeping for years—he wondered if it was still the same day that he'd dropped into this netherworld. He turned away from the water to peer into the passage—he could feel wind blowing through it. He hoped that meant it led somewhere, or else he'd fallen a long way for nothing. He stared into it, wishing he had a torch. Then he remembered: "I'm a powershaper!"

—So you've been saying, said the House. Instead of talking about it, why don't you do someth—but not that!

Pelmen was extending his hand, and a violet ball of flame appeared over his palm. A puff of wind blew it out.

—Try that again and the next one will be snuffed out as well!

Pelmen did. And it was.

"Come on," he said with some frustration. "I need to see!"

Pelmen said it to himself, really, but the House sniffed a response anyway:

—Very well. That's reasonable, if irritating.

The sphere of green flame Pelmen summoned up next was smaller than the others, and notably cooler.

—Thank you, the House replied, through a creaking of the door jambs on the third floor. Naturally, Pelmen didn't hear that.

"Where am I?" Pelmen wondered aloud as he started down the craggy corridor.

—You're under the doorway into the offices of trade, the Imperial House answered, where that verminous pest with the pyramid supposedly does his work—*when* he works—which isn't often, since he prefers to pester this House . . .

The castle gazed scornfully at Jagd from all the walls that the creature hadn't covered with a smelly coat. Jagd lay on his bed, trembling with a chill. Purely for spite, the Imperial House lowered the temperature of Jagd's room perceptibly, and the merchant shivered harder.

Pelmen noticed that that curious condensation formed on the walls of these subcastle caverns as well. He walked thirty-five feet and came to a juncture. The corridor branched off in two directions.

—Now you're under the great hall—under the stairway from the platform to the floor. Of course, it's forty feet above you . . .

Pelmen hesitated, obviously pondering which way to turn.

—If you want out, go left. There's a stairway up into the infirmary that no one seems to know about . . .

But Pelmen didn't want out, he wanted in, into the dungeon. And it seemed that from the location of the grate and the cistern, the right hand tunnel would take him closer to it.

—On the other hand, some people can't accept advice from anyone, the House said crossly, and it resolved to offer no further suggestions.

Pelmen went on another twenty-five feet, and stopped. This seemed to be a man-made section of the passageways, for the rock walls bore chisel marks, and the floor was smoother.

He now had three options. He could continue straight ahead, but carved galleries extended to his left and right as well. "Now which way," he mumbled.

—That all depends on where you're going, the Imperial House huffed. That is, if you know.

"The dungeon," Pelmen said, biting his lip. The sound of his own voice in the moody silence reassured him. "Which way to the dungeon?"

The castle could scarcely contain it's excitement at finally being consulted. It had only expanded its consciousness into these caverns in the last week and now felt quite knowledgeable.

—To your right, of course. Then listen closely, for it gets very complicated from where you . . .

But before the House could finish, Pelmen plunged straight ahead. The castle was incensed.

—All right! Go ahead and get lost!

Pelmen took little time in doing just that.

He went a hundred and forty feet, pausing only briefly at other branchings off to the left, deciding to keep to his right. The corridor seemed to make a long bend in that direction, and he felt hopeful that it might take him straight to the dungeon. But it ended in another gallery that crossed from left to right. He was confused.

—Of course you're stuck. You're under the platform in the Chamber of War! But will you ask for advice? No. You wouldn't listen, anyway!

Pelmen decided to go left. That branch ended in a wall of blank rock fifty feet beyond. He retraced his steps and went the other direction. The passage curled back and forth, ending in another fork. Pelmen went left again, and found another dead end. Pelmen was lost.

The Imperial House laughed.

The Drax table had been knocked aside, and the pieces lay scattered on the floor, forgotten. Jagd had not returned, and Ligne had tired of waiting. She was presently in hot pursuit of Rosha, and the young swordsman sweated freely as he fought to restrain his fists from permanently altering the woman's lustful expression.

Actually, the pursuit had run its course. She'd cornered him against the far wall and was struggling to insinuate her lithe, perfumed body inside his bound arms. Rosha flattened his hips and back against the wall, but it wouldn't yield. Nor would Ligne, as she succeeded in slithering into his unwilling embrace. She stretched her neck up to steal a kiss, and Rosha banged the back of his head trying to jerk away.

"What's the matter, my darling?" she cooed. "You certainly weren't so shy earlier in the afternoon . . ."

"I—I—I—" Rosha could think of no meaningful way to end the sentence. Ligne ended it for him by plastering her lips over his. He fought to hold his arms away from her writhing form, thinking how easy it would be to slip his arms up around her scented throat and choke off her kisses entirely. Instead, he forced a wide, toothy grin onto his face—a hideous grin, more snarl than smile, that caused her to lean away.

"You're mad at me," she pouted. "Because I didn't let you win the game, is that it?"

"N-n-no, no it's n-n-n—"

"Are you still upset about that silly old hood?"

"I c-c-c-c—"

"You can't talk, I know that," she sneered. Rosha jerked her tightly against him in reflexive rage, and she smiled broadly and sighed. "Ahhhh. Now that's more like it." Once again he fought the urge to strangle her, and managed to spread his arms away from her hips. She studied him with a sultry, self-confident smile. "So. Never been with a woman before, is that it?"

"I-I-I—" Once again his voice faltered, and Ligne sighed with exasperation.

"Come on, talk to me!" she demanded.

"M-m-m-maybe a-a-another sp-sp-sp-speech lesson—"

"What for?" she snarled. "What good's the first one done?"

"It t-t-t-takes t-t-time—"

"Who told you that? The clown? I don't doubt the fool did." She ducked out of his arms, and Rosha drew in a welcome breath of unscented air. "To cover his own incompetence. Where is that fool? I've not seen him all day!"

Rosha sucked in another clean draught and shrugged his

shoulders. When he saw the way the woman eyed him, he had a sudden insight into how a hunted beast must feel when finally run to ground.

"You are so good looking," the woman purred, her voice husky.

Rosha swallowed hard, and smiled. "I'm s-so p-pleased that I p-please you—"

"Do you want to please me, Rosha?" she asked pointedly, her blue eyes glowing.

"P-p-perhaps I'm not p-properly p-p-prepared—"

"You look thoroughly equipped to me."

"I mean," he hurried on, "that I f-f-feel so inadequate—"

"Let's find out!"

"—to be a proper escort!"

Ligne paused in her pursuit. "By that you mean what?"

"That—that I'm n-not worthy of you! Look at m-me!"

"I am," Ligne growled.

"I c-c-c-cannot speak, I can't c-c-carry on a p-proper c-conversation, I'm ungracious, unlettered, backward—"

"As well as broad chested, bull-necked, curly-haired . . ." The woman hummed, reaching out to stroke each feature as she listed it. Rosha jerked aside and walked away. When he stopped to look back at her, she was frowning. "Why did you walk away from me?" she demanded.

"I—I n-need more t-time. By all the powers in the Mar, woman, I was ready to kill you two days ago! P-p-perhaps—a day or two, a week . . . more speech lessons . . ."

"You're putting me off."

"No!" Rosha lied. "I'm not! I—I like you." He turned his face to the wall and forced himself to say "I . . . I even begin to—to—love—you." Suddenly he whipped around to face her. "I've heard you and Kherda talk about the acting troupe here in the ca-c-c-castle. Let m-m-me j-j-join with them!"

"Acting troupe!" Ligne exploded. "What for!"

"I know they're d-d-doing a p-play in p-praise of you. I c-could be in it! Grow more c-confident!"

She stared at him a moment, a hand on her hip, then strolled over to the spilled Drax pieces and picked one up from the floor. She studied it a moment, tossed it in the air and caught it, and then looked at him. "Maybe I'm expecting too much of you. Maybe Gerrig could teach you a thing or two about women, at the very least." She thought for another moment, then dropped the piece on the floor again. "Come along. We'll find your actors. And maybe I can reclaim my lost clown as well. This palace has been dull all afternoon." She marched smartly out of the game room, snapping her fingers at Carlad, who leaned on the wall outside the door.

It took several inquiries for them to find the rehearsal hall in this labyrinthine palace. Ligne had never bothered herself to seek it out before. Her arrival took the troupe very much by surprise. She slammed open the door and stalked in, leaving Gerrig dangling in midspeech.

"Why—why, my Lady, what a pleasant surprise," Gerrig stammered, panicked by the thought of having to perform immediately. He hadn't seen Pelmen since their encounter in the garden the day before and had no idea where he was now. "Ah—what can we do for you?"

Ligne waved her hand, and Rosha walked into the room, followed by a bored Carlad. "This is my consort," she announced. "Give him a part."

"Why, ah—" Gerrig swallowed. "We don't normally do that kind of thi—but certainly, of course, we'll surely find a part for him to play in our little entertainment, won't we, friends?" He raised his eyebrows at the others and nodded vigorously. They all chorused their approval of the idea.

"And, Gerrig," she added, leaning toward him, "while you're teaching him to use his tongue, show him a few things about using his body as well, hmmm?" She winked at him.

Gerrig smiled anxiously, hoping it looked as if he understood what she was talking about. "Certainly! We'll do it."

"Another thing. This room's too cramped, and too far away from my apartments. From now on, you rehearse in my throne room."

The big actor gagged, then recovered quickly to protest. "My Lady! This play was to be a surprise. How can we—"

"I'll not be there when you're rehearsing, idiot!" Ligne snapped. Then she looked around. "Where's my fool?"

"Ah! Yes! Your fool. Ah, Parmi, where *is* that fool?" Gerrig asked nervously.

"He's not with you, my Lady?" Parmi asked.

"If he were with me," Ligne said with a mocking patience that dripped sarcasm, "do you think I'd be looking for him? Where is he?"

"He is . . . perhaps . . . indisposed . . ."

"By what."

"Ah . . . natural causes?"

"You mean he's sick?"

"Perhaps . . ."

"When you see him, send him to me. If you're going to have my Rosha, I need some entertainment, don't I?"

"Most certainly you do, my Lady." Gerrig grinned. "And I'll see to it that you get that entertainment just as soon as the clown reports to rehearsal. And, of course, we'll work your fine young man into the script!"

Ligne didn't hear the last of his speech. She'd already disappeared out the door. Gerrig smiled and nodded at Carlad, then sidled up to Yona and whispered, "What do we do now?"

"Apparently we move to the throne room." Yona shrugged. To himself, he added, "And perhaps a little closer to the truth."

The House was still laughing at Pelmen hours later, when the exhausted shaper finally slumped against one of its walls. As near as he could tell, Pelmen had crossed his own path three times. He couldn't even find his way back to the cistern. In frustration, he raised his head and appealed to the Power. "I don't suppose you know the way out of here, do you?"

—Of course, cackled the Imperial House. But if you won't lis—

The House was interrupted by a shocking event. A powerful wind whistled through its caverns—a wind it neither initiated nor permitted.

—Where did that come from? it bellowed in amazement.

Pelmen shook his head and muttered, "You make it seem so easy." Then he hopped up and let the wind rush around him. He turned his back on it and let its pressure guide him down the tunnel.

—Magic? the Imperial House wondered. If so, this

magic felt like nothing it had ever experienced. It was painless—and cleansing.

Pelmen was impelled by the wind past branching corridors that were free of even the slightest breeze. He had no light to walk by, but he made no effort to kindle any. He knew that now he wouldn't be able to.

—This wind knows these caverns! Amazing! the castle gasped. For the wind was guiding Pelmen to the very tunnel through which Admon Faye had penetrated the lower dungeons.

Pelmen walked on boldly, passing yet another intersection of passages. Then the wind died as suddenly as it had come. At the end of the corridor he could make out a dim light. He walked swiftly toward it, and found it was shining through a small hole, just large enough to crawl through. He got down on his hands and knees and listened.

Pelmen had spent more time in dungeons than he cared to remember. During Talith's reign, he'd even been a guest in this one. He knew that prisons sounded different when there were guards present than they did when the warders were gone. He listened for the telltale sounds of soldiers. Sure, at last, that the way was clear, he shoved his shoulders into the small opening and wiggled through.

He saw immediately why the hole had never been plugged. It was hidden under a low outcropping of rock in a dark corner of this cell. As he pulled his feet through, he noticed three skeletons dangling from the walls, each still held in place by an ancient collar and chain. Pelmen wondered briefly if these were his predecessors in the office of court jester, but they'd been here too long for that. This cell had long gone unused. The door was ajar. Torchlight flickered in the hall beyond. He listened, then slipped out to investigate the corridor. It was cemetery silent. Most of these cells were clearly vacant. These were the lower dungeons—there was another floor of cells above him. It made sense that a lazy warden would pack those above to capacity before filling these lower rooms, thus saving himself extra trips up and down the stairs. Besides, it seemed Ligne preferred killing her enemies to holding them captive. Would Bronwynn be on the upper level? Or could she already be dead?

He decided to search this floor thoroughly first. He

crept down the hall, listening at each door and peering through its food slot. He paused at each only long enough to assure himself there was no one inside, then moved on to the next.

He stopped—he heard a chanting. He glanced toward the spiral stairway that led to the upper floor, but that wasn't the source of the noise. He traced the sound past the stairs to a cell door beyond them. He slipped cautiously toward it, then knelt to listen. It was a woman's voice.

"Bronwynn," he whispered, wishing immediately that he hadn't. The chanting within stopped, and there was a long period of quiet shuffling within the cell. Pelmen tried to listen to that and watch the stairs as well.

A woman's voice suddenly came through the oaken barrier. "I'm sorry to disappoint you, Prophet, but I'm not your initiate. I have been expecting you, though."

Pelmen forgot all caution, as her name tore from his lips. "Serphimera!"

Many miles to the north, in another dungeon cell, sat the Prophet of Lamath.

He wasn't a prisoner. Erri the Prophet, formerly Erri the sailor, had simply taken over the prison of the King of Lamath as the headquarters for the new faith that Pelmen had established. He never called himself the Prophet—that honor he reserved for Pelmen. But Pelmen called him that, and so did everyone else. Like it or not, Erri answered to the name.

But he never really felt worthy of the title. He missed Pelmen and longed to see him again. The longing to be near his absent friend had caused him to choose this cell for his private residence. Here they had spent their most fruitful hours together when he, Rosha, and Bronwynn had been imprisoned with Pelmen by the command of the Priestess, Serphimera. As they'd awaited Pelmen's certain execution, the real Prophet had taught him to read the weird runes in which the ancient book had been written.

The ancient book! It sat on a simple table near the small, barred window. The sun streamed in upon it, throwing the table's shadow on the straw-covered floor. The day was cloudy and, as the clouds passed overhead, the light around the table seemed to dim, then brighten, then dim again.

"My faith is like that," Erri murmured honestly. For though he was now the most respected religious leader in Lamath, there were times when the Power seemed very remote. He had learned to tolerate silence from the Power. He hadn't learned to tolerate faithlessness from himself.

He roused himself out of his ruminations and looked at the cluttered desk before him. This and the table of the book were the only additions he had made to the cell—and they were its only furnishings. The desk was a necessary addition, for it seemed these days his life was filled with paperwork—sending and receiving messages from the vizier of the King, answering requests for skyfaith initiates to come educate new masses of the population, appointing supervisors of new work, authorizing the destruction of dragon statues—all coming or going on paper. Sometimes his old sailor's tongue grew exceptionally salty as he reviled the absent Pelmen for sticking him with this responsibility. But he usually meant it all in good-natured aggravation, for Pelmen had been right about Erri's gifts. Erri had spent his life on the sea, but in his heart he had ever been a man of letters. It irked him, though, that he had to spend so much time writing, and so little reading! From where he sat, his sharp eyes could see the dust settling on the book's ornate cover!

He was also a man of action. He'd been first mate too long to shirk a duty when he saw one. He'd quickly learned that the King was as dependable as any of the host of captains he'd served under—that is, not very. He had met the King only once, when he returned from Dragonsgate with the news of Vicia-Heinox' death, and he remembered that the man had trembled throughout the interview. The vizier had explained later that Erri was the first person the King had seen in over three years. It seemed the man was scared to death of people. Asher, the Chieftain of Defense, had run the country in the King's place. But Asher had been killed by the dragon. Erri had seen the need and accepted the responsibility. All of Lamath had been turned upside down in the turmoil. Erri set about righting it again.

One of the first orders of business had been the smashing of the dragon statues. He'd marched from one end of Lamath to the other, leading a troop of idol-smashers who destroyed every symbol of the old Dragonfaith that they could find. His light blue robe, the color of the sky, had caused Lamathians to term this reformation movement the skyfaith. Erri agreed to the term, so long as it was made clear that he and the others clad in sky blue did not worship the sky, as those of the earlier religion had worshiped the dragon.

This destruction was not accomplished without incident. There were occasional clashes between skyfaithers and those of the old order—followers of Serphimera, who signaled their allegiance with dark blue gowns. Erri was hard pressed to prevent bloodshed—at one point he'd only stopped it by clubbing his own people over the head with the book. His gracious treatment of those who held other views seemed to contradict his image as a statue-smasher, but soon it began to dominate Lamath's conversation about him.

Erri sighed and looked over at the door. Though his love and tolerance had carried the day at last, he hadn't prevented the disappearance of Serphimera. That woman had traveled through the land as quickly as he had; rallying the surviving unionists with a new theology. He'd heard it everywhere. "The dragon is us! We are the dragon!" What it meant, exactly, he couldn't fathom. He hoped Pelmen would pop back around sometime soon to fill him in.

But mostly he hoped Serphimera would be found. Though he'd tried, Erri couldn't be everywhere at once. Though he'd beaten his sky-clad followers off one day, he'd been somewhere else the next, and religionists of both light and dark hues had clashed and wrestled and bled. The tales of intolerance made him weep. The stories of persecutions made him rage. In the name of the Power, people had killed people, and Erri learned during long, bitter nights of mourning that he couldn't reform a nation in a moment. By the time the dust had settled, Serphimera had disappeared. Murdered, he wondered? Imprisoned in the basement of some so-called believer? Erri sighed.

He heard a flutter of wings at the window, and glanced up in time to see a blue blur dart into his cell and settle onto the cover of the book. "Here now! You can't do that!" he shouted, pointed toward the bird, and it obligingly left the book and shot over to perch on his extended finger. "Well. I guess that means you're for me." Erri raised his finger and peered under the creature, looking for a message on the flyer's legs. "Where's your letter? Did you lose it?" The bird just looked at him, and Erri shook his head. "Probably wasn't properly tied on. Go on with you," he ordered, and he tossed the bird toward the window. The blue-flyer circled the cell, and came back to land on Erri's shoulder. "I said, go *on!*" the former sailor growled, and he pulled the little bird off its perch and marched to the window. He tossed it out the bars, and returned to his stack of work. A moment later it was back again, settling comfortably onto his head. "What's your problem, bird?" Erri roared, and he started to grab the flyer again. Then it registered. "Oh!" he nodded. "You're from Pelmen!" He let the creature maintain its perch in his graying locks and concentrated, trying to read the thoughts Pelmen had placed in its little mind. He cleared all other concerns away, and waited . . .

It took only a moment for the flyer to rid itself of its mental burden. Its mind erased, it swooped out the window, seeking some seeds and some sleep. It left a perplexed Prophet in its wake.

Erri thought for only a moment, then he sprinted for his door, hurled it open, and shouted, "Send me Naquin!" Then he walked back to the book, and fingered its ornate covering. He said nothing—he was trying to cull the salt out of his speech—but his thoughts were dark and angry. The picture of Rosha, bound and hooded, infuriated him, and the mention of Serphimera deepened his fears. He tilted his head back to glance at the beams of light that illuminated the dancing dust. "I hope you know what you're doing," he muttered. The book felt reassuring under his palm.

"Prophet?" someone called from the door.

"Come in, my friend." A gaunt skyfaither entered the room, and stood humbly before him. "Don't do that," Erri said, waving his arms toward the piles of straw. "Drop on the straw, sit on the floor, but don't stand there looking at me so formally." As he watched the initiate find a seat, Erri chuckled and added, "If I'd wanted formality, Naquin, I would have moved into your place to begin with."

Naquin smiled piously. "You would have found it terribly boring. I did."

"That's why you took to the drinking?"

"In part. Partly it was the great pressure I was under to try to sustain the worship of a self-serving, destructive monster I didn't really believe to be a god."

Erri lowered his eyes. By now, everyone in Lamath had heard the story of Naquin's transformation. Formerly the High Priest of the Dragonfaith, he had worn the jewelled hood of office through the final days of Vicia-Heinox' destructive life. By the time Erri returned from Dragonsgate with the news of the dragon's death, Naquin had disappeared. Mobs of angry citizens rushed toward the temple to destroy it, but found that Erri had boarded it up. The High Priest couldn't be found.

One night, on a walk through those ancient alleyways he'd come to know well as a sailor, Erri had found Naquin drunk in a mud puddle—and cursed him for a fool.

"I certainly got hot at you that night, didn't I?" Erri chuckled.

"It was necessary, Prophet, that I see the error of my ways, and be set on the proper path—"

"Pardon me, Naquin, for interrupting you, but you've lived around religion all your life, and you know a lot of these religious terms that don't mean much to the rest of us. I know you want to sound pious, but just speak your mind, as you did the night I found you. May not sound holy, but you'll make a lot more sense."

In actual fact, Naquin had struggled to his feet that night and cursed Erri right back. Then the two had gone off together for a long discussion about religious matters. It was a curious conversation. Naquin knew all the words and concepts, and Erri knew almost nothing. But Erri knew the Power—and Naquin didn't. Naquin didn't discover until the next morning that he'd been talking to the Prophet himself—and later on that same day he put on the sky robe for the first time.

"I apologize, Prophet. My past experience—"

"Forget it." Erri shrugged, meaning more than just to forget the moment. But men don't change overnight either. "Any news of Serphimera?" Erri asked.

"No direct word—just the same information we've been hearing for weeks. She traveled so fast that it's hard to be sure, but it seems she was last seen in the southern region.

I'm beginning to believe like everyone else—that she passed Dragonsgate." Erri nodded. "Why not just let her go?" Naquin asked. "I met the woman and had a chance to see how very dangerous she could be! Do you really want to bring her back?"

Erri graced Naquin with a slow smile. "I'd wager that if the Priestess could see you now, she'd say you were dangerous, too!" He stood up, and walked behind his desk. He picked up a piece of straw and absently began cleaning his ears with it. "Trouble is, in the face of the dragon's savagery, she still maintains her devotion to the beast. I can't understand it. I only know that Pelmen said we must love her out of it, and we can't do that if we don't know where she is."

Naquin said nothing. Though he'd never revealed it to his master, he did not care for Pelmen—never had liked him since the first night he laid eyes on the man, here in this very dungeon, and found he was a disguised powershaper. Naquin's priestly father had bred him to despise powershapers, and Pelmen was no exception. Never mind that Erri considered the man a Prophet—Naquin knew better, and if the opportunity ever arose, he intended to expose the man for what he truly was.

Erri sighed, then went on: "Much as I hate to admit it, I fear you're right about her passing Dragonsgate. But which direction? Did she go to Chaomonous or to Ngandib-Mar? I don't have a hint. That's why I've decided to send you as my envoy to one of the royal courts—to find out."

Naquin's eyes widened in surprise. "Which one?"

"A good question, and one I've been studying for days. Now, Ngandib-Mar is a land of free-spirited folk who are terribly superstitious. Certainly the woman would find a hearing there, more easily than among the cocksure, cock-eyed Chaons."

"A reasonable guess."

"On the other hand, the woman loathes powershapers, as we both know . . ." Erri studied Naquin's reactions as he went on. ". . . A feeling I believe you share with her?"

"Never trust a powershaper, my master. They'll turn on you every time."

"So you've said before. And Ngandib-Mar seems to be full of them. Has she gone south instead? That's what I want to know. There's more to it than that, however. We have . . . friends . . . in Chaomonous who inform me that the land is ripe to be claimed for the skyfaith."

"Then I'm bound for Chaomonous?" the former High Priest asked.

Erri nodded. "I want you to take a group of initiates with you to scatter throughout the countryside. Let them begin spreading the precepts of the book and explaining the Power. I want you, however, to report directly to Queen Ligne's castle. Chaomonous has a court full of snobs. Please take no offense in this, Naquin, but you'll fit right in. Your manners and training—even your fancy words— suit you admirably for the court of that Queen." Erri's eyebrows knitted, and he leaned down toward Naquin. "Besides, you're experienced at intrigue, and it seems that's essential to life in her castle. Once inside the Imperial House, you are to find the fool. Do whatever he tells you."

Naquin's eyes flew open. "What?"

"That's right, the fool—whoever answers to that name. He's our . . . friend." Erri gazed into Naquin's eyes. "Will you do it?"

"How could I refuse my Prophet?"

Erri smiled, clasped Naquin's hands warmly, and pulled him to his feet. "Go with my blessings," Erri ordered. "And remember. You represent the Power now—not yourself."

"It seems we always meet in dungeons," said the woman.

"Shh . . ." Pelmen hissed, looking up at the stairway.

"Don't concern yourself with the noise. Those above us can't hear what takes place down here. That's why the Queen had me put in this lower dungeon. So she and I could speak privately."

"But—why are you here?" Pelmen whispered. "Why are you in her prison?"

"It appears that I am the Queen's . . . confidant. She's a woman with deep spiritual needs—she comes to me for comfort."

"She keeps her confidant in the dungeon?"

"She is also a woman of great insecurities."

Pelmen peered through the bars that crosshatched the window in Serphimera's door, and gazed into those emerald eyes that had entranced him so many months before. His mind wandered, stunned by the sheer joy of seeing her face once again. Then he remembered where he was, and his white forehead knitted in concern. "How did you know me?" he asked cautiously.

Her half-grin took him by surprise. He had never before seen Serphimera smile. "How indeed? How do you think, Prophet? Or should I say player? The silly white grease on your face doesn't befit a supposed holy man."

Pelmen's heart sagged. "You know . . . so much . . ." he began.

"Oh, I know a great deal about you. Ligne's told me all she remembers, and I've given her an earful as well." Serphimera's eyebrows arched disdainfully. "I let her know exactly what I thought of you. And of course, she agreed." Serphimera walked back into her cell. Pelmen had a chance now to see into it, and was surprised again. It was well furnished, with a hand-carved headboard and a large bed, a desk, several chairs, and a rich rug. A dozen silver candlesticks lined the walls. Ligne obviously kept her in style.

"You still blame me for the death of the dragon," he said softly.

"Shouldn't I?" she asked over her shoulder. Her long black hair coursed down her back, and the flickering candlelight enhanced her delicate beauty. Hers was not the blatant prettiness, the sophisticated sensuousness of Ligne. Serphimera's features were at once mysterious and innocent. Where Ligne called out of men a hot, objective lust, Serphimera warmed the spirit. Her eyes were open windows to her feelings, for Serphimera never hid anything she thought. She broadcast her emotions to any who would listen with their eyes—and Pelmen listened now to her anger. "You killed him."

"He would have eaten you."

"I longed for him to!"

"You longed to be one with the Power. That wasn't the way."

"The Power!" she spat. "What has this Power done for Lamath? Stripped her of her god and cast her spinning into a sea of faithlessness! Every shrine is destroyed, every monastery scattered! Is this what your Power does?"

"If it must—to reach through to the people—"

"I was reaching the people!" the woman cried, and she turned away from him again to walk to the blank wall on the far side of the room.

Pelmen looked nervously behind him at the stairway. It occurred to him then that in all his days in dungeons he'd never once seen a guard respond to a prisoner's shouting with anything other than apathy. He looked back into the cell. "And that's why you're here?"

"I came to urge the Queen to march on Lamath, to rid the land of heretics and reinstitute the worship of Lord Dragon."

Pelmen waited through a long pause.

"She laughed at me," Serphimera finished.

Pelmen waited another moment before he spoke. "I never did that," he said.

Serphimera sat on the bed. "When I told her the Lord Dragon would burn her palace for her disobedience, she laughed again—but she also ordered me to be brought here. It was only later that she began to come and talk to me."

"Made you her confidant."

"Exactly." Serphimera gestured at the room. "She treats me well."

Pelmen smothered his rage at the Queen, and whispered resolutely, "I'll get you out."

"Oh, no need of that," Serphimera said. She stood up and walked toward him. "I shall leave this castle as I came in . . . walking freely."

"But how do you—"

"How do I know? The same way I knew you were coming, Prophet. I had a vision."

Pelmen had brushed with Serphimera's visions before. Whatever their source, they tended to come true. Her words made him feel very vulnerable. "Serphimera . . . do you . . . tell the Queen your visions?"

The Priestess looked away. "Most of them. That's one reason she comes to call. Among other things, she seems to see me as some sort of—fortune teller." Serphimera bit down on the words. "The humiliation of it! Priestess of the dragon, viewed in the same light as a Mari witcher woman!"

"Have you told her about my—disguise?"

Serphimera met his eyes. "No."

Pelmen experienced a flood of relief. "Why not?"

Her gaze remained fixed. "I think we both know the answer to that."

Her lips looked lovely. He wanted to kiss them.

As if reading his mind, Serphimera backed away and crossed her arms. She fixed her features in an imitation of scorn—but her eyes told a different tale altogether.

"I don't suppose your vision told you how you'll manage to walk out as freely as you came?"

"No."

"Then is it possible that I might play some part in that event?"

"Perhaps."

"Fine. Then—"

"But I doubt it."

Pelmen looked at her, puzzled. "Why?"

"Because you came crawling in through a tunnel. Knowing something of your previous antics, I daresay you would expect me to crawl out of this dungeon on my belly."

"And you wouldn't do that," he countered.

"That wasn't in the vision."

Pelmen bit his lip in consternation, and thought for a moment. "You knew I was coming. Is there anything else you know that might help me?"

Serphimera smiled. "That all depends on what it is you're trying to do."

"I came down here expecting to find the Lady Bronwynn. She's the rightful heir to the throne of this arrogant land, and I'd like to see her on it."

Serphimera's nostrils flared slightly at the mention of the Princess' name. "Bronwynn. Isn't she the rude little girl who followed you so devoutly?"

"She was one of my initiates, yes—you met her with me in the dungeon of Lamath."

"And if she's crowned, what will that make you?" Serphimera asked, her lips curling into the tiniest of sneers. "The new king?"

Pelmen laughed aloud. He hadn't meant to, it just came out. He clapped his hand across his face and stepped swiftly to the base of the stairwell to listen. Then he came back, still chuckling at the idea. He laughed harder when he saw the glare on Serphimera's face.

"Well?" she snapped angrily.

"No," he chuckled. "There's a lad upstairs who'd take my head off in a stroke if I tried." Pelmen's smile softened from mirth to one of concern. "I just want to restore to this land a little peace and security."

"As you did to Lamath?" she snapped.

"If you know anything of Bronwynn, my Lady, I urgently request you share it." His face had turned grim—as grim as was possible in white face, anyway. Serphimera had to smile at that. His serious expression remained, however, and she grew solemn as well.

"She spent many days in the pit at the far end of the corridor. The Queen treated her as badly as she's treated me well. I heard her groans each night. Then one night I heard them no more. I feared she was dead, but the Queen shared with me later the information that someone had snatched her out of the dungeon. She told me whom she suspected, and I'm dismayed to have to relay it, for I travelled with the man and know him for a cruel, lying unbeliever. His—"

"How wonderful!" Pelmen snarled, for he knew immediately whom she meant. "We're stuck in Ligne's dungeon, and Bronwynn's in the hands of Admon Faye!"

CHAPTER THIRTEEN

An Ancient Spell

"MY ARM IS TIRED!" Bronwynn yelled.

"Do you think an enemy will hold off and let you rest it?" Admon Faye challenged, then he swung his mock blade around savagely to crack across Bronwynn's left shoulder. "Come girl. Parry or feel pain."

Bronwynn hurled her wooden weapon away, and it clacked off the stone floor several times before coming to rest against the wall. "Now both my shoulders ache," she snarled, and she grabbed them with opposing hands and began massaging. Admon Faye raised his weapon as if to strike again. "Go ahead!" she screamed belligerently. "Beat me black and blue!"

He lowered his practice sword and grinned at her. "I'm just trying to teach you to defend yourself—"

"Maybe I don't want to learn to defend myself today!"

"Pick up the sword and return to work!" he ordered her. "We haven't much time!"

"You haven't much time," Bronwynn snarled, turning her back on him. "I have plenty. Ow!" she yelped suddenly as the slaver whacked her across the rump.

"You're lazy," Admon Faye grunted. "I'm offering you

a kingdom, girl. Don't you consider it worth a bruise or two to be the Queen?"

"Queen!" she snapped. "What kind of rule could I have, with you and Flayh constantly looking over my shoulder? That's no reign—just a new kind of captivity!"

"You're a child. You still believe it possible to be free."

Bronwynn rubbed her shoulders and sulked. "No, I don't."

Admon Faye glanced up at her jutting lip, and snickered. "Pining for your boyfriend? He's not pining for you."

"You shut up about Rosha!"

"Why should I?" the slaver sneered. "I speak only what I heard from the magic glass . . . perhaps my lady missed that?" he mocked.

"I didn't miss it!" Bronwynn flared. "I just don't believe it!"

"And why is that?" he baited her. "Oh, don't tell me. Let me guess. Your Rosha lad is too pure to sully himself with such a scheming, wicked woman. Right this minute he's in a room somewhere in your father's old castle, weeping romantically for you, his only love."

"Rosha doesn't weep," Bronwynn muttered, her head turned away from him.

Admon Faye hooted. "You believe that?" he laughed harshly. "You actually believe he's faithful and pure?"

"Why shouldn't I believe it?" she roared.

The slaver's face turned incredibly hard. "Because that's not the way life is, little girl. And underneath that pout, you know it's not."

Bronwynn whirled away from him and walked over to stare angrily out at the sleazy gray sky. This practice session had been scheduled for the courtyard, but the weather had refused to cooperate, dropping showers on the keep from early morning throughout the afternoon. The snow that had frosted the ground for months had melted away, leaving behind a thick, black muck in place of the court. The change in climate made it as miserable inside the castle as it was outside. Bronwynn's soaking practice garb clung uncomfortably to her sticky back. But if her body felt as if she'd been swimming in a swamp, it couldn't compare to the murky wasteland inside her soul. She fought to hold the tears down, but they were there—salty tears that struggled to push their way into her cheeks, to add their small contribution to her misery.

"Face it. That boy is having the time of his life!" the slaver cackled lustfully. "He's learning things that—"

Bronwynn shot like a blur across the room to scratch viciously for the slaver's eyes. She was no match for Admon Faye. He slung her past him to ram into the wall. She slumped to her knees in pain and leaned against it. Those tears that had threatened to drizzle now fell in a flood.

Admon Faye walked over to stand above the sobbing Princess. "Get up," he snarled contemptuously. "Get up, and pick up that weapon. I'll teach you how to take some hide off that woman! Wouldn't you like that? To have Ligne's delicate neck at the cutting edge of your blade?"

Bronwynn's tears subsided, but the hot pain in the back of her throat remained. She thought for a moment of Ligne. She focused her mind on a mental image of the woman's mocking smile and hated her. But when Rosha edged into that picture alongside Ligne, Bronwynn's feelings of hurt and betrayal overpowered her hatred, robbing her of the will to fight. Her tears flooded anew.

Admon Faye stepped back, a bit chagrined. He'd never seen the girl weep before, and it surprised him. As waves of despair swept Bronwynn's body, raising the pitch of her sobs, the slaver turned his attention to other matters. He'd caused a host of people to cry in the course of his career and recognized that point when tears made further work impossible. He left her sobbing and went hunting for Flayh.

Finding the powershaper took some time. No one seemed to know where he was. Pezi suggested the library, but if Flayh were inside, he didn't respond. Admon Faye strolled slowly through the hall, looking carefully at each of the dogs who scrambled up to meet him, but saw no unusual intelligence in the eyes of any of them. He wrapped his cloak around him and walked out into the drizzle.

As he stepped carefully around the deepest puddles, he noticed a small figure standing on the battlements above him. The man didn't even bother to cover his bald pate. It took a few moments for Admon Faye to climb up to him. "Enjoying the rain?" the slaver asked with cruel humor.

"I was enjoying the privacy," Flayh responded without looking at him.

"We have business to conclude, you and I." Admon Faye frowned. "I thought you were interested in haste."

"I was," Flayh mumbled. "I was. Until I destroyed all possibility of my plan's success with my too hasty temper."

"Why, I thought you acted with great moderation," Admon Faye mocked.

"The Council in an uproar, the conclave dispersed prematurely—" Flayh shook his head. "A tragedy. And all because of this young Tahli-Damen."

"You surprise me, Flayh. For a powershaper, you seem to have a limited imagination."

Flayh looked at the slaver and raised an eyebrow. "Explain."

"So the rest of the merchants know, now, that you're a wizard. Why should that matter?"

"The houses are split!" Flayh's eyes flashed indignantly. "Nothing could be worse for business than interhouse rivalry. Tahli-Damen was right about that, at least."

"You merchants." Admon Faye snickered. "So tied up in your cliques and Councils that you can't see the world as it is. Take a hard look, Flayh!" The slaver gestured across Westmouth Plain. "The world. It's free for the taking. And you and I, we have the power to take our share. I never played any of your merchant games, and I've done all right."

"And yet you wanted a seat on the Council," Flayh reminded him.

"On my own terms and for my own purposes. I still do. Relax, Flayh. You've done no irreparable damage to your precious Council, just shook it up a bit. A power shift was inevitable, after the dragon. Your little fireworks display just let these others know what kind of forces they're dealing with."

"You are bold and inventive, Admon Faye, but you lack experience in dealing with merchant minds. The Council of Elders is damaged, and if it should be reconstituted in the days to come, I fear the house of Ognadzu will no longer be welcomed. Jagd and Ligne have locked me out of Chaomonous, Pelmen the Prophet has chased me from Lamath, and our dominance in this land is threatened by this same Tahli-Damen."

"Since when have you concerned yourself with mere business matters?"

"That's just it. I've spent so much time improving my skill at shaping that I've let my family business fail."

Admon Faye smirked, and shrugged. "So it fails. Don't worry, Flayh. You can always get work as the court powershaper in the High Fortress."

"What?"

The slaver shook his head. "Pardon my jest. It just seems so out of character to see the ruler of the mighty house of Ognadzu bemoan his family's fortunes."

"What were you saying about a High Fortress?"

Admon Faye chuckled. "Over a year ago, the family of Pahd asked me to find them a powershaper to heal King Pahd of his laziness. They wanted Pelmen, actually—"

"Pelmen." Flayh spat.

"He's not my favorite either," Admon Faye said grimly. "This twisted visage of mine is a gift he gave me long ago."

"Pelmen did that?" Flayh asked.

"Let's say he played a role in its shaping. But that's another story. I came out here to—"

"Did you find them a powershaper?"

"The Pahds? No. Why such interest in this? I was only making a joke!"

"So you were. You were trying to assure me that our plan will succeed, in any case, and that the fortunes of my house will soon be restored."

"I guarantee it. Perhaps these other houses do mistrust you, but with my band in control of Dragonsgate, they're in no position to threaten us."

"You're unafraid of the combined might of the merchant Council?"

"Not if I have as an ally the most populous of the houses." Admon Faye grinned back. "For all your moaning, you certainly don't deny that you could field a formidable army from your cousins alone. And which merchant would be fool enough to challenge it, when he knows it's led by a proven wizard?"

Flayh nodded. "You're probably right."

"I am right," snorted Admon Faye. "You may depend on it."

"I do, slaver!" Flayh said quickly. "Indeed, I do. For if this plan fails, I may be forced to seek employment elsewhere, doing dragon-knows-what. I assume your roughnecks are already in place?"

"You mean the members of my house?" Admon Faye asked.

Flayh chuckled—a malicious laugh coming from low in his throat. "Yes. I mean your family. Are those your chosen colors?" He nodded toward the sweaty garments Admon Faye wore. The slaver's tunic was a dull gray. His leggings were an equally drab green.

"I thought them appropriate." Admon Faye grinned.

"Brutally ugly," said Flayh, meeting the slaver's eyes.

Admon Faye smiled no longer. "As I said. Appropriate. Also practical. These are the colors of the Great South Fir. A hundred times I've watched your riders move through my forest, completely oblivious to my presence. But of course, they looked so noble, so prosperous in their blue and lime tunics. Very favorable targets, to be sure."

"What you wear is of no concern to me. What you *do* is." Flayh raised an inquiring eyebrow.

"Yes, my band is in place."

"Fine. And the girl?"

"I'm working with her."

"Don't rush her. I learned that with Ligne. I paved her a path to the throne room of Chaomonous because she seemed empty-headed and pliable enough to be controllable later."

"Oh?" Admon Faye smiled. "Ligne believes she came to her exalted position entirely on her own."

"I realize she does. And the mudgecurdle Jagd has encouraged her to think so, milking her at will. That's why I want him dead as soon as possible, and her, too." Flayh sighed. "I never guessed things would turn out as they did. That's why this time, I want to be certain the girl knows who her masters are before we give her the crown!"

"She's learning." Admon Faye snickered.

"Be certain, before you move. Speed is important, yes, but not as important as success!"

"You're talking to me, Flayh, not Pezi," Admon Faye responded, annoyance showing in his voice.

"Forgive me," Flayh said, shaking his head. "I've been surrounded by my dense relations so long, I've had to make a habit of double-checking their every move. When the girl is ready—and I leave that decision to you—notify me by flyer. Of course, once you've disposed of Jagd, we'll have a more direct link of communication."

"You mean the other pyramid."

"I do. Pezi will retain his. He's an oaf, of course, but an occasional burst of savage cunning has convinced me to keep him around. Besides, he's in the family, and thoroughly tame, and he shuts up when I tell him to. I didn't enjoy the period of Tohn's possession of the object. My dead cousin had an inflated moral sense—something I trust you've never been plagued with?" The slaver guffawed at that, and Flayh nodded. "Nor have I. Three nights after you toss the bird to say you're ready, Pezi and I will be watching our pyramids. That should give you time to capture the castle and seize Jagd's crystal . . . ?" Flayh left the question dangling, his eyes asking for yet another assurance that this plot would succeed.

"I'll be there. And our little Lady Bronwynn will be on her throne."

"I do hope so." Flayh nodded "I've been surrounded lately by people who have disappointed me. I have confidence you're made of sterner stuff. You're leaving for the pass in the morning?"

"That's the plan."

Flayh looked at the skies. "Maybe the weather will clear up. If I don't see you before then, I wish you well in your journey. Now if you'll excuse me, I have some urgent business in my library."

Admon Faye watched the wrinkled merchant scurry away, and scramble eagerly down from the battlements. Flayh puzzled him. He wondered if he should be worried, then dismissed the thought. "He's a powershaper," the slaver said to himself, "and all powershapers are a bit strange."

He made his own way down the slick steps, and back into the practice hall. He found Bronwynn still lying on the floor. He decided to try the soft approach. He walked over and knelt beside her, reaching out to touch her shoulder. "I don't suppose you've cried yourself to sleep, have you?"

"No."

"You've been thinking about what I said."

"Yes," she said after a moment.

"I've been thinking about what you said, too. And I think I can understand. Of course you don't feel like recapturing a crown when you've lost your lover. But tell me this. After what we all heard Jagd say the other day, if you could have your Rosha here right now, what would you do?"

Bronwynn sniffed, and growled, "I'd kick him in the teeth!"

Admon Faye chuckled. The low, soothing tone of his voice contrasted sharply with his words, as he said, "Oh, but I'm going to teach you how to get much better vengeance than that. Here . . ." He handed her the wooden practice sword again. His calm manner planted the seed deeply in Bronwynn's mind. Like the grass outside responding to the warmth of spring, the notion of vengeance took root and grew.

The next morning the sun came out. The rain was gone, blown eastward in the night to Ngandib. Strong, cool winds continued to rip the plain this morning. Bronwynn had been bundled aboard her horse by Flayh's servants, and now she and Admon Faye rode from Castle Tohn against a heavy gale that seemed resolved to blow them back inside. She squinted against the whistling gusts, looking up at the crags of Dragonsgate, outlined sharply against the cloudless sky. Snow still topped those peaks, but the hills below bore the unmistakable signs of early spring. There was green everywhere—across this Westmouth Plain as far as she could see; up in the high valley that formed the heart of the pass itself; and tufting every patch of ground that clung tenuously to the faces of the cliffs. The wind made her eyes blur and, in the same breath, stirred every branch and blade. For a moment it seemed that all the world was astir with the writhing and twisting of living green beings. Amid the emerald shimmer of life, the mountains stood cold and firm. But the shrubs and the grasses bore brilliant witness to an immutable truth proven anew with each cycle of the sun—that life will not be denied. Less than a year before,

Vicia-Heinox had burned every green thing from this, his ancient home. Only a few short days ago, the pass had been clogged with snow. But the snow had melted—the dragon was dead—and the grass lived on and grew.

Freed of the castle's stifling closeness, Bronwynn inhaled a deep draught of the heady new possibilities before her. She was alive, she was young, and after months of hopeless captivity she at last had a chance to claim her rightful inheritance. For the few moments of their windswept ride she forgot Admon Faye completely and dreamed again the dreams of her girlhood, dreams that had been born long ago in the warm security of her father's court. But her exhilaration was fleeting. Thoughts of her father's house led inevitably to thoughts of Rosha, and the fresh, clean air of freedom turned stale and lifeless in the wake of those memories.

Her tears of the day before had been an exception. Bronwynn had never been much of a crier. She didn't weep now, though the hard lump in her throat might have been eased by the cleansing of tears. Instead she set her jaw and scorned the self she'd been when she'd loved the stuttering warrior. "He'll pay," she muttered between clenched teeth. Then she lashed her horse needlessly and leaned low over its neck.

Admon Faye glanced over at her in time to see her lips move. His grim smile went unseen, and he turned his attention back to the oncoming pass. Already a knot of gray-clad riders formed a line abreast the narrowest stretch of Dragonsgate's Westmouth. They knew him and the girl. They were only following his explicit orders not to let anyone approach the pass without stopping them with a show of force. As his sharp eyes searched the line, he saw a struggle evolving among a group of unmounted warriors to his right. He turned his reins in that direction and spurred his horse toward the disturbance.

"I tell you I belong to Admon Faye!" a lank character he didn't recognize was shouting. The man wrestled to free himself from the sure grip of two of the slaver's trusted comrades. Another stranger, a squat fellow who wore an expression of sheer disgust, no longer struggled against his captors. It was this short bandit who first noticed Admon Faye's approach. The man seemed to sigh in resignation.

"You belong to me?" Admon Faye asked. The tall stranger twisted around to smile up at his hero. Pinter's smile froze on his face at his first glimpse of the slaver's monumental ugliness. Admon Faye let him stare a moment. Then he demanded, "Well?"

"Ah—yes!" Pinter said with forced brightness. "That is, I long to be—"

"These two attacked us when we rode into the pass," a wrinkled old slaver grunted. "Claimed they were members of your band and demanded tribute in your name."

"I told you they were cutthroats," Tibb whispered to his wildly grinning companion.

"And we meant it!" Pinter defended. "We have some tribute to offer you!"

"Don't—" Tibb snapped, trying to stop his cohort before Pinter got the words out. Failing, he winced, sighed, then shook his head.

"Tribute?" Admon Faye asked. "Show me."

Pinter grinned proudly. "Show him, Tibb."

Tibb's expression of rueful disgust returned, as he jerked an arm free from one of his captors, reached into his shoulder pouch, and pulled out three copper coins. He held them out to the slaver.

Admon Faye gazed at Tibb's palm. "That's it?"

"That's it," Tibb muttered matter-of-factly.

"We would have had more," Pinter explained sheepishly, "but somebody robbed us."

Admon Faye still stared at the coins. "I could get more than that just by selling your bodies for tugolith fodder!"

"Didn't I tell you?" Tibb sighed to his friend.

"Please, Lord Faye!" Pinter begged, dropping to his knees at the slaver's feet. "I realize we don't appear very likely prospects for your band, but you've got to understand—you've arrived at a difficult time for us. We're actually much better outlaws than we appear!"

Admon Faye winked at his fellows. "Lord Faye. I like that."

"We actually had a tidy sum accumulated to present to you. We were just outsmarted by a fiendish Mari freetrader, who got us so interested in one of his metal pots that we didn't notice when he took off with our bag of gold!"

"I see." Admon Faye nodded with mock gravity. "And you still have this pot?"

Pinter and Tibb exchanged pained expressions, then Tibb blurted out, "Actually, we sold it the next day to another trader for these three pence." Tibb shrugged. "We're not bad thieves, really. Just terrible businessmen."

"But we can handle our swords," Pinter inserted proudly.

Admon Faye raised a hairy eyebrow at his grizzled lieutenant. The man nodded. "They gave us a go before we overpowered them."

The slaver glanced back at the two forlorn thieves, obviously amused. "You want to join my band, yet battle with my warriors?"

"How were we to know they really belonged to you?" Tibb barked. "Just because they said so doesn't make it so. We're living proof!"

"Presently living," the brutal slaver corrected. "With no guarantee that will continue." Admon Faye stalked around the two would-be recruits, examining them as a horse trader inspects his livestock. Finally he snorted and muttered, "Very well. You may present your swords to me."

Pinter cleared his throat. "We would, however——"

"However what?"

"Your men took 'em away from us!" Tibb growled.

Admon Faye glanced at his warriors, and they quickly passed the two thieves their weapons. In a time-honored gesture the two knelt and held their blades out before them. They contrasted sharply. Lanky Pinter offered his polished sword proudly, a smile of victory lighting up his face. Barrel-shaped Tibb, on the other hand, still wore his look of disgust as he offered his bent and battered blade to his new master. Admon Faye noted the odd angle of Tibb's weapon and chortled uncontrollably, slapping his companions, who also cackled at the sight. Then the slaver clamed himself and asked in ritual fashion, "Your names?"

"I am Pinter," Pinter said grandly.

"I'm Tibb," his friend grunted.

"Very well. I accept your service . . . Pinter the proud, and Tibb the twisted . . ." Here he convulsed again with mirth, and couldn't continue.

"Go on with you," instructed Admon Faye's wrinkled

companion. "You know where the soup pot is." Pinter and Tibb rose hurriedly then, and made their way up the pass to the spot where the slavers had pitched camp.

Admon Faye wiped the tears from his cheeks and grinned at his lieutenant. "Other than that, how did you find things here?"

"Undisturbed. The two bunglers had not discovered our cache of weapons—"

"Evidently!" Admon Faye cackled, still thinking of Tibb's sword.

"—and all is ready for us to move, whenever you choose."

Admon Faye nodded. "Very good. The young lady seems to be coming along well. If I can increase her combat confidence, I think she'll be ready as well."

"Who will you assign to build her confidence?"

"Who better than our new recruits?" Admon Faye snickered, and the other slaver laughed aloud. They slapped one another's backs as they made their way to the soup pot.

Flayh's hands trembled. He stared at the ornate page spread before him, awed by the crystalline clarity of the words scratched upon it. How many years had this book sat on a dusty shelf in this library? Power unheard of, power beyond the imagination, hidden between these gilt-edged sheets, patiently enduring the passage of time! Surely Tohn had never read it. Tohn, the man of action, Flayh thought to himself as he winked contemptuously at the flickering candle. Tohn had probably never entered this room, much less plowed doggedly through its stacks of musty tomes to find the jewels of precious thought buried here. But Flayh had. The powershaper lifted his shaking arms in exultation. His ultimate victory was assured him, for he now owned a copy of an ancient master's spell-book!

No one had instructed Flayh in how to shape the powers. He'd learned everything he knew on his own, through hard work and ceaseless experimentation. His own library in Lamath had been worthless, for those volumes had been filled with religious garbage, more concerned with miracles than magic. But this was Ngandib-Mar, land of wizards! Here—its pages caked with choking dust, some of them shredding with age—sat a teacher. And what a teacher!

Flayh's old eyes rested upon the most spectacular spell of all. With this knowledge, added to that he already possessed, Flayh could bring a castle to life!

He rose and paced the tiny sliver of floor that was not clogged with still more books. "I'll need the High Fortress of Ngandib, of course. That's a castle of substance, an unassailable citadel that will soon be able to defend itself from attack, leaving me free to concentrate on my craft without interference." No longer would he concern himself with the unpredictable maneuvering of the Council of Elders. Oh, he would keep his hand in, of course, but with Admon Faye as his ally and this new found spell-book, the Council was no longer necessary to him. He would go to Ngandib and volunteer his services as court powershaper. With this new ability he could quickly control Pahd—and with his puppet Queen on the golden throne, he'd control two-thirds of the world! "*Then*," he muttered, "I can turn my attention to Lamath—and Pelmen."

He summoned Pezi to meet him in his apartments. Pezi entered Flayh's room as he always did—cringing, expecting a tongue-lashing, uncertain as ever about why. Flayh smiled sweetly, making Pezi even more anxious. "Have a seat, my boy!" said Flayh. Pezi obeyed. Flayh beamed. "How are you doing, nephew?"

"Fine, uncle," Pezi replied. If Flayh was expecting any elaboration, he was disappointed.

"Getting along well, are you?"

"Fine, uncle," Pezi said.

"Are you enjoying Ngandib-Mar?"

"It's fine, uncle," Pezi replied.

"Liking the climate?"

"It's fine, uncle," Pezi answered. Pezi was suspicious. What was his uncle driving at?

Flayh kept on smiling, staving off exasperation. How to get the lad's attention? He had a sudden inspiration.

"Had any good meals lately?"

Pezi's interest immediately picked up. "Oh yes! I had a stuffed pheasant leg this afternoon with a dish of mallinsok pudding, and a—"

"Fine, nephew," Flayh cut him off. He knew from long experience that Pezi could wax positively rhapsodic on the subject of an onion soufflé, and he'd already accomplished his purpose. The fat merchant was at least listening. "I've been studying you, Pezi. You have potential."

"I do?" Pezi asked. He quickly altered that to a quasi-firm expression of self-confidence. "I do."

"Yes," Flayh smiled, carefully avoiding the subject of what Pezi had potential for. "That's why I'm placing you in charge of this manor."

Pezi nearly swallowed his tongue. "You what?" he exclaimed.

"You were a competent enough manager in Chaomonous—not brilliant, but so few of us in the family really are—and I believe you can handle the responsibility. If—"

"If what, Uncle Flayh!" Pezi was excited.

"If you'll concentrate with your brain instead of your belly." Flayh stood. "I'll be travelling for a while, and someone needs to handle the Mari accounts. Trade will soon be returning to normal, with control restored to the pass. Of course, Admon Faye is readying a strike for Ligne's heart, and you'll need to notify me by flyer immediately when you've received word. After his conquest of Chaomonous and his recovery of Jagd's pyramid, we'll be able to converse regularly."

"Yes, uncle!" Pezi responded. He was flabbergasted. He, Pezi, in charge of the Mari accounts! But Pezi was suspicious by nature, and he wasn't a dummy. Obviously his uncle was planning something. And knowing Flayh, it would be deliciously sinister. "What are you going to be doing?"

"What business is that of yours?" Flayh snarled. Pezi sank back into his pitiable chair, chastened. "That's not for you to know . . . yet," Flayh went on, a bit more cordially. "All you need to know is where to post the flyer, informing me of Admon Faye's move."

"Fine, uncle," Pezi replied. "Ah . . . where will that be?"

Flayh got a faraway look in his eye and appeared to stare through the room's western wall. "I'm bound for the palace of Pahd mod Pahd-el—the fortress of the High City of Ngandib."

CHAPTER FOURTEEN

Drax

BURIED IN THE TIMELESS DARKNESS, they couldn't know that they had talked away the morning and most of the afternoon. Pelmen and Serphimera knew only that they found each other's presence enchanting, and neither wanted to be first to break off the conversation. For the first time in their unusual relationship they felt really free to talk. She teased him, her emerald eyes flashing warmly as she charmed him with her mischievous smile. Again and again, his quick wit and self-mocking humor pulled trills of unexpected laughter from within her. They leaned on the door, clinging to the bars that parted them until their legs could stand no more. Then they slumped to the floor, propping their heads in their hands as they continued their rapt discussion through the door's narrow food slot. Mostly they compared backgrounds. His experience as a cosmopolitan traveler contrasted sharply with the memories of this small-town girl from the Lamathian farm lands. They were as different as their origins. It was no surprise that they seemed to agree on almost nothing. The surprising thing was how little their differences mattered at the moment. They skirted the issues of religion and faith entirely, realizing that a chasm too deep for even love to bridge separated their two views. While that difference loomed as a giant question mark between them, they both ignored it, preferring for the moment the warmth of one another's eyes, and the halting hope that perhaps even that wall could someday be breeched. Occasionally verbal conversation ceased entirely, and their lips communicated silently by touching. The food slot permitted little contact, so they stood again and kissed between the bars.

Their kisses saved Pelmen from discovery, for it was during one of those sweet silences that they heard sandals slapping on the stairway. Serphimera's eyes shot open in shock, and she whispered, "My dinner!"

"I'll be back," he whispered intensely. Then he streaked down the hall, past the stairway toward the half-open cell door at the far end of the corridor.

"Ho!" he heard someone cry behind him. "Is someone there?" He slipped into the cell and wasted no time slithering head first through the narrow gap into the caverns beyond. There he paused and listened. There was no sound of scuttling soldiers, no shouts of alarm. Evidently Serphimera had succeeded in covering his escape.

Pelmen sat in the dark, contemplating this new situation. He was hungry. He was tired. And now that he'd at last been forced out of the warmth of Serphimera's gaze, the seriousness of her circumstances finally impacted on him. Now he had to evolve some plan to extricate both Serphimera and Rosha from Ligne's grasp—and then to deal with Admon Faye. And he didn't even know his way out. "I hope you're still around," he mumbled fervently, then crawled to his feet and started down the corridor in the dark.

He tried to concentrate on solving the maze, but his thoughts kept drifting back to Serphimera. He'd be counting his steps, trailing one hand along an uneven wall, then would realize suddenly that for the past ten or fifteen paces he'd been replaying some snatch of their lengthy conversation, and that his count was hopelessly off. From time to time he would stop and wave his arms above him, searching for some drafty sign of the Power's presence. He felt none. He wasn't surprised.

The Power did not jump when he called. He had no assurance that his every request would immediately be met.

If past experience were any guide to the Power's actions, Pelmen could count on no assistance until he'd exhausted his own resources. Often in the past, when he'd felt he had no other alternatives, a silence from the Power had demanded that he seek new ones—and he'd found new alternatives in every case. Other times, the Power had come unbidden, before Pelmen realized his own inability to cope with the particular struggle at hand. The relationship was complex and constantly puzzling, forcing him into continual reevaluation of the Power's nature . . . and sometimes even of its existence. At other times, the Power's presence was so overwhelming as to brook no doubt whatsoever. There seemed no logical consistency to the Power's participation in his life, and yet—a perplexing patterning appeared to run through all of their relating. It was not quite capricious, but certainly unpredictable—beyond him, somehow. All in all, it was easier to shape than to be shaped, but far less exhilarating. He had learned to live with the ambiguity between the two.

At the moment, it appeared he had not exhausted his own resources.

His foot sloshed into water, and he froze against the wall. Like a shaft of light in this dark tomb, a long-forgotten memory broke into his consciousness with a force that left him gasping. He saw before him the book, spread open to the pages of prophecy he had come to term the "cryptics" because of their hidden purposes. A single phrase stood out boldly for him to read: "Deal gently with the House that speaks, lest it make the waters rise." The line had been meaningless when he'd first read it, meaningless when he'd memorized it. But the cryptics were always meaningless until they were needed. This one had suddenly become so.

"House?" Pelmen asked tentatively. "Are you listening to me?"

For once, it wasn't. It had done a very good job of shutting the fool and his lady out of its thoughts completely. And for very good reason.

The castle had watched manifold love affairs blossom, flourish, and fade within its walls. Long ago, the high drama of such involvements had been intriguing. It had watched with some amusement the initial stirrings, listened intently to the inevitable counsel of friends, sniggered with the naughty glee of a Peeping Tom at the final consummation. Thus involved, however, it had been drawn unwillingly to witness the often tragic outcomes of one affair after another—the miscommunication, the pride, the jealousy, stubbornness, the selfishness that presaged broken heart after broken heart. And though it often knew far more about these relationships than either participant and could clearly see the pathways to reconciliation, it was powerless to help. No one took its advice.

The house had tried then, for a time, to view love as a broad comedy, and the broken hearts as merely comic pratfalls that soon would heal, their causes forgotten. That paled too. It grew tired of the sameness of it all—the same ritual, repeated infinitely, from the crown through the craftsman to the crassest of slaves. It concluded at last that human love was an insidious disease, excessively communicable, universally endemic—and thoroughly depressing to one utterly and hopelessly alone. The Imperial House dismissed love affairs as unimportant. It found that easier than wishing there were another castle nearby that could think, and speak—and love.

So when Pelmen and Serphimera had drifted into the same predictable patterns of conversation the House had heard so many times before, it took care to look elsewhere. At the moment, there was a mystery unfolding, and it was trying to find answers to some questions. There had been several conferences between the Queen and her Lord of Security in the past two days, and it had missed the most critical of these, being distracted by the pain from the pyramid. Now it followed Joss from room to room, trying to account for the burst of troop activity within its walls since the General's return. But the castle was discovering Joss to be a tight-lipped individual. For whatever reason, the Lord of Security had spent the afternoon cross-examining his dungeon guards, but the Imperial House couldn't tell exactly why.

—Perhaps he's going to tighten security, the House muttered hopefully. The castle hoped so. Internal defense had grown terribly sloppy when a fool could penetrate the dungeon at will!

Joss dismissed an anxious guard, then folded his hands

before him for a moment and leaned back in his chair. Abruptly he shot out of it and stalked up his private staircase to the upper levels. He found the Queen where he expected to find her—at the Drax table. Ligne kept her eyes fixed on the board as the General stooped to whisper in her ear.

—Here now! Speak up! the castle snapped.

Ligne frowned and looked up at him. "You think he's who?"

Joss whispered again, then looked at her meaningfully. She stared at him, then ordered, "Go away. I need to think about this." Joss returned to his offices in the same way he'd come. A moment later Ligne rose from her Drax table and marched across the hallway to the throne room.

For Pelmen there had been no answer. Perhaps he hadn't understood the cryptic after all. At least the water helped him find his way back to the cistern. It was overflowing, evidently the result of heavy rains up river. From there, it was a simple task to find the galleries that climbed toward the front gate of the castle. Pelmen quickly made his way up the ramps, noting how the tunnels broadened out as he ascended. He turned a corner, and stumbled on the lowest step of a stairway. He looked up and saw a thin box of light above him. "An entrance," he whispered to himself, and he started climbing up the stairway that led to the infirmary.

Rehearsal was in full swing when the double door slammed open. Silence dropped on every occupant of the room as the Queen pointed at Gerrig from the doorway and shouted, "Where's the fool?"

"The fool? The fool. Ah, ah, as we told you, he's sick—"

"With what?"

"Ah, ah—"

"I suppose he's had the wisdom to report to the infirmary?" the Queen asked, her tone suddenly softening.

Gerrig saw an opening, and sprinted through it. "Oh yes! Of course! He may be a fool but he certainly has good sense when it comes to—"

"Why isn't he there then?" Ligne demanded. Her eyes sliced Gerrig like a pair of knives.

"Perhaps he's in his quarters," Parmi offered.

"I've had his quarters searched!" Ligne snarled, whirling to glare at Yona. Then she casually wheeled back to Gerrig, who was wishing he'd never even heard of the acting profession. "But you said he was in the infirmary, didn't you?" She smiled sweetly. "Sick, is he?"

Gerrig could do nothing but nod.

"Shall we go look?" she inquired with that same sarcastic sweetness. Gerrig swallowed, and nodded again. "Go!" she shouted, pointing to the doorway, then her long finger whipped around to Yona and she ordered, "You, too!" As the two men turned to walk into the hall, they shot each other anguished looks. "Come along, Rosha. We're going to get to the bottom of this, or I'm going to fry me some actors!"

Rosha's hands formed fists and he glanced at Carlad's sword. He could take it and decapitate the Queen in a stroke—

"Come *on*, Rosha," she shrilled. She started out of the throne room. Rosha took a deep breath and clamped down on his emotions once more.

By the time they reached the door of the infirmary, Gerrig, too, had controlled his feelings and had donned his toothiest smile. He slung the door wide, shouting a hearty, "Hello!" at the back of the spindly Lord of Herbs. The man leaped off his stool and swung around in horror. "He's not here, my Lady, perhaps we"—Gerrig stopped and stared at a bed in the corner, as his false smile turned genuine. "I mean—he *is!*"

"I'm what?" asked Pelmen.

"You're here!" Gerrig beamed.

Pelmen frowned in the character of Fallomar. "You don't have to sound so pleased at my illness!"

Ligne drifted into the room and looked at him in disbelief. "You're sick?" she asked. She turned to her Lord of Herbs, whose mouth hung wide open. "What's he got?" she demanded.

"Wha-wha-why, I've never seen this man in here before!"

"It really is hard to get a doctor to look at you these days," Fallomar offered, as he hopped off his cot. "In spite of the lack of care, I feel much better now."

Ligne gazed at him suspiciously, as if making up her

mind what to believe. Suddenly she smiled. "I've missed you, fool. I want you in the game room immediately. But change your clothes! You smell as if you've been in the garbage—or the dungeon!" She spun on her heel and marched out.

Pelmen stared after her, feeling a heaviness in his chest. "Are you all right?" Parmi asked quietly.

Pelmen nodded. "I think so."

"Wonderful," snarled the Lord of Herbs. "Then I'll thank you to get out of my infirmary!"

As they moved into the hallway, Gerrig groused, "Next time you choose to drop out of sight, would you take the time to inform your friends?"

"My drop came as quite a surprise to me too, Gerrig. I had no chance to tell anyone."

"What did you learn?" Yona Parmi asked him quietly. Rosha pulled up close behind to hear as well, which prompted Carlad to edge closer.

"Nothing any halfwit doesn't already know. Stay out of the mouths of fishes, don't think you can walk in the dark without running into the walls, and never trust a woman to be where you expect her."

"What?" Gerrig asked.

Carlad, at least, was chuckling. "I know what you mean, fool."

Pelmen glanced back at him and smiled brightly. "I'm sure you do!" He looked back at Rosha. "Who decided to make you an actor?"

"I d-d-did," Rosha responded carefully.

"A wise choice," Fallomar nodded, his eyes holding onto Rosha's as he added, "I'll wager a Queen's consort has a lot of acting to do."

"He does indeed." Carlad laughed, missing the exchange of looks entirely. "And this lad's already done a fair share of it!"

Now the clown looked at Carlad. "Has he now? And how about you? Aren't you also an actor of sorts?"

"Of some sort, I suppose." Carlad chuckled.

"Then perhaps we should find a role for you as well." The clown smiled, catching Yona Parmi's eye. Parmi nodded.

"Me?" the guard asked. "No . . ." he went on, shaking his head, but it was clear he could be cajoled.

"Why don't you two go on to rehearsal while the three of us think you up a part?" Fallomar suggested, and Carlad, charmed by the idea, eagerly led his young charge up the stairs.

"What are you getting us into?" Gerrig demanded. "First we get stuck with this young stutterer, now a castle guard! You miss rehearsals without a word to anyone! Are you trying to scuttle this performance altogether?"

"Why not teach Carlad my lines," the fool suggested. "He seems eager enough, and it appears the Queen is determined to dominate my time. That'll keep him from staring at you suspiciously when you're trying to rehearse."

"Let a guard play the role of the clown King?" Gerrig asked, incredulous.

"Why not. You've always said any oaf could act as well as me. Hasn't he, Parmi?"

"He has, indeed." Parmi nodded. "But what about the lad?"

"Let him play himself—suitor to the Queen."

"Stuttering suitor to the Queen," Gerrig snarled.

"I wouldn't say that around him, Gerrig," Pelmen advised. "Not if you fancy keeping your head where it is."

Gerrig's eyes widened, then he nodded. "Very well. But I don't mind telling you all this is making me very nervous! I'm ready to get out of this place."

"Funny," said Yona. "You wanted so much to get in."

"Close it up, Parmi, or I'll stuff this in it!" Gerrig shook his ham-sized fist in Yona's face, but the round-faced actor seemed unconcerned.

"Do it and I'll kick you in the shins," he replied honestly. Yona had never been a fighter. Nevertheless, his association with Gerrig had at times involved him in unsought, yet unavoidable, altercations. He often got his face punched, but no adversary left a fight with Parmi without rows of blue bruises on each shin. Parmi looked at Pelmen. "Can we help in any way?"

"Not yet, my friend. Take care for what you say," he added. "I think the walls may be listening." Pelmen then stalked up the stairs toward his tiny cell.

"What did he mean by that?" Gerrig asked.

"What does he ever mean?" Parmi shrugged. "Come on, we have to rewrite a play."

As Pelmen walked toward the game room a sense of dread built inside him. Something had roused Ligne's suspicions, and Pelmen wondered if he were walking into the jaws of a trap. There was little he could—

—Got you!

Pelmen scrambled around to face the speaker, his heart in his throat. There was no one behind him.

—Not that! Don't do that!

Pelmen felt a little dizzy. He was hearing words that weren't words at all. He listened to the fluctuations of temperature in this corridor—and comprehended them as thoughts.

—Are you blind? Her red column is sitting on your flank!

Drax. The castle was talking the language of Drax. And Pelmen understood it.

If the House found any redeeming feature in the vain woman who presently wore the crown, it was her compulsive urge to spend hours at the Drax table. Of course, the game had advanced considerably during the castle's extended nap. The openings were now far more sophisticated and the end game much more subtle, but it was still the same vicious pastime the castle had enjoyed so long ago. It was fortunate for the occupants of the palace that the board's shape and the basic moves had not been altered in the last thousand years. The Imperial House was a Drax purist, and would have been enraged at such trifling with perfection.

It was studying an animated match being played by the Queen, her Prime Minister, and one of Ligne's ladies' maids. "Come on," Ligne goaded the woman. "I'll loan you the gold!"

"But I'm already so deeply in debt," the maid protested. "Oh please, my Lady, can't we just play this game for fun?"

—Absurd! the House sniffed. Drax was played for blood and gold—not fun. The castle reflected back on ancient

games, played with powershapers not so dense as this Fallomar fellow. It chuckled, recalling how one night it had lost
one of its gold-inlaid floors, but won it back the following
day, along with the wizard's tunic, vest, and pants!

—Savage game, the Imperial House snickered.

"Ah-ha!" Kherda said with satisfaction, as he made his
move and removed a red piece from the triangular table.

Ligne cursed, and her azure eyes devoured the board,
searching for a move that would take this sudden pressure
off her disc. Kherda always made sure she won, but she
inevitably had to work at it. The Prime Minister considered
his skill far superior to the Queen's—often it was a difficult task just to avoid winning. Occasionally he daydreamed about actually beating her . . .

—Deliciously wicked! the Imperial House crowed in
praise, as Ligne found the soft underbelly of Kherda's defense and slashed into it with her star. The Queen's eyes
gleamed. She did not hide her glee.

"Fallomar, my Lady," Pelmen said, ambling into the
game room. "At your hand."

"You took your time, didn't you, clown?" the Queen said
archly. "But no matter. I'm winning."

"She always wins," the maid explained, smiling at the
jester flirtatiously.

"Indeed, Queens usually do," Fallomar said.

"Do you play?" Ligne asked, eyes on the board.

"I am a player by profession, my Lady. Does a seam-
stress sew? Does a sewerman slough?"

"Such a graphic expression!" Ligne smiled, wrinkling
her nose at her maid, who giggled merrily. "But do you
play games?"

"Life is a game, my mistress, and I am alive, thus I must
play it well."

"Answer me directly," Ligne said sharply. "Do you play
Drax?"

"A pennyless player?" he responded, his eyes wide. "Not
without a wealthy patron to pay my bills."

"Then you know the game?"

"Vaguely. Play on, and I'll watch. You'll find I pick up
new moves quickly." He winked at the ladies' maid.

The game had often been described as something akin to
a three-sided dagger fight in an alley. With lightning speed,

the pieces whizzed around the board, each move drastically altering the subtle balance of power. It was a game both of cutthroat diplomacy and studied tactics, changing far too rapidly for any player to develop a grand strategy. And it was quickly over, with Ligne the victor. The maid hid her eyes behind her hand.

"How much do you owe me now?" Ligne demanded of her, and the woman shrugged and smiled helplessly in response. "Too much to pay, I realize. And you, Kherda, I suppose you must owe me the entire treasury by this time!"

"My Lady, as you say. I am flat of purse."

Ligne looked at the painted fool and smiled scornfully. "You see the kind of stakes I play for? We might as well wager handfuls of dirt!"

"Ah, yes." Fallomar sighed. "There's a price to be paid for owning everything. Of course, that means you can always afford it—"

Ligne stood and brushed past him, toward the double doors of the game room. "It's boring, playing for nothing! What I want is a real game, with real wagers! Fortune riding on every move!"

—Hear hear! cried the House in absolute agreement.

Ligne cocked her head, and looked at the door frame. "Did you hear this thing crack?"

"This castle is full of curious noises lately," the maid observed, clearing the reference plank of pegs.

"It's a very old House," Kherda snorted, looking at the ceiling. "Looks as if it could all fall in any minute!"

The castle said nothing. But it had heard.

"Pity it doesn't fall on you, Kherda," Ligne said. She couldn't know the House was contemplating such at that very moment. "Don't you agree, clown?"

"If it crushes Kherda, I hope it'll crush me as well."

Ligne looked at him. "Why would you hope that?"

"Why, if he were gone, you might make me your Prime Minister, and any fate is better than that." It was a skillful remark, one designed to chop either way. Ligne took it as more abuse for Kherda, and threw back her head to laugh aloud. The Prime Minister, however, caught the fool's wink, and just for an instant remembered how to smile. He was coming to like this clown.

Ligne slapped her hands together. "Very well. Kherda, you may go bury your nose in your bureaucratic burrow. I have my clown back!" Kherda left the room quickly as Ligne walked over to seat herself at the board again. "Well, fool, what will you wager on a game of Drax?"

"Only my antics. They're all I own."

"Then plant your antics in that seat and let's begin," the Queen commanded.

Pelmen's mind raced. He was gauging the quickest way to lose.

"You want me to play what?" Carlad asked incredulously.

"Just give it a try," Danyilyn coaxed him in candy-coated tones. "You don't know, you might find you like it."

"But do I have to put that white stuff on my face? No. No, not for me. My sergeant would take one look at that and—"

"He'll never see it." Danyilyn smiled. "Come on, try it. It's a large part . . ."

"It is?"

"One of the most critical roles," Gerrig broke in.

"Well . . . all right," Carlad grumbled, but he was smiling as Danyilyn started coating his face. "You know, I'd kinda like my wife to see this . . ."

Yona Parmi and Rosha had drifted toward the door of the room, and now Parmi whispered, "The clown has informed me of who you are, Rosha, and your connection with him."

"Oh?" Rosha responded guardedly.

"Your secret is safe. I wish I felt the fool himself was."

Rosha studied Yona's face. "I've heard them call you Yona. Are you the Yona Parmi who's travelled with—this fool—all over Chaomonous?"

"I am. Unfortunately, he's not allowed me to help him as much as he has your father. I suppose he hasn't needed help . . . But I have a sinking feeling that this business is too large for him to handle alone."

"He's not alone," Rosha said flatly, his eyes on Carlad. The guard was laughing now as Danyilyn read him his lines.

"You mean the Power, of course." Yona nodded.

"You know the Power?" Rosha asked him, shifting his dark eyes to Yona's face.

"I know *of* the Power, only."

"So far," Rosha grunted, and Yona smiled.

The door clacked open, and Maythorm popped his handsome head inside. He was grinning. "There you all are." He glanced around the room. "But where's Pelmen?"

Yona stiffened in shock. "Where's who?" he asked quietly, glancing at Carlad to be sure the guard hadn't heard.

"You thought I wouldn't catch on, didn't you." Maythorm smirked. "Who were you trying to deceive? Me?" Maythorm showed them his dimples. "Surely not the Lord of Entertainments! I'm the one who discovered you, Parmi, in the days when your Pelmen was but a pitiful, pennyless playwright with verses to flog." Maythorm sneered. "You may fool Ligne, and you may fool Joss, but you'll not fool the premiere critic of Chaomonous with your little masquerade!"

Yona had caught Danyilyn's eye and jerked a thumb at Carlad, and the actress quickly picked up the cue, hiding her anxiety as she walked the grinning guard to the far side of the room. Now Yona turned back to face the arrogant courtling. "What do you want from us?" he growled.

"From you? Why, nothing, little Parmi. What I crave is the head of your pompous Pelmen! Oh, I don't know how he did it—his special effects were excellent! But he'll pay for that particular performance!"

"I don't know what you're talking about," Parmi rasped, his round body trembling with rage.

"Oh, I think you do." Maythorm grinned. He nodded toward Carlad. "Be glad you've found another clown. After I meet with General Joss, you're going to need him!" The Lord of Entertainments swept his cloak aside and left the room.

Parmi whipped around to Rosha. "Do you think we could—" He stopped. Rosha was gone.

Maythorm swept past the closed door of the game room and around a corner. That was as far as he got. Rosha clubbed him once in the gut, twice in the face, and a final time across the back of his neck. A crackling of bone assured him Maythorm would say no more. He caught the man as he fell and lowered him to the floor, then glanced around for a place to hide the body.

His eyes met those of a startled slave, who stood five feet behind him, leaning on his broom. Rosha gazed up at him a moment, slack jawed, the blood draining from his face. His muscles tensed, and he prepared to spring.

"Was it your wife or your sister?" the slave whispered.

"What?" Rosha asked.

"No matter. I'll sweep up the remains." The slave swiftly leaned his broom against the wall and stooped to grasp Maythorm's body under the arms. Then he glanced up. "Well, get on!" he snapped. "You waiting for someone to give you a kiss?"

Rosha blinked, then slipped around the corner and back into the throne room. A quick glance around relieved him. Carlad was still busily engaged in learning his lines.

Yona Parmi drifted around in front of him, anxiety etched in his face. Rosha sighed. "Relax, Yona Parmi. He's made his last speech."

It didn't take long for Pelmen to lose the first game— nor for the House to begin abusing him for it.

—Stupid move! Stupid move! jangled the bells on the wall.

"Ignore those silly bells," Ligne instructed. "Just play."

That was easier said than done. The castle's comments were starting to effect his concentration. While Drax was a rough game frequently associated with fistfights and murders, there were some things one simply didn't do. One of these was to mock a player at the board.

—Insipid, pasty-faced actor! Too proud to accept expert advice when it's offered you!

Pelmen shifted in his seat as the bells clanged on. Finally he clamped his hands over his ears. "They're a nuisance, to be sure," he admitted to Ligne.

"What difference does it make?" She shrugged. "You're going to lose anyway. Move."

—Why not sweep your cube, the Imperial House suggested sarcastically, and slit your own throat?

Pelmen smiled to himself, and did just that.

—And you did! Oh! Fool! You've lost it now, though doubtless you're too dense to know it!

"Got you!" Ligne crowed, as she slammed her disc into Fallomar's sole remaining piece, sending it flying off the table. That was another of those things one didn't do at Drax, but Ligne had already demonstrated that she had little concern for manners.

"What a surprise," Fallomar lied. "I didn't even see that piece sitting there!"

—Try opening your eyes! the House snarled.

Pelmen stood, bowed politely, and asked, "Could I take a moment's break?"

"Where are you going?" Ligne snapped.

"Just out in the hall to collect my thoughts."

—What thoughts? the castle growled.

"Five minutes," Ligne told him. She seemed in a terrible humor. Pelmen hoped he didn't know why.

He nodded at the pair of guards who opened the door for him, then walked fifteen feet down the hallway and leaned against the wall. The guards craned their necks to watch him. After a moment, one asked the other, "Is he talking to himself?"

The other, who had already had some strange experiences with Fallomar, nodded wisely and tapped his head. "With this one, expect anything."

—You're undoubtedly the most miserable Drax player to set foot within—

"That's not sporting, you know," Pelmen said quietly. Everyone in the castle was relieved by the sudden cessation of the bells.

—Do you address this House?

"You think I talk to walls to hear my own echo?"

—You *do* understand! the House shouted, and a whistling wind of joy whooshed down every hallway, blowing tapestries off of walls and vases off of tables.

"I certainly do, and I'm appalled! If you are the expert Draxist you claim to be, you ought to know it's poor manners to mock a man at the board."

—It's bad manners to ignore the Imperial House! the castle responded defensively.

"Actually it's only been in the last hour or so that I've understood your speech. It's remarkably easy to pick up."

—Naturally, the House sniffed. It makes infinitely more sense than your human gruntings and snortings.

"Nevertheless, it is distracting to play with such vile language ringing in one's ears. Literally."

—Then pay attention! You've forfeited one golden opportunity after another!

"Because I'm trying to lose." The Imperial House was shocked. It responded with a frosty silence. "I realize that's offensive to a purist like yourself, but I'm losing these games to keep the Lady relaxed and happy. There's something far more critical at stake here than the outcome of a Drax game."

—If you're speaking of your trivial little plot to deceive the Queen, how could you possibly compare them!

"Misplaced priorities?" Pelmen shrugged sardonically.

—This House could not agree more!

"In spite of what you think," Pelmen whispered, "it's more important to me than Drax." The House echoed with an angry ringing.

—That's a form of cheating! To throw a Drax game is repugnant behavior, far more unsporting than to mock a horrid Draxist at the board!

"It bothers you that much?"

—There is only one thing worse than a Drax cheater, and that is a Drax welcher! I suppose you're one of those as well?

"Well, I really didn't bet anything—" Pelmen was unprepared for the explosion of outrage that greeted his words.

—Then why play at all? bellowed the Imperial House. The castle took its Drax quite seriously.

"If it's cheating to lose a match deliberately, isn't it also cheating to intimidate your opponents so that they fear winning worse than losing? That's what this Queen does."

The House was silent for a moment.

—This demands some consideration.

"Fine. You think about it. I've got to go back inside and lose another round, and I'd appreciate it if you'd keep your opinion of my play to yourself." Fallomar turned away from the wall and walked back to the door of the game room. The guards regarded him curiously as he passed between them and stalked back to the table.

"Where have you been?" Ligne demanded.

"Telling the walls to shut up."

"Oh, you talk to walls, do you, clown?"

"Only when they talk to me."

"I see. And are the walls amused by your jesting?"

"You hear them laughing, don't you?"

"Did my warders laugh at your jests today?" Ligne asked pointedly. "I was told you paid them a visit."

"To the warders? Oh, the dungeon! Certainly. I frequently visit prisons. They're always good for a laugh." Pelmen studied the board. The game it represented would quickly be lost and forgotten, but he suddenly found himself in a game he needed to win.

"You were trying to follow me in. Why is that?" She turned a harsh stare at him.

Pelmen maintained his composure, smiling smoothly and saying, "To amuse you, my Lady. As I said, I know dungeon life well—all jesters do. I sought only to entertain."

"I see. I've decided to give you your wish."

"My wish? My Lady, in my work I utter many meaningless phrases, which live in my listeners' ears only briefly, and in my own memory not at all. Which wish is this?"

"Why, to see my dungeon, of course." Ligne smiled cruelly. "I do hope you truly are entertaining. Otherwise, I might be tempted to leave you there." She tapped the board, then swept her hand across the pieces and stood up. "I tire of this. I'm off to bed." The maid quickly hopped up to follow her. "After breakfast, clown," Ligne called from the doorway, "I promise you the grand tour. I'm sure we'll both find it amusing." She swept out, followed by the maid and the pair of guards.

Left alone, Pelmen contemplated this new twist. One thing was sure—he could do no more today. He felt exhausted.

CHAPTER FIFTEEN

Defending the Faith

"WHAT DID I DO to deserve you?" Bronwynn spat down at Tibb, who lay at her feet. She had just tossed him against the wall of the canyon and was threatening to inflict more damage if he got up.

Tibb rubbed his aching back. "You know, Lady, I was just asking myself the same question."

"Would you get up," Pinter urged his short companion as he cast an anxious look over his shoulder. "Admon Faye is watching us!"

"Fine, he can watch me lie here awhile."

"He's laughing." Pinter frowned, his gaunt face flushing.

"Let him," Tibb grunted.

"But he's gonna think we're fools!" Pinter cried.

"Then he's half-right already. I'm not proving I'm one by standing up and getting my head split open." Tibb gazed up at Bronwynn. "You're good, Lady. You'll make a great murderess."

"Murderess," came Bronwynn's dull echo.

"You're a natural. I even feel a little sorry for the fellow."

"A natural murderess," Bronwynn repeated grimly.

"He's wondering why we're just standing around," Pinter

said nervously, still gazing over his shoulder. He spun around and charged Bronwynn earnestly. She responded with a quick grab of his arm and a flip, and Pinter cartwheeled off the wall, just as Tibb had done.

Tibb raised his head to watch, then smiled. "He's all arms and legs, hunh." Bronwynn didn't smile back, but leaned thoughtfully against the wall. "Why so glum?" Tibb asked. "Being a cutthroat is great practice for ruling—"

"Wonderful," the girl snarled, staring at her hands as if they were filthy. "Now I'm a cutthroat."

"What's the matter? You got something against being a cutthroat?"

Bronwynn looked at Tibb, surprised. "Well, of course I do!"

"What?" he demanded.

"It's . . . it's just . . . wrong!"

"What's wrong about it?"

"Why . . . ah . . . what's right about it?" Bronwynn challenged.

"Listen, Lady. It's us cutthroats that make this economy go. Why, without us robbing people along, and kidnapping, and murdering—the nobles and the merchants would have all the gold by this time, instead of just most of it."

"But . . . to murder someone! To be a murderer! That isn't—"

"Ladylike?" Tibb finished for her. "Some of the best women I know are murderesses."

"Really?" Bronwynn asked.

"Sure. My mother—"

"Your mother!"

"Right. Sister, too . . ."

"But . . . if they were brigands . . . no wonder you turned out as you did."

"What do you mean by that?" Tibb snarled, starting to get up.

"Don't upset her, Tibb," Pinter suggested, as he got shakily to his feet. "She'll bang your head against that wall—most unpleasant—"

"I mean, they must have taught you it was *right*, or you—"

"Listen to me, my Lady! I know right from wrong, for sure. Right's what helps me, wrong's what don't."

"But don't you see? That's so far from the real difference between right and wrong that I . . . I wonder . . . if you'd ever be able to understand . . ."

Tibb snorted. "Maybe not. But I know this. As a cutthroat, I kill a man in an alley. As a Queen, you'll order a war and kill a thousand. As a cutthroat, I'll steal all the gold a man can carry in his saddlebag. As a Queen, you can make a single proclamation of a new tax and rob a thousand peasants of their life savings. Now, my Lady. You tell me what's the right and wrong of that!"

"Ah, Tibb," Pinter mumbled in his friend's ear, "we're supposed to be training this girl to take the throne, not talking her out of trying. If our master—"

"Well, someone has to rule!" Bronwynn blurted out. "Someone has to make decisions for the good of the whole nation."

"Fine," Tibb said, hitching his pants. "Let them do it. But don't try to convince me that their right and wrong is any different from mine."

"Tibb," Pinter whispered, "would you please shut your mouth before this girl decides not to—"

"Why?" Bronwynn interrupted. "He's just telling the truth." She struggled to her feet, sliding her back up the wall of the cliff, and brushed between the two of them on her way to find a private place to think.

"Now you've done it!" Pinter snarled. "Admon Faye gives us a chance to join him, and you kick it away!"

"What did I do?" Tibb asked, confused.

"You just talked her out of playing her role in the master's plan," Pinter roared, and he, too, stalked away.

"I did?" Tibb asked. "Now wait a minute, Pinter," he called, stomping after his friend and grabbing him by the shoulder. "You tell me how I did that."

"You called her a cutthroat!" Pinter snapped. "No one wants to be called a cutthroat."

"But that's what we are," Tibb pleaded.

"That's what you are, maybe," Pinter replied archly. "I'm an outlaw."

"But what's the difference?" Tibb begged.

Pinter paused and looked back at him disdainfully. "If you don't know, I'm sure I couldn't explain it to you."

Shouting in the northern mouth of Dragonsgate cut short

their debate. They looked at one another in surprise, then
bolted toward the noise. Pinter's longer legs carried him to
the site of the confrontation well before his comrade, and
he was full of news when Tibb came puffing up behind
him. "What is it?" Tibb shouted. "What's going on?"

"Some pale believers," Pinter smirked. "Some of that
Prophet's band. Look." Pinter pointed, and Tibb watched
as slavers dragged one blue-clad initiate after another off
of their horses. The missionaries didn't resist, yielding passively to this brutal treatment.

"Always was easy to bag a dragonfaither," Tibb snickered.

"These aren't dragonfaithers," Pinter corrected him,
"though I'm not surprised you can't tell the difference.
They're members of that new heresy."

"I know that," said an annoyed Tibb. "You think I've
lived this last year with my eyes closed?"

"Wouldn't surprise me."

Admon Faye's companions were experts at fast-binding
new victims. It took only moments for them to tie the entire group of Lamathians, which Tibb estimated as at least
a score.

"What will we do with 'em?" Tibb asked. "Kill 'em here?
Sell 'em in the south?"

"No. These fellows say we'll skin them and send them
home as an example. Say, the Princess is a Chaon! Maybe
watching a few Lamathians getting skinned would get her
blood boiling to be Queen again! Let's go!"

Tahli-Damen lay on his back, staring into space. The
wounds that Flayh's alter-shape had inflicted on his leg
had proved to be more spectacular than substantial. He was
walking without any difficulty. But Wayleeth had noticed
that a strange dread had settled over him. He refused to be
cheered by anything she said.

"Tahli-Damen," she called from the doorway. "The man
who's been watching Flayh's castle has brought you a report—"

"Flayh's castle!" Tahli-Damen blurted, as if the words
themselves touched a raw nerve within him. "I set no
watch on Flayh's castle!"

"I know that," Wayleeth answered patiently. "I did."

"Why did you do that!" he demanded. "Didn't I tell you? That man is a powershaper! He hurls balls of fire! He—he—he changes his shape at will! Look at my leg!" The young merchant frantically waved his leg in the air and pointed to it.

"I know all about your leg, my love," Wayleeth answered him evenly. "I'm the one who has bathed and dressed it, remember?"

"Of course," he mumbled, and he rolled over, turning his back on her, as well as the strange powers that suddenly threatened him anew.

"I set that watch because I know that's what you would do—if you were being yourself."

Tahli-Damen rolled back to face her. "If I were being myself. Wayleeth, look at me! I am being myself—and myself is terrified."

"You're going to let a little dog bite prevent you from seizing your rightful place on the Council of Elders?"

"Oh, Wayleeth," he moaned, covering his ears.

"To prevent you from seizing one of those precious pyramids you've talked so much about?" Tahli-Damen swung himself off the bed and limped toward the door. "Where are you going?"

"I told you before, I'm frightened and I don't want to talk anymore about Flayh!"

"Flayh's gone."

Tahli-Damen stopped and looked back at her. "What?"

"He left a day and a half ago for the High City, for powers know whatever reason. What's important is that while he's off to visit the sloth-King, he's left guess who in charge of his castle?"

Tahli-Damen raised his eyebrows incredulously. "You mean—Pezi?"

Wayleeth giggled. "Old barrel-bottom himself!"

The young merchant dashed to a closet and grabbed his cloak, shouting, "Dispatch a bird to Jagd at once and give him the news!"

"Where are you going?" Wayleeth smiled knowingly.

"I've got to plan a visit to our new local lord of Ognadzu!"

* * *

"What's happened to me?" Bronwynn whispered to her reflection. She gazed into a little pool, fed by the melting snow that trickled off the mountain. This pass was bare of the trees Bronwynn loved, and she had despaired of finding any private place where she could think. This quiet pool, at the base of the cliff opposite the dragon's old lair, wasn't really beautiful, but it was the nearest thing to beauty she could find.

Bronwynn was amazed at herself. Only a few short months before she had bid good-bye to Rosha in this very pass—she could see the exact spot from where she sat— and had ridden away with Lord Joss, expecting to recapture her throne by sundown. So naïve, so trusting. It was good she had learned something of the world.

But was it right? Tibb had struck a soft spot within her. Until she'd met Pelmen, her own attitudes toward moral evil had been the same as those of these outlaws—perhaps even worse. Her father Talith had exercised his power with the same savage expertise as Tibb wielded his knife—well, probably more skillfully than poor Tibb—and he'd taught Bronwynn to do the same.

"But I thought that had changed," Bronwynn breathed, remembering conversations with Pelmen that had extended far into the night, and the sudden unveiling of a spiritual sensitivity that had long laid dormant within her.

"My Lady! My Lady!"

She glanced up. Pinter and Tibb both raced toward her. She'd become well acquainted with these two in the past few hours. Thus it didn't surprise her at all when Pinter's legs tangled and he fell in a pile at her knees. Tibb tripped and landed on top of him.

"Yes, Pinter?" she asked wearily.

"Get offa me!" Pinter growled, and Tibb complied quickly. Both struggled to their feet.

"We've caught our first unauthorized passage!"

"Twenty of them, actually," Tibb corrected.

"They're being held in the north mouth. Hurry!"

"Why should I?" Bronwynn asked pointedly. "I told you, I don't relish the thought of indiscriminate killings."

"Oh, we're not going to kill them," Tibb protested.

"No?"

"Of course not. What good would that do? Would it keep anyone else from trying to come through?"

"I would think so—when word got out."

Pinter laughed, and winked at Tibb, who winked back. Bronwynn didn't much care for their patronizing looks. "But who would carry that word out?" Pinter asked, as if of a child.

Bronwynn frowned at this, and Pinter looked away. "So you'll send them back," she said, looking down at her reflection in the puddle.

"Right!" Tibb crowed, a big smile spreading beneath his bulbous nose. "Of course, we'll skin 'em up a little first. Come and watch. They're Lamathians—"

"No, thanks. Beatings don't interest me any more than killings."

"Might do you good," Tibb wheedled. "Help you see the real world. Our boys have already begun the job, stripping off a few of their funny blue robes and stretching them on the—"

"What?" Bronwynn asked sharply. "What kind of robes?"

Tibb was puzzled. "They're just robes, my Lady, the usual kind—"

She spun around to Tibb's companion. "Pinter, what kind of robes?"

"Nothing for you to be alarmed about, my Lady. We've just captured a group of religious fanatics that you would know nothing about—"

"What color robes?" she screeched, and Tibb, wide-eyed, answered:

"Pale blue—" He broke off, as Bronwynn sprinted between them and raced toward the northern mouth.

She arrived, breathless, at the side of Admon Faye, just as the skyfaither leader was being brought before him.

"What are you going to do with them?" Bronwynn demanded sternly, before the slaver could open his mouth.

Admon Faye turned his ugly face toward her and frowned. "I'm going to beat them and send them back where they came from, to discourage further—"

"No, you're not."

Admon Faye gazed at her. "What!" It wasn't a question, it was a threat.

"You aren't going to beat them, nor will you send them back."

Admon Faye grew conscious of the watching eyes of the rogues who ringed them. His initial thought was to slap the girl's face and have her arms bound behind her for still more instruction later. He resisted the impulse, but his frown stayed fixed in place. There were many who would have preferred a slap to that stare. "Are you ordering me, little girl?"

"I'm no little girl, I'm your Queen—or so you claim I *will* be. And perhaps I'll be more compliant with your wishes than Queen Ligne has been—but there are *some* things that I demand!"

"You're hardly in a position to demand anything," said the slaver.

"Oh?" she replied. "It was my understanding that you needed me, as legitimate heir to the throne you plot to steal. Suppose I choose not to take it?"

"Then we'll use someone else."

"Ah," Bronwynn said. "But what of the wasted time? Another heir to be found and trained, rechecking the plans with Flayh—are these few worth it to you?" She gestured to the two skyfaithers who stood before them, soundly trussed and gagged.

"Are they that important to you?" Admon Faye wondered.

"Yes."

The slaver stared at her, then chuckled. At the sound of his laugh, the tension broke. He glanced around at his fellows and winked, and they began dispersing, echoing his laugh. He looked back at her. "Then they're yours—for all the good it does you."

"I see you've already begun your vicious game," Bronwynn growled as she ungagged Naquin.

"Just a little lesson to help would-be freetraders to think twice before crossing this pass. Perhaps this group will be willing to convey our message?" he asked Naquin, raising his eyebrows and grinning crookedly.

"We carry only the message of the Prophet and the book—none other," Naquin answered proudly.

"Oh-ho!" Admon Faye cackled. "A proud one. Too proud to save the skins of some of your fellow travelers?"

"Salvation is our purpose," Naquin announced, "but your threats are meaningless in view of the Prophet's words. The changes will come—so says the book and the Prophet."

Admon Faye wrinkled his nose in disdain and sneered at Bronwynn. "Never could understand these religious crazies. You're sure you wouldn't rather just send them home?"

"No!" Bronwynn shouted, and she turned to smile hopefully at Naquin. "The Prophet sent you?"

"He did. With instructions to proclaim the message throughout Chaomonous."

"You're sure?" Admon Faye snickered. "Means nothing to me. They're harmless enough. But if you let them through now, it means you'll have to put up with this garbage from now on."

"I don't think it garbage!" Bronwynn snapped.

"Oh that's right. You got a whiff of it yourself while in Lamath, didn't you? Very well then, I'll leave you two to ponder worshipfully the wonders of theology." The slaver turned his back and strode away, trailing his laughter as he left.

Freed now to mention his name, Bronwynn whipped around to whisper, "How is Pelmen? Where is he?"

Naquin stared at her, then his face assumed an expression of pious distaste. "I certainly have no knowledge of that man's whereabouts—and I wish none."

Bronwynn stared back at him. "I thought you said you were from the Prophet!"

"Indeed we are, from the true Prophet of Lamath. We have no dealings with the Mari imposter you mention."

"Mari imposter!"

"That is what he showed himself to be when he abandoned the land to chaos."

"He didn't abandon the land!" Bronwynn fumed. "He put Erri in charge of Lamath and moved on to other things."

"What other things?" Naquin demanded, and Bronwynn hesitated. "You see, you don't know his whereabouts," Naquin said smugly.

"But I know him," snarled Bronwynn. "I was with him!"

"That may be," Naquin said evenly in the face of Bronwynn's clenched teeth. "But where are you now? In the company of cutthroats, outlaws and brigands. And by your dress, obviously one of them. That doesn't say much for this Pelmen, does it?"

Bronwynn's fist flew toward Naquin's face, and he flinched. She managed to stop it in midflight, however, and backed away, amazed at the violence of her own reactions. Naquin smiled a pitying smile that made her want to vomit.

"Go ahead and strike," he urged. "We skyfaithers are prepared for persecution."

"Persecution!" Bronwynn gasped.

"Of course. I'm not fooled by your pretended mercy. If you truly stood with us, you'd untie us and let us get on with our task. Moreover, you would don a robe yourself and follow me into Chaomonous."

"Follow you!" she spat. "I'd not follow you anywhere!"

"I cannot say that shocks me." He sneered. "Since you've chosen to follow Admon Faye."

Bronwynn glared at him, her eyes blazing. "You can't make me believe Erri thinks as little of Pelmen as you do."

"But he does," Naquin lied. It wasn't so much that he meant to lie. It was simply that Naquin had debated this point so many times since Erri found him that he'd convinced himself it was the truth—even if Erri didn't realize it as yet.

"That's a lie!" Bronwynn roared.

"Child, you're speaking about things you simply don't have the experience to comprehend. The land has been changed a great deal since we've rid ourselves of Pelmen. Untie me, and perhaps I can explain the words of the Prophet to you more fully, and—"

Bronwynn didn't give him a chance. She jammed his gag back into his mouth and whipped out her knife. "The next sentence you utter in my hearing will be your last!" she warned, as she held the blade to his throat. "You listen to *me*. I once wore a robe like yours. Wore it proudly. I followed Pelmen as he led me to the Power, and I did that proudly. But I find no pride in these colors now. So Erri thinks Pelmen was an imposter? Well. Maybe he was. I only know that if you're what's become of the reborn faith

Pelmen espoused, I want none of it!" She gazed around the cluster of bound skyfaithers who stared at her, their anxious eyes bulging above their gags. Then she looked over her shoulder. Admon Faye leaned against the cliff face a hundred feet away, watching her and laughing with his cronies. Her face flushed, and she looked back at Naquin. "If I hadn't made such a fuss about saving you, I'd give you back to Admon Faye. Since I did, I'm going to cut your bonds and send you on through. Interpret it as you will," she continued sarcastically. "Say that the Power moved me to do it. But I swear, if you so much as touch your gags before you reach Chaomonous, I'll send every slaver in Dragonsgate down on your heads, do you hear me?" she shouted at the group. They nodded eagerly, and she started cutting through their bonds, leaving Naquin for last. "Begone!" she shrilled as she cut his last rope, and she booted him in the rear. He joined the rest of the pack as they raced down the sourthen mouth on foot. Then she sheathed her knife and walked off to find Pinter and Tibb. As usual, they squatted on their haunches, arguing. They stopped when the Princess joined them and looked up at her expectantly.

"I'm ready," she announced. "Teach me how to murder."

"Pahd! Pahd, get up!"

"Hmm . . . humph . . . hunh?" said Pahd mod Pahd-el, as he crawled out from under a favorite pillow. "What the . . . what's (yawn) . . . the trouble, mother? Is it breakfast already?"

"It's midafternoon, Pahd!" Chogi lan Pahd-el, his mother, replied scornfully. "You had half a duck for your midday meal. Don't tell me you don't remember?"

"Remember? Do I remember?" Pahd asked blearily, rubbing his eyes.

"Yes, you remember!" Chogi yelled impatiently. This drew Pahd's wife, Sarie, to her husband's defense.

"Please, Chogi, let him alone. He got hardly any rest last—"

"Ridiculous!" Chogi blustered, throwing out her generous chest and stomach and propping her fists on equally generous hips. "All he does is sleep."

"Why, that's not true," Sarie protested. "Is it, darling?" she called sweetly to her husband.

Pahd snored.

"You see," Chogi growled.

"Why not let him alone? It's hard business running a kingdom."

"I should know," Chogi replied vehemently. "I've been running this one ever since his father died."

"And probably before that," Sarie huffed to herself.

"I heard that!" Chogi said, thrusting her bulldog's visage into Sarie Ian Pahd's pretty, if vacant, face. "You just tell me where we'd be if I didn't take steps to administer this realm."

"We'd be living peaceful, ordinary lives right here—as normal people do," Sarie answered. "People in Ngandib-Mar don't need to be ruled, any more than Pahd needs to rule them. We'd all get on very well if you just left things alone."

"I know why he married you." Chogi scowled. "It's because you're content to let him sleep his life away, in exchange for your court and your crown!"

"Why not?" asked Sarie sensibly. "It's what he wants."

"Well, it's not what I want!" Chogi finished, and she walked over to jerk the covers off her slumbering son. "Get up!" she roared again.

"Hmm? What? What's that? Breakfast time?"

"I've brought someone to see you, Pahd."

"Fine," said Pahd as he snuggled down again. "Let him look as long as he likes."

"Oh, no," Chogi said, grabbing his shoulders and pulling him upright. "This one you're going to talk to."

"What about?" Pahd yawned.

"Remember months ago, before the crisis with the dragon, when you asked me to find you a court power-shaper?"

"I did?"

"You did."

"Certainly I remember." Pahd nodded. "Where did the fellow go, by the way?"

"We never found one," Chogi roared.

"We didn't?" Pahd asked Sarie.

"No, dear," she replied.

"Most inefficient," Pahd mumbled. "Remind me to make a decree deploring inefficiency . . ." He was eying his favorite pillow longingly.

"No need," Chogi snorted. "I've found one for us."

"Really!" Sarie said, genuinely delighted.

"I thought that would get your attention, Sarie . . . at least . . ." Obviously it hadn't gotten Pahd's. His eyes were closing, and his head listed to one side. "Wake up!" Pahd came back to attention. Momentarily.

"Where is he?" Sarie bubbled.

"Send in the powershaper!" ordered Chogi lan Pahd-el, and a servant lazily moved to obey. "He's outside," Chogi explained, not troubling to hide her own excitement. "He's a most dynamic man—if a bit short . . ."

"Announcing Flayh," said the servant as he reentered.

"Flayh?" asked Sarie.

"Just . . . Flayh? That's all?" Pahd said drowzily. "Rather unimpressive title."

"I have others, but why be redundant?" Flayh had stepped into the room and suddenly commanded the attention of everyone. Even Pahd. "I am Flayh. Let's leave it at that." He wore his splendid red and white cape. He'd thrown back the hood, and it stood upon his shoulders like a high collar.

"Certainly looks the part," Pahd mumbled.

"Pay no attention to the King," Chogi said apologetically. "He often says things he doesn't mean."

"I do not." Pahd snarled. "Do I?" he asked Sarie.

"No, dear," she replied.

"You see," Pahd said.

"Yes, you do," said his mother, staring him down.

Pahd raised an eyebrow, shrugged, and looked at Flayh. "All right. I do. So . . ." He sighed, and bit his lip. "Shape."

"Pahd, we don't want to rush the man," said Chogi, smiling at Flayh.

"I'm not offended," Flayh interrupted, and he threw his cloak aside.

He was a lean, powerfully built hound.

"A puppy!" Pahd said, clapping his hands. The two ladies were awestruck.

Flayh was again a man.

Pahd looked a bit crestfallen. "I rather liked the puppy, myself . . ."

"Pahd, I'll not play word games with you," said Flayh as he walked brusquely to the side of Pahd's bed-shaped throne. "I understand that you need a court sorcerer."

"That's what my mother says."

Flayh examined the man closely. This was the first time he'd ever met the one they called the sloth-King face to face. Always before, he had discounted the stories of the man's laziness, but Pahd was certainly living up to his reputation today. It was hard to imagine that this lump on the bed could also be one of the foremost swordsmen in the world. "I've come to offer my services," Flayh explained.

"Flayh," Pahd said to himself. "I know of Joooms, and that troublesome Mar-Yilot . . . Terril . . . Pelmen of course. Never heard of a powershaper named Flayh. You new to the trade?"

"I am." Flayh nodded.

Pahd yawned and rubbed his eyes. "Ah, what will you need? What are your requirements?"

"All I ask is a tower of my own to practice my arts and free access to every part of your fortress."

Pahd smiled in surprise. "Free access? Is that really necessary?" The King chuckled. "I somehow can't feature walking into my private chamber and finding you casting a spell on it."

"I can't feature you walking anywhere," Chogi snorted.

"Chogi!" Sarie scolded.

"Well, I can't," the square-jawed matron replied. "We've gotta carry him everywhere he goes."

"Perhaps I should retire and let you decide," Flayh suggested.

"Oh, no." Pahd smiled. "Why not decide, then I can retire." The King studied Flayh carefully, then looked at his mother. "Well, what do I decide?"

Chogi wheeled around to Flayh. "Your wishes are granted. I know just the tower for you, it's right by this one. You'll love it. And of course it is very convenient to the kitchens and the library so that you'll be able to—" Her voice faded away as she escorted Flayh from the room, her sizable forearm wrapped around his thin shoulders.

Pahd was still chuckling. "I think mother's got a new beau. Poor fellow—" he added.

Sarie regarded the door uneasily as she strolled over to sit on her husband's bed. "Did you really want him here?"

"Why not? Mother's obviously taken with him. And if she's with him—" Pahd grabbed the sheets and pulled them over his head. "—maybe she'll let me sleep."

It was hours later before Flayh was finally able to shake himself from the demanding admiration of Chogi lan Pahdel. Free at last, Flayh paced through the uppermost room of his new tower and out a doorway. A tiny balcony, not more than four feet from tower to balustrade, ringed the spire, and Flayh stalked this circle, gazing down on the awesome view spread below him.

Except for the blocky citadel occupied by King Pahd and his family, this was the loftiest point in the royal fortress—which meant it was lofty indeed. Flayh had the sensation that he stood on the top of the world. The spring rains had cleansed the air of dust, and he could see to mountain peaks on every horizon. It thrilled him, this powershaper life, and he vowed never to return to that other existence, where power was nothing more than the shadowy possibility of political influence. From this vantage point Flayh could see that his new power need know no bounds. "I stand atop the greatest fortress in the world," he whispered to himself—and he was right.

The High Fortress of Ngandib was founded on a small rock plateau, which sat in turn in the middle of a much larger plateau. The city of Ngandib covered the eastern half of this larger tableland from its very edges to the base of the castle's rock. The western half of the plateau was a gigantic basin carved of stone—a man-made reservoir dug to contain the city's precious water supply. To reach the city, a traveler had to climb a switchback road carved into the eastern cliff face, which rose five thousand feet from the valley floor below. Theoretically, this road could be defended from above so easily that no army would ever be capable of taking Ngandib by storm. The theory had gone untested throughout the centuries, since no one had ever thought it sensible to try such a thing. The residents of this lofty plain boasted smugly that they lived in a city without walls—their cliffs were all the defense they needed.

Should an invader by some miracle reach the city, he would find yet another insurmountable obstacle to conquest in the positioning of the fortress. Since it was built atop that smaller outcropping of rock, its parapets extended another six hundred feet above the plateau floor—far too lofty to scale. The only entrance was through a cave chiseled into the rock beneath the castle, and up a long flight of interior stairs. Of course, Pahd never climbed the stairs. He rode, instead, on a primitive lift, operated by slaves from the upper chambers.

"Absolutely inaccessible," Flayh breathed, staring beyond the palace walls, past the larger plateau, to the far distant valleys more than a mile below. From this height the view was partially blocked by clouds. Flayh had never seen the upper side of a cloud before. The very thought made his heart pound. "Invincible," he muttered. It wasn't clear, even in his own mind, whether he meant the fortress or himself. No matter, for soon they could be one. He slipped back inside the tower and pulled a couple of precious treasures from his luggage. The first was his pyramid, which he slipped from its velvet bag and placed on the table. The second was the ancient grimoire. He sat down, laid the book open before him at the proper page, and began to chant.

As the light in Dragonsgate waned, Admon Faye watched Bronwynn defend herself. He could barely contain his pleasure. What he'd been unable to accomplish with threats and arguments, one self-righteous skyfaither had done in a matter of minutes. "I'm amazed at your transition," Admon Faye grunted, as he watched Bronwynn make short work of an attacking slaver.

"I learn quickly when I choose to," she replied grimly.

"You do, indeed," he cackled. "Your stuttering bull has met his match." In answer, she smoothly attacked and disarmed another brigand. "But I wasn't meaning your battle skills. Your instincts for that have always been good; it was just a question of tapping that hostility bottled inside you. No, I'm more interested in your—ah—spiritual transformation."

Bronwynn shot the slaver an ugly look. "Don't push it."

"But you were such a stalwart defender of the skyfaithful," he mocked.

"I said don't push it!" Bronwynn shouted, spinning to face him and whipping her dagger from its scabbard.

Admon Faye gazed up at her coolly, uncowed by her fierce expression. "Still threatening me," he murmured. "That's not a good sign. You haven't yet learned who gives directions in the new family of Faye." He got slowly to his feet. "What do you choose, Bronwynn? Knives? I'll flay a patch of skin off your back—not where it will show, you understand, except to yourself in a mirror. You prefer swords? Then I'll take off—let's say—four of your toes. A six-toed queen is just as much a regent, isn't she? Or would you rather choose staves? I'll leave you with one ear delicate and shapely, the other the size of a melon. Your choice, child. Which?"

Bronwynn blinked twice, then sheathed her knife.

The slaver nodded. "I take that to mean you yield?" Bronwynn bit her lip. "Do you yield?" Admon Faye demanded, stepping to her and grabbing her under the chin.

"I yield," Bronwynn whispered. The words tasted bitter.

Admon Faye's twisted smile spread across his ravaged face once again. "Good. Then we ride." At that single word, the host of gathered slavers sprang into a whirlwind of activity.

"Now?" she asked. "The sun's almost gone."

"Right." He nodded. "That makes it the best time of the day."

Less than an hour later a hundred and seventy riders pounded down out of Dragonsgate. Not, however, before Admon Faye had tied a note to the leg of a blue-flyer and tossed it into the purpling sky.

CHAPTER SIXTEEN

❧   ❧

Words with the Walls

PELMEN WAS SOUND ASLEEP when the castle made its decision. It might have let the matter rest until morning, but the Imperial House had been longing for company for weeks. It decided to wake the powershaper up.

—Very well. Intimidating an opponent is another form of cheating, said the House.

Pelmen fell out of bed, for the castle had communicated this through a dreadful creaking in the beams that supported the ceiling. His initial instinct was to get under the cot.

—Did you hear?

"I . . . did," Pelmen responded, a bit shakily. He crawled back out onto the straw covered floor and looked up at the darkness. "I . . . appreciate your understanding spirit," he went on, rubbing his eyes and yawning.

—Don't mention it.

"Can I go back to sleep now?"

—There are things that should be said.

"I want to talk to you, too, but it's night. Don't you sleep?"

—There's been too much sleeping. A thousand years too much.

"You mean you've been asleep for a thousand years?"

—Since the coming of the dragon to the Great Gate, and the cutting off of magic from this land.

Pelmen felt a rush of intense excitement. Sleep was forgotten in the face of the incredible opportunity. "But what woke you up again?"

—The death of the twi-beast, said the Imperial House. A wind stirred through the room, rustling the straw.

Pelmen felt it on his face, and smiled. "You're laughing about that," he murmured.

—Wouldn't you? the castle chortled.

"I read about you in a cryptic sentence in a book composed in the ancient times!"

—Ancient times! scoffed the Imperial House. It was yesterday! If you'd like to speak with the true ancients, look to the hills!

"Unfortunately, I don't know their language."

—Few do, replied the House through a change of the room's temperature. They speak so dreadfully slow that your human lifespan could not contain a sentence . . .

"But what of you? Tell me of yourself!"

—This House woke under the spell of Nobalog—a wizard of some renown, though often taken less than seriously by his peers. He was a practical joker, you see, and got more pleasure from his little tricks than from the major works of his art.

"Such as yourself."

—Of course! the House thundered through the groaning beams.

"Did he not keep some record of his achievement?"

—He kept a book of spells, but that is all.

"No wonder I'd never heard of such, then," Pelmen muttered, biting his lip. "That book has most certainly been lost for centuries."

—So it has. Was found recently, however.

"Found!" Pelmen exclaimed. "By whom?"

—That information you must discover for yourself, powershaper. This House only knows that at this moment, another House is stirring.

Pelmen stared into the inky room, dumfounded. "Where? What structure?" he asked earnestly.

—Such questions humans ask! the House replied. Always talking of where. There is only one place, and that is this place.

"The—the other living House is also you?"

—Fool! How can there be a House and a House in a House? The other House that wakes shares this world, that's all. It is semi-conscious now, but it already is clear that the shaper who wakes it is of a malevolent turn.

"But who?" Pelmen asked himself. The House ignored the question.

—Why can you suddenly hear? the House inquired. For days you've ignored everything that was said to you.

"I've known for some time that there was something different about you—since the night you teased me out of my sleep and blew out a torch in the hallway."

—Apologies.

"Accepted. But though I knew you were a power, I didn't know you were the castle itself. I recalled that cryptic saying about you after talking with a woman in your dungeon."

—Her words were heard.

"Do you hear everything that takes place within these walls?"

—Of course.

"Simultaneously?"

The House puzzled over the word for a moment.

—Everything is heard and known. At this moment the Queen snores in a bed carved of ivory and inlaid with gold, beneath piles of fish-satin sheets. The man with whom you alternately plot and argue, Gerrig, is not in his room, but in the room of—

"I have a good idea what Gerrig is doing," Pelmen interrupted. "But what of the woman I mentioned? The lady named Serphimera?"

—That lady paces the floor and invokes for your protection the name of the dragon. Rather silly, the House added needlessly.

"That . . . cheers me, nevertheless." Pelmen thought for a moment. "Has she ever spoken aloud about me?"

—The woman has a great fondness for you, power-shaper. She calls upon the twi-beast to protect only those whom she regards highly. Why does she? That lizard is long dead.

"That's just her—understanding. I confess, I don't understand it either, but it's nice to know I'm warmly remembered."

—Then her understanding isn't yours as well?

Pelmen was surprised. "Why do you ask?"

—Because you, too, invoke such a power. Or was it the House you cried out to for aid, when trapped in the jaws of the fish?

"Since I didn't know you existed at the time, I could hardly have been shouting for you."

—The dragon, then? asked the Imperial House. Pelmen was rapidly growing more sensitive to the castle's inflections. The House seemed troubled.

"As you've said, the dragon is dead."

—Then . . . what?

"Better *whom*. I called on the Power, not on a power."

—I know nothing of this Power, replied the House.

"Really?" Pelmen asked. "You didn't feel the wind that was sent to guide me? You didn't feel the heat that boiled the big fish in the cistern?"

—This House boiled the fish, the Imperial House corrected.

"Oh," Pelmen said, a bit startled. "Well, I thank you, but—"

—But what?

"But why did you?"

The House was quiet for a long time. Then it said:

—Does this Power make you do things you might not ordinarily do?

It was Pelmen's turn to ponder. At length, he replied, "I think it's rather that the Power leads you to do what you should—and furnishes the energy with which to do it."

—This must be considered.

"Wait! Don't go yet, there's so much I want to know!"

—Ask, then.

"Why were you wanting to talk to me?"

—Two reasons. Loneliness and pain.

"Pain? You?"

—Excruciating agony. It occurs whenever some show-off sorcerer like yourself shapes power in the hallways.

"But I didn't shape you," Pelmen replied evenly, "though I had the chance."

—Not the night you were teased, no. Thank you.

"You're welcome."

—But you did shape the airs of my dungeons into ulcerous balls of light!

"When I was in the caverns," Pelmen remembered. "I had no idea—then it was you who kept blowing them out."

—Every time.

"I . . . I'm sorry. If I'd known, I certainly would have stopped."

—You were told enough times! roared the House. Its tone softened, however, and it went on:

—But that wasn't the real pain. The agony comes from that miserable parasite of a trader, the scarlet-and-purple-clad Jagd of Uda!

"Jagd? A powershaper?" Pelmen asked, alarmed.

—No, fool! the House shouted back. This Jagd causes pain by use of that savagely pointed pyramid of his.

"Ah," Pelmen breathed, understanding at last. "I've had experience with those three devices before."

—Three? There are six of the magical objects. Or were.

"I only know of three."

—Powerful magic is contained in each, embedded there from the days of their making, in the last days of the one land.

Pelmen's mouth opened in wonder. This was a tale he'd never heard. "Go on," he urged.

—They were formed by all the parties in cooperation: those of faith, those of magic, and those of observable nature. The task was to shape a weapon that could destroy Vicia-Heinox, while forming a new unity of all parties in the process. The craftsmen of natural laws operated complicated devices wrought of steel and glass, and produced the six objects in their proper shape. Then the six were intrusted to Sheth, the foremost magician of that age. It fell his lot to pour each crystal full of power, then knit them all together with a mystic bond known only to himself. Thus prepared, the finished object was to be passed to the men of faith, for them to add their contribution.

"And what was that?" Pelmen begged eagerly.

—No one ever knew. Sheth went into meeting with those of the faith, and emerged with the bonded crystals still in hand. It was said that, along with his craft, he'd poured himself into those crystals. He couldn't give them up to be used by anyone else. Alone he scaled the Central Gate, intent on destroying the beast that had made the place its own.

"And?" asked Pelmen—sadly, for he'd already guessed the tale's unhappy conclusion.

—The dragon devoured him. The magical bond that had melded the crystals into one shattered in the instant of his passing. And in the final conversation this House recalls before falling into slumber, someone told of seeing the dragon tossing the sparkling crystals from one mouth to the other. These magical objects contained the sum of the one land's wisdom, and the fool dragon was playing catch with them.

"Not quite the sum," Pelmen muttered.

—What's that?

"They lack, evidently, the contribution from the party of faith."

—So they do. The House was silent for a moment. Perhaps that was to have been the Power's contribution?

Pelmen nodded to the damp darkness. "I'm sure of it."

—This must be considered.

"Then the crystals were never made for communication at all?"

—You've been told the story of their construction, said the House, a bit peevishly. Was anything said about communication?

"No."

—Very well, then. When they're used in a task for which they weren't intended, they scatter waves of magical nausea that cause this House dire distress. It would be greatly appreciated if you would remove this magical thorn from within these walls.

"I'll do my best. But I must have your cooperation if I'm to succeed."

—Gladly offered. With one condition.

"Which is?"

—No magic.

The phrase thundered at Pelmen from every side.

"Done," said Pelmen, and he meant it.

The conversation extended into the early morning, ending at last only because of their mutual need to absorb what had already been discussed. House and man fell silent, but with an implied promise to renew the contact as soon as possible. Pelmen lay awake thinking for a long time, but finally slipped into sleep, leaving the House alone. It pondered a new idea that seemed at the same time very ancient:

—What is this Power?

A heavy, wet mist clung to the heights of Dragonsgate. The band of slavers wore it like a cloak in the darkness as they pounded down out of the southern mouth and onto the flatlands of Chaomonous. At the head of the column Bronwynn rode, her jaw set in hatred, her eyes aflame. At the base of the mountains the fog cleared, and the stars could be seen clearly above them. But she didn't tilt her head back to look. She peered straight ahead, down the road to the capital, driven by her determination to murder Ligne— and her lover.

Pinter and Tibb also rode with determination—they were determined not to get lost in the dark. They rode horses stolen from the skyfaithers, and fortunately these mounts were proving equal to the task. But the two made a point of staying toward the center of the pack. They had not experienced universal acceptance among this band of outlaws, and it would have pleased some of their companions to abandon them along the road. In spite of Tibb's insistence that "a cutthroat is a cutthroat wherever he's from," their differences with these Chaons grew more pronounced with each passing hour.

The moon rose blood-red over their left shoulders, dimming the stars and throwing eerie illumination before them. But the strange light did not reveal the forms of twenty sleeping figures until the column was already upon them. The campers woke to the terrifying sound of an onrushing wave of hooves. Most were alert enough to scatter out of the way, but a few unfortunates were deep sleepers. These never woke again. The charging army never stopped. It soon had disappeared to the south.

The moon was long gone, and the sun's glow was just beginning to light the horizon, when the small group of blue faithers finished burying their dead. Already, these four who had left them in the night seemed a little less human and a lot more holy than the living. On a green knoll only a few hundred feet from the site of the midnight tragedy, Naquin committed their bodies to the ground. A few moments later, as the sky turned from pink to gold, he quietly dismissed the survivors. The tiny group of missionaries dispersed in every direction, more determined than ever to share their Prophet and their book.

Naquin turned back to gaze at the freshly turned dirt one last time, then spun on his heels to follow the band of outlaws to Chaomonous.

Pelmen awoke refreshed and alert and immediately jumped off his cot. He zigzagged through the corridors to the wide hallway that circled the outer perimeter of every floor of the castle and found a window. It was early still— the sun was not yet up, but the red sky above the horizon painted the day with promise. He raced to the gardens, found a secluded spot behind a bush, and addressed the House again: "Good morning."

—It may prove so.

"Or it may not. The Queen has promised me a trip to the dungeon this morning."

—Her words were heard.

"Any idea what's behind it?"

—Perhaps it's the result of the Lord of Security's suspicions.

"Do you know anything specific? Does either Joss or the Queen suspect that I am more than just a fool?"

—The Lord of Security is secretive as well as suspicious. He says little, and this House cannot read thoughts. Actually, the man is proving a relatively responsible General in spite of his failure.

"Failure?"

—He allowed a captive to be stolen from the dungeon of this House! the castle snorted. Pelmen heard bells ringing in the distance.

"That angers you?"

—Certainly. Escaping prisoners threaten the integrity of this House as a fortress. Such failure on the part of the warders is intolerable.

Pelmen felt alarmed at the castle's fury. "Would it anger you if I were to rescue someone from the dungeon?"

Every soul in the castle was awakened by the Imperial House's clamorous reply. Pelmen couldn't translate the curses, but he could tell they were curses. He set his jaw, and plunged ahead:

"That disturbs me, since I intend to do just that. But before you break into another chorus, hear me for a moment." The castle was silent. "You asked me to remove the painful pyramid from within you, and I'll do my best to help you. But I want something in return."

—And that is? the Imperial House demanded.

"Freedom for the woman in the lower dungeon, and a route of escape for myself and my friends." Pelmen expected another barrage of bells, but none came. The House was silent. "Are you thinking?"

—This must be considered.

Pelmen nodded and settled back on his rock to wait. As he waited, the castle came awake—or rather, the people in it did. He became aware of the birds chirping above him and leaned back to enjoy their beauty.

—Can you do anything about them? the House grunted, making Pelmen jump.

"About what?" he asked when he recovered.

—These infuriating fowls!

"You don't like birds, either?"

—They besmirch the roof and terraces of this House. Daily.

Pelmen nodded. "I see. Very well, you help me plan my escape route, and I'll steal the pyramid and free the birds. Fair enough?"

—This goes against the nature of this House!

"Your requests go against my nature too. I'm no thief and I like birds."

The House thought for several more minutes.

—Very well.

"You're agreed?"

—You remember the condition?

"I do. No magic."

"Good morrow, clown," said a voice above him, and Pelmen whirled around in shock to look behind him. "Up here, fool."

Pelmen tilted his head up. On a balcony that had gone completely unnoticed until this moment sat the Queen, still clothed in her nightgown. She was scarcely fourteen feet away. "Greetings, my Lady." He smiled woodenly.

"Why are you out there talking to yourself this morning?"

"I—am—rehearsing a part, my Lady," he covered.

"Ah. For the play about me?"

"That is correct. I have little free time to rehearse, so I—"

"Very responsible of you. Come, join us on this balcony for breakfast," she invited. Then she added, "Now," turning it into a command.

"How do I get to it?"

"Come to the door of my apartments. They'll let you in. Ah, here's Rosha already!" she gushed, turning away. She popped her head over the balcony once again before she went on into her room and ordered him, "Get up here." Then she was gone, back inside.

How much had she heard? Probably made little difference, he reassured himself, since she only heard one side of the conversation. Nevertheless, he reviewed his words as he made his way down out of the gardens and into the hallway, then back up the stairs towards Ligne's multileveled suite. He met Yona Parmi on a stair-landing.

"Good morning, Fallomar. What's the matter?" Yona quickly added as he saw the expression on Pelmen's face.

"Nothing. Ligne's taking me to the dungeon, that's all." Yona's face turned nearly as white as Pelmen's, and that made the powershaper chuckle. "Relax—I don't believe it's intended to be permanent. Besides, I've found us a powerful ally within these walls, one that I think can get us all out of this place. Is Gerrig still anxious to leave?"

"I don't know how he feels about that this morning. He met another young lady last night—"

"So I heard," Pelmen interrupted. "I have to hurry, but listen. During rehearsal today, arrange some signal to gather the troupe quickly in one place. It may be necessary to move fast."

"Are you finally going to involve us in your plans?" Parmi smiled.

"I'm afraid you're already involved because of your connection to me. I hadn't intended to become so well-known

to the Queen. Since I did, if I disappear with Rosha, she's
certain to take her vengeance out on you."

"So we go out with you." Parmi nodded. "Through the
infirmary?" he added, then smiled at Pelmen's surprise.

"How do you know about that?"

"Give me credit for some power of observation," Yona
snapped.

Pelmen nodded. "I do, Yona. I just wanted to keep you
out of any danger."

"Worry about yourself, not us. Maythorm announced to
us last night that he knew who you were." Pelmen's eyes
widened. "Rosha took care of it for you. He broke the
man's neck."

Pelmen heaved a relieved sigh. "That sounds like his father. Yona, please try to help him hold his temper just a
few more days." Then he charged up the stairs toward
Ligne's apartments. As he walked, he asked the House,
"Why didn't you tell me Ligne was listening to me in the
garden?"

—Was that part of the bargain?

"If it wasn't, it should be from now on."

—She didn't hear a great deal. However, the woman is
acting curiously today. Perhaps you had better take care.

Pelmen nodded. He had at last reached the Queen's
door, and he knocked on it.

"What kept you, clown?" Ligne asked sharply as he was
escorted onto the balcony.

"Your palace is so vast, my Lady—I lost my way."

Ligne raised a disbelieving eyebrow. "I had thought you
got around quite well—perhaps too well. Unfortunately,
you seem to have missed breakfast while you wandered the
halls. Joss and Rosha have just finished the last crumbs."

Pelmen glanced now at the two men who sat flanking
her. To one side was Rosha, looking more distressed than
usual. Had Ligne discovered their relationship? On her
other side sat General Joss, who studied Pelmen's face with
patient, emotionless suspicion. Pelmen ignored his own discomfort and smiled brightly. "No matter. Are you ready
for me to take you slumming below?"

"I had rather thought I was taking you," Ligne replied.

"Whether I take you or you take me, what difference?
We're all sure to be taken by someone, eventually."

"Maybe not, clown."

"And yet maybe. The possibility of being taken is more threatening than the certainty of it." Pelmen pointed toward her door with a flourish and shouted, "To the dungeon with you!"

Ligne's face suddenly grew hard. "You overstep yourself, fool," she murmured dangerously.

"Again?" Fallomar responded. "I'm forever doing that. Perhaps that explains why I so frequently fall on my face?"

"Come along," Ligne snapped as she stood up and stalked past him. She stopped when she got to the balcony door, and looked back at Joss. "General," she said, "you will see that Rosha is moved to his new quarters?"

"I will, my Lady."

"Bye-bye, Rosha. See you after your rehearsal," she sang, and Rosha managed a shallow smile. Pelmen took comfort that he was at least still trying. "Come, clown," Ligne snapped, and she left the room with Pelmen striding swiftly along behind her.

Throughout their descent to the lower levels, Pelmen talked and joked, earnestly gauging Ligne's responses for some change in her attitude toward him. As they descended to that final level, the lower dungeon where Serphimera was housed, he grew quiet.

"What?" Ligne asked him. "No quick-witted remark for this level?"

"To be forthright, my Lady, this hall is so drafty that the chill bumps have extended to the tip of my tongue. You see?" he said, thrusting it out at her.

"Put your disgusting tongue back in your mouth! Your impudence begins to gall me."

"Such cold makes my tongue thick and slow to wag."

"Stick it out again and I'll have it extracted! It certainly won't bother you then."

"Missing it might . . ."

"Stay here." She pointed her finger at the floor and the jester made a show of rooting himself in that precise spot. Ligne ignored him and walked down the corridor to Serphimera's door. Pelmen hoped his loud remarks had alerted the Priestess to his presence. He was confident he could maintain the pretense of not knowing her. He felt no such assurance, however, that Serphimera could do the same. He strained to hear their conversation.

"Priestess!" Ligne called through the bars, and Serphimera uncurled herself quickly from her bed and padded across the floor to face her.

"My Lady. I'd not expected you to return so soon."

"Then perhaps I've been too predictable in the past. Come come, any news for me?"

"News, my lady?" Serphimera said guardedly.

"Visions! Predictions! What may I expect?"

"You can expect me to freeze if we stay down here much longer!" Pelmen interrupted, leaving his spot to come toward her.

"I told you to say there!" Ligne ordered, pointing her finger at him. "Do you want me to leave you behind?"

The fool didn't slow his pace. "Why, look!" he shouted as he turned to peer into the Priestess' cell and feigned surprise at seeing Serphimera. "Here's a captive to remain behind for! Such radiance is like a light in this darkened world! Tell me, my Lady, who is she?"

"You don't know her?" Ligne asked, keeping her eyes fixed on Serphimera's face to judge the woman's reactions.

"Know her?" Pelmen gushed. "Why, if I did, I'd have quit this costume long ago and followed her, hat in hand!"

"You are taken with her, then?"

"As I said, we all must at last be taken or forfeit our humanity. I'm taken, indeed! Do you pen her here because her beauty is the only rival to your own?"

"You ask too many questions, clown." Ligne turned and explained to the staring Serphimera, "He's an insolent creature."

"I see that clearly," the Priestess responded, and she clamped her jaws tightly together, freezing her expression in place. Serphimera's head swam. What was she supposed to do?

"Like a cur, he'd been sniffing out my dungeon—I wondered if he belonged, somehow, to you?"

"To me, my Lady?" Serphimera said faintly. "Queen Ligne, my business has nothing to do with jesters, and certainly not with this fool!"

"But surely," Pelmen murmured, "such beauty as the two of you share makes a fool of every man . . ."

Ligne smiled. "You see why I like to keep him around. He has such a lovely tongue—" Here she looked at Pelmen. "—when he keeps it in his mouth."

Serphimera looked at them both uncertainly, and it seemed to Pelmen that she made some sort of decision. He braced himself.

"There was a vision . . . that . . . that came in a dream. I saw two plots against you, Queen, but neither plot succeeded."

"Indeed!" said Ligne, startled. She turned to Pelmen. "Clown, get out."

"Then I'm not to be behinded?"

"Get!" the Queen roared, and Pelmen scrambled up the stairs. Over his shoulder he saw Ligne lean into the cell window and demand: "Tell me more." He wished he, too, could hear that revelation, but he felt less uncertain of his standing now than he had throughout the morning. Ligne evidently had found no clear link between himself and Serphimera, and that relieved him. He also felt confident Serphimera would not willingly betray him. In fact, he was convinced she had just passed him a pointed warning.

"Two plots," he muttered to himself, "and neither one will succeed." The news was certainly troubling. But if Serphimera had seen it in a vision, he didn't doubt it for a minute.

Carlad maintained his formal, cool manner as he and Rosha walked down the hallway side by side. Once in the throne room, he dropped that pretense and raced over to join himself to Danyilyn, laughing and clapping the other players on the back. Rosha stood near the doorway, trying to control his rage. Yona Permi quickly joined him.

"I saw Pelmen in the hall this morning," Parmi said quietly. "He says he has an ally in the walls, as well as a way out for all of us. Patience, Rosha. Just a few more days."

"I don't have a few more days," Rosha snarled.

"What?"

"The woman has moved me into the room next to hers," Rosha said grimly. Then he looked at Parmi. "She's going to marry me, she says." Yona nodded. "What am I supposed to do?" Rosha pleaded.

"Stall her."

"I can't do that forever. Yona, if that woman chases me around the room again, I swear I'll break her neck!"

"Don't do it!" Yona snapped. "You'll bring the whole castle down on us!"

"I can't help it! The woman makes me ill!"

"That's it!" Yona smiled brightly.

"What?"

"Get sick! Everytime she comes near you, get sick. It's hard to maintain passion for someone who is retching."

Rosha stared at him. "You mean—"

"It's easy. I'll teach you," Yona said, and he took Rosha aside and began his instruction. By late morning, the young warrior had mastered the art.

Pelmen quickly climbed the stairs to the upper level of the dungeon, and started for the doorway. He stopped short when he saw Joss blocking it. The General appeared to be staring at him, and Pelmen felt some of his uneasiness return. He shot the aged soldier a quick smile. He was not greatly comforted when the Lord of Security returned it. "Pardon," he mumbled as he brushed through the door and into the hall. Joss made no effort to stop him—but neither did he get out of the way. Pelmen quickly put some distance between them.

Moments later he slammed the door of his cell and sat on the floor before one of its walls. "What are they saying now?"

—They? the castle replied casually. There are at least four hundred conversations currently in progress. Perhaps you could be more specific?

"The Queen and the woman Serphimera! What are they saying?"

—Nothing at the moment. Their conversation ended only moments after you were dismissed, with the captive woman pretending ignorance of any further details of these two plots she mentioned, and the Queen cursing her for a liar.

"You say she's pretending—she does know more about them?"

—She fears she does.

"Does she think that my presence within the walls constitutes one of the two?"

—She does.

"How do you know," Pelmen demanded.

—At this moment she addresses a long supplication to the dragon on your behalf. Since that scaly beast is dead, he surely cannot mind if this House eavesdrops.

Pelmen stared at the wall, his mind as blank as its surface.

—This woman's appraisal of your so-called plot seems to bother you, the Imperial House chortled.

"She's not the crazy woman you seem to consider her," Pelmen said quietly. "I know her. And her visions come true."

—Then your plan is doomed to failure. While this House can sympathize with your frustration, this certainly cannot be allowed to interfere with the contract agreed upon this morning.

"I'll still get your pyramid," Pelmen said wearily. He lapsed into silence for a moment, then quickly demanded, "What's the best—the most unobtrusive—way out of you?"

—You plan to press on in spite of her words?

"If I make no attempt, I prove her vision true already. What route?"

—It grieves this House to make this confession. It was a crack in the foundations that permitted that thief to steal away a captive. It may be reached through those same tunnels you became so thoroughly lost in.

"But you could guide us to it?"

—Naturally.

"That'll have to do. How do I—"

—There is a problem.

"What problem?"

—The crack opens onto the river. Unless your friends are all excellent swimmers, it would seem necessary to have a boat positioned below the crack. There is no boat there.

"I see."

—There is another alternative.

"And that is?"

—The rulers of this House have long kept a boat secreted in a cavern beneath the northern face of this castle. This cavern can only be reached through a concealed passageway, which can be entered only through the royal

apartments, the throne room, and several other strategic
locations within these walls. These entryways are evidently
closely guarded secrets, since the spiders who make the
passage their home have not been disturbed in years.

"But you know the secret?"

—This House watched while the cavern was carved! the
castle snarled.

"Very well." Pelmen nodded. "But how do I get Serphimera out of the dungeon and up to one of these entry
points in order to escape?"

—That is a problem you must solve. While this House
might permit the theft of another captive, you cannot expect it to suggest how such might be done!

Pelmen nodded—and spent the rest of the afternoon
grilling the castle about possible escape routes and planning
possible scenarios for their grand attempt. The castle was
intrigued by this fool's errand. So intrigued, in fact, that it
paid no attention to a brief encounter that took place between Joss and the Queen as Ligne left the dungeon. It
never heard the General mutter, "Now?"

Nor did it hear Ligne swiftly reply, "Not yet."

CHAPTER SEVENTEEN

With Violence and Guile

THE LAZY OCCUPANTS of Pahd's fortress took little notice of Flayh, except to observe that he seemed unduly industrious, and to suggest that he take life a little easier. Flayh responded to each of these comments with a silent smile so false and threatening that no one had yet dared to address him twice. Chogi lan Pahd-el was the only one who engaged him in conversation. She, however, was certainly enough. The old girl pursued him through the castle like a bulldog—short of wind and stubby of legs, but long on determination. He'd been forced to repeat a dozen spells due to Pahd's mother interrupting him at a critical juncture. It had happened again just a moment before, and he was contemplating what slimy denizen of the deep he'd like to change the woman into as he accompanied her up the royal tower's steps.

The woman banged open the door without stopping to knock, and stalked to the foot of Pahd's bed. "Get up. We have a crisis."

"What?" asked Sarie groggily, raising her head and gazing bleary-eyed at her mother-in-law. Then she looked at a nearby window. "It's still morning!" she scolded. "We never get up in the morning!"

"We do when an army marches against us!" Chogi snapped, and suddenly Pahd's head popped up off the pillow.

"Battle?" he asked hopefully.

"It appears so." Chogi sighed.

Flayh was shocked to see the King dance out of bed, skip across the fur-covered floor, and jerk a great sword out of a scabbard hanging on the wall. "Wonderful!" Pahd cried, as he thrusted and parried, quite oblivious to the flapping of his nightshirt.

"Your joy may be premature," Chogi said soberly.

"Why's that? Whom are we fighting?"

"Mar-Yilot and her man."

Pahd stopped dancing. "Oh." He looked at Flayh expectantly, and the former merchant suddenly discovered that Chogi and Sarie were gazing at him too.

"Am I supposed to say something?" Flayh asked.

Sarie's eyebrows raised with just a hint of disapproval. "Well you might offer us a bit of encouragement. After all, you *are* the court shaper."

"I hadn't realized lending encouragement was part of my task," Flayh responded evenly.

"What the girl is saying," Chogi explained apologetically, "is that since you are our shaper, and since Mar-Yilot is a witcher woman, we would like to know how you intend to protect us." She folded her hands on her ample belly and waited for a reply, her eyes fixed demurely on the floor.

"Oh, that." Flayh nodded, endeavoring to appear nonchalant in spite of the sudden pounding of his heart. But Flayh had not been a longtime success at merchandising without learning how to use shifting fortunes to his advantage. He beamed his false smile at them and said, "Don't be alarmed. I can assure you that I can provide total protection for you by nightfall."

"Total protection?" Pahd asked. "From Mar-Yilot? That's a rather grandiose claim, considering the woman's past successes in shaper battles. Why, in the last war of confederation, the only wizard to control her was Pelmen the powerful, and that only by outwitting her. For raw strength in bending powers to her will, no one can match the woman." Pahd said this in awe-filled tones approaching hero-worship, and Sarie looked at him sharply.

"That may be," Flayh murmured confidently. "But she has yet to meet with me—or my knowledge." He laid his hand over the place where his spell-book was concealed in his tunic. "If you will permit me to work throughout the rest of this day—" Here he looked at Chogi to add, "—*undisturbed*—" He looked back at Pahd. "—by the time you take to your bed again this evening, this fortress, already formidable by all human standards, will be totally impervious to magic attacks as well."

"Really? You can do all of that while I'm out of bed? That is fast."

"But only if I'm undisturbed."

Pahd nodded and pursed his lips. Then he looked at his mother, who was quite obviously preparing to pout. "Ah . . . mother? Weren't you planning to visit Aunt Razel sometime soon?"

"Are you telling me to get out of this house?" Chogi challenged her son, her jaw jutting forward.

"Why, no, mother." Pahd shrugged. "Just suggesting that—"

"I'll not interfere with you, Lord Flayh," she promised the powershaper in a voice thick with sarcasm. "Just see to it that you do your job and that we are protected." She banged her way back out the way she came in, heading for her own quarters to weep away her feelings of rejection.

Pahd misinterpreted Flayh's look of scorn as an expression of concern. "Don't worry, my friend. She won't give up on you that easily." Pahd slipped his sword back into its holder and eyed his pillow. "Don't, ah—don't let me keep you from your work . . ." he hinted.

"I certainly won't. Good day, my Lord—my Lady." Flayh bowed slightly, then left the tower, pulling out his grimoire as he went.

Pahd started for the bed, then stopped, and sniffed the air. "You smell something funny?"

"It's your mother's perfume," Sarie told him with a droll smile.

"Ah." Pahd nodded, stretched, yawned, and scratched his side. "I guess that takes care of the crisis, so . . . I think I'll take a little nap."

"You do that." Sarie smiled sweetly. "Everything here is under control."

And by nightfall, everything was under control. Flayh's.

"I'm in charge here," Pezi yelled at the cook, "and unless you'd rather be working the docks in southern Chaomonous, you'd better keep that in mind!"

"I shall, *Lord* Pezi!" the cook roared back, ramming a wicked-tipped fork into the rump roast that lay on the cutting table before him. Pezi could hardly miss the implication. The cook was obviously wishing it were Pezi's.

Pezi drew himself up to his full height, hitched his pants—a futile gesture he repeated a hundred times daily—and sauntered out the door of the kitchen into the courtyard. He immediately wished he hadn't.

A sugar-clawsp hung there in the air, eying him menacingly. Its membranous wings were a-blur with motion, yet it held its position in his face, unyielding, offering no quarter. Sunlight glinted off its iridescent violet body, adding to the illusion of armor-plated invincibility. Never mind that it was only half an inch long—Pezi was terrified of these things! He gulped and backed toward the kitchen door. The sugar-clawsp slowly followed him.

Pezi stopped. He couldn't let a clawsp chase him back into the presence of the cook. He already faced enough difficulty in establishing his authority over this manor. He refused to add this indignity to the list of Pezi stories he knew was making the rounds. Yet the suger-clawsp just as adamantly refused to let him pass. When he stepped to the right, the tiny insect zipped over to meet him. When he stepped back to the left, it buzzed back to its original position.

Pezi reviled himself silently. Why hadn't he left the kitchen through the hall? Why had he chosen this back door, where he knew sugar-clawsps would be swarming this time of year? Clawsps loved sugar and lived wherever it was readily available. They formed it into the inverted castles of silvery crystal that hung from the eaves above him. Kitchen help throughout the three lands encouraged these insects to swarm, as a convenient way of storing sugar supplies. Whenever more of the substance was needed for the table, some unfortunate servant was delegated to tear down a clawsp castle and grind it to powder. This miserable task usually fell to the servant currently in deepest disfavor, for

invariably he would need to pluck a host of the tiny creatures out of their crystal courts first—and when aroused,
sugar-clawsps exuded an oily acid that produced nasty
burns on human skin. Touching an angry sugar-clawsp
could be compared to thrusting a hand into an open flame.

And all clawsp seemed angry around Pezi. Perhaps they
were instinctively aware that his great girth represented
scores of demolished sugar palaces. Perhaps they were jealous, for it was evident that Pezi got all the sugar he
wanted. For whatever reason, the fat merchant had never
met a clawsp he didn't hate.

A voice came from the kitchen. "I'm looking for the
Lord Pezi—have you seen him?"

"Go right out that door—" Pezi heard the cook reply.
The fat merchant's face flushed as the cook continued with
a snicker: "He's outside dancing with a clawsp."

"Lord Pezi?" said the voice behind him.

"I'm right here," he retorted, visibly impatient.

"I . . . can see that . . ." the voice replied. Pezi identified it as belonging to the chief watchman at the gate.

"Well, get around here where I can see your face!" Pezi
was not about to turn his back on the tiny violet creature.
He'd tried that before, and more than one hostile sugar-
clawsp had taken advantage of the huge target thus provided. As the watchman stepped cautiously into his field of
vision, Pezi grabbed the man by the collar and swung him
around as a shield. The clawsp buzzed angrily, but did not
strike the guard. "Now what is it?" Pezi demanded, his
eyes focused beyond the man's head.

"I . . . there's someone in the courtyard to see you—"

"Who is it?"

"Tahli-Damen, the local lord of Uda in this region—"

"What!" Pezi yelped, suddenly focusing his eyes on the
guard. "And you let him in!"

"Of course, Lord Pezi. Why, he is a merchant—"

"Without asking me?"

"You weren't in your office, Lord Pezi!"

"You knew that it was time for my afternoon snack."

"I know that all afternoon is time for your afternoon
snack—"

"Then why didn't you seek me out?"

"He told me that he bore an emergency message specifi-

cally for the Lord Pezi. Besides, he's a merchant, and common courtesy demands that merchant houses admit any un-
accompanied merchant who asks entry—"

Pezi snarled and shoved the guard backwards. The man
screamed in pain and clapped the back of his neck, for the
fat merchant had pushed him into the clawsp. Pezi didn't
linger to hear the guard's angry curses. He waddled rapidly
around the corner of the kitchen toward the courtyard—
and away from the clawsp.

Tahli-Damen waited in the dusty court. Instead of the
velvet and fish-satin robes his office entitled him to wear,
he had donned the simple costume of a trading captain.
His expression was almost penitent.

Pezi jellied toward him, regarding the Udan merchant
with puzzled suspicion. "What are you doing here?" he
blustered.

Tahli-Damen's reply astonished him. The man dropped
to one knee and mumbled, "I've come to beg your forgiveness."

"Hunh?"

"I've had several days, Lord Pezi, to review my behavior
at the conclave. I offer my apology, if I caused you and
your uncle any discomfort."

"What do you want?" Pezi's eyes narrowed to mere slits
in his fleshy face. He was keen enough to know no merchant ever acted like this unless he wanted something.

"Lord Pezi, you see right through me," Tahli-Damen
confessed. "As you've guessed, I've come seeking a favor—
a rather . . . delicate favor . . ." Tahli-Damen lowered
his voice and glanced around. Several occupants of the castle had stopped to watch this curious spectacle unfold.

"You want privacy?" Pezi whispered.

"When you learn my business, I'm sure you'll want privacy as well . . ." Tahli-Damen replied mysteriously.

Pezi straightened up, his expression of consternation
masking the gloating pride welling up inside his belly. He
liked the idea of commanding the whole castle's attention.
He enjoyed being addressed as Lord Pezi by his chief competition in Ngandib-Mar. And he exulted in the picture of
this competitor kneeling at his feet in the dust. He wasn't
in any hurry to move out of the public eye.

"I don't have any secrets from my employees," Pezi said

grandly, gesturing around at the large court. "If you have business, speak it plainly." Pezi propped his hand on his hips and splayed his feet wide apart.

"As you choose, Lord Pezi, but I—" Tahli-Damen looked up then and suddenly broke off.

"What's the matter?" Pezi grunted. "Forget what you were going to say?"

"No, my Lord," Tahli-Damen replied humbly. "It's just that I noticed a sugar-clawsp buzzing around your head—"

"On the other hand, my offices are cool and quite private," Pezi suggested earnestly, and he dragged Tahli-Damen to his feet.

"You'll not regret this choice," Tahli-Damen said as Pezi hustled him into a dark hallway and away from the insistent violent pest.

"I'm sure I won't," Pezi puffed, hurrying along the hall's cobbled floor. In the dark of the passageway, the fat merchant completely missed Tahli-Damen's gloating grin.

Erri cleared his throat and pointed to a wall. "That one first, Dolna."

The tugolith keeper nodded, and began explaining to his assistants where they would attach their chains to the walls of the temple. Nearby, a dozen tugoliths waited impatiently for the destruction process to begin.

Erri had decided weeks ago that in order to eradicate all memory of the Dragonfaith from the minds of his people, this central symbol of the ancient religion had to be destroyed. It was a pity to tumble such a grand construction. But if symbols couldn't be changed, they had to be removed—and this was one symbol he had no intention of the new skyfaith adopting. Scores of initiates had urged him to reopen the delicately crafted cathedral and make it as central to the new faith as it had been to the ancient religion. But Erri resisted. "The Power cannot be contained in a house," the Prophet snapped when anyone suggested it. If this place had to come down in order to make that clear, then come down it would. Today.

Erri felt a lingering sense of depression, however. He had been wakened in the night by horrible screaming—only to find the screams had been in his dreams alone. Even so, he felt a malaise that couldn't be denied and that wouldn't go away in spite of the attention he gave to this project. He had been talking to the Power about it all morning. "Is Naquin in trouble?" the Prophet asked.

"What's a Naquin?" asked a curious tugolith. Erri turned around to stare up at the horned monster. The tugolith's huge green eye, easily the size of small wagon wheel, gazed back at him curiously.

"It's . . . a man." Erri answered carefully.

"I don't know a Naquin man," the gigantic beast explained.

"I see. That's all right." Erri smiled in a soothing tone.

"But you asked me," the puzzled tugolith pointed out.

Erri looked at it. "Oh, about if Naquin was in trouble? I was talking to someone else, child. Don't worry about it." It was impossible to think of a tugolith as anything other than an enormous baby. The beasts thought at the level of human toddlers.

"But if he's in trouble . . ." the beast began.

"If he's in trouble, what, Chimolitha?" asked Dolna as he rejoined Erri. The Prophet felt great relief at the keeper's return.

"Then . . . you'll be angry," Chimolitha explained.

"I'm not angry at anyone, sweetheart," Dolna said. "Are you ready to pull down this building for me?"

"Yes!" trumpeted Thuganlitha, an aggressive beast who liked nothing better than to bury its gigantic horn into something—or someone.

"I know you are, Thug. Riganlitha? Pulanlitha? Are you ready?"

"I want to play," Riganlitha whined.

"Why, this will be fun!" Dolna exclaimed. "You'll really like it!"

"I like killing people," Thuganlitha interrupted.

"I know that, Thuganlitha—"

"Are there any people inside?" the beast asked hopefully.

"No," Dolna replied wearily. "None inside."

Thuganlitha muttered a brief obscenity, shocking both its keeper and Erri. "Where'd it learn that?" Erri asked, wide-eyed.

"Thuganlitha," Chimolitha chided. "You're not supposed to."

"I don't care!" The aggressive monster sniggered.

"Dolna, what does that word mean?" Pulanlitha asked.

"Never mind!" the overseer shouted, and he looked apologetically at Erri. "I think I'd better get them in place right now or we could have a problem on our hands . . ."

"Go to it," Erri told him, dismissing him with a wave. The Prophet turned to go back to his tiny cell, but was startled when a voice—a tugolith voice—called out to him.

"Prophet?"

The Prophet spun around, his eyes wide. The same green eye gazed down at him. "Ah . . . yes . . . Chimolitha?" he replied, hoping he had the right name. He did.

"Is that Pelmen man all right?"

Erri remembered then that this was one of the two beasts that had nearly torn Pelmen in two. His face softened. "Yes, child. The Pelmen man is all right."

"Good," Chimolitha said with a kind of giggle. "I like him."

"I like him too." Erri grinned, then he waved at the beast, and walked across the vast city square. As he reached the far side, well out of earshot of the tugoliths, he inclined his head to look at the fluffy clouds drifting high above him. "He *is* all right . . . isn't he?" Erri asked. Then he went inside, to await the same assurance from another source that he'd so easily afforded the tugolith.

"I see," said Pezi, nodding in what he believed was a dignified manner. Tahli-Damen returned Pezi's sober expression, while in his mind stifling a guffaw. This task promised to be simpler than he'd ever imagined. Already he'd identified the corner where Pezi stored his precious pyramid. Though the office was dark, with only the flame of a single candle for light, the triangular contours of the bag behind the desk had broadcast its contents to Tahli-Damen's eyes. The only problems left to solve now were how to get Pezi to leave the room, and then how to get safely out of the keep.

"It's quite clear," Tahli-Damen explained. "I think you can see the advantages. The actual trade is perfectly aboveboard, and if the other local houses are caught in the resulting squeeze, we can hardly consider it unfair. After all, we are the two most competitive houses in this mountain-

ous nation." The young merchant leaned forward to place a
hand on Pezi's balloonlike knee. "And think, Pezi—think
of the respect we'll win. These old codgers who've ruled the
Council for ages—they aren't prepared to cope with this
new situation. They've spent all their lives saying 'yes sir'
and 'no sir' to the dragon—what do they know about this
modern world?"

"You have a point." Pezi nodded wisely.

"Your uncle. Where is he? Off someplace playing magician, that's what. And Jagd, my supervisor? All he does is
sit in the palace of Chaomonous playing table games. I tell
you, Pezi, that pair is senile, they're long past their prime.
And as you and I both know, the other ruling Elders are all
fossils as well, so accustomed to copying either what Flayh
does or what Jagd does that they've no minds of their own.
They're ripe plums, ready for us to seize and swallow."

Pezi smiled broadly. He liked the plum analogy. Pezi
liked plums.

"But it's essential that we move quickly—before your
uncle returns or Jagd regains his courage. Otherwise, we'll
soon go back to being what we've always been—abused
slaves, standing in the shadows of two old men."

"Ah . . . yes." Pezi nodded. "I can see that. But . . ."

"But what, Pezi?"

Tahli-Damen never heard Pezi's objection. There was a
heavy pounding at the door. "Go away!" Pezi shouted.

"A flyer, Lord Pezi," someone called from the corridor.
"We just discovered it. I'm afraid it's been here all night.
It's from Admon Faye."

"Admon Faye!" Pezi stopped himself, looked at Tahli-
Damen, then struggled to his feet and hustled over to the
door. "Give!" he commanded, and he was handed a small
scrap of paper that wanted to roll back into a cylinder. He
scooted to the candle and unrolled the scrap to read it. He
made a point of hiding the scribbled message from the eyes
of Tahli-Damen, but might just as well have handed it to
him in the first place, for all the good that did. Pezi moved
his lips when he read, and Tahli-Damen simply read them.
It was a terse message—AM RIDING TONIGHT—ADMON
FAYE—but it was enough to send Pezi into tailspinning confusion. "You—ah—you remain here." Pezi ordered, and he

started from the room. Then he stopped. "No. Leave. You must leave."

"But Pezi, what about our plans? Our future?"

"Oh. The future." Pezi pondered for a moment. "Ah, stay where you are, I have to send a message to my uncle—"

"What's it about?" Tahli-Damen asked innocently.

"The invasion of—oh, never mind," Pezi covered hurriedly. "It's nothing of importance, believe me." Pezi rushed into the corridor, the sudden beads of sweat popping out onto his head a clear indicator that the fat man was lying. An invasion by Admon Faye? Must be of the palace of Chaomonous, Tahli-Damen thought to himself. Jagd would certainly be pleased to have some advanced warning—

"On the other hand," Tahli-Damen said to himself, remembering his own words of a few moments before—perhaps Jagd didn't need to be warned at all. Certainly, there would be no question who would head the family of Uda if Jagd were gone . . .

Tahli-Damen dove under the desk and scooped up the bag. A quick check of its contents assured him it was the item he'd come to pilfer, then he was out into the corridor and running through the courtyard. "Your Lord Pezi needs you," he cried to the gatekeeper. "It's an emergency!"

"Let him wait," the porter responded angrily. The back of the man's neck still burned from his contact with the sugar-clawsp. Then, without Tahli-Damen's even asking, the man opened the gate and let him out.

It was really almost too easy.

A single flame sat on the table before Flayh in the darkened room. He stared into it, breathed deeply, then chanted: "By the powers of the sea, by the powers on the wind, by all powers that may be, let this castle's life begin!" His volume built quickly through the brief rhyme that formed the linking spell of all the work he'd done. Then he waited in silence, watching intently as the smoke curled up from the candle—listening. At last it came:

—Awake! the High Fortress of Ngandib snarled, and wind whistled through its corridors. Doors slammed and age beams cracked, bells rang, and the horses housed in the cave beneath the castle screamed in terror. It was late, and most of the palace-dwellers had long ago retired, but everyone woke up now. Even Pahd mod Pahd-el.

"What in the—" he began, then his voice left him as he gazed at the tall window. The room was dark, but moonlight streamed in, illuminating the terrifying inrush of wind that caused the long drapes to stream out from the wall and up toward the ceiling.

"Pahd," Sarie whispered, "do you think . . ."

"Yes, my love," Pahd murmured, hugging her trembling body close to his own. "I think our shaper has made good his promise."

"It scares me," Sarie whimpered.

Pahd licked his lips and didn't reply. There wasn't a warrior in the world who could cause him concern. But this scared him witless.

"Stop!" Flayh commanded.

—Why? the castle sneered, and Flayh's own window blew open with a bang.

Undaunted, he chanted again: "By the powers of the wind, by the powers of the sea, by my powers you begin, all your powers rest in me!"

The High Fortress laughed aloud. Flayh was ready for that. Without a word he altered shape—and his magic transformation turned the laughter of the Fortress into a long howl of pain. Flayh did not hurry to resume his human form. When at last he did, it was Flayh who was laughing and not the Fortress.

—Who? the High Fortress asked him.

"I am your master," Flayh said quietly, and he blew out the candle. For the rest of the long night, Flayh sat in his black room—smiling.

CHAPTER EIGHTEEN

From Troupe to Troops

THE ONRUSHING SLAVERS did not stop with the coming of daylight. They just left the main road and spent the entire day in the saddle. No words were exchanged, not even during the infrequent pauses in their journey. This trip had a very different flavor from Bronwynn's exhilarating ride through the Great South Fir. Raucous laughter had been replaced by muffled grunts. Wild careening over bushes and brush had given way to disciplined, orderly riding, the kind one would expect from a crack equestrian brigade. Every slaver present knew he had entered the territory of a deadly enemy. No one was foolish enough to take the Golden Throng of Chaomonous lightly—especially not when he considered the reputation of Lord Joss. Several of the slavers had spent time as Joss' captives and had shared sobering stories of his cruelty. It was in deference to Joss' skill as a tactician that the troop divided at midday. While the bulk of the riders forded the river twenty miles north of the capital, sixty of the finest horsemen continued southward. They were to make a carefully planned raid on the city's northwestern suburbs. Admon Faye felt confident that the raid would draw Joss out of the castle and cover his larger contingent's entry into the city sewers.

After twenty-seven hours of nearly nonstop riding, the larger unit of the house of Faye abandoned their exhausted horses at the northeast edge of Chaomonous. In minutes all were underground, Bronwynn included. She plugged her nose with cotton against the fetid odor and took her appointed place in a low, lean boat. An hour later, just a few minutes after midnight, they were all assembled in a subterranean cavern beneath the warehouse of one of Admon Faye's many "business associates"—one who knew how to keep his mouth shut.

Several lamps guttered in the close, foul cave, casting a flickering light on Admon Faye's face as he stood to address them:

"Here we sleep. Five hours—no more. We're within a few hundred yards of our target, so keep silent and get some rest. You'll be awakened by squads and ferried across to the point of entry at the base of the fortress. Once inside, wait in the cavern until all have assembled."

"Only one boat at a time?" a boatman asked. He knew the answer, but wanted to be sure everyone else did too.

"As planned," Admon Faye grunted. "One boat the guards won't take notice of. Fifteen boats at once would insure us all of a grave at the bottom of the river." Admon Faye searched the faces of his fellow cutthroats, seeking any signs of undue nervousness that might indicate duplicity. He found none. His eyes lingered on the face of Bronwynn. Angry? Bored? Or just sleepy and cross? Whatever, it was clear from her grim look that she was far from happy. The slaver dismissed it. He didn't expect her to be.

"We wait in the corridors below the house until after its occupants have had breakfast. Breakfast within the walls is a feast—as we shall all discover, when our little Bronwynn is the Queen," he added with a wicked grin. "After the meal, the guards will be stuffed and sleepy from their long night of defending the suburbs—totally unprepared for our invasion. We'll have diminished their number still further, I hope. I've scheduled a second raid on the western side of the city at a little after dawn, and Joss should be reacting to squelch it just about the time we attack. Sleepy, full, lulled by the false security of knowing where the enemy is, Ligne's guards will be raw meat for our cutting." Admon

Faye paused and allowed himself a satisfied smile. "It's a good plan," he affirmed. "There's not a thing that can stop us."

Bronwynn stared absently beyond the slaver at the garbage and dung drifting atop the surface of the waterway. It somehow seemed the only appropriate backdrop to this entire episode.

A few hours later, the boat was pushed away, off to deliver its first load. Bronwynn fingered the hilt of her dagger and waited her turn.

The night had come and the occupants of the Imperial House had long been still, when Pelmen suddenly awoke, his body drenched with sweat. He raised himself off the cot and felt the steam rising off the floor. He reached out in the pitch darkness to touch the wall he knew was there and snatched his hand away from the hot stone. "You're steaming!" he gasped.

—Seething, actually, the Imperial House growled from its bowels.

"Angry?" Pelmen whispered.

—Infuriated! the House thundered, and the steam continued to rise.

"Why? And where's this steam coming from?"

—While you've been slumbering, an army of thieves and robbers has crawled through the crack in these foundations! the Imperial House roared. As to where the steam is coming from, you will find the water is rising in the caverns.

"Water?" Pelmen asked. The cryptic sprang immediately to mind: "Deal gently with the House that speaks, lest it make the waters rise." "Are you causing the water level to rise?"

—Certainly. In the same way in which this House cooked the fish.

"You have to stop!" Pelmen shouted, and he leaped from his cot. He jumped back onto it immediately, however. The floor singed his feet. He quickly found his sandals and strapped them on, even as the castle snarled back:

—Why should this House wait! Do you expect the Imperial House of Chaomonous to permit an invasion from without? Why do you think this castle was summoned to life in the first place? It was to protect this castle's occupants against vermin like this.

Pelmen crawled into his garments as he asked, "How many are there?"

—Less than a hundred. No! More of the scum seep in at this very moment! The Imperial House seethed in fury.

"Who leads them?"

—This House knows few human faces—

"Is it the man who took Bronwynn from your dungeon!" Pelmen asked. The House was silent for a moment.

—It is that very rodent.

"Admon Faye." The powershaper nodded; he stood in the middle of the room and tried to clear his head to make plans. Obviously this was the other plot Serphimera had envisioned—one of two doomed to fail. Dismissing for a moment this reminder that his own scheme was similarly destined, he appealed to the House to recognize the outcome of its heated solution to the problem. "I take it you're planning to cook these invaders out of your tunnels in the same way that you boiled the fish."

—You guess rightly.

"But these tunnels connect to the lower dungeons. Won't that boil the Lady Serphimera as well?"

—It will, as well as several of those in the upper dungeon. But a House cannot consider individual lives when its entire populace-is threatened from without.

"May I suggest an alternative?"

—You're free to speak.

"Let my friends and myself drive these attackers from your lower galleries." It was the only idea that came to mind. But he had to do something.

The steaming stopped briefly, and a puff of laughter whistled down the hallways outside.

—That appears a ludicrous suggestion.

"Not so ludicrous if you recognize that we will need your help to do it."

—This House needs no powershaper's assistance to rid itself of robbers and blackguards. It shall do to this Admon Faye what it should have done the first time—what it would have done, had these lower galleries been under control!

"Very well." Pelmen nodded, feigning disinterest. "But the House does seem to need my help in ridding itself of a certain magic splinter of crystal." He folded his arms upon his chest, and shrugged. "If the woman in the dungeon is unnecessarily boiled, I see no reason why I should rid you of the pyramid."

Pelmen waited through the cascade of curses that tumbled upon him, following his threat. When the House was finally calm again, it asked:

—What do you plan to do?

"Is that an agreement to help me do this my way?"

—Get on with it! A hundred and twenty now wait in the lower galleries.

"Fine. I'll need a detailed plan of those corridors in your belly."

—Belly? huffed the castle. Rather, foundations.

"You call it what you like. Just give it to me." Pelmen bolted out the door of his cell and raced toward Yona Parmi's room. To his surprise, Parmi met him in the hall.

"Yona! What are you doing up!"

"The whole castle is up, it seems. First there was a general alarm to the palace guard—some kind of sneak attack on the north of the city—then this strange steam. I was on my way to wake you. Were you coming to wake me?"

"I was."

"Are you finally going to ask for some help?" the round-faced player asked with a touch of amused pride.

Pelmen thought for a moment. Was he being fair? Was it just for him to ask his friends to risk their lives to save a Lady they didn't know? "I . . . wonder if it's fair to involve you—"

"Would you let me be the judge of that?" Yona snapped.

"This is a dangerous task—"

"Wonderful." Parmi nodded. "You want me to circulate the signal to gather?"

Pelmen sighed. There was more involved here than just the salvation of Serphimera. Admon Faye could well have brought Bronwynn in with him. If the rightful Queen was boiled as well . . . "Yes," he grunted suddenly, and once again Parmi saw in Pelmen's eyes that strange fire that had illumined them backstage in Pleclypsa. Without another word from Pelmen, Yona Parmi scampered away.

"Now," Pelmen mumbled, "to get myself into the infirmary without being seen . . ."

"Ohh!" Danyilyn moaned, rolling and tossing on her thick mattress. "Ohh!" she wailed louder, hearing the approach of sandals flapping on the stone floor beyond her open door.

"I'm coming, I'm coming," snarled the Lord of Herbs impatiently as he turned the corner and entered the room. The man looked terrible—deep, dark bags sagged under his eyes, and his gray hairs pointed in every direction but down. The stubble that lined his bony chin added to his generally unkempt appearance. "I suppose you think you're sick as well," he growled, and he ran a hand through his unruly mane as Danyilyn groaned again. "You're the third one in this past hour. Everytime I get back to my infirmary door, there's someone else standing there, ready to tell me of another case. What's the problem with you actors. You eat something rotten?"

Danyilyn shook her head, then rolled her eyes dramatically and grabbed her stomach. "Ohhh!" she moaned.

"Trouble is, not a thing I can do about it, and it's the fault of one of your fellows!" The old man stretched his lengthy neck and scratched behind his ears. "After I got back from my first call this morning, I found someone had swiped all my balderberry juice! How can I treat a sick stomach without balderberry juice!"

Danyilyn shrugged and rolled her eyes again—quite thankful that Parmi had successfully made off with that particular concoction. Balderberry juice was an extremely potent purgative that tasted horrible. "I'll . . . I'll be . . . all right . . ." the actress gagged.

"Very well." The herbalist nodded, suddenly becoming aware of the young woman's curves. His bedside manner abruptly improved, and he sat next to her and felt her forehead. "You don't seem fevered," he murmured, growing a little fevered himself. "Perhaps it's just a mild case, but one can never be sure. I'd suggest a thorough examination, in order to—"

"Maybe we could do that . . . tomorrow?" Danyilyn asked coyly, and the old man's heart palpitated. She was far and away more lovely than the merchant's daughter he usually dated.

"Right. Certainly. Tomorrow. Try to rest, and come and see me in the morning. That is—" He interrupted himself. "I'll come and see you. Night-night!" he called, and he floated out of the room, now fully awake and already planning the morning's activities.

Danyilyn groaned again as he left the room. She waited until she could no longer hear his footsteps, then hopped off her bed and danced to the doorway. "Parmi's surely found Gerrig by this time," she muttered sourly, then she tiptoed into the hallway to follow him. She kept well out of sight until he had reached the infirmary door again. She heard his groan, then sighed with relief as she heard Gerrig direct him to the room of yet another "sick" actor. Gerrig had arrived—they were all finally gathered. She hugged the wall as the grumbling Lord of Herbs shuffled past her. She smiled with satisfaction as she imagined the old roué's reactions when he found her room empty in the morning. Served him right. He would find his present trip up the stairs frustrating, too—Gerrig had sent him to Yona's empty room. Danyilyn darted into the infirmary, shot a dirty look at Gerrig, and slipped swiftly through the trapdoor.

"We're all clear," she murmured waspishly. "Finally!"

"Any trouble getting here?" Pelmen asked Gerrig as the bulky actor lowered himself through the infirmary floor into the presence of the others.

"I told you," Danyilyn snapped, "the only trouble was finding where he was sleeping tonight."

"Silence!" Pelmen ordered, and the actors and actresses clustered around him obeyed without a question.

"No trouble," Gerrig whispered after a moment.

"Good. We're all here then, safely."

"And you're going to get us out now?" Gerrig grinned.

"Not exactly. Jamnard, Magrol—close off the doorway."

A pair of younger players moved quickly to seal off the portal, hiding once more this nether stairway from the infirmary. Pelmen waited until the task was done, then explained: "I have information that somewhere down with us in this maze of passageways is a small army preparing to take control of this castle."

"And we're going to join them?" Gerrig asked incredulously.

"No. We're going to drive them out."

There was a long, high-tension pause. Pelmen could hear several of the troupe gasping. Then Gerrig made a move for the door.

"Gerrig. We all agreed to do this together—" Yona murmured.

"And now I've decided to leave, *alone!*" the big man replied, trying to free his shoulders from Parmi's surprisingly strong grip.

"Do you want out of this castle alive?" Pelmen snapped fiercely, and Gerrig stopped struggling.

"Of course I do. But is what you're suggesting any way to do that?"

"Perhaps not," Pelmen admitted. "But if that army succeeds, I can't guarantee you'll live through the day."

"I'll take my chances. I'm going back to bed."

"As you choose. Parmi, let him go. For the rest of you— remember how disgusted you all were with my play praising Ligne? It's possible that the rightful Queen of this land is among this silent army of invasion. If so, she comes as a puppet—a slave of Admon Faye." Pelmen waited until the anxious mutterings faded. "I'll not explain all the reasons, but if we can chase this force from these dark caverns, we'll do them a favor, as well as ourselves. Don't feel ashamed if you chose to follow Gerrig back upstairs. After all—" Pelmen glanced at Gerrig's back. "—you're only play actors. You've trained yourselves to imitate heroes on stage, not to be heroes in the pitch-black face of fear. I don't blame you. Turn back."

No one moved. Though Gerrig stood with his hands resting on the door back up to the infirmary, he didn't thrust it open.

"On occasion, though," Pelmen continued with a peculiar lilt to his words, "a chance arises—and I think such moments come quite unexpectedly to most—a chance to be a hero, instead of playing one. The chance to do something worthy of the playwright's immortalization."

Silence greeted his words. Gerrig broke it. "I remember that speech well," he muttered.

"I thought you would," Pelmen replied softly. "It was

your line, after all, from *Shadows of a Night at Sea*." He waited for a moment, then asked, "Are you coming?"

Gerrig looked at him and frowned. "I'm scared," he breathed.

"So am I." Pelmen chuckled. "Exciting though, isn't it?"

"You said an army," Danyilyn whispered. "There's only a handful of us."

"Yes, but we've got a big friend." Pelmen smiled back. "Maybe two," he added to Yona Parmi.

"You don't make any sense," she grumbled.

"Since when has he ever made sense?" Yona Parmi asked her.

"We don't have any weapons," Gerrig said. His voice had changed in texture and tone—it was deeper, more mellow. The gravity of this situation had caused him to slip without realizing into stage speech.

"There's an armory through the side door of the infirmary—only fifteen feet away."

"But what if there are soldiers there?" Danyilyn asked nervously.

Pelmen held up a hand for silence and cocked his head to listen. "No soldiers right now," he said; then he smiled and added, "Believe me." He waved at the two young players who had closed the trapdoor, and they opened it up again and climbed through.

While they were gone, Danyilyn tugged anxiously on Pelmen's arm and asked, "What if these adversaries are just around the corner? We're helpless—"

Pelmen hushed her again. "They're still on the far end of the castle."

"How do you know?" she demanded. She was cross and wanted to be sure he noticed.

"You'll see."

Jamnard and Magrol hustled quickly back down the stairs, their arms laden with odd armor pieces and assorted weapons. These were distributed quickly around the small circle.

"Just a shield, thank you," Yona Parmi said, "and those." He pointed to a pair of armored shoes, and swiftly took them from Magrol's hands. By the time he had fitted them onto his feet, the door was once more in place, and the other players were armed and ready to move.

"Stay near me," Pelmen ordered. "I'd rather not lose any of you." He took their single candle and led them down the passageway toward the cistern.

"Feel as nervous as opening night—" Gerrig began, and someone shushed him. Then there was silence, broken only by the *clink-clink-clink* of Yona Parmi's metal boots.

CHAPTER NINETEEN

Bloodshed and Bathwater

"IT'S TIME," Admon Faye murmured, and he moved out, leading a long train of fierce, dangerous-looking men and one frowning Princess. He'd ordered them to leave their swords sheathed to prevent the noisy scraping and clanging that would naturally result from carrying drawn weapons through a narrow, dark tunnel. As always, he travelled without a light, relying on his memory of the twisting maze.

He was in no way prepared for an ambush.

"Now!" someone grunted, and something whispered past the slaver's face. He knew the sound of a blade cutting air far too well to hesitate. He threw himself to the side and jerked his own weapon free. Before he could swing it, though, he was sent crashing to the ground, crying out in pain. Something had slammed into his shin!

"Ambush!" someone behind him cried, and a thunder of scrapes and clatters echoed through the tunnel as the House of Faye armed itself for battle.

"Oww!" Admon Faye roared a second time, and someone nearby chuckled:

"I got him again."

"Get back!" another voice warned sharply, so the ugly

slaver thrust his sword savagely at the voice, venting his rage with a full-throated scream.

None of the survivors could ever adequately describe what took place after that. Like enraged cats sewn into a sack, the frustrated combatants struggled to fight each other, but found themselves battling the cavern instead. Scores of swords were broken on the walls. Knuckles were scraped raw. Faces were trodden underfoot. Some people screamed, while others seemed at times to laugh. The entire situation lent itself to description in expletives—the black darkness turned blue with curses: muttered, grunted, hollered, screamed, spat and sighed.

One of the maidservants preparing breakfast heard something strange as she passed by the cistern and reported it to the cook.

"Just boatmen, arguing with one another over some trifle. Fishing rights, probably. Set the table."

The cook served a baked pig that morning.

Ligne missed the actors at breakfast. "Where's the fool?" she asked airily. "Where's the rest of your tedious players?"

"They've b-b-been working hard lately. Let them s-sleep," Rosha said as he downed a helping of steaming ribs. His acting was improving. The Queen didn't realize just how anxious their mass absence made him feel. Had he been left behind?

"They've been working you too hard as well," Ligne snarled.

"Why, n-no, m-m-my Lady, it's only that it t-t-takes practice to d-d-do a play well."

"You've not been rehearsing," the Queen spat. "Your speech isn't a bit improved for all your practice."

"Yes, but the p-p-play—"

"The play had better be ready today," Ligne announced, and she twisted in her seat to look him in the eye as she added, "Since it's going to be performed tomorrow night, as part of our wedding celebration." She saw Rosha's eyes widen. The young man choked down the piece of pork he'd been chewing.

"Wedding?" Kherda broke in, leaning out over the table to try to look at Ligne's face. "Why is it that I have not been informed of this?"

"Because I just now made up my mind," Ligne shrugged. "That is satisfactory with you, Rosha, is it not? Your friends are ready to perform?"

Rosha nodded, but his swarthy complexion seemed unusually waxy. "Y-yes, my Lady."

"But this is highly irregular," Kherda protested, "to plan a royal wedding while the city is under attack!"

"Ah, but Joss has assured me that Admon Faye will be apprehended before noon. Tomorrow at dinner I will have a celebration of my victories, Kherda. All of them." She looked pointedly at the Prime Minister, then rose from the table. "I'll be in my bath," she announced. "Send Joss to me as soon as he arrives. And Rosha," she added, "I'll see you later." Then she turned to climb the grand spiral to her apartments.

The gallery abruptly emptied before them, as Admon Faye's crew finally responded to their leader's screams for retreat and got moving in the right direction.

"Follow them!" Gerrig shouted, flourishing his sword. Though he'd often brandished blades coated with imitation blood, this weapon wore a patina of the real substance. They had experienced real battle—and Gerrig had found that he liked it.

"Let them go," Pelmen ordered, and his tiny troupe stopped their pursuit.

"But we've got them on the run," Gerrig protested.

"Quiet," Pelmen snapped, and he cocked his ears to listen.

—They've gone around to the left-hand gallery. Back up twenty yards and to your right. You'll cut them off.

"Did we lose anyone?" Pelmen demanded briskly. The troupe took a quick roll call in the dark.

"No," Danyilyn answered, "though we've got some cuts and scrapes—mostly from each other."

"There do seem to be a number of bodies scattered around, though," Jamnard said, and Pelmen nodded.

"I expected that. Most of them killed by their own mates. They're trying to get around behind us—back that way." As the powershaper herded his charges backward to their new position, he couldn't shove from his mind the implications of the past few moments. Could one of those

bodies be that of a young woman? For the first time in
many weeks, he missed the gentle life of the monastic—
and the morning had barely begun.

Only a few minutes separated the clashes, but the second
skirmish had a far different flavor from the first. Slavers
were accustomed to this type of warfare, though they were
normally the ambushers, not the ambushed. This time they
were ready and, when the fray was finally rejoined, fewer
swords scraped the walls and more rang on steel. Pelmen
and Gerrig, though untouched by enemy metal, were
driven steadily backward by waves of fresh warriors. As
one pair tired, Admon Faye sent another pair past them.
Soon the two players could no longer effectively return
their attackers blows, and Pelmen shouted, "Break off!"
The actors behind him quickly vacated the corridor, and it
was Admon Faye's turn to hold his troops back from pursuit.

"Slowly!" he shouted to the men on the point. "There's
no telling how many warriors Joss has scattered through
this cavern, and this retreat may only be a lure into further
ambush." The pressure of this pitch-black struggle with
what he assumed were superior forces had given him a horrible headache, but he shook it off and endeavored to plan
his next move. They couldn't turn back—there was only
one boat. Of course, he thought, one was plenty—for *him*.
"Bronwynn!" he shouted. "Someone get Bronwynn up here
to me!"

After a minute of chaotic discussion, the news was finally passed back to him:

"The Princess is no longer with us."

"So you failed to apprehend him—again?" Ligne asked
as she soaped her beautiful arm with perfumed bubbles.

"I cut his raiding party to half its size, my Lady. Admon
Faye wasn't with them."

"Joss, I'm very unhappy with this. I'm to be married
tomorrow noon—had you heard?"

"The Prime Minister informed me."

"And I want the mood to be lavish, cheery, and romantic. I won't be pleased if my party is interrupted by attacks
on this castle. Soap my back," she ordered a maid, who
swiftly obeyed.

Joss ignored the Queen's bathing. It pleased the woman's vanity to summon him here and berate him from her scented tub. But her vanity was no greater than that of the King who preceded her, nor of Talith's father, who had ruled when Joss was but a page. The General expected quirky behavior from his monarchs. He tried not to let it interfere with security.

"I apologize, my Lady, that I've not as yet caught the slaver. I do know that he's in the city, and my forces are combing the streets and sewers, searching for him."

"You told me yesterday that my borders were secure," she snapped.

"Yesterday, my Lady, they were," Joss replied patiently.

"Yet today?"

"Today I am securing them."

A slave girl entered the bath chamber, bowing as she came, obviously uneasy with her role as the bearer of bad news. "My Lady, Lord Joss—there's been another report of an attack west of the city—"

Joss was across the tiled floor and gone before Ligne could say another word. "I didn't dismiss you!" she shouted after him, then she whirled around to face the timid slave, sloshing water across the tiles. "You!" she ordered, pointing with a bar of soap. "Send in that strange character in the blue robe who arrived this morning, then go have yourself beaten for interrupting my bath!"

"Yes, my Lady," the young slave mumbled, as she bowed herself backwards out of the presence of the queen.

The tiny troupe had taken up a new position and waited breathlessly for the slowly advancing column of slavers to reach them again. Pelmen listened intently as the Imperial House kept him posted on their approach.

—Twenty yards from you now, but around several sharp turns.

"Can't you do anything?" Pelmen asked.

"What?" Gerrig answered, puzzled. Pelmen laid a finger across the brawny man's bearded lips to still him, as the House replied:

—Such as?

"I'm open to any suggestion."

"Maybe we could—" the perplexed Gerrig began, but

Pelmen again covered his mouth. He jerked Pelmen's hand away. "Why ask for suggestions if you—"

"Hush!" Pelmen ordered. "I'm talking to someone else."

"Oh," Gerrig replied. He shrugged elaborately and made a face at the darkness.

—No suggestions come to mind.

"Well, friends," Pelmen sighed, "perhaps we should quit doing what we're not good at and try doing what we do well." For the next few minutes he murmured quiet instructions.

"How did we get in front of this line?" Pinter asked Tibb tremulously. He suddenly had serious doubts about being an outlaw.

"I just want to know how we get to the back of it again," his comrade replied.

"Move ahead," someone behind them called, and Pinter called back:

"Why don't you? We'd be happy to let you . . ." But those behind them just pushed them forward, ever forward into the dark. They marched tentatively, stepping, stepping—

"At them! At them now!" cried a voice from very nearby on their left, and another voice, that of a woman, shrilled from their right:

"I command you, Joss! Kill every last one of them!"

There was a blood-curdling screech from directly ahead, and the sound of metal-shod feet sprinting toward them.

"Back!" Pinter cried out in terror. "Tibb, go back!"

"Oww!" Tibb screamed, and Pinter heard his fellow clank to the ground.

"Are you hit? Are you hit?" Pinter yelled hysterically.

"Somebody just kicked me in the shins!"

"Somebody wha—Oww!" Pinter hollered, as his own shins became targets.

"Bring up the reserves! Finish them off!" shouted the woman, and Tibb heard as someone far down the corridor relayed the message on.

"There are hundreds down here with us!" he gasped.

They could hear swords whizzing before their faces, and one whispered across Pinter's hand. He swung that fist blindly at his attacker—then stopped, puzzled, for somehow the sword it had held was gone. It took a moment for him to realize that he'd lost the hand as well. He screamed in shock. The passageway once again rang with the chaotic clamor of a rout.

Naquin hid his eyes from this woman who seemed intent on exposing her body to him. Nothing in his experience in the temple of the dragon had prepared him for this. Never had he seen a woman so brazen—nor so beautiful.

"What's the matter, my friend?" Ligne teased. "Haven't you ever seen a woman before?"

"I . . . I come in the name of the Prophet—" Naquin began for the third time, and for the third time Ligne refused to allow him to get the words out.

"Don't you want to look at me, holy man? Come on, show me your eyes. Are they the same rich blue as your lovely robe?"

"Please, my Lady!" Naquin sighed. "I am unused to such treatment. Since I left Lamath I've been tied and threatened, lectured by a child and booted in the backside, trampled under horses' hooves and chased by a hundred dogs. I ask only that you let me perform my task and return to my Prophet."

"Ah yes. Your Prophet. I'm curious about this Prophet of yours. What kind of man is he?"

"The Prophet? Why he's the greatest of men! A careful leader, with a vision for our nation unequaled in the long history of Lamath! Through his programs of—"

"Enough of programs," Ligne snapped. "You sound like my Prime Minister." She slipped back into the water, covering herself with bubbles. Her eyes fixed intently on Naquin's face, she asked, "Do you know Pelmen?"

"Pelmen?" Naquin blurted, almost dropping his covering hand. "Why would you ask such a thing?"

"Why, I thought he was the highly praised Prophet of Lamath." Ligne smiled knowingly. "You mean he's no longer your leader?"

"He never was!" Naquin barked. "The man's nothing but an imposter, a powershaper who uses his guile to entrap and confuse others. We drove him from our land."

Ligne had been smiling until she heard the word power-shaper. "You mean you believe this Pelmen can actually alter events by magic?"

"Of course not," Naquin snapped. "He's a trickster, that's all."

"Ah." Ligne smiled. "Something of a fool, one might say?"

"Fool?" Naquin echoed uncertainly.

"You spoke of your task. What is it?"

"To find the Lady Serphimera, and retrieve her to Lamath."

"Retrieve her?" Ligne smiled. "Like a dog retrieves a bird?"

"That is my charge."

Ligne raised a carefully sculpted eyebrow. "I'd wondered if Serphimera might be the cause of your coming. She wears a robe just like yours."

"My Lady, unless she has recanted, she wears a habit of midnight—mine is the color of noon. Do you know where she is?"

"I'd intended for her to join my wedding celebration tomorrow. Perhaps you'll be willing to escort her?"

"You mean she's here?" Naquin asked excitedly. He suddenly realized he'd dropped his hand. He clapped both hands over his eyes again and squeezed them tightly.

"You peeked." Ligne giggled. "Tell me. How does the beauty of your Serphimera compare to that of the most powerful woman in the world?"

The fleeing slavers found their way back to their point of entry by following a trail of slippery blood and groaning bodies. Each faced the same dilemma when he finally thrust his head through the crack into the sunshine—there were no boats. Admon Faye had abandoned them. One by one, they all came to the same, inevitable decision. One by one, they dove into the river.

Many drowned. A few were hauled aboard passing boats. The strongest swimmers survived the river's tortuous currents and made their way to shore. But no one died by the arrows of the guards above them. The soldiers of the Imperial House—who hadn't seen them arrive—never saw them leave, either. As panic-stricken slavers dropped into the water far below them, the soldiers talked of gambling and traded jokes.

One slaver who had made it to the crack turned back to find his friend. "Pinter?" Tibb said softly. The corridor was now as silent as a tomb. It had become that for many. "Pinter?" he said again. He thought he heard a sobbing some yards away, and crawled over bodies toward the sound. "Pinter?" he asked again.

"I lost my hand." Pinter sniffed; then he sobbed again.

Tibb felt helpless to answer. He struggled around to sit by his friend, leaning against the cool stone wall.

"It isn't fair." Pinter wept, and Tibb reached out to squeeze his friend's thigh reassuringly.

"We're alive," he suggested meekly. He thought that was worth something, at least. He slipped an arm around Pinter's shoulder and held onto the man for a few moments, then he cleared the lump from his throat and spoke. "I've been back to where we came in, so I know the way out. We'll just sit here until you feel better. All day, if we need to."

Pinter sniffed. "We'll get left behind," he said, his voice cracking.

"Just rest," Tibb soothed. "Just rest." He patted his friend's shoulder until Pinter was calm again. "When you're better, we'll go. I'll help you." Then he cleared his throat again, and added, "We'll have to swim, though. It seems there was only the one boat—and Admon Faye took it."

Pinter nodded, and his head lolled over on Tibb's thick chest. "It isn't fair. I only wanted to be someone, Tibb. To be an outlaw. With Admon Faye . . ."

"Shh, Pinter. You are. You are, lad."

"I am?" Pinter asked weakly.

"Of course you are. Why, they'll sing about us in the pubs back home—about Pinter and Tibb, of the House of Faye. I can hear it now, as pretty Gerlywa draws the ale, Maknor the tenor is singing of you. He sings of Pinter the long, and his side-man Tibb, who dwelt in the lair of the twi-beast. He's singing . . . you know what he's singing, Pinter? He's singing about how you . . . Pinter?" His friend did not respond. Tibb leaned his head down against Pinter's chest, listening for the sounds of life. They were gone. He laid Pinter's body carefully against the cave wall, wiped the wetness from his face with his sleeve, and murmured solemnly, "They'll sing of you, lad. They will. And when they sing, they'll sing of how you lost your hand for nothing—and of the man who let you die." Tibb crawled to his feet, and gritted his teeth against the tears. Then he gasped, and formed a fist before him in the darkness. "And as long as I keep this hand, and can hold a blade— Admon Faye, beware of Tibb the twisted!"

He gave his friend a child's kiss, then left him in this dark tunnel, and crawled away toward the crack—and daylight.

A much-sobered acting troupe collapsed in the corridor beneath the infirmary and waited for Pelmen to give the all clear. They'd been through a battle and looked it, but the stains on their garments would quickly wash out. It would take years to clean the stains the carnage had left on their minds. It had turned into a morning of desperate madness, and they'd left at least one of their number behind. Jamnard was dead.

Pelmen still spoke to the strange ally that had won the battle for them. They ignored him, each fighting a battle inside with the inexplicable loss of a friend. All would be relieved to return from the inky nightmare to what was for them the real world—the stage.

"Are they gone?" Pelmen whispered.

—A few stragglers remain.

"Then we did it." The Powershaper sighed in exhaustion.

—Not quite, the Imperial House responded accusingly.

"What do you mean?"

—It appears you let one of these rodents slip past you!

CHAPTER TWENTY

The Falcon and the Hound

CARLAD NAPPED against the door. The long night had been very strange, and while he'd not been dragged off to battle, he had been temporarily assigned to the front gate. He was sleepy.

"Wake up!" Ligne screeched in his ear. At the same time she stamped on his toes, and between stamping and shrieking he did just that. "Open this door," the perfumed beauty ordered, and he hastened to obey, sniffing her sultry aroma as she passed and good-naturedly cursing Rosha's luck.

"Hello, darling!" Ligne sang, and she leaped onto Rosha's bed and crawled atop his chest. The warrior grunted in shock as he awoke to her lips pressing onto his and her arms locking around his neck. He grabbed her and wrestled, rocking left and then right trying to dislodge her. Finally he broke her grip with a powerful heave and rolled off one side of the bed as she tumbled off the other side. Her head popped back up quickly, and she glared at him.

"Why do you keep rejecting me?" she demanded.

"Why, we, t-t-t-tomorrow is our—"

"Yes. Our wedding. And you will be my lover, Rosha. I will no longer tolerate this simple-minded resistance."

"B-but I've n-not—"

"You have. But you'll not anymore." She scrambled to her feet and circled the bed toward him, her eyes locked into his. "We are going to settle this right—"

Rosha got sick. He did it with an artistry that would have amazed even his teacher. And the ploy certainly succeeded. Ligne stopped where she was, then backed to the far side of the room. "You're sick!" she shrilled, and Rosha nodded. "Why didn't you tell me you were sick."

"I tried." Rosha shrugged.

"And I just took a bath," the Queen moaned. Then she glared at him again. "I'm going back to bathe again. You go to the infirmary."

"On my way," the young warrior assented, and he hustled out the door. He was halfway down the hall before Carlad woke up enough to pursue him.

A few minutes later he was begging the Lord of Herbs for some word of his friends. "I tell you, I don't know where they are," the harried chemist screeched. "I know they were all sick, that's all, and that I had no medicine to give them. And then, when I made a call this morning on the little woman with the ample figure, she was gone. They're all gone. And if you want my opinion, we're well rid of the nuisances," he added nastily. He was most unhappy about being stood up.

Rosha nodded, postive that he knew where the troupe was now—or at any rate, where they'd gone. He forced himself not to glance over at the low cot that hid the door into the tunnels below. Obviously, Yona Parmi had passed the word to gather, and the plan had succeeded in drawing the herbalist out of his infirmary long enough for them all to make entry. Rosha had certainly expected to be included in that summons. Had Pelmen and the others abandoned him to Ligne?

Rosha took deep breaths as Parmi had taught him to do, seeking to control his anxiety. Pelmen wouldn't abandon him. Logically, there was no way they could have passed the word to him, since Ligne now posted a pair of guards outside his apartments on a permanent basis, in addition to assigning Carlad to dog his heels wherever he went in the castle. Carlad presently stood napping just outside the door of the infirmary.

Rosha shook his curly head to rid himself of these distracting fears and tried to think clearly. If they were in the passage below, as he believed they must be, they couldn't safely get out while the pharmacist remained in the room. Rosha wondered if he could assist them . . .

"M-my apologies for b-b-bothering you," Rosha said. "I'm sh-sure that it was n-nothing—just a bit of undigested b-breakfast."

"Humph," the gaunt man grunted, and he turned back to his pestle and his bottles of herbs.

"I imagine you are s-s-summoned often in the m-m-middle of the n-night . . ."

"Too often," the Lord of Herbs snorted. "Especially last night."

"M-must get very little s-s-sleep . . ."

"Too little."

"P-perhaps you sh-sh-should take off this morning, and c-catch a nap—"

"And leave my post?" the man exploded self-righteously. "Never!" He turned back to his mixing bowl.

"What are you m-making? A love p-p-potion?"

The Lord of Herbs spun around and backed up against his table, aghast. "Wh-wh-what a ridiculous notion!" he shouted. "Ah-ah-ah—of course not." Once more the blood filled his old cheeks, and they radiated warmth. A love potion was exactly what he was making, and once this young intruder left him alone, he planned to steal away and slip it, somehow, to a merchant's lovely daughter. Not that he actually believed it would work, of course . . . "Ah-ah-ah—why do you ask?" he demanded.

"You really ought to d-do something about that s-stutter," Rosha goaded. Then he turned on his heel and stalked out of the room. He decided if he couldn't push the chemist out of the infirmary, he would summon him from it. Carlad fell into step behind him as he climbed the spiral stairs to return to his apartment. As he passed the door of the throne room he glanced in, just to check if the troupe might have somehow eluded his search and gathered here. It was empty but for the brocade-swathed dais and the ornately carved throne. Rosha blanched, then, for he saw something had been added—a smaller throne, carved exactly like Ligne's, now sat on the floor to the right of her

platform. Rosha knew who the chair was intended for, and
his sudden nausea truly warranted his calling the doctor.
He continued down the hall to his new apartment, thankful
at least that Ligne had moved him out of his rooftop prison
and down to this level. He was that much closer to the
gate—and freedom.

As he passed alone through the double doors into his
room and closed them on his weary guard, he was contrast-
ing Ligne to his thoughtful, sensitive Bronwynn. Then
something slammed into his back.

Bronwynn had grown up inside this castle. While she'd
known nothing of the nether tunnels until Admon Faye
had revealed them to her, once she was through the infirmary floor and into the House proper she was loose on her
home territory. She'd explored these halls as a child, had
stuck her turned-up nose into every corner and closet.
She'd learned thereby all the secrets to moving into and out
of the hidden passageways that laced through the upper
levels. Fortuitously, she escaped the infirmary without
being seen. Mere seconds later, she was safely hidden in
the walls.

She brushed cobwebs aside as she walked. Evidently,
Ligne had either not discovered all of these narrow aisles,
or else she used them infrequently. Either way, Bronwynn
thought grimly, they would prove the wanton imposter's
downfall. Whether Admon Faye and the others survived
the battle below her feet or not, Bronwynn was resolved to
dispatch Queen Ligne by nightfall—after she'd dealt with
Rosha, of course. She made that vengeance her first order
of business. Methodically, she searched the rooms of the
castle for him, quite unnoticed behind the drapes and panels.

She'd already determined that he could most easily be
killed in his bed—which she assumed would be in Ligne's
own apartments. She climbed a dark ladder, barely a foot
and a half wide, to peer through a crack into the royal
apartments on the second floor.

She watched as a trio of maidservants made up Ligne's
vast bed. She bit her tongue in rage, to think that the usurp-
er of her throne now slept here, in her parent's room. She
choked back hot tears as she remembered crawling up into

that very bed between them, when common sounds made strange by the night drove her, frightened, from her own. She strained to hear the words of these servants, but the room was vast, and the sound didn't carry through the walls. She shifted position, circling through the darkness to a tiny portal closer to the women, arriving in time only to see them leave. One half-heard comment was enough, however. As they left the room, the senior of the three said they would need to do a complete cleaning the next morning, when the new young master moved in.

It was fortunate for Bronwynn that the ladies made their exit then, for she couldn't contain her boiling temper, and any occupant of the room could have heard her vent her rage on the walls. Once she'd controlled herself, she concluded that Rosha must either be in one of the guest rooms beside the royal suite, or else in the rooftop room where her father had himself placed Ligne. She shuffled sideways around the perimeter of the wall to check the guest rooms.

The first room she reached puzzled her. The cracks and eyeholes that would normally permit her to look into it had all been filled or masked. She thought for a moment, remembering the trick to getting into this particular apartment, and twisted a carved knob. A panel swung open, and Bronwynn stepped into the room of Jagd of Uda. Fortunately, he wasn't home. She knew instantly to whom it belonged, by the scarlet and purple cloaks that draped from all the walls. Bronwynn smirked. Jagd had ever been the suspicious type. In this environment he did well to be.

Bronwynn slipped back into her hiding place and closed the panel behind her. She squeezed around another corner, making her way by the dim light that filtered through tiny cracks from the rooms on either side of this aisle. She checked a second guest room and found her vision unobstructed. Once again, it was unoccupied at the moment. She recognized nothing that gave any hint of the one to whom it belonged. A quick pull on a hidden latch, and Bronwynn danced lightly inside, moving quietly to the closet. She found it filled with new clothes, imaginatively styled and richly colored. She held up a tunic to measure the size of the shoulders and felt a fierce satisfaction. These were Rosha's new clothes, specially tailored for the consort of the Queen. At the moment, this was where the mudgecurdle was living. Well, here he would die as well. Bronwynn swiftly hung the garment back onto its hook, slipped her dagger from its sheath, and backed into the closet. She only had to wait a few moments.

The blow should have killed him. It didn't. The summer before, when Rosha first left his father's manor in the company of Bronwynn and Pelmen, Dorlyth mod Karis had given his son the chain-mail shirt he had worn himself throughout his adventures. Now, that shirt saved his son's life. It turned the dagger, though Rosha's covering garment was sheared into tatters, and Bronwynn cursed her own poor memory for not having planned a better stroke.

Rosha didn't think. He simply grabbed his assailant by the arm and tossed her across the room. Only after he'd launched her past his head did he realize who she was. "Bronwynn!" he grunted. More emotions were summed in that one grunt than in any phrase the young man had ever uttered before.

"Did you call me?" Carlad shouted from the hall.

"No!" Rosha called back, stepping over to hold the doors should the man attempt to investigate. "N-nothing. G-g-go back to what you were doing."

Bronwynn had by that time rolled to her feet and, seeing his back turned, charged him again. Rosha heard her coming and sidestepped her at the last moment. The blade of her weapon thudded heavily into the wood of the door jamb. The young warrior knocked the girl's hand away from its haft before she could jerk it free, picked her up, and once again tossed her across the room. This time, however, he made sure to aim her for the bed.

"Are you sure everything's all right?" Carlad shouted again, and Rosha opened one of the doors and stuck his head into the hall. His sleepy guard looked rather perplexed. Rosha gave him a friendly smile. "No p-p-problem," he said cheerfully, and he waved. Then he slammed the door shut and whirled in time to see Bronwynn's foot heading for his forehead. He ducked, and it thumped noisily on the wall behind him. He caught her on the way down. She clawed for his face as he carried her once more to the bed and dropped her there.

The pounding on his door grew more animated, and

Rosha rushed to swing it open. "What do you want?" he demanded angrily.

"Is there someone in there with you?" Carlad squinted suspiciously, craning his head to peer around Rosha's large bulk.

"If there is, whose fault would it b-b-be?" Rosha responded.

"Ah . . ." The guard didn't know quite what to answer, and Rosha rushed on:

"There's n-no one in here b-but me, as you well kn-know! Now leave m-me alone, or I'll tell your sergeant about your acting career!"

He slammed the door and turned to face Bronwynn once again. He'd heard her scuttle across the floor behind him and knew she was working to free the knife from the wall. Once again he grabbed her, this time less gently, and hurled her at the bed with a grunt. She bounced over it onto the floor. By the time she could recover, he was standing over her, her knife in his hand and a savage frown darkening his features.

"Well, go ahead," she flared. "Stab me with it."

"What's the matter with you?" he demanded.

"You might as well. I'm sure the Queen will reward you richly—though of course, since you have her, what other reward could you want?"

"Would you keep your voice down—"

"Why should I? You'll give me to her anyway—"

"Shut up!" he spat, slamming his free hand over her mouth. He tossed the dagger aside and grabbed the back of her head with his other hand and held her quiet while she did everything in her power to make noise. She beat at his head, kicked his legs, rolled from side to side, and tried to bite through his hand. Through it all, Rosha held onto her, absorbing the blows without blinking, staring fiercely into her face.

She couldn't keep it up forever. Finally she relaxed, and he began in a heated whisper: "I get the impression you think I want to be here. I don't! You think I want that witch? All I can think about is you, yet you try to stick a knife in my b-b-b—in me." He sighed in exasperation. "Why do you think I've got guards at my door? It's because I'm a prisoner here."

All he could see of her face were her eyes. They suddenly watered over, and he decided to let her speak.

"You're moving into her room tomorrow," she spat out, and he clamped his hand back in place and looked at the door.

"Not if Pelmen and I can help it," he muttered. Her eyes widened. He lifted his hand.

"Pelmen is here?" she asked. For the first time, she whispered.

"He is. Disguised as a jester, and using the name Fallomar." Rosha frowned, as he remembered his friend's absence. "That is, I hope he's here. He went below the castle last night, and hasn't yet come up."

Bronwynn's face clouded with concern. "But there's a battle below the castle going on right now. That's how I got in."

"A battle? Who's battling whom?"

"Isn't Joss down there—"

"No," Rosha blurted. "Joss is out chasing Admon Faye all over the countryside."

"But Admon Faye's in the caverns—" Bronwynn stopped, and stared at his long face. Rosha suddenly looked very tired. And once again, someone was pounding on the door.

Rosha sighed. Then he stood up. "Hide," he told her, and Bronwynn quickly got within the wall again as Rosha stalked to the doorway. "Who is it?" he shouted.

"Fallomar the fool, my Lord, come to entertain you and teach you fancy words—if the time be appropriate?"

Rosha swung the door open, his face beaming. "Under the circumstances, I c-can't think of a time that would be b-better. Carlad, let this fool past." Pelmen swept into the room, and Rosha winked at his guard and patted his cheek. "Remember . . . disturb us again and I'll tell him about the whiteface too . . ."

As soon as Rosha closed the door behind him, Bronwynn burst from her hiding place and raced to embrace the clown. Pelmen hugged her to him, and both wept—but quietly, each one keeping a cautious eye on the door. Bronwynn cried out of her months of loneliness and frustration, while Pelmen wept in thanksgiving for her safety. Rosha stood to one side, his arms folded across his chest, maintaining a reserved smile, but wishing someone would include him in all the hugging. Soon Bronwynn turned and reached out to him, and Pelmen passed the girl to her young warrior. In a few moments she had completely reversed the poor opinions of these two she'd formed over the months of separation. The clandestine nature of Pelmen's arrival had totally convinced her of Rosha's sincerity, and if that hadn't, the bear lock he wrapped her in surely would have. In more than one way, Bronwynn finally felt she'd come home.

"You don't seem surprised to see me," she whispered to Pelmen, wiping her cheeks with the back of a hand.

"I knew you were on your way. My only worry was in getting here before you split this one's skull." He jerked his head at Rosha.

"How did you know about that?" she asked, suddenly suspicious.

"The House told me."

Bronwynn stared at him. "What?" she finally asked.

"This ancestral home of yours is alive, Bronwynn. And it has ways of communicating its thoughts. It watched you climb up through its walls, and gave me a running description of your attack on Rosha as I raced up here to stop you." Pelmen glanced at Rosha. "It's fortunate your weeks of inactivity haven't dulled your reflexes."

"Reflexes had nothing to do with it. It was my father's mailed shirt." Rosha turned a hard look onto his still-puzzled Princess. "Why did you try to cut me open?"

"They told me you'd gotten cozy with Ligne," Bronwynn snapped. Then she advanced a step on him, suddenly grim. "Have you?"

"Not by choice," Pelmen interrupted, squeezing between them to prevent a renewal of hostilities. "Tell me—who is 'they?'"

Bronwynn shrugged. "Admon Faye, Flayh, Jagd. All of them."

"You've been with Admon Faye?" Rosha demanded. It was his turn to be suspicious.

"Not by her choice," Pelmen said evenly, turning to stare Rosha down. "Admon Faye helped her escape from this place—"

"How do you know?"

"Serphimera told me—"

"Serphimera!" Bronwynn blurted out. "Is that witch here?"

"Why didn't you tell me you knew where Bronwynn was?" Rosha asked stonily.

"Would you two please quiet down?" Pelmen ordered. When they were silent, he turned first to answer Bronwynn, then to Rosha. "Yes, she's here, but she's not a witch—and—I didn't tell you because I didn't think it would help matters any."

"But if I'd known she was safe, I would have killed Joss days ago."

"You call being with Admon Faye safety?" Pelmen frowned. "Besides, that's what I expected you'd do. You might have succeeded in killing him, but neither you nor Bronwynn would have been any better off."

"It doesn't matter now, anyway," Bronwynn whispered. "I'll take you through the walls and you can kill him while I slaughter Ligne." Both of the men turned to stare at her. "I think it's a good plan," she added defensively.

"Maybe for Admon Faye," said Pelmen. "Is that what he intended?"

"I never really listened to what he intended." Bronwynn shrugged. "I was busy planning my own revenge."

"I can't believe you really thought I—"

"That's what Jagd said."

"When did you speak with Jagd?" Pelmen interrupted. "He's been inside this castle for weeks."

"Flayh talked to him—Flayh and Pezi. Through the little blue pyramids."

"You were there? You heard that conversation?"

"Sure."

—Which brings up an important point, said the Imperial House.

"Yes. I hadn't forgotten."

"Hunh?" Bronwynn asked.

"Talking to the House," Pelmen explained. "I'll go and get it now. I assume there's a secret way into his room?"

—Ask the girl. She just visited it.

"Were you in Jagd's room a few minutes ago?"

"How did you—"

"I already told you. Can you take me there?"

"Of course, but aren't we going to make some plan of attack first? I came into this castle to kill a Queen, not to stand around and talk to the walls."

Rosha's nose wrinkled as he watched Bronwynn speak. Dressed as she was in close-fitting leather fighting clothes, she looked very little like the girl who'd bid him good-bye in Dragonsgate, less than a year before. Her language was harsher, less thoughtful. He wasn't sure he liked the change. In fact, he knew he didn't.

"There's no need for a bloodbath," Pelmen said, "especially not when we could all end up its victims. Bronwynn, you want to murder Joss and Ligne. In spite of your secret panels I consider that no easy task. Joss is cut of the same cloth as our treacherous Admon Faye; what if he knows of those same secret panels and guards himself against them? Nor does the leopardess Ligne appear the type who would allow herself to be casually butchered in her bed. And should you manage to kill them both, what then? Before tomorrow night you'd discover half a dozen members of the court who deem themselves just as worthy to rule as you, Bronwynn—and possibly, they'd have enough friends to make that happen."

"Then what do you suggest?" Bronwynn demanded.

"Patience?" The way she spat out the word indicated how little use she had for it herself.

"I suggest we let the House help us. With its assistance we routed Admon Faye this morning—"

"You routed him?"

"The castle says all but a few of the army we battled are dead or have escaped into the river. I know it could help us to destroy Ligne and her supporters as well."

"Well, ask it then. I'm ready to get on with this."

"Be patient, Bronwynn!" Rosha broke in. "There are more people involved than just the three of us."

"Really?" she said, and she turned back to Pelmen. "Who?"

"A group of old friends I used to perform with, who agreed to fight Admon Faye this morning out of loyalty to you. Who do you think attacked you in the darkness?"

"You . . . you conquered Admon Faye with a troupe of players?" she asked, incredulous.

—They had some assistance, huffed the House.

"The House just reminded you that we had its help, and that made all the difference. It will again, when the time comes to overthrow Ligne. Because of its help, we lost only one in the caverns this morning. I want the rest alive to see your coronation as well, Bronwynn. So yes—be patient. If all goes well, we'll be out of here tonight, planning your triumphant return."

—And what about the pyramid?

"I was getting to that. I made a deal with the House and I need to hold up my end of it now. Would you show me the way into Jagd's room?"

Bronwynn nodded. "You'll need to be careful," she said. "He's covered the walls with his clothes—you can't tell from the corridor if he's in there or not."

"We'll let the House worry about that. Rosha, we'll be right back." Pelmen ducked then, and followed Bronwynn into the hidden corridor.

Flayh sat in an armchair and struggled to relax. It was an impossible task. "Where are they?" he demanded of the pyramid that sat before him.

—Not here, replied the High Fortress of Ngandib.

"I know that. I'm waiting for them to contact me through this pyramid."

—Must you? the Fortress grumbled.

"Yes, I must," Flayh replied snappishly. "And you'd best accustom yourself to it, for I don't intend to stop using magic just because it gives you heartburn."

—Yes, master, said the palace. Far below Flayh's tower, in the slave quarters, a child suddenly got her finger caught in a slamming door and screamed for her mother. The Fortress smiled with satisfaction, wishing only that it dared do the same to Flayh.

"Where are they?" the bald sorcerer roared, pounding an arm of his chair. "Pezi, if you've fouled up again—" Flayh cut himself off. There was a flicker of brilliant blue inside the pyramid. The other two must be showing interest in theirs, Flayh thought, and he leaned forward to stare . . .

"Wayleeth, be quiet," Tahli-Damen whispered, but his admiring Lady would not be silenced.

"He did it so easily," she told their dinner guests. "Just

walked in one afternoon, and walked out with it that night.
Just like that." She snapped her fingers, then turned to hug
her blushing merchant's neck.

"Please, Wayleeth," he admonished her softly. "This is
supposed to be a secret—don't press it . . ." Tahli-Damen's
grin belied his words, however. He was proud of himself,
and it was difficult to maintain his modesty when Wayleeth spoke nothing but the truth.

"He just doesn't like for me to brag on him," she told
their beaming guests. They were entertaining the local
Lord of Myfa, a very small trading house that had hooked
its fortunes to Uda so many years before that it was now
considered little more than a satellite of the purple and
scarlet.

"That's attractive in a young leader," chuckled Maywar
mod Maywar-el, "but you needn't be so modest, Tahli-
Damen. Secrecy is important, and I know Jagd is probably
insisting on it, but we're all friends here, after all. The
news that you've gotten away with one of these precious
pyramids is a secret not likely to keep long, in any case. I
expect you'll be getting a formal protest from Flayh any
time now."

"I've been expecting one all day," Tahli-Damen nodded,
sampling a pastry. "The fact that I haven't makes me wonder if Pezi's neglected to tell him." This comment drew a
round of giggles. Pezi stories were not confined to the fat
merchant's own house. He was gaining quite a reputation
among all the merchant families.

"May I see the object?" Maywar asked. "I've heard so
much about it from my brothers that I'm quite curious."

"Weren't you at the conclave?" Wayleeth asked.

"No, child," the older merchant responded. "A touch of
emphysema kept me bedridden. But I would like to see
it . . ."

Tahli-Damen looked at his plate. "Jagd's orders were to
keep it hidden," he mumbled.

"Pah!" Maywar snorted, then he chuckled. "Jagd's never
going to know unless you tell him. I certainly won't. Bring
it out."

"Yes, Tahli-Damen, please do," Wayleeth pleaded, and
she looked across at Maywar's wife. "He hasn't even
showed it to me yet. Come on, Jagd won't ever know."

Indeed, he might not, Tahli-Damen was thinking to himself. Especially if this invasion of Flayh's had succeeded. Tahli-Damen trembled involuntarily with a mixture of guilt and thrill.

"What's wrong, darling?" Wayleeth asked earnestly. She'd been alarmed by his strange behavior ever since his return from Pezi's castle. "Are you sick?"

"No, not sick," he muttered. Abruptly he stood. "I'll go fetch it." He started for his room.

His pace increased with each step he took toward the object. By the time he reached his inner chamber he was running, and he had to stop to catch his breath. Then, just as he had done time and again throughout that day, he fell to his knees and lifted the pyramid out of its place of hiding. He stripped its protective bag away and fondled it again, amazed that he actually possessed such a wondrous object. He sat on the bed and stared into it for a moment, wishing he hadn't promised to show it to the others. As he thought of excuses for not bringing it out after all, it came alive in his hands. He stared . . .

—It's under the bed.
"And Jagd is . . ."
—On the roof with the birds.
"You'll warn me—"
—Yes.

Pelmen turned to Bronwynn and put a finger to his lips, then nodded. She turned the knob that opened the panel to Jagd's room, and Pelmen slipped inside. He closed the hatch behind him, as they'd agreed, and knocked one of the purple cloaks from its peg to allow her to watch him while she remained hidden. Then he walked to the bed and knelt beside it. "Under here?"
—That's right.

Pelmen leaned over and looked. There was the case. He tugged it out, unlatched it, and found the bag inside. He fetched it out quickly and opened it up to be sure it was the right thing.
—Don't! screamed the House, but it was too late. Pelmen stared into Flayh's face.

"You!" Pelmen shouted in surprise.

Without a moment's hesitation, Flayh squinted his eyes

and chanted an incantation. It appeared to both Pelmen and Tahli-Damen that the bald wizard's eyes filled the crystal completely. Pelmen tossed up a hand to catch the blow and deflect it, but Tahli-Damen had no such power. The young merchant found his eyes locked into the magic crystal, helpless even to scream.

—Stop! roared the Imperial House of Chaomonous, in agony. Through its pain, it could hear the echo of its own scream in that of a distant palace:

—Agony! cried the High Fortress of Ngandib, but Flayh ignored its ravings. He muttered another incantation and peered into the faces of Tahli-Damen and a curiously powerful clown.

"You fear me!" Flayh ordered, expecting instant submission from these two unexpected visitors.

Tahli-Damen would have cried out, "Yes!" if he'd been able, but his vocal cords seemed frozen by an abject, all-consuming dread. The eyes that had locked onto his sucked dry the wellspring of his courage.

"No!" Pelmen reacted, and he bent his energies to the struggle.

Suddenly two pairs of eyes filled the object Tahli-Damen held, the second more terrible than the first. Both pierced completely through him. The young merchant felt sure he was bleeding from every orifice of his body, but he couldn't tear his eyes away to check.

With the screams of his own castle echoing through his mind, Flayh shouted, "Who are you?" at the clownish eyes that filled his vision.

"You know me, Flayh," Pelmen murmured quietly. To Flayh and Tahli-Damen, his words pierced like a shout. "Yield now, before I kill you both."

—Stop! Please! anguished the Imperial House of Chaomonous, and Pelmen was dimly aware of the renewed chorus of bells throughout the hallways, and of pounding feet outside in the corridor. He was helpless to stop the conflict now. He could only end it by winning it.

Then Pelmen recoiled from the crystal, squinting in revulsion. The bared fangs of a savage dog seemed to lunge out of it for his face. Those jaws snapped on his neck, but his neck was suddenly gone, replaced by the widespread beak of a screaming falcon. The dog jerked away, terrified by the razorlike talons it saw diving for its eyes. Those claws hooked flesh, and sliced six long red gashes into the dog's muzzle. The beast howled.

Tahli-Damen reeled. A dog had nearly severed his neck, only to be knocked aside by a falcon which slashed its face. Yet the merchant's eyes remained fixed on the surface of the glass. He was unaware of the cries of his woman, who called to him from the stairway.

The Imperial House ground its stones together. It would have thrown itself asunder, had it been able, but the energy necessary to do so was all being focused through a tiny sliver of crystal in its heart. Powerless, it bellowed its agony.

Bronwynn cowered in her hiding place. When the bells began through the castle she'd jerked away from her eyehole, feeling sure they had something to do with her. Someone had discovered her presence, and had called for a general search. Or was it that Admon Faye had returned and, with Pelmen occupied, had broken out of the lower level into the castle? As they continued, she stood up and looked into Jagd's room again. Her mouth fell open in shock— Pelmen was a falcon.

The dog disappeared as quickly as it came, and Flayh— newly marked with six red stripes on his cheek—breathed, "Pelmen!"

Once again the clown peered up at him out of the crystal. "That's right, Flayh. Yield yourself and end this madness."

Flayh grunted with effort, and Pelmen gasped and threw up his hands to shield his face. A ball of yellow flame hurtled up at him out of the pyramid.

"Return," he cried, and the ball bounced off his hands and back into the object. Then, as he closed his eyes, it engulfed the pyramid in flames; under the pressure of both shapers, it exploded with a silent flash into a blazing ball ten times its original size. Then it was gone, and the pyramids suddenly went cold.

Wayleeth dashed into her lover's room to find him lying on their bed, hugging the pyramid to him and weeping aloud. "Why, darling, what's the matter? Did something we say upset—" She stopped. Tahli-Damen opened his eyes to stare up at her, and she staggered away in horror. There were no pupils, no irises, no whites—just a solid background of pale, powder blue.

"Wayleeth," he sobbed, as he gazed up toward her face. "Wayleeth? Are you there?"

"Yes," she finally managed to choke out. "I'm standing right in front of you."

"You . . . are?" He stared sightlessly into space a minute, then cleared his throat. "Wayleeth," he gasped. "Flayh's had his vengeance at last."

"My darling," she sobbed, wrapping her arms around him to get away from the ghastly blue tint of his eyeballs.

"I stole a vision-maker from a wizard . . . and the wizard stole my eyes."

Flayh reeled away from the table, and lurched toward a drawer in one of his several desks. He jerked it open to pull out a mirror, and examined himself in it. The sight dragged a strangled moan from his lips.

Across his cheeks were the six red gashes—hideous, to be sure, but clearly not as disfiguring as the other new feature. He looked at the back of his hands, and groaned in understanding. He'd managed to get them to his face in time to prevent blindness, but the backs of them had been stained a light blue by the flash. He looked back at the mirror. Two hand prints had been tattooed onto his face. That skin protected by the shield of his hands was the same milky-white as the rest of his body. But that part exposed to the blast now wore the same light blue tint as his hands, all the way up to the top of his bald skull.

—No one can say you're not unique, said the High Fortress of Ngandib, and windy laughter whirled through the room. Flayh gave it cause to regret that, long into the night.

Bronwynn had ducked when Pelmen threw up his hands and had missed the flash. When she looked again, he was lying prone on the floor, unmoving. She gave the knob a savage twist and bolted out to look at him. Then she grabbed up the pyramid, stuffed it into its bag, and scrambled back to her corridor. A moment later she burst in on Rosha, who'd been waiting impatiently by the moveable panel.

"Well?" he whispered.

"Pelmen's hurt," she snapped. "Come on." She tossed the pyramid onto the bed and dragged him back with her into Jagd's room. After several minutes of grunting and tugging, together they hoisted Pelmen onto Rosha's bed beside the object.

"What happened?" Rosha begged, finally free to ask the question safely.

"I don't know. I'm afraid it has something to do with Flayh. Can you get him back to his room?"

"I'll summon Yona Parmi and the others—they can."

"Fine." she nodded. "Isn't this stuff on his face supposed to be a disguise?" she scrapped off a bit of his grease-paint.

"Of course—"

"Better tell these friends of his to have him change it when he wakes up. Look," she said, holding up her finger to show him. "It's turned blue."

CHAPTER TWENTY-ONE

Curtain Call

"SHH," Danyilyn whispered. "Go back to sleep."

Pelmen groaned. His whole body arched. "I'm exhausted."

"We know. That's why you need your sleep."

He heard a muffled sound coming from the corner and sat up on his cot. "Who's that?"

"Never mi—"

But Danyilyn couldn't stop him. A weak ball of soft orange flame blazed above the corner in question, revealing the struggling form of a bound and gagged Princess. He ignored Danyilyn's gasp of surprise as he murmured, "Bronwynn?"

"You *are* a sorcerer!" the actress whispered.

"Why is she tied up?"

"Rosha told us to," Danyilyn said apologetically. "He said it was the only way to keep her from knifing Ligne before you woke up."

"Rosha knows her well," Pelmen murmured, and he groaned. "What time is it?"

"Early morning."

Pelmen sat up and stared at her. "Morning!"

"Just lie back and—"

"No time. We've got to get Serphimera out of the dungeon and then get all of us into the escape tunnel before the castle wakes. If the House—the House!" Pelmen exclaimed suddenly, and he swiveled toward the walls and listened.

"What are you—"

"Shh!" Pelmen strained to hear.

Silence.

"Imperial House?" he whispered. Silence was the only reply he received.

"Anything wrong?" Danyilyn asked.

"Maybe everything," Pelmen sighed, and he rolled off his cot. "Here—help me put Bronwynn on the bed."

"But—"

"She's going to have a long day tomorrow and she doesn't look very comfortable in that corner."

"What about you? You need some sleep."

"No time," he answered her from across the room. "I've got to figure us a new way out of here."

Several hours later, as dawn coated the eastern face of the castle with the illusion of golden mail, Pelmen was still sitting in the corner. Danyilyn had long since returned to her own room, and the heavy breathing from the trussed girl on his cot assured him that Bronwynn finally slept.

Did the castle sleep too? "Are you asleep?" he pleaded quietly for the fortieth time. "Or just keeping silent because you're angry? I've offered you every kind of apology I know—I had no idea such a confrontation would take place. I realize it was agonizing for you—it was agonizing for me as well, but I could only end it by winning it. My friend . . . you've known powershapers throughout your whole existence, many more than I. Surely you witnessed shaper battles, in the time before the dragon? Did you ever once see a shaper turn his back on the sorcerer who attacked him? If you did, I'll wager you witnessed his burial as well, and I have far too many people depending on me to let myself be taken without a fight!" He paused then, and listened.

The Imperial House was as silent as the sunrise.

"Or did I kill you," Pelmen sighed, rubbing a hand across his face and smearing further his blue-tinted greasepaint. "It could be. The powers unleashed between us would take an incredible toll on armies of men—did our battle kill you as well? I guess it's possible—since a power-shaper gave you life . . ." He waited, hoping to hear something—a creaking in the wooden door, a sigh of stone—a change of temperature in the room—even bells would be welcome.

But the Imperial House was as still as the dawn—that kind of stillness so deep, so pervasive that it drags one into sleep. Pelmen finally yielded to it and dozed. He could do nothing else.

He was awakened by a fierce pounding on the door. He jumped to answer it and was met by Danyilyn and Yona Parmi. "Change your makeup now!" Danyilyn spat as she raced to the cot and slipped a knife-blade under Bronwynn's bonds.

"Hurry!" Yona Parmi added. "Ligne's dispatched soldiers to summon you. We've got to get her out of here."

Danyilyn dragged the groggy Bronwynn to her feet as Pelmen scrubbed the old makeup from his face and slapped on a new layer of white. "What time is it?"

"Past breakfast," Yona mumbled as he helped Danyilyn walk the Princess to the door.

"Where are you taking her?"

"Gerrig says to put her in the play—who's going to notice another ingenue? Hurry!" They were out the door and gone.

Pelmen was still trying to clear his spinning head when the soldiers arrived. They slammed open the door without knocking.

"Good morning," Fallomar said cheerily. "Did you bring me breakfast in bed?"

"The Queen has summoned you, fool. Now."

Pelmen made the journey through the halls and into the throne room without speaking again. There seemed little point in trying. These were not the relaxed guards who kept a casual watch from the castle's towers. They were hard-faced warriors—probably the pick of Joss' own crack brigade. They showed little inclination toward joviality.

When he was ushered into the throne room, he found it that much more difficult to smile. There, facing him, sat the Queen herself, along with Joss, Kherda, Jagd, and a

host of other courtlings whose names and offices all
merged together in his mind. To Ligne's right, on a small
version of her own throne, sat Rosha, his jaws locked and
his lips forming a tight frown. But the most distressing
sight of all was to Ligne's left. There stood Serphimera,
bound in heavy chains, and standing beside her was a man
Pelmen dimly remembered as Naquin, the High Priest of
the old dragonfaith, a man who had long ago ordered his
death. Pelmen assumed it was for that same purpose he'd
been summoned this morning.

Yet Fallomar the fool found a smile and jerked three
balls from his pocket. "What will it be, my Lady? Juggling?" He tossed the balls into the air and juggled them
until, at a nod from Joss, a warrior knocked them bouncing
across the room. Fallomar grinned. "No juggling?"

The Queen smiled back primly. "No juggling."

There was a weighty silence. "Well?" Fallomar asked at
last.

"Are you ready to perform your wonderful play, Fallomar?" the Queen asked.

"Certainly. Tonight you'll witness a performance that—"

"Not tonight," she interrupted. "Now."

Pelmen glanced at Rosha. The young warrior gazed up
at him, his eyes filled with despair.

"Now?"

"The rest of your troupe is all assembled, but they informed me that you were—sick last night. They wondered
whether you had recovered enough to perform this morning." Ligne smiled a bright, wicked grin and husked, "Evidently, you are!"

"My Lady, the entertainment would be better if played
tonight—"

"I have other entertainment scheduled for tonight,
clown." At this, Ligne looked down at Rosha, and stroked
the back of the young man's neck. To his credit, Rosha
didn't stiffen under the caress.

"Why, if the others are in place, certainly I am ready,"
beamed Fallomar. He glanced casually at Serphimera's
face. The distress evident there disturbed him, but at least
Ligne hadn't ordered his immediate execution. Perhaps she
still hadn't recognized him. The play was two hours long—

there might yet be time for Bronwynn and Rosha, at least, to escape.

"I hear the role you play was modeled after King Talith. Is that true?"

"Most correct, my Lady." Fallomar smiled.

"I made a fool out of him—perhaps you remember?" Ligne gazed into his eyes.

Fallomar gazed back. "I certainly do—that's why we play him as a fool."

"Appropriate," Ligne said meaningfully. "Take them to prepare."

Rosha and Pelmen were marched down to the great hall by the same squad that had fetched Pelmen from his room. There was no chance for conversation, but he could tell from the young swordsman's dull expression that Rosha had already surrendered the fight. What had transpired through the night? Had some slip finally revealed them all to Ligne? As they turned into the great hall and climbed the steps onto the stage, the soldiers began dispersing to the lower doors. The other actors, their faces creased by worry, clustered around him.

"What are we going to do?" Gerrig whispered.

"Where is Bronwynn?" Pelmen demanded, and someone ushered the Princess to him through the crowd. In sharp contrast to her outfit of an hour ago, she was now swathed in yards of lace, and her hair was tied up in bows. They'd layered on the greasepaint until her skin looked like porcelain—in fact, almost as white as his own. She looked every inch the dainty, innocent ingenue. She shattered that illusion as soon as she opened her mouth:

"Why didn't you let me stick her when I had the chance?" she spat.

He ignored her. "Rosha and Bronwynn," he began crisply, "since you really have little to do in the early part of the play, maybe we can get you out of here. When the act begins, make for that door behind you and into the kitchen. There are no soldiers blocking it yet and perhaps they won't. Once there, jump feet first into the cistern. It connects with the underground passages, and Bronwynn can lead you out."

"What about us!" Gerrig pleaded.

"I have a long soliloquy at the close of this first act—I'll make it longer. Much longer."

"And we take the same route?" Danyilyn asked.

"I can't swim," Gerrig murmured.

"Don't worry," Yona Parmi whispered, looking at Gerrig's belly, "you'll float."

"What about you?" Danyilyn asked.

"What *about* me?" Pelmen snapped. "I'm a powershaper, aren't I?" Danyilyn nodded. Suddenly they were all slamming their hands over their ears, as trumpets blared above them on the grand spiral. Any further conversation was impossible in the wake of that deafening noise, which grew louder as the heralds descended the stairs. They were followed by the ladies of the court, who smiled courageously in the face of their own pain. Each resolutely refused to cover her ears, though it was obvious that all would have liked to.

As the the heralds reached the stage, the castle's other inhabitants began pouring into the great hall through the guarded doors. Pelmen was cheered by the sight of the cook and his helpers—that signaled that the kitchen might be empty and the getaway a real possibility. He glanced over at Yona Parmi and saw that the man watched him grimly. Pelmen smiled encouragement, but Yona Parmi's expression didn't change. He hadn't been fooled by Pelmen's grand speech to Danyilyn about powershaping. In their many late night discussions, Pelmen had told him much about shaping the powers. If Yona remembered nothing else, he'd learned at least that shaping demanded energy—and he knew Pelmen was too exhausted for the task. Less than a day before, Pelmen had wrestled a rival sorcerer in a perilous contest of power—and that on top of a morning-long battle of more conventional character. Pelmen couldn't defend himself against this horde of soldiers, and he knew it. Evidently, so did Yona. Pelmen shrugged then, slightly, and Yona nodded and looked away. They would all have to make the best of it. "House," Pelmen muttered, "are you there?"

If the House had given an answer, it would have been lost in the renewal of the fanfare. Pelmen continued to hope . . .

The Prime Minister made his entrance then, followed by

a pair of servants bearing the Queen's throne between them. They walked across the stage and down onto the floor, placing Ligne's chair in the center of the front row. Then there was another trumpet announcement, and Ligne made her own entrance on the arm of Jagd of Uda. The assembled throng stood to welcome her and, in keeping with custom, began clapping. Pelmen joined the applause, searching out Bronwynn to see what she would do. She'd had the same idea, and their eyes met. Pelmen glanced down at her hands, and she finally lifted them to her waist and patted them together. Her eyes, however, never left his. She gazed at him accusingly.

When Ligne was seated in her place, the trumpeters quit blowing, and scrambled for their own seats. A flurry of bench scraping and coughing ensued, until all had found places. Then the audience was silent.

"Are you there?" Pelmen asked softly.

The House was silent.

Ligne enjoyed the stillness for a moment, then she clapped her hands together twice. "Let it begin," she commanded. She leaned back in her seat to watch.

The play opened with a conversation between a merchant, played by Gerrig, and a scholar, played by Yona Parmi, plotting the overthrow of the clown King. The parts were loosely modeled on Jagd and Kherda, and Pelmen watched these men carefully for their reactions. They gazed at the stage with identical expressions of disinterest, and it soon became clear that they failed to recognize themselves in these characters. Ligne did, however, and it was she who began the laughter. So lightly did she take it all that Pelmen grew steadily more convinced. Of course she could enjoy it, for she was firmly in control. Pelmen shifted his eyes to look at Serphimera. As she stared at the floor between her feet, he recalled the message she had passed him in Ligne's presence. Two plots against the Queen—and both would fail. Once again, she'd proven right, but it seemed to bring her little satisfaction. The kidnap scene was quickly over, and Pelmen made his entrance, shouting in character:

"What? No Princess? Search the roof! Search the halls! Search the dungeon! Search the walls!

Search every room within this house—
Except my mistress' room,
For I'll be searching her myself—
That is, I mean, her *room,* this afternoon."

He heard a cackle from the front row. Ligne, at least,
seemed to be enjoying it.

"Through here," Rosha murmured, and Bronwynn rushed
past him into the kitchen.

"Come on," she said as she grabbed him by the hand and
they raced toward the cistern.

They quickly skidded to a stop.

"Going somewhere?" asked Lord Joss. He had perched
his foot on the lip of the cistern and was casually sipping a
cup of water. The warriors clustered around him did not
appear so relaxed. Their pikes were leveled at the young
pair, menacing them as the guards moved to encircle them.

"We . . . n-needed a c-c-cup of water," Rosha stammered.

"Easily handled. I have a whole basin full right here,
that I was fetching for the Queen. You, young lady—
would you be good enough to carry it in for me?"

"But what of the King? He'll know, for sure," said
Yona.

"The King? Clown King? Why the fool is pure as driven
snow." Gerrig gestured to his face, drawing a laugh. "You
say he'll know? Then are you the clown! For it's noised
around, through all the—" Gerrig suddenly broke off. Pelmen, who had been following the scene attentively, traced
Gerrig's gaze to the source of the interruption and his heart
stopped. Bronwynn, carrying an ornate basin, had just
come back in the rear door of the stage, followed by a
crestfallen Rosha—and General Joss. As they crossed the
stage to a stairway and down onto the floor, Bronwynn
kept her eyes humbly lowered. But after she'd stooped to
place the bowl before the Queen, she made a telltale grab
for her hip, and Lord Joss leaped on top of her, knocking
her to the floor. The first few rows screamed in shock, and
some of them jumped to their feet, but Ligne kept her seat,
beaming happily up at Pelmen. Rosha jumped on Joss'

back in turn, but guards swarmed everywhere by that time, and he and Bronwynn were both swiftly subdued. The crowd came alive with animated expressions of disbelief and amazement, and Ligne was obliged to nod at the trumpeters. Their piercing blasts stunned the audience into quiet, and Ligne smiled at the players.

"Go on," she said. "Finish it."

"We . . . ah . . . we . . ." Gerrig gazed across the stage at Pelmen. His expression was far from kind.

"We can hardly finish it, with two of our players bound like that," Pelmen said. "Release them, and we'll continue." It was fruitless, he realized, but it seemed Ligne had decided to play out this cat-and-mouse game to the bitter end.

"Release them? Why, this girl just tried to kill me! And as for the lad, well . . . I have plans for him later. I don't want him to injure himself." She smiled fondly at Rosha, who jerked toward her in rage. "Ah, Rosha, you can't imagine how I've missed that side of you." Ligne looked back at the stage. "You can't go on? A shame. I did so want to see it. I know. Why not let me play a part?"

"What part do you choose, my Lady? The stage is yours." Pelmen bowed as he spoke.

"It is mine, isn't it?" Ligne gloated, and she mounted the steps to look him in the eye. "Why don't I play myself?"

"Type-casting, to be sure," Pelmen responded. He wondered how much energy he could muster, and glanced over to watch Bronwynn struggle against Joss. A great sadness swept through him. Struggle—that's all the girl had been allowed to do for months. It wasn't just. Pelmen thought of the Power, and murmured, "Are you seeing this?"

"What?" Ligne asked. The audience listened in rapt silence.

"Nothing, my Lady. I take it you want to play the scene where the mistress kills the King. I'm ready."

"Oh, not kills," Ligne smiled. "I didn't kill Talith. Didn't need to, he accomplished that all by himself. No, I only made a fool of him. Kherda, the bowl of water."

The Prime Minister rocked up to his feet and scooped up the basin off the floor. As he bent, his eyes swept across those of Princess Bronwynn . . .

"Kherda! Now!" Ligne waited until Kherda brought the

bowl of water to her. "I made a fool of Talith," she said to
Pelmen then. "I intend to unmake a fool of you." Pelmen
stood in his place as Ligne dipped a cloth in the basin and
washed the white grease paint from his face.

"The first Prophet!" exclaimed Naquin, and he twisted
around to Serphimera. "Look, it's that Prophet who caused
us both such misery." Serphimera didn't respond.

"She knows, Naquin," said the Queen, walking down-
stage toward him. "She's known for days. And last night at
dinner when you berated Pelmen in her presence, so did I."
Ligne turned to face Pelmen, a sneer curling her pretty
lips. "Oh, you managed quite well, Pelmen. I honor your
talent for deception—you had me fooled completely. But
your little Priestess there is a revealer of secrets, not a
hider of them. She'd told me before of her intense feelings
for you, be they love or hate. She couldn't hide those feelings from me. Not from *me!*" the Queen finished with a
dramatic flourish of her hand.

"You missed your calling, Ligne," Pelmen said quietly.
"You should have been an actress."

"Should have been? I am an actress. Mustn't every regent be a player of sorts? As your little play makes clear,
the halls of state are no place for the guileless innocent."
Ligne smirked. "And that's what you've surrounded yourself with, Pelmen. Innocents. Fools." Ligne turned to Joss
and shouted, "Take them!" The armed warriors didn't wait
for their commander to pass along the order. They scrambled onto the stage immediately, and soon every player in
the troupe was trussed as soundly as Bronwynn. During
the interval, Ligne strolled gracefully off the dais and resumed her throne. The captives were then led to stand facing her along the apron of the platform. Obviously, she'd
choreographed her triumph quite carefully.

"Now then." She smiled. "What's next? Pelmen, don't
we get some kind of speech from you?"

"To what effect, my Lady?"

"Why, I assumed you would attempt to arouse the rabble
against me. Wasn't that your plan, your reason for ingra-
tiating yourself with each of my servants?"

"There was no plan, my Lady, save to escape from you."

"No plan. Oh, come now."

"It's true. I only wanted to protect my friends and loved ones."

"Then how did this little Princess get back inside my castle?" Ligne jumped up, crossed to Bronwynn, and grabbed the girl's chin.

Pelmen had hoped Bronwynn might go unrecognized under her makeup, but he was disappointed even in this. "She was brought into this house by the same man who took her out. Admon Faye."

"Ah yes." Ligne nodded. "And where is that ugly slaver?"

"I've no idea."

"Don't lie to me. You know exactly where he is. You've been working together with him."

"You're mistaken, my Lady."

"You deny that you plotted my downfall together?"

"I would plan nothing with Admon Faye, my Lady. Not even an enterprise as necessary as your demise."

"You watch your tongue!"

"You asked—I responded."

"You want me to kill you here?"

"It matters little to me where I die, my Lady, if you've determined already that I shall."

"I thought I might give you a chance to decide that." Ligne smiled. Then she laughed at Pelmen's puzzled look.

"I don't know what you mean."

"Perhaps a little wager is in order."

"A wager?"

"On a game of Drax. If you win, you may take this rubbish heap of an acting troupe with you. If you lose, I kill each of you personally—"

"Done!" Pelmen snapped, without a moment's hesitation.

"Pelmen," Gerrig began, but the powershaper cut him off.

"Gerrig, it's clearly the only alternative—and it's surprisingly fair." He looked back to Ligne. "I thank you, my Lady, for the opportunity you offer."

"You seem so eager, Pelmen. How is that, after six straight losses against me?"

"You may find I play quite differently when my life depends on it. As is customary in accepting the life-death challenge, I offer you choice of red or blue."

"Red or blue?" Ligne asked in mocking innocence. "Not green as well?"

Pelmen's eyes narrowed. "Such a challenge traditionally means the green will be played by the dummy." More needless words, Pelmen thought. He was indeed an innocent to think Ligne would challenge fairly! It was clear, now, what she intended.

"And I have just such a dummy in mind. Kherda, my Prime Minister."

Her words touched off a wave of quiet protest among the crowd, for Pelmen had been quite correct in assuming she'd offered him a challenge to Green Dummy. Kherda was stung, not only by Ligne's insult, but by her injustice as well. He shuffled to his feet. "My Lady! Is this fair?"

"To term you a dummy? Certainly it's fair."

"To issue such a challenge. Tradition clearly calls for—"

"This miserable actor came into my house to steal my throne! I've offered him the opportunity to free himself and his friends, and he's accepted the wager."

"Yes, but—"

"Kherda be silent!" Ligne commanded, and the old man gulped and closed his mouth. "You, of all people, should know that your Queen *never* plays Green Dummy." Ligne spun gracefully to face Pelmen. "Or do you back down?" Her blue eyes mocked him.

"That would be a breach of etiquette, my Lady," Pelmen replied tonelessly, "and we certainly can't have that. Shall we play?"

Ligne clapped her hands in delight. "Oh, let's do!"

CHAPTER TWENTY-TWO

Razor

THE PLAYERS WERE HELD ONSTAGE by a circle of guards while the Queen preceded them up the stairway. They watched helplessly as Rosha was dragged up the grand spiral after her, kicking and jerking all the way. Serphimera, too, was led up the stairs, followed by Naquin. The pitiful skyfaither looked puzzled. Though he'd lived his entire life in the presence of political power, never had he witnessed such eccentric behavior as that he'd been exposed to in this court.

Pelmen watched them out of sight, then glanced at Yona Parmi. "What do you think?"

"What can I think?" Yona mumbled, shrugging. "Winning at Drax is hard enough when all three are battling each other. Two against one is impossible."

"Why doesn't she just kill us and get it over with?" Danyilyn muttered.

"What?" Gerrig snorted. "And forfeit her afternoon's pleasure?"

"I'm sorry," Pelmen said quietly, and they all turned to look at him.

"What for?" Yona asked him. "We all chose to come."

"Gerrig didn't."

"I did, too!" Gerrig blustered, and Pelmen looked up at him in disbelief. "Before you go thinking this is your fault, you just remember it was I who led the battle in the caverns. And I'd do it again this morning."

"We're here," Danyilyn broke in, her temper flaring. "What concerns me is how we're going to get out. Pelmen, you're a powershaper. Is there any—"

"What you don't realize is that he's exhausted," Yona Parmi interrupted. "There are limits to what a powershaper can do—and he's reached his."

Danyilyn looked back and forth between them. "That's it, then? It all depends on Drax?"

Yona Parmi looked at Pelmen. "Maybe not."

Pelmen read his mind. "The Power works through people, Yona. Perhaps there are limits even to what the Power can do."

"Well," Danyilyn said glumly, "I hope you're on your game."

"The Queen is ready for you now," announced a servant from the stairway.

"I'll bet she is," Danyilyn snapped, and, herded by their guards, they all plodded up the stairs.

Spectators crammed the game room full and spilled out both its doors in the hallways. The troupe's escort had to shove people aside to get the players through. Once inside, guards were no longer necessary, for the mob of courtlings crushed back together in their wake, leaving no possible avenue of escape. The press of jabbering people, combined with the visual impact of their multicolored garments, served initially to disorient Pelmen, and he twisted around in confusion, looking for Ligne and the game table. The clamor prevented him from hearing Ligne's summons, and a servant was sent to grab his hand and fetch him into the open space in the center of the room. His appearance there served as a cue for the gathered host to hush. Pelmen happened to glance at his feet, then stared down at the intricate patterns that had been painted on the floor. He'd been in here only two days before, but the room had been altered considerably in that short space of time. This section had formerly been covered with mats, and had served as a kind of gymnasium for the practice of throws and falls and of fencing. A glance at the walls told him many of the practice swords still hung there, a fact that would probably do him no good, since he'd never be able to get to one. His eyes were drawn back to the floor.

"What's all this?" he asked, as the Queen gave instructions to her guards to clear the throng back off of the design.

"What does it look like, fool?" she replied. "You're standing on a giant Drax board. You think these people could witness my triumph if we played on that tiny table?"

He recognized it as the crowd surged back out of the way and noted, too, that Ligne's throne had been positioned along the red flat. Rosha, a gag in his mouth, sat in the smaller throne next to her, struggling against the bonds that secured him to it. "I take it you're playing red," Pelmen murmured, his eyes on the lad.

"You did offer me the choice," the queen sneered. Not only had she teamed herself with Kherda to outnumber him, she'd claimed the advantage of the first move.

Pelmen turned to his left to look at Kherda. "And the Prime Minister is green." Kherda gazed back uncertainly.

"Which leaves you with blue." Ligne smiled. "I thought that might please you, since you seem to have a certain affinity for the color." She turned her gaze in the direction of Serphimera, whose expression of dismay hadn't changed.

"Where are the pieces?" he asked.

Ligne grinned, and clapped her hands. Guards blazed a new path through the crowd, leading ten tired looking creatures into the open area. Half were clothed in robes of bright crimson, the other half in kelly green, and each wore strangely shaped headgear. One man of each color wore a tri-cornered hat, another pair wore tall, conical caps, and so on. It was clear they had been costumed to represent Drax pieces. "Intriguing, isn't it?" the queen purred. "I call it my living Drax set."

"I must say, Ligne, you've stage-managed your triumph quite professionally," Pelmen murmured.

"Why thank you, fool. It took me several days, but I did so want it all to be right."

"But where are the blues?" Pelmen asked.

"Kherda and I drew our pieces from the dungeon, but I thought it might be fun to assemble yours from the ranks of those dearest to you. Perhaps it will add dimension to

your play to realize that every move you make risks the life
of that piece."

Pelmen gazed at her, his face as calm in defeat as if he
had won. "How very fitting. For to you, it's all a game,
isn't it? Your power, your crown—just a game to while
away your time."

"And a splendid game it is." She smiled, her teeth flashing. "Pity Admon Faye couldn't be here to enjoy it with us.
Robe Gerrig in blue," she ordered her servants, "and put
the tri-corner on his head!"

Pelmen glanced around the game room as he took stock
of his own energy level. There were some things he could
do—he just couldn't guarantee the results. Shaping was
dangerous in any case—and weariness made it more so.
Still, if he could make the act explosive enough, perhaps
someone could get away.

"The round-faced one," Ligne said, pointing at Yona
Parmi. "Make him the column. And make this actress the
disc," she continued, grabbing Danyilyn's wrist, "in appreciation of her miserable impersonation of me."

"Of course it was miserable," Danyilyn snarled at her,
fiery to the last. "I had such a miserable subject to imitate."

Fire would be the most compelling, Pelmen thought. He
could probably empty the hall in a moment. Of course,
they'd all be consumed along with Ligne, but perhaps it
was worth their lives, to rid the world of this dangerous
Queen . . .

Ligne paced across the floor toward Bronwynn and
jerked the heavily bound Princess out onto the board. "I'd
thought to make Naquin the cube—"

"I say," Naquin gasped. "I'm not with the man."

"—he is, after all, dressed in blue already and is block-
headed enough. But since you've so kindly brought Bronwynn to me—" She shoved the girl toward a servant. "—
we'll make her the cube instead."

An explosion of wind? Pelmen reasoned. Blow out the
ceiling and crush all the spectators. That was the trouble
with magic—it killed indiscriminately.

"And of course, Serphimera."

Pelmen whipped around to stare at her. "Serphimera?"
he said aloud.

"Certainly Serphimera," Ligne snarled.

"She never threatened you."

"She didn't forewarn me either. Put the star on her head," Ligne ordered. "She already has the blue robe."

But Serphimera had told him she would walk out the gate unharmed. For the first time all day, Pelmen brushed shoulders with hope. For if Serphimera was destined to live . . . "And I'm to understand that all of these will lose their lives if I fail to defeat you?" he asked.

"That is the wager." Ligne sneered smugly.

A year before, Serphimera had prophesied that Vicia-Heinox would rip a blue-clad figure in two. She'd been right. She'd been right about two plots against Ligne ending in failure. And Serphimera had seen herself leave this castle on foot through the front gate.

Ligne made her first move, and flung the reference plank toward Pelmen. "Play the game, fool. That is, if you remember how."

Just then it happened again.

Pelmen always had difficulty expressing the experience in words, but he instantly knew what had happened. Erri would have understood completely, while Ligne might have laughed herself breathless at the very idea. Naquin might have comprehended, while Jagd would have dismissed it as the kind of delusion all Lamathians were subject to—a simple result of their upbringing.

But Pelmen knew what it was. His spirit soared with an elation born from far beyond human experience. At the critical instant, at the moment he'd started his last desperate act of shaping, he'd heard, "Wait." No one nearby had said it, and the House was as silent as ever. Yet it had come, and Pelmen felt again that curious mixture of elation and terror that had seized him so many times before. No longer was he the shaper—he was being shaped, and his ultimate destiny, be it life or death, seemed trivial in the face of this rushing presence.

Bronwynn saw it. Gagged as well as hobbled and cuffed, she could only smile with her eyes. But that she did. Her eyes radiated excitement. She recognized the face that Pelmen now wore and knew its strangely compelling nature came from beyond him.

Serphimera saw it too, and it startled her. She had long

denied the possibility of this happening to anyone outside her own circle. It seemed incredible she should be witnessing this transformation now—but she did. And it thrilled her beyond words.

Ligne regarded Pelmen's strained expression with a contemptuous sneer. "Are you going to move, fool?"

Pelmen drew a deep breath and forced himself to stare at the gameboard. This was torture. He longed to surrender to the enormous warmth that engulfed him, to slough off responsibility for himself and his friends and soak in the Power's presence. Yet he could not. In the midst of this abundant joy, there was not necessarily any hope. The Power was shaping him, he knew—but he knew as well that what he might choose might not be the choice of the Power. He fought only briefly to retain control, then acquiesced. "Very well," he muttered quietly to the One who had made him a Prophet. "I hope you know how to play this game." Then he made his first move.

From the beginning, the pattern of play took on new and puzzling shapes. This game didn't follow any of the classic forms—or if it did, no one could tell. The size of the board and the rocking and whispering of the pieces prevented any real perspective. As the three players wove in and out between their brightly attired armies, guiding living pieces across the board, Ligne's frustration level grew. She moved a disc ten feet across the floor, only to have it taken immediately by an unseen column concealed behind Pelmen's star. "I can't see what I'm doing," she shouted.

"At the moment," Pelmen told her with considerable effort, "you appear to be losing." That wasn't quite true. They'd both lost two pieces to Kherda's three, and the game hung in the balance. Yet Pelmen had realized that he was playing far beyond his own capacity. He'd detached himself from the fearsome outcome of the exercise and watched his own play with objective admiration. It was a necessary mental adjustment, for the near future was too horrible to consider. Somehow, the Power helped him make it.

"What's happening?" the spectators muttered to one another. But for all their confusion, it seemed most of them had a better grasp of the dynamics of this match than did the befuddled Prime Minister.

"Kherda," Ligne screamed, "are you trying to make me lose?"

"No, my Lady," Kherda called back raggedly, and Pelmen almost felt sorry for the man.

The reference plank changed hands a dozen times in rapid succession, noting a dazzling exchange of blitzing moves that left everyone a little dizzy. Then it stopped, and Kherda loudly announced, "Razor."

The crowd gasped, then cheered.

Pelmen frowned. It was uncanny the number of times this situation arose. So frequently did it happen, in fact, that the merchants had long since given this configuration its own name. Pelmen had lost Gerrig and Serphimera, and had three remaining pieces. Ligne, too, had three pieces left on the board. Kherda had lost all but one, but he had done so with the consummate skill of one who has practiced only to lose. His one piece now controlled the outcome of the game. He held the deciding position—the Razor—and the way it cut would determine the winner.

Ligne chuckled. "Well, well."

Kherda smiled at her. He could take Bronwynn on this move, and Ligne would then be free to take Danyilyn—three to one to one, a victory for the Queen. Or he could take one of Ligne's pieces, and her succeeding move could not prevent Pelmen from seizing that same winning margin. The cry of "Razor" was normally the cue for a vigorous round of negotiations between players to begin. Often the player with a Razor walked off with more gold in his pocket than the winner himself. But Pelmen felt no desire to negotiate. He had lost. He only wondered why, this time, Serphimera had been wrong.

"Go ahead," Ligne ordered. "Take her."

Kherda looked Bronwynn straight in the eyes—and took Ligne's piece instead!

Queen Ligne stared. The act was so incomprehensible, she could think of nothing to say. Pelmen grunted in surprise, and stared as well. Unbelievably, he had won. He turned his head to gaze at Kherda, and found the man was looking at him. Whether or not he understood the import of the change in Pelmen's face, Kherda remembered the befriending of the fool—and Ligne's back. Now, he'd repaid them both.

"Kill them!" screamed Ligne. "Kill them all!" Before she finished the phrase, swords were whistling out of their sheaths and armed warriors were advancing on the players.

—Not only does she cheat, she's a welcher as well! bellowed the Imperial House suddenly, and the bells on the wall broke into a horrendous clamor.

Pelmen threw back his head and laughed joyously. "I wondered when we'd finally hear from you."

Joss did not pause an instant. Already his sword was in the air, and he charged forward, intent on dispatching Bronwynn first, then the rest. Ligne's game had gone on far too long. It was time to restore some cold-steel discipline to this castle. "Hold, Joss!" cried someone on his right, and he whirled to see who challenged him. He stared down the blade of Rosha mod Dorlyth.

"How did you—Carlad!" Joss roared, as he watched the guard sprint for the wall to tear another sword from it. The lad's guard had proved himself a mudgecurdle!

"Yes, Carlad cut me free," Rosha shouted as he whirled the guard's blade into motion above his head and leaped between Joss and the knot of players. "And Queen Bronwynn will reward him for it."

—No welcher dwells within this House! trumpeted the castle, and the room started quaking. The House was angry—and it finally found the energy to express its rage.

Rosha kicked a sword from one warrior's fist and slammed shut the visor of another as the floor shuddered and then buckled. Soldiers and spectators alike tumbled to their knees, and the room filled with panicked screeching. People scrambled for the exits, jamming the hallways beyond the doors just as tightly as they'd jammed the game room. Many warriors dropped their weapons and raced to join them. Others, fearing their lords' reprisals worse than falling stones, staggered to their feet and struggled forward. The floor shifted again, and the walls shimmied, and still more guards chose to abandon the fight to join the flight. Those few who kept shoving forward through the scattering mob suddenly faced a dilemma. Ligne's piercing voice still rose above the roar, but once they got into the open space where the troupe clustered, they faced the whirling blade of Rosha mod Dorlyth. Steel clashed on steel only by accident, as warriors seeking to brake their charge came into range of his weapon. No one wanted to battle the brawny savage.

None save Lord Joss himself. "Come then, young warrior," Joss called grimly. "We shall see if the Golden Throng might be avenged for the battle of Westmouth on the son of the Mari commander."

"There is some vengeance I crave as well, Joss," Rosha snarled back. "Vengeance for a broken promise and a cowardly betrayal!" As the room rocked from side to side and the screeching became intolerable, the two warriors clashed together over the giant Drax board.

Pelmen spent these chaotic minutes whispering reassurances and struggling with knotted ropes. "Relax," he soothed, "the House is angry at Ligne, not us."

"Maybe so." Gerrig quaked in terror. "But are you sure it can control on whom it drops its walls? Look out!" A chandelier came crashing to the floor, crushing half a dozen unfortunate spectators.

Pelmen turned his attention to the sword battle. Joss was letting the younger warrior do all the work, circling him warily and parrying each blow with a skill born of experience. Rosha attacked him doggedly, his face twisted by a fierce scowl. Their swords rang together twice before they tangled in one another's arms, and Joss quickly booted Rosha in the thigh and jabbed him under the breast with his elbow. Rosha hurtled backward, his chest unhurt but his leg suddenly cramping. He planted that leg to dodge the General's onslaught, but it couldn't hold his weight, and Rosha tumbled to the floor. Joss grinned and plunged his sword through the sprawling lad—

At least, he thought he did. But when he pulled back on his haft, he felt no resistance—then he noticed his blade had liquefied. He stepped back in astonishment, then quickly tossed the useless pommel aside and dragged out his dagger. Before he could raise it above his head, its blade liquefied as well, and he staggered, staring at yet another useless haft. He glanced up then, and saw Pelmen standing ten feet away, his arms extended, his palms up. "Are . . . are you doing this?" Joss choked out.

"Oh, not I," Pelmen said. "But it is being done."

Joss threw up his hands and backed away. "How can a mortal withstand such powers?" he shouted. Then he knelt and bowed his head. "I'm ready to die," he called. Throughout his life, Joss had been a gloating victor. But somewhere through it all he had learned how to lose gracefully.

Pelmen sighed. "That's the nice thing about miracles," he told Bronwynn and Serphimera. "They're so very specific."

—She's getting away, announced the Imperial House, and Pelmen jerked his head up to listen.

"How?" he demanded.

—Through the walls.

"Bronwynn, she's leaving through the walls!"

"I know where she's going. Get me loose!" Pelmen nodded, and dropped to his knees to tear at her knots with his teeth.

"Here," Rosha grunted, and he pushed Pelmen aside to slash through her bonds with Carlad's sword. Another quick slash and her hobbles were cut, and Bronwynn dashed to the wall to rip down a practice sword. Pelmen sprinted right behind her and grabbed off a pair of blades.

"What about us?" Gerrig hollered. Right above them a chandelier identical to the one that had fallen swung wildly. Gerrig's eyes never left it.

"You'll be all right," Pelmen called as he raced back and stooped to hack at Gerrig's bonds. Carlad quickly joined him, and soon the actor was free. "Here. Protect the rest of them." Pelmen shoved one of his swords into Gerrig's hands and took off after Bronwynn and Rosha, who had disappeared into a gaping hole in the wall.

"There's a tiny dock on the northern face!" Bronwynn was calling as Pelmen started down a dangerously steep stairway in the dark. "She's headed for the escape craft."

—Actually, she's already in it, the castle corrected.

"The House says she's there," Pelmen shouted as he stumbled. It was impossible to move quickly and cautiously at the same time. "Can we stop her?"

"If we hurry—" Bronwynn started to yell back. Then there was a heavy thud, and Bronwynn groaned. "She's bolted the door!"

"Stand back!" Rosha bellowed. With the snort of an enraged bull he hurled his weight against the barrier and broke it down. The three of them tumbled over one another onto the wet dock—in time to see Ligne's boat slipping out onto the river.

"We've lost her," Pelmen sighed. Bronwynn moaned aloud, and Rosha slammed his heavy hand onto the dock in frustration. Pelmen sighed again, helpless to stop the woman's escape. He'd pushed his body to its limit.

But the House wasn't finished. Just as Ligne's boat slipped out from under its walls, an overgrown pigeon relieved himself on the roof once more.

—Enough! the Imperial House thundered and in its rage gave its mightiest shudder yet. The iron aviary had never been bolted to the roof, and it began to rock on its base. The excited House shimmied once more . . .

Ligne, rowing with every shred of her remaining energy, could hear the tremor, and glanced up the face of her former home in time to see the aviary fall. She had the chance to scream once before the massive cage impacted on the water. Her tiny launch was shattered into splinters as the twisted structure buried itself in the ancient mulch of the riverbed. Ligne was buried with it.

The three figures on the dock stared in shock as they watched the metal sink. Bronwynn and Rosha shouted in exultation, and Pelmen felt a slow smile of relief spread across his face. Then he heard behind him the castle's windy laughter, as the Imperial House chortled:

—How fitting, that the welching Queen should be buried under such a weighty—dropping!

CHAPTER TWENTY-THREE

The House Retires

WITH A FEW SHARP COMMANDS, Bronwynn took charge of her realm. In bursts of staccato instructions she dispatched messages to the mayors of all her major cities, reconfirmed most of the petty courtlings in their roles at court, and summoned the guards to bring her erstwhile enemies to the gardens to face her judgment. As she and Pelmen made their way through the floating dust up the debris-strewn spiral walkway, she suggested that Rosha might want to dispatch a flyer to Erri. "If there's going to be a wedding"— she smiled confidently—"I think we might want him to be present."

"Since there will be," Rosha beamed back, "I'd better go summon him. I think I recall that my father wanted to be informed, too . . ." Then, dropping his studied nonchalance, Rosha bolted up the ramp with a shout of boyish exuberance. Bronwynn turned her head to look at Pelmen, her face a study in regal self-assurance. "How am I doing?"

"Admirably." Pelmen nodded. "You've grown up a lot in these months of suffering."

Her expression softened, then turned pensive. "Perhaps."

"Something troubles you, though?" Pelmen asked hopefully.

"Shouldn't it? I may have been through a lot since we met, but I don't think anything's prepared me to reconstruct a country."

"Then you've taken the first step in being a success at it. You realize you need some help. Ligne never got that far."

"You'll help me, won't you? Please, Pelmen, stay on as our Prime Minister!"

He gazed at her fondly for a moment. "Thank you, my Lady. But no."

"Why not? You know more about this than I do, and—"

"But there's one who knows far more about it than either of us. And today he saved our lives."

Bronwynn wrinkled her nose. "Kherda? But he overthrew my father."

"Which you've said yourself probably needed to happen. I'll not make the decision for you. You're the Queen." The two of them stepped out onto the lowest terrace of the garden. With the displacement of the aviary, the sunlight burned down brilliantly on the luscious green foliage, forcing them to stop and breathe the air. It seemed fresher, somehow, and Pelmen said so.

—Of course this House smells better! the castle snapped. The birds have flown.

That wasn't wholly true, for many of the aviary's occupants remained. No longer caged, these stayed by choice, for this was the only home they had known in this northerly land. "Not all, evidently," Pelmen said.

—The others will leave with winter, the House said smugly.

"And so will the plants." Pelmen nodded sadly. "But changes must come."

"What are you two talking about?" Bronwynn asked.

"Birds and change," Pelmen said quietly. Then he nodded over her shoulder. Kherda and Joss stood with several others, awaiting the news of their fate. Bronwynn looked at Kherda grimly, then motioned him to her. He cleared his throat nervously, then walked forward. "My Lady, I can ask for nothing save your mercy. While I know—"

"Kherda, can you give me some idea of what's happening in the provinces?"

Kherda looked at her, puzzled, then rapidly responded, "Drought in the east, though perhaps the rising of the rivers signal some rains have finally come. Insects in the north have ravaged seed stocks, but we have enough in storage here in the city to replenish supplies, once the order is given to move them. It's been a poor year for farmers—the dragonburn, of course, and the battle at Westmouth—but we're not facing a major famine, for the fields in the far south produced—"

"Can you prepare the orders to ship the necessary goods?" Bronwynn asked.

"Certainly. They're in my office awaiting signature. Just let me—" Kherda started out, but stopped and came back. "However—it's—not my office anymore—is it?"

"Who moved you?"

Kherda's wide eyes grew wider. Then he scooped up his skirts and flapped out of the room, shouting, "I'll be back in a moment."

Bronwynn glanced back distastefully at the remainder of the group, then settled her gaze on Joss. He was being diligently guarded by a fierce-eyed Gerrig—whom he ignored completely. The warrior met Bronwynn's gaze passively. Bronwynn glanced back at Pelmen.

"Yes?" he asked. "What of Joss?"

"My recent experience as an almost murderess has convinced me that—somehow—I don't think a Queen should be one."

"And?" Pelmen asked.

"And I don't want to start my reign with a full dungeon." She gauged his reactions. "Joss has so much experience in affairs of state. Why not make him Ambassador to Lamath?"

Pelmen raised his eyebrows in surprise. "Certainly a creative idea," he said appreciatively.

"He's loyal to Chaomonous, we know that. And it would keep him in a position of responsibility which might prevent him from raising an army against me. He and Kherda would be separated—that's important; those two have been fighting all my life—" She stopped when she saw Pelmen smiling at her. "Besides," she smiled back, "if he spends time in Lamath, he might learn something. I did."

Pelmen nodded, still smiling. "You're the Queen."

Gerrig led the General to them and turned Joss around to face Bronwynn. "My Lady, would you have me dispatch him here?" Gerrig asked dramatically.

"Gerrig, this isn't a play. You can put up your sword and leave us. But gather the troupe and meet me at the table tonight. I think you'll like the rôle I have picked out for you."

"A new rôle!" Gerrig said brightly. He stalked out of the garden smiling grandly. Nothing pleased Gerrig more than a new rôle.

"Now, Joss," Bronwynn began, "what shall I do with you?"

"I ask no favors, my Lady. I chose wrongly. I'll accept my death as my due."

"How about accepting appointment to the court of Lamath instead? As my Ambassador?" The General blinked. Then his hard eyes softened. He remembered when this woman had been but a bright-eyed baby girl—and she'd stolen his battle-hardened heart with a smile. "Joss," she continued quietly, "this past year has been a nightmare for all of us. Perhaps we could . . . wake up?"

"I'll serve you faithfully," Joss said with a solemn frown, and Bronwynn knew he meant it.

"Here's the (puff) documents." Kherda panted as he raced up to Bronwynn. "Ready for circulation."

Bronwynn took the stylus he offered and quickly signed them, asking as she did, "What's happened to Jagd?"

"I saw him leaving the castle. I can call him back if you—"

"Oh no," Bronwynn said, shaking her head. "I'm glad he's gone. I would, however, like to meet with the other local merchant lords tomorrow, as well as all the freetraders you can assemble."

"Freetraders?" Kherda frowned.

"I expect to be increasing our dealings with Lamath very soon. Here." She handed the documents back to him and the Prime Minister wandered away, shaking his head and muttering about freetraders. Bronwynn winked at her mentor. "I believe I'm going to like this."

Pelmen smiled, but his eyes were serious as he replied, "I hope so. I certainly hope so."

"The flyers are on their way," Rosha mod Dorlyth told them as he came down the spiraled terraces.

"And the two of you have much to discuss. I'll let you be." Pelmen started for the doorway back into the halls.

"You have some discussing to do, too?" Bronwynn guessed.

"Perhaps." He nodded. Then he left them alone.

He searched several floors before he finally had the presence of mind to ask the House where she was.

—In your cell, waiting for you.

Pelmen raced to meet her. "Serphimera?" he asked as he opened the door.

"I'm here," she called.

"I know. The House told me."

The woman looked at the walls. "Is there no place— private?" she whispered.

"There *are* some things it can't hear," he whispered back, and he leaned over and kissed her. She held him briefly, fiercely, then abruptly pulled herself away. He looked at her with surprise.

"I suppose your two initiates will marry," she finally said.

"They're planning that now. And—what of us?" He asked the question tentatively.

Serphimera's dark green eyes transfixed him. "Are you finished yet?"

"Finished?"

"With your tasks."

Pelmen gazed at her. "I don't know."

"I know. And you're not."

"More visions?" Pelmen asked, a bit harshly.

"You're not. Nor am I. And we both must care for those things first."

"You're going to keep on telling of Lord Dragon?" Pelmen didn't mean to sound angry, but he did.

Serphimera smiled forgiveness, bit her lip, and looked beyond his head. "Lord Dragon," she sighed. "I think, for a long time, the dragon has been more a symbol for me than anything else. The image is familiar—it has a comforting power that's rooted in my childhood. But I've long since cast aside any relation between those soothing terms and the scaly monster you killed in Dragonsgate." Pelmen stared at her, his mouth open. "And that one you serve? The Power? I serve that One, too."

"But when—"

"When did I change?" Again Serphimera bit her lip and tried to express what she felt. "I don't know. Not when I saw the lizard die. Before."

"Before! But just the other day you said—"

"Perhaps when I first saw the beast, and realized that the one I served was not there, in those huge heads. Or perhaps when I first met you on the road to Serphila, and called you a heretic while your eyes loved me." She looked back at him. "I couldn't admit it to myself until today. But the change has come." She sighed and scooted toward him. "Still, there are other changes yet to come—other heartaches." She bent forward until her forehead rested in her hands. "I *know*."

"And . . . what about us?" Pelmen whispered, longing to hear, but fearing her answer. She was silent. "Tell me what you know!" he demanded.

"I know there are things we each must do, which may at any moment part us. Can we know anything beyond that?" She stood, and started for the door. He caught her by the hand.

"We will talk again," he said firmly.

Serphimera's emerald eyes dazzled him. He saw a longing there, an eagerness that thrilled him. Then she blinked her lashes, and suddenly the look was gone. "Perhaps," she said. Then she left the cell.

Erri arrived a week later to a city festooned with drapes and garlands. With the assistance of Pelmen's old acting companions, whom Bronwynn had appointed as heads of various cultural ministries, the Prime Minister had hurriedly organized a national festival to celebrate both the coronation and the wedding of Queen Bronwynn lan Rosha. Chaomonous, sensing the dawning of a new age, awoke into a most colorful spring, as befitted a city long known as the Golden. The whole population turned out to watch the arrival of the Prophet from the north.

If they wanted pomp, however, Erri disappointed them. He rode into town on a dark mare, flanked by Naquin, who had met him at Dragonsgate. And while he smiled and

waved as much as was necessary to keep up appearances,
his mind was engaged in explaining to Naquin firsthand
the rôle Pelmen had played in the remaking of Lamath.
Erri was followed by a long column of riders gowned uni-
formly in pale blue, but the parade did not have the preci-
sion of a military unit. Instead, riders kept slipping off
their horses and joining themselves to the cheering crowd
to walk along the parade route in conversation. Toward the
middle of the procession a solemn-faced contingent of riders led four wagons, each wagon carrying a blue-draped
coffin. Erri was bringing the bodies of those trampled by
the slavers to rest here, in the capital city of the land he'd
assigned them to evangelize. It seemed fitting.

He and Naquin were laughing by the time they reached
the gate of the Imperial House, and Erri's smiles grew
broader as he greeted first Bronwynn, then Rosha, and finally Pelmen with bearhugs. He shared some quiet words
with Serphimera, who answered him shyly, then took her
hand and slipped his other arm around Pelmen's shoulder
as they turned to follow the new Queen into her palace. It
was a joyful day.

Rosha's joy was muted, however. He still hadn't heard
from Dorlyth.

Another week passed. They could wait no longer. Everything was ready in the city, and Erri needed to return
home. Bronwynn and Rosha agreed, finally, that they had
to go ahead. Even so, Rosha still made frequent trips to the
roof, hoping for some word from Dorlyth. When it came
time to clothe himself in the fancy garments Bronwynn
had commissioned for this occasion, he sent Pelmen to the
roof in his place.

Now Pelmen leaned against the battlements, gazing
sadly out at the road that wound down from the gate into
the city. In his hand he clutched a crumpled parchment
sheet.

—This news is sad, but perhaps not unexpected, said the
House.

Pelmen agreed. "I just didn't expect the trouble to develop so quickly."

—Any powershaper skilled enough to breathe life into a
castle must be a person of great ambition. And if the wak-

ing of the High Fortress of Ngandib is any indication, this Flayh you speak of will waste no time in taking what he chooses.

Pelmen opened the parchment again and reread it.

SON—BLESSINGS ON YOU! WOULD COME IF I COULD, BUT FLAYH CONTROLS PAHD AND WE HAVE NEW WARS OF CONFEDERATION. MUCH LOVE—DORLYTH MEL ROSHA.

The signature was significant. It meant Dorlyth, father of Rosha, and was the salute a Mari father gave when acknowledging his son's manhood. Pelmen smiled grimly at that. Dorlyth had always been the most mannerly of swordsmen.

The news was more than sad. It was threatening. Wars of confederation—again. "New magic wars," Pelmen breathed.

—Indeed they are that, the House agreed. Already this House is feeling the aftershocks of the shaping taking place in the Mar.

"In what way?" Pelmen asked.

—Just a warmth, at present. If the battles move into this region, the pain will become intense—as you must know.

"I . . . apologize again for what I inflicted on you—"

—It is past, if not forgotten, said the House. Your apologies—all of them—have been accepted. But the one you battled is most insensitive to the pain he causes his own castle. The High Fortress may be a malevolent place, and poor company, but not even it deserves such misery.

Pelmen sighed. "I can imagine how it feels—"

—No, you can't, said the House. No one can—no one but this House. And you are perhaps the only one who can do anything to aid it. You, and the Power, of course.

"You believe what I've told you of the Power?"

—No need. This House has met the Power. It is to the Power that this House withdraws.

"What do you mean?"

Before the House could answer, Pelmen was grabbed by the elbow and spun around. "You have the news?"

"Look at you!" the powershaper exclaimed, and he followed his own instructions. Rosha glistened in the light of the sun. His basic garments were shades of blue, Bronwynn's reminder to him of their time as Pelmen's initiates in the skyfaith. What sparkled was the trim. The entire costume was frosted with a glaze of diamonds set in gold. Rosha was frankly embarrassed by it.

"The news!" he begged. "A messenger told me you had some."

Pelmen frowned and handed Rosha the parchment. Then he leaned over the battlements again as the lad read it. Rosha soon leaned on the low wall beside him, and they stood together in silence for several minutes.

"I'm sorry," Pelmen said finally.

"He just couldn't make it, that's all." Rosha shrugged. He struggled to hide his concern.

Pelmen put an arm around Rosha's shoulder. "I know what you're thinking, but it wouldn't do any good. You've got a bride waiting for you down below—and your father can take care of himself."

"You're going," Rosha muttered.

"How do you know that?"

"I know you."

"Well. We'll talk about it. Right now Bronwynn's waiting, and I'm sure Erri is anxious to get this ceremony out of the way."

"Right." Rosha nodded and started toward the gaping hole where the aviary once stood. "You coming?"

"In a bit," Pelmen called back. Rosha nodded again and left the roof. "Now. What were you saying?"

—This House is withdrawing to be with the Power.

"I don't understand."

—It is apparent that castles are not made to live. These stones, these walls, this House—all of these have their own existence, quite apart from that of man. The hills, the river—these don't aspire to copy man. Nor should this House.

"But you're alive!"

—In imitation of human life, and not by choice. This House lives rather by human device and ambition. Yet men can move. This House cannot move. Men enjoy the company of others. This House has no company, save you and the High Fortress. But that castle has a cruel spirit and all the dangerous ambition of the very young among men. And you will soon be leaving, because of that Fortress. Men may live in happy ignorance of the magical forces being shaped around them. This House must endure the necessary pain such shaping creates without recourse. That pain makes these coming wars that much more frightening. For all these reasons, it seems better for the House—for the life in this House—to withdraw.

"But where will you go?"

—Back to the Power. For it's from the Power that all life is shaped.

"All?" Pelmen asked, thinking of the life now in the High Fortress and its evil genesis.

—All. Either by the Power . . . or artificially, *through.*

"Then I'll not speak with you again?"

—Only if the Power permits. The peace of this House be on you, Pelmen Dragonsbane. Attend your task. And your Lady. She slips away this very moment through the front gate. Perhaps you can catch her.

"Serphimera?" Pelmen shouted. He raced to the battlements and looked down. Five floors below, he could see the flowing navy robes of the Priestess as she quickly made her way down the cobblestones toward the city. "Serphimera, wait!" he cried, and he vaulted on top of the parapet and leaped off.

Maliff, the falconer, stepped out of his mews just in time to observe Pelmen disappear. "Here now!" he cried in horror. He raced to the wall and looked down to see the falling man spread the wings of a bird. It glided upwards, then down to settle on the shoulders of a blue-clad woman. Maliff stared for a minute, watching as woman and falcon disappeared among the throngs of shoppers in the market. Then he clucked his tongue. "Why didn't you just *terr* me you were a farcon in the first prace? You birds," he mumbled. "You've arways got to pray your rittre tricks." As Maliff ducked back into the cool darkness of his falcon house, he was still chuckling.

About the Author

Robert Don Hughes was born in Ventura, California, the son of a Baptist pastor. He grew up in Long Beach, and was educated in Redlands, Riverside, and Mill Valley, gaining degrees in theater arts and divinity. That education continued and he finished a Ph.D. in Missions, Religions and Philosophy in Louisville, Kentucky.

He has been a pastor, a playwright, a teacher, a filmmaker, and a missionary, and considers all those roles fulfilling. He has published several short plays, and presently teaches drama. He spent two years in Zambia, and while there was bitten by the Africa bug. His two passions are writing and football—not necessarily in that order, especially in October. He is married to Gail, a beautiful South Alabama woman who loves rainbows, and fills his life with them. Currently, he and Gail, with a beautiful baby daughter, are living in Africa where he is doing missionary work.

Most of all, Bob likes people. The infinite variety of personalities and opinions makes life interesting. The sharing of self makes it worthwhile.

Enchanting fantasies from